KNOT PLAYING FAIR

FAIR

BOOK ΩNE

Other Books by Ember Blaze:

The Secrect Pack Trilogy

Hide or Die
Fight or Fly
Truth or Lie

The Packverse

All for Knot: Book One
All for Knot: Book Two
Knot for Sale

EMBER BLAZE

Knot Playing Fair: Book One

ISBN: 978-1-955073-88-2 (paperback)

For information, contact the publisher at www.otherlovepublishing.com/contact/

Cover art by Ember

First Edition: March 2025

Author's Note

Knot Playing Fair is a human omegaverse duology where the main character doesn't have to pick one person in the end. It features protective alphas and the omegas who love them, but no shifters. The series contains steamy LGBT content, and is intended for a mature audience.

Table of Contents

1

ONE

Mia Dimitriadis

BEING ANGRY IS *always better than being hurt.* That was my new personal motto, and it had been in force for the last two weeks. I sat at the polished oak bar, rubbing idly at the smooth band of tender skin where my wedding ring had sat for the past five years, two months, and eighteen days.

"This isn't fair to me, Mia." Nat's words from our last argument had been playing on a continuous loop, living rent free in my head every hour of the day and night. *"My needs aren't being met, and they haven't been met since business at the restaurant started to take off last year. I want to open up the marriage."*

My hands shook. I reached for my wine glass, throwing back a generous swallow. The bar stool next to me creaked, a broad, heavy figure settling on it.

"You looking for company, Flower?" It was a man. An alpha. He was the sixth one tonight to lead with a similarly bad pick-up line. "Pretty little thing like you shouldn't be sitting here drinking all alone."

He smelled like cigarette smoke and guava nectar. Hopefully the tobacco scent was because he smoked. If it was part of his natural pheromone cocktail, that seemed like a pretty cruel genetic joke.

"I'm good, thanks," I told him.

"I'll just *bet* you are."

He waggled bushy eyebrows in case I hadn't caught the double entendre. If he was younger than sixty, I'd eat my chef's hat.

"That'll have to remain a hypothetical, since I'm not interested," I told him. "Good hunting, though."

The alpha grunted and heaved himself from his stool, off to find more tractable prey. I returned to my merlot, debating the pitfalls of ordering another glass.

21 Oak was a singles bar that catered mostly to alphas and omegas. Aside from a decent wine collection, its main selling point was that it lay within walking distance of my restaurant, the Elderflower Inn.

I'd come here with a nebulous plan to flirt outrageously with a couple of attractive alphas, completely fail to go home with them, and then hurl an embellished version of the evening's entertainment in Nat's face the next time we fought.

I pondered whether being hit on six times in ninety minutes was enough to call it a night. I didn't think I could bring myself to engage in any more conversations that began with, '*I hope you know CPR — because, baby, you just took my breath away.'*

God. What was I even *doing* here?

I should be curled on my sofa at home, wrapped in a blanket and watching mindless TV. Trying to recover enough energy to get up and go do my job tomorrow. I'd dragged myself here out of some twisted idea of tit-for-tat. Like, if Nat insisted on making connections outside of the marriage, then I would, too.

Was he even home tonight? Would I be going to bed alone? Would I be *waking up* alone?

Two weeks of this, and I still hadn't told anybody else about it. I already knew what most people would say. *Have some self-respect, girl. You need to leave his cheating ass.*

It wasn't that simple, though.

Nat and I weren't just married. We were also business partners. Together, we'd launched the first Michelin-star restaurant not only in St. Louis, but in the entire state of Missouri. In addition, the Elderflower Inn was only the third Michelin-star restaurant in history with an omega head chef.

I'd worked my ass off to achieve that honor. I wasn't about to throw it in the dumpster just because Nat had taken a meat cleaver to my heart.

A new presence slipped onto the stool next to me. I steeled myself to deliver yet another brush-off. But instead of heavy alpha pheromones, the sweet scent of honeysuckle and fresh-mown grass tickled my nose... like a childhood summer captured in a perfume bottle.

Startled, I turned to meet the olive-green eyes of the slender male omega who'd sidled into my space. Tousled black hair topped a pale, angular face. His cupid's bow lips twitched into a smile so brief I might have missed it if I hadn't been staring.

"Hey," he said in a light tone. "I couldn't help noticing that you don't seem to be enjoying the meat market all that much. My friend and I have a table if you'd like to come sit with us instead."

I blinked, following the jerk of his chin toward a table tucked in the back corner of the room. A pleasant-faced, broad-shouldered man sat facing us. He was dressed casually, with dusky skin and long dreadlocks gathered up in a messy half-bun. One hand casually cradled a glass of beer. He caught my gaze and inclined his head in a tiny nod of acknowledgement.

The jolt in my chest as his eyes pinned mine instantly identified him as an alpha.

"Um…" I said stupidly, trying to kick my wine-muddled brain far enough into gear to decide if there were any reason *not* to join them. I couldn't come up with anything. "Sure?"

"Cool," said the omega. "I'm Luca, by the way. That's Zalen."

"Mia," I replied. "Thanks for rescuing me. I wasn't really prepared for the level of creepy on display in this place."

He snorted a small breath of laughter through his nose. "With a bar like this, it's best to travel in a pack." The moment the words left his mouth, though, he seemed to catch himself, a flush of pink rising to his cut-glass cheekbones. "Well... I mean... I suppose most omegas who already have a pack wouldn't be here in the first place, right?"

The sudden awkwardness didn't quite match the vision of porcelain, put-together perfection seated next to me.

"Are, uh... are you and Zalen together?" I asked, not wanting to blunder into anything without first knowing the lie of the land.

"*No*," Luca said quickly. The color staining his cheeks deepened, and he cleared his throat. "I mean, not exactly. We work together, and... it's kind of complicated."

"Gotcha," I said, despite having no clue what that was supposed to mean in this context.

Luca slid off the stool and ushered me toward his *complicated* alpha, his hand hovering a few inches behind my lower back. I clutched my mostly finished glass of 2015 Leonetti and spared a nasty thought for my absent husband.

Suck it, Nat.

Zalen rose as we approached, offering me a faint, reserved smile. It crinkled the skin at the corners of his dark brown eyes, but he had the air of someone distracted by other worries.

I could relate.

"Hello," I said, taking the initiative. "I'm Mia. Thanks for offering a refuge."

I transferred the wine glass to my left hand and reached across the table with my right—an automatic gesture after too many meetings with investors and members of the press. Zalen accepted the handshake with a murmured greeting. His palm was cool and dry despite the stifling heat of the bar; his grip pleasantly firm without being overbearing.

"Have a seat," he said, hooking Luca's chair out for him before retaking his own.

Not together, my ass, I thought, mildly amused by the display of chivalry.

I settled into my own seat, placing my glass in front of me. As I did, Zalen's incisive gaze flicked down to my hand… where, I abruptly realized, the paler band of skin at the base of my ring finger would be easily visible.

As stupid as it was, I jerked my hand down to rest on my lap, where it would be hidden by the table. Then I silently berated myself for the guilty reaction. *I wasn't doing anything wrong, damn it.*

Thankfully, Zalen was too polite to say anything. Or possibly, he simply didn't care that I normally wore a wedding ring.

"So, Luca says you two work together?" I began, in an oh-so-cool and natural segue into conversation.

Smooth, Mia. Real smooth.

"That's right," Zalen said, playing along. "My pack runs the Hope Project in East St. Louis. Luca's our grant writer, among various other talents."

The idea of anyone voluntarily running *anything* in East St. Louis was a bit hard to wrap my head around. St. Louis, Missouri had a pretty bad reputation for crime. East St. Louis, Illinois had a *horrible* reputation for crime.

"I haven't heard of it," I said. "Don't really get across the river much. What do you do?"

"It's a center for at-risk youth," Luca said, drawing my attention back to him.

For the first time, I noticed that his heavy-lidded green eyes were accented with guyliner as well as thick, dark eyelashes. I'd always had a bit of a thing for pretty, male omegas — at least from an aesthetic standpoint. Luca certainly wasn't doing anything to cure that tendency.

"There's some heavy gang activity in the area," Zalen said. "It's where we're needed. We do our best to offer the kids an alternative. Free classes, tutoring on life skills, that kind of thing."

"And martial arts," Luca put in.

"And martial arts," Zalen agreed.

"What about you?" Luca asked. "No offense, but you've kind of got that '*I just finished a brutal shift at work*' look."

I let out a short laugh. If I'd been in any doubt that these two weren't pick-up artists, that would have sealed it. '*Wow, you sure look tired*' wasn't exactly prime seduction material.

"Restaurant chef," I said, not mentioning the name of the establishment. The nice thing about being a local celebrity chef was that people didn't generally recognize your face on the street… or in bars, for that matter. But there'd been enough press coverage of the Elderflower over the past year that specifying *where* I was a chef sometimes made things awkward.

People seemed to have all sorts of passionate opinions about a female omega running a prestigious restaurant kitchen, for reasons I couldn't begin to fathom.

"Yep. That'd do it," Luca said. "Do you enjoy it?"

I used to. These days, I could still honestly say that I enjoyed the sense of accomplishment at achieving that first Michelin star—but the actual day-to-day grind was slowly wearing me down. More so over the past two weeks since Nat dropped his bombshell on me.

I settled on, "It can be stressful. But probably not as stressful as dealing with gang members."

Zalen shrugged. "They're mostly good kids."

I drew breath to reply, but a prickle at the back of my neck alerted me to approaching trouble an instant before Zalen frowned at something behind me, his brow furrowing.

"*Mia!*" The barked name wasn't quite a shout, but it carried clearly over the ambient noise of the room.

A sick swirl of dread mixed with hot resentment twisted my stomach as Nat stomped over to the table.

"Nat," I said through gritted teeth.

My beta husband looked incredulously from me, to Zalen, to Luca, and then back to me.

"What the *hell*?" Nat demanded… and this time, it was *definitely* a shout.

Around us, heads turned curiously as nearby patrons were drawn toward the promise of drama. With a scowl still wrinkling the skin between his eyebrows, Zalen rose slowly from his chair, squaring up to Nat across the table.

TWO

Mia

"PROBLEM?" ZALEN asked, with the kind of scary alpha calm that did absolutely nothing to imply an epic beat-down in the middle of a singles bar wasn't on the table if it became necessary.

Luca and I both froze like startled rabbits. It was more or less hardwired in when confronted with unexpected shouting and alpha dominance vibes, but the unwanted omega reaction still pissed me off.

"That's my wife," Nat snarled, at least making an effort to keep his voice down this time.

"And?" Zalen prompted in a bland tone. "Do you always try to police who your wife talks to in public places?"

I managed to wrest my instincts under control, rising from my own chair with gritted teeth. "No. He *doesn't*. What do you want, Nat?"

He had the gall to look hurt, like I'd betrayed him somehow.

"What are you *doing* here, Mia?" The question had a bewildered air to it, like he couldn't possibly imagine why I might feel the need to get revenge on him for breaking my heart.

"Having a drink," I told him, pointing to my wine glass. "What are *you* doing here?"

Nat's eyes darted nervously to Zalen. The alpha was still standing with crossed arms, radiating the timeless patience of a hundred-year-old oak tree. I knew perfectly well why Nat was here… although I was a bit surprised he hadn't chosen a singles bar that catered to betas.

"We need to talk," Nat told me, rather than answering the question.

"Do we really, though?" I asked.

"Yeah," he said flatly. "We do. Come back to the house, Mia."

With a final hard glance at my tablemates, he turned on his heel and walked out of the bar. Around us, the gawkers gradually lost interest as it became clear the drama was wrapping up. I willed the hot flush of humiliation to drain from my cheeks.

I was still hovering awkwardly in front of my chair. Wrenching myself free of my paralysis, I stepped to the side and pushed it into place beneath the table.

"I'm really sorry," I muttered, not able to meet Zalen's dark brown eyes. "I should… um… I should go. Thanks again for offering me a break from the meat market earlier. It was nice talking with you."

I started to turn, but Zalen's voice stopped me.

"Wait," he said. "Are you safe? If you're not, we can help."

I paused, confused for a moment until his meaning penetrated. When it did, my mortified blush returned at triple strength.

"Oh! Oh, good *Christ*, no—it's nothing like that." The idea of being physically afraid of Nat was so far-fetched as to be laughable. "We're going home to have an overdue fight about the fact that he demanded an open marriage, and apparently it never occurred to him that it might go both ways."

Damn.

Was that too much information?

That had probably been too much information.

I snuck a look at Zalen's expression. There wasn't an ounce of reaction visible. I wondered idly if he played poker. He'd probably be good at it, if so.

"I see," was all he said. "You have a way to get home?"

To an outside observer, it must seem like a red flag that I wasn't riding home with Nat. Personally, I was just relieved we wouldn't be fighting while he was driving. Sharing a car with my husband after these last couple of weeks wasn't something I was in a hurry to do.

"Believe it or not, they let omegas ride alone in cabs these days," I said mildly, trying to banish the part of me that liked how concerned he was for me. *Really* liked it, in fact. "Yes, I do have a way to get home."

Luca, who'd been letting all this play out without inserting an opinion, cleared his throat and stood. He reached over and picked up my handbag, slipping something into the outside pocket so casually that I might have missed it. I took the clutch when he handed it back to me.

"Sorry. Zalen's not *actually* that much of a neanderthal," he said conspiratorially. "He just gets overprotective when people around him act like dicks."

"No offense taken," I said, desperate to get out of there before I managed to plumb any additional depths of embarrassment. "Seriously, thanks again. It sounds like you guys are doing important work."

And before either of them could answer, I fled.

Phone in hand, I flagged down an Uber and stood shifting from foot to foot as I waited outside the bar. This was the fight I'd been wanting, right? It was past time Nat got a wake-up call about how selfish he was being.

The promised silver Hyundai Sonata pulled up to the curb. I got in and let it take me north, navigating the eleven-mile commute from Soulard to Jennings. Nineteenth-century red brick facades gave way to abandoned factories, then warehouses, and eventually Depression-era bungalows.

Unlike Nat, I wasn't willing to risk blaring news headlines of *'Local Restaurant Owner Charged With DWI!'* on nights when I planned to go out drinking. And normally on days when I didn't drive myself, I'd have taken the Metrolink—but this was quicker.

The driver dropped me at an unprepossessing white three-bedroom house off Jennings

Station Road. Light filtered through the living room window. Nat had beaten me home.

I squared my shoulders and marched up the front walk, preparing for battle. Letting myself inside, I closed and locked the door behind me before turning my full attention to the rumpled figure sitting on the couch.

Jacket gone, sleeves rolled up over well-defined forearms, Nat peered up at me from beneath jet-black hair that had escaped the day's styling. His brown eyes—deep set and heavy lidded thanks to whichever of his biological parents had been Chinese—were lined with stress and exhaustion.

"What the *hell*, Mia?" he asked, in a much softer tone than the one he'd used at the bar.

I tossed my clutch onto the small table in the entryway.

Where to fucking start?

"Are you *seriously*," I snapped, "going to give me a hard time for going to a bar and talking to strangers after you basically told me that I wasn't enough for you? That you needed to find other people to fuck?"

"You said," he began plaintively, "that you were okay with what we had! That it wasn't a problem for you! You as much as told me that you were *fine* with no sex! *That's why we're in this situation in the first place!*"

My anger surged, thin and sour like bile. I could smell the way it curdled my scent, announcing my emotions to anyone with a functioning nose.

"I'm an omega! I'm not a beta! If you want sex that we'll both enjoy, you need to let me know so I can have synthetic alpha pheromones ready to kickstart my libido. I have always been *very clear about that!*"

Nat scrubbed his hands through his hair in frustration, mussing it further. "And do you not see any reason why a man might start to resent the fact that his own wife needs to take drugs before she's willing to have sex with him?"

The unfairness of this might have been easier to take if he'd gotten off the damn couch and paced around angrily rather than just continuing to sit there, looking pitiful and wronged.

I blinked at him. "They're not *drugs*, they're *pheromones*! What the *fuck*, Nat? Did I somehow miss the part where you stumbled into this marriage having no clue about omega sexual biology?"

"I don't know," Nat said coldly. "Did you miss the part where you haven't had a natural heat in more than a year?"

Disbelief flooded me, and all I could do was stare at him. "Nat… how the hell am I supposed to randomly disappear for a week every few months when I'm the head chef at a *Michelin-star restaurant*? For that matter, how the hell are we *both* supposed to disappear? Who do you think is going to run the place?"

He threw his hands up in disgust. "I don't *know*, Mia! But for the third time, why the *fuck* were you in a bar picking up alphas when you're so quick to tell me that sex means nothing to you?"

The words *'to make you jealous, you complete asshole,'* were born and died behind my lips.

"To make a point," I said instead. "And don't you *dare* act like you found me riding some alpha's knot in the men's room. I was sitting at a table with two people that I'm pretty sure were already together, having a glass of fucking *wine* and talking about *youth centers.*"

"In a singles bar," Nat grated out.

"A singles bar *you* just happened to walk into," I shot back viciously. "This may come as a shock to you, but I'm not exactly getting my needs met in this marriage either."

A look of combined horror and petty victory twisted his features. "But you *just* said—"

"My *emotional* needs," I snarled. "For god's *sake*, could you think with some other body part besides your dick for *one goddamn minute*? When was the last time you talked to me about *anything* that wasn't related to the restaurant... or to your need to fuck other women because I'm not enough for you?"

Nat went cold and still. "I don't know. Probably around the same time you last made an effort to put on some pretty lingerie and be intimate with me. When was that, exactly?"

My throat grew tight and clogged. My stomach felt like it was in danger of eating itself, not helped by the wine earlier. That was my excuse for not managing a decent comeback before Nat surged up from the couch, grabbed his jacket, and stormed out of the house. A minute later, I heard the rumble of his Jeep rolling out of the driveway and disappearing.

I stood in the middle of the cramped living room for an embarrassingly long time, tasting stomach acid. Eventually, I unclenched my fists, picked up my handbag, and zombie-walked to the bathroom. The harsh fluorescent lights illuminated a pale face with lines where there hadn't been any a year ago. Dark bags underlined bloodshot eyes.

Desperate to distract myself from the flaming wreckage that was my marriage, I dug my fingers into the side pocket of my tasteful black clutch, indulging a dull throb of curiosity. I came out with a rectangle of stiff cardboard.

It was a business card, simple but elegant in dark, jewel-tone green with pale gold text. *Luca Doyle*, it said. *Grant writing, freelance project research and management.* And below that, a phone number.

THREE

Mia

"TABLE SEVEN SAYS these lamb medallions were supposed to be medium rare, but they're well done." Trinn, one of the waitstaff, brandished a partially eaten plate of food through the kitchen pass.

Quashing the little adrenaline jolt of guilt that always hit me when an order went out wrong, I took the plate and confirmed that, yes, the medallions didn't have a hint of pink in the center.

"Okay," I said, trying not to let on how harried I was, with the dining room packed and a line of diners waiting to be seated. "Do we know which table was supposed to get the lamb well done?"

"One with bad taste in meat?" Trinn muttered. "Who orders lamb *well done?*"

I shot her a narrow, quelling look — but before I could tell her to go find out, Paul hurried up, holding a nearly identical plate.

"Table eleven says—" he began.

"That they ordered well done lamb and got it medium rare," I finished for him, taking his plate as well. "Apologize to both tables and tell them their meals will be out as soon as possible. Give them a twenty percent discount on the checks."

I scraped the contents of both plates into the trash and handed them off to be washed. "I need two lamb medallion plates, one medium-rare, one well-done, on the fly!" I called to the line.

"Yes, chef!" came the immediate reply.

No sooner had I retrieved four more lamb medallions for the grill than one of the sous-chefs came rushing over. "Sorry, chef—we're out of asparagus! What do you want us to do?"

"We're *what*?" I snapped, harshly enough that the poor kid flinched. "How the hell can we be out of asparagus?"

"I… I don't know, chef?" he stammered.

More guilt and stress piled onto my shoulders. It wasn't like the sous-chefs were responsible for ordering produce.

"Sorry, Isaiah. Not your fault." I scrambled for the best work-around. "Substitute a medley of summer squash, carrots, and parsnips with mint."

"Yes, chef," Isaiah said, and scurried off.

Christ—now not only would the two tables with the switched lamb have to wait for their meals, but they wouldn't even get what they'd originally ordered. Seriously, how the *hell* could we be out of asparagus?

I gritted my teeth and seasoned the lamb medallions, tossing them on the grill where they sizzled at me accusingly.

"Mia?" Nat's voice cut through the bustle of the kitchen, and my shoulders tensed further.

"Bit busy," I called back.

"What's this about orders going out wrong?" he demanded, ignoring the words.

"Why are we out of asparagus at seven p.m. on the busiest night of the week?" I shot back.

"We can't be out of asparagus," said the guy in charge of making sure we didn't run out of asparagus.

"So, my sous-chef is lying, then?" I asked sharply. "Or maybe he suddenly forgot where we keep the produce. I mean, he's only been working here for a year-and-a-half."

Nat burst into the kitchen, making a beeline for the walk-in cooler. I clenched my jaw and flipped two of the lamb medallions, taking a quick survey of the line to make sure everything else was nominally under control.

"Dress that salad for table three," I said. "It's been sitting there too long. And finish that charcuterie board so it can go out!"

The bustle around me increased, orders flying out just barely fast enough to keep up with the hungry crowd on the restaurant floor. Once upon a time, I'd thrived on this controlled chaos. Now, all I wanted to do was crawl under a giant pile of blankets and hide there for a week.

Nat stomped out of the cooler, two high spots of color on his cheeks. "There's clearly been some kind of mistake."

"Yes, *clearly*," I agreed, in a tone that could have stripped paint. "Tell the waitstaff to warn customers about the substitution, will you? I'm a bit swamped back here."

Trinn approached again, looking like she expected to get yelled at. She was holding a salad bowl this time. "Um… sorry. This wasn't supposed to have parmesan. The customer's allergic."

I took the bowl and thanked her, feeling my blood pressure ratchet up another few degrees as I binned it and called for a replacement.

———◆———

Three hours later, I returned to the house and flopped back on the sofa with my laptop, intent on distracting myself after the worst Saturday dinner service I could remember having since the restaurant opened.

Nat's Jeep was in the driveway, but he wasn't in the living room, the kitchen, or the bedroom. The door to his office at the end of the hall was firmly shut, a strip of light showing through the gap at the bottom. I left him to it, in no hurry for a conversation after an evening spent snapping at each other across a busy kitchen.

I knew I should be browsing something mindless, but my brain wasn't ready to turn itself off yet. Without really intending to, I found myself scrolling through the private forum where a bunch of the newer Michelin star recipients hung out and traded intel.

Maybe I was looking for reassurance that other high-end chefs had off nights, or maybe I was just torturing myself with yet more work-related shit. Whatever the case, the post I stumbled over was one titled *'Michelin inspector spotted in Chicago'* and dated two days ago.

A terrible, sinking feeling made my stomach dip, irrational though it was. St. Louis would likely be the next stop after Chicago on an inspector's list, and we were the only starred restaurant in the area.

It was ridiculous. Just because an inspector might be hitting St. Louis this weekend, it didn't follow that they'd been at tonight's dinner service... or that they happened to have a bad dining experience when the vast majority of orders had gone out just fine.

Still... I steeled myself and set the laptop aside, heading for Nat's office. Whatever else was going on between us, we were business partners. I knocked on the door.

Silence settled for a long moment, but then I heard footsteps and a lock clicking. The door swung open. Nat looked about like I felt — exhausted and overwhelmed.

"Yes?" he said neutrally.

The queasy feeling in my stomach grew. "You should know that a Michelin inspector was spotted in Chicago two days ago." I tried to match his flat tone. "There's a chance they might be in St. Louis this weekend."

I didn't have to spell it out for him. He knew what that could mean as well as I did.

He stared at me for a long moment—the face I'd loved so ardently now cold and distant.

"I need to be alone for a bit," he said eventually. Then he took a step back, and the door closed in my face. Not slammed. In fact, it closed very gently, barely making a sound as the latch slipped home.

Somehow, that was worse.

I stared at the blank wood surface for a few seconds, then turned and walked back to the living room. Without realizing, I was moving like a thief, sneaking silently through my own house as though I didn't have every right to be there. My queasiness had turned into full-blown nausea. I sank down on the couch, clutching a pillow to my stomach as I stared blankly into the middle distance.

I thought I should be feeling more. Anger, or frustration, or fear, or sadness. Not this terrible, sick nothingness. A dull whisper in the back of my mind told me I shouldn't be alone right now... and yet, in that moment, I felt more alone than I ever had in my life.

Rising on numb legs, I shuffled to the empty bedroom and came to a stop before my dresser. My makeup case was in the top drawer. I pulled it out and opened it, slipping the green business card from its place between a compact and a flat of eye shadow. I stared at it for a long time before pulling my phone from my pocket and unlocking the screen.

The text window stared at me blankly as I silently debated.

Finally, decision made, I entered the phone number and texted, *"Hi. This is Mia from the bar last night. You gave me your card. Are you awake?"*

Nothing happened for several moments. Then three dots marched across the bottom of the screen.

"Hi. I wasn't sure you'd use it. What's up?"

I bit my lower lip, rolling it between my teeth.

"Been a bit of a rough day. I know it's late, but could we maybe meet up?"

More dots.

"Sure. I don't sleep much at the best of times. Want to come over?"

The guilt that washed through me was predictable and unwanted. But this time, hard on its heels came something new.

I could say yes. I could get in my car and go see Luca, because my husband, who should have been my rock, was probably sitting in his office right now, contemplating who he was going to fuck next outside of our marriage.

My breath caught in my lungs, a dizzy, untethered feeling making me briefly lightheaded.

"I'd like that," I texted. *"What's your address?"*

FOUR

Mia

THE ADDRESS LUCA texted me was in *freaking Ladue* — only one of the richest places in the entire damned *state*. As I drove along winding, wooded roads barely wide enough for two cars to pass in opposite directions, I fought a surprising surge of imposter syndrome.

I'd been here only a handful of times in my life, most recently during a trip to see the Christmas lights at Tilles Park with my parents a few years ago. While driving around the area afterward, we'd laughed at the almost obsessive habit of hiding giant mansions at the end of long private drives, behind so many trees that we mostly only got fleeting glimpses of tasteful white decorations in the heavily branch-shrouded distance. Eventually, we'd given up and gone to a different part of the city for our infusion of holiday cheer.

There were no Christmas lights now. The roads all looked alike — trees and more trees. I was fully reliant on my phone's map at this point, the cheerful female voice calling out left and right turns until I had absolutely no sense of where I was.

"Your destination is on the left," the voice said with an air of digital finality, as I pulled up to a paved driveway with a mailbox set in a neat brick pillar with an arched top.

For the last fifteen minutes or so, I'd been silently mulling over the apparent disconnect between someone running a youth center for gang members in East St. Louis while living in a mansion in Ladue.

This, despite the fact that it was A) none of my business, and B) a reassuring sign that I wasn't about to be kidnapped at gunpoint and sold into sexual slavery. Maybe I'd ask about the apparent contradiction at some point, if doing so didn't feel too awkward—because as far as I knew, nothing in the area sold for less than a cool million.

This house must have cost a *lot* more than that. It was huge, my headlights scrolling across a massive two-story Neo-Georgian façade as I negotiated the final turn in the driveway. I parked in the generous circle drive, pausing to take it all in as I wondered once again what the hell I was actually doing here.

Coach lamps illuminated the flagstone walk leading up to the entryway, which was brightly lit by two matching glass lantern-style porch lights. I wavered for a moment before deciding that the only thing stupider than driving all this way to hang out with someone I'd met for, like, fifteen minutes in a singles bar, would be to drive all this way, then turn around and drive back to my crappy house and my crappy husband in Jennings.

I turned my phone off and pocketed it—mostly to conserve the battery, but with the added benefit of ensuring I didn't end up on the receiving end of a series of increasingly angry *'where the hell are you'* texts from Nat. Slipping out of the car, I locked it and pocketed the fob, as well.

No sooner had I started toward the imposing front door than it swung open, a slender figure silhouetted inside.

"Hey," Luca said, holding it open for me while I hurried up the low steps leading to the porch. "Come on in. Did you have any trouble finding the place?"

"Nah," I told him, sliding past his thin frame and into an elegant yet welcoming foyer. "I think I startled about half a dozen deer on the way over, though."

He laughed. "They're a bit of a nuisance around here. It's worse in late fall and early winter, unfortunately."

"Look on the bright side," I quipped. "If society collapses, you'll be dining on venison while the rest of us are scraping by on wild nettles and squirrel meat."

"Hopefully not," Luca said, waving me down a short hallway. "Zalen's a vegetarian, and I faint at the sight of blood."

I nodded, pursing my lips against a smile. "Right. I suppose that would complicate matters in most post-apocalyptic zombie scenarios."

"Personally, I'm holding out for an alien invasion, with advanced outer-space overlords who are a step up from the clowns running the show currently," he said. "Here… come back to the kitchen. I can't offer venison, but I thought if you wanted to watch a movie or something, I could nuke some popcorn for us."

"Oh, my God—that sounds *amazing*," I said, the words heartfelt.

I followed him toward the back of the house. He led me through a space that seemed a bit small to be a proper dining room in a house this large—though it might have been a breakfast room with its wall of airy windows on one side. Beyond lay a large and well-appointed kitchen. I took it in with a professional eye.

"This place is absolutely gorgeous," I began, as Luca stretched up to retrieve a packet of popcorn from a high cupboard and popped it into the microwave. He was barefoot, clad in emerald-green track pants and a faded black Depeche Mode T-shirt. His dark hair, which had been artfully messy at the bar, looked more like a slightly squished dandelion puff now. "It's also *huge*. Do you and Zalen live here alone?"

It was a guess on my part—but after the way Luca had talked about Zalen being a vegetarian who wouldn't appreciate the culinary potential of the local deer population, it seemed like a reasonable question.

Luca snorted. "Not alone, no. The house is Zalen's—he was in corporate finance before… erm… before he came back here and started the Hope Project."

It sounded as though he'd been about to say something else, then thought better of it. I didn't comment, but I filed it away as interesting.

He cleared his throat as the sound of popping kernels increased to a steady rhythm in the background. "He has a tendency to… how should I put this? *Collect* people. In a knight-in-shining-armor way, I mean. Not a creepy serial killer way."

"That's reassuring," I said wryly.

He hooked a shy half-smile at me over his shoulder, and *Christ*, this man was pretty to look at. The fact that he seemed to have no clue about his own attractiveness made him even more appealing.

"Sorry," he said. "Some days it feels like I've just barely mastered adulting. Learning how to 'people' is next on the list."

"From where I'm standing, you're doing fine on both counts," I reassured. "Also, your popcorn is about to burn."

"*Shit*," he yelped, whirling back to the microwave to hit the cancel button.

From the smell of things, it was just in time. There might be a few scorched kernels in the bottom of the bag, but the rest would hopefully be fine.

Risking steam burns, my sheepish host tugged the top of the bag open and then shook out his hands to cool them. "Salvageable," he decided, retrieving a bowl and dumping the popcorn into it. He tossed out the handful of blackened kernels. "Drink?"

"Whatever you're having, as long as it's non-alcoholic," I told him.

He grabbed a couple of sodas out of the fridge, handing one to me and then gathering up the bowl, along with a couple of paper towels. With a jerk of his head, he indicated the direction we'd entered from. I followed him back into the main part of the house. When I'd first come through, I'd noticed a formal living room just beyond the foyer, but I hadn't paid much attention to the darkened family room further down the hall.

Now, I saw the low flicker of a television coming from inside. Luca led the way in, and I startled slightly as I realized there was a man seated on the sofa, his attention focused on his phone as the TV played some kind of MMA-style cage fight in the background.

He was a very *large* man.

"Emiel, this is Mia," Luca said, plopping the popcorn down on a coffee table in front of the couch. "She's going to hang out for a bit. Mia, Emiel."

Emiel glanced up from his phone, looking nearly as startled as I'd felt. From his size and appearance, I thought he must be an alpha, but I couldn't catch any scent from him. There was only Luca's summery honeysuckle, along with some older background scents from other people. I thought I recognized Zalen's lime and vanilla among them.

"You've had that show on for hours, dude," Luca said, "and you're not even watching it. I'm commandeering the TV."

Emiel grunted. "Okay," he said easily, rubbing a huge hand over his shaved head.

He rose without another word, his eyes skating over me without quite sticking. By contrast, I couldn't help staring at the mountains of muscle on display. Emiel was dark-skinned and broad-shouldered, contrasting sharply with Luca's delicate paleness. He looked like the kind of person who could snap someone in half, but he walked out of the room as meekly as a lamb, not looking back.

Sudden self-consciousness pierced me. "I didn't mean to evict anyone inside their own home," I said.

But Luca only picked up the remote and flopped down in the space Emiel had just abandoned. "Don't mind him, and don't take it personally. Emiel's not what you'd call a sociable guy. Besides, he really *wasn't* watching the TV. So, we might as well use it."

Setting it aside, I let some of the tension drain out of my shoulders and lowered myself onto the couch next to Luca with a gusty sigh. I cracked open the soda can and grabbed a handful of popcorn as he navigated to one of the many streaming channels on the home screen.

"Have you seen *Red, White, and Royal Blue?*" he asked. "That's been my go-to comfort watch lately."

"I haven't." I wracked my brain for a minute. "Wasn't that a book?"

He nodded. "Mm-hmm. It's a surprisingly good adaptation, believe it or not."

I shrugged agreeably, reaching for more popcorn. "Comfort viewing sounds perfect tonight."

He shot me a sidelong glance. "Rough day, you said?"

I wasn't sure how far into the weeds I wanted to get… not when there was popcorn to be eaten and mindless TV to be watched.

"It was a really bad night at the restaurant," I said. "And also, my husband is a dick."

"Yeah," Luca agreed. "From what little I saw, he kind of is."

We settled in and started the movie, munching popcorn and watching the deeply unlikely but undeniably appealing gay romance between the second in line to the British throne and the son of a US President.

"God, Nat would *hate* this," I muttered, only half aware that I'd spoken aloud.

Luca raised an eyebrow at me. "Not a fan of Hallmark-style romantic comedy? Or not a fan of queer people getting happy endings?"

I flushed as I realized how bad this was going to sound.

"All of it, really," I mumbled. Then, not sure why I felt the need to try and soften it, I added, "He's adopted. His mom and dad aren't exactly what you'd call tolerant people. Born-again Christians. I think they fucked him up pretty bad, in some respects."

Luca made a considering noise and paused the screen, the two protagonists locked in a passionate clinch inside the tack room at a polo match.

I picked at a seam on my jeans—not looking at him, or at the male flesh on display on the television.

"So… feel free to tell me to mind my own damned business," my companion said tentatively. "But if you're so incompatible, and you're both completely miserable in the marriage, why don't you leave him?"

FIVE

Mia

GOD, WHAT A QUESTION. "It's... complicated?" I hazarded.

"Yeah, it usually is," Luca muttered, and I couldn't help thinking he was talking about something other than my own mess.

I could have let it go at that. I *should* have let it go at that, and I had no earthly clue why I didn't.

"We own a restaurant together," I said. "It's our sole source of income, and... uh... there's a fair amount of debt involved."

So much for not getting any deeper into the weeds.

"Ah." Luca's olive-green gaze focused fully on me once more. "Okay, that *is* complicated." He hesitated. "Anyplace I've heard of?"

I sighed and slumped back against the well-worn sofa. "The Elderflower Inn. Soulard." Apparently, I'd needed to talk to someone about this more than I'd realized.

Luca's eyebrows drew together. "The one that's had all those lifestyle articles written about it lately?"

I nodded, a bit sheepishly.

"So, you're not, like, a chef at some random Olive Garden," he went on slowly. "You're the chef-owner of the only Michelin star restaurant in the Midwest?" He blinked. "Damn, girl. Way to go. That's *awesome*."

"Co-owner," I muttered, picking at the seam of a random decorative pillow.

"Right." Luca sobered. "So, you can't ditch the marriage without also sabotaging your crazy success in the restaurant industry."

"Pretty much," I agreed, still laser-focused on the pillow's loose thread.

"Only," he went on, "it seems like your ball and chain *has* pretty much ditched the marriage, except maybe on paper."

I looked up sharply, and he raised a defensive hand — palm out in a placating gesture.

"Again, feel free to tell me to go to hell," he said. "None of my business, etcetera, etcetera."

My throat felt tight and hot with unprocessed bitterness, but I made myself swallow it like I always did.

"It's your business to the extent that you had to rescue me in a singles bar, and now I'm curled on your sofa eating your popcorn and drinking your Dr. Pepper. But… I don't really have any answers for you. Or, y'know, for *myself*."

Luca's green-eyed intensity ratcheted down several notches, and so did his rich, floral scent.

"You came here for escapism, not an interrogation," he said. "Sorry. Zalen says I have a tendency to insert myself into other people's problems as a way of avoiding dealing with my own. Movie?"

There was a fair amount to unpack in that statement… but it wasn't my luggage.

"Movie," I agreed.

Without meaning to, I found myself becoming invested in the implausible third-act romantic misunderstanding, to the extent that I teared up a bit during the messy and emotional reunion on a grand palace staircase. When the final, unexpected twist allowed the star-crossed lovers to be together despite the odds, I had to cover a sniffle.

Clearing my throat, I turned to my host. "I can see why it's your comfort watch. Thanks for sharing it."

He smiled. It was a nice smile.

"Something about the unlikely fairytale ending appeals to me. Reality is deeply over-rated a lot of the time."

I snorted. "Amen."

A rustle of movement drew my attention to the doorway, where a tall figure leaned languidly against the frame.

"Oh, dear. Did I miss evening prayers again?" The scent of sweet fennel and aniseed hit me at the same time as the words.

My eyes landed on trouble dressed in a three-piece suit. Or, more accurately, trouble partially *out* of a three-piece suit. The blond alpha lounged at the edge of our space. The sleeves of his pale rose-colored shirt were rolled up to the elbow, baring well-defined, tattooed forearms. Tailored maroon trousers clung to a lean, swimmer's frame, his matching vest highlighting the breadth of his shoulders and his narrow waist.

He held his discarded suit jacket draped casually over an elbow, and his pale, tousled golden hair had escaped its product to curl over his forehead on one side. More tattoos marched upward from the open shirt buttons at his throat. There was no sign of a tie. An earring glinted in his left ear.

"Yes, we're converting to Pastafarianism," Luca said. "Sorry you missed the ceremony."

"Sounds exhausting," said the alpha. His eyes were some undefined pale color in the light of the television—gray or maybe light blue. He glanced at me with interest before flicking his gaze back to Luca. "Is Zalen here? I need to talk to him."

Luca's body language closed off. "No. He's staying at the center with that kid who was having… er… *trouble at home.*"

The alpha nodded in apparent understanding. "Right. Okay, it can wait until tomorrow. Who's this, then?"

Pale eyes returned to me, and the little jolt I felt somewhere behind my ribcage took me by surprise.

Luca relaxed. "Yes. Sorry. Mia, this is Byron Harper. Byron, this is Mia… uh, I don't actually know your last name."

"Dimitriadis," I said reflexively. "And, no, there won't be a spelling test later."

Sultry lips twitched in a half-smile, and holy *shit*, what the hell kind of place had I walked into? The jolt in my chest rippled, spreading lower… growing heated and heavy.

"Good to know," said the lickable sin-sicle propping up the doorway.

"Mia's a friend," Luca said. "She's hanging out tonight to watch a movie. She is not—I repeat, *not*—a pick-up. Mia, sorry about this. You remember when I told you at the bar that Zalen wasn't actually a neanderthal? This one is, but if you swat him with a rolled-up newspaper, he'll go away."

"Um," I said, caught out at the realization that I wasn't sure I *wanted* him to go away.

"You wound me," the alpha—Byron—said. "And you're also mixing your metaphors pretty badly."

Luca pointed a forefinger at him. "Do *not* harass the omega who came here to chill out and watch movies with me. She isn't on the menu."

I felt like I should probably be saying something on my own behalf, but I had the feeling that if I tried to, it would come out as some fresh variation of *'Um.'* And I didn't think that was the kind of competent, no-nonsense aura I wanted to project.

The situation wasn't helped when Byron looked at me like he wanted to eat me for a midnight snack.

"Pity," he said, holding my gaze unblinkingly. "Because you look like you could use some better stress relief than a cheesy romcom. If you ever change your mind, let me know."

I swallowed hard, hiding a cringe when I realized my scent had just spiked.

Byron gave me a knowing half-smile. It said loud and clear that he had a nose as well as eyes, and he saw right through me.

"Enjoy your evening," he said, and disappeared into the massive house.

Luca sighed. "Okay, that was awkward. Again… sorry about that. He's… well, I guess *harmless* isn't really the right word. But I promise he's not a creeper or anything."

What was it about this place that made me want to pick at things when I knew I should be letting them go?

"You said I wasn't a pick-up. And… you were at a singles bar with Zalen when I met you. Is that something you do?" I asked, willing my pulse to stop beating like a drum in my ears.

Why was I not letting this go?

Luca looked suddenly wary. "Sometimes, yes. Not Zalen, I mean—he was just there to play bodyguard. I mentioned how overprotective he can be."

I licked my lips, taking that on board.

"But seriously, that's not why I invited you to come over," he said quickly. "You just sounded like you needed a friend, that's all."

He was so obviously worried about offending me that I felt bad for pursuing it further. Yet, I couldn't seem to ditch the thoughts racing through the back of my brain—the ones whispering about how my marriage was in a shambles, and there was quite literally nothing stopping me from taking Byron up on his offer.

Rather than the reassurance that should have come out of my mouth when I opened it, I heard a voice that sounded an awful lot like mine asking, "Out of curiosity… if I *had* been a singles bar pick-up, and I was here because I wanted to have sex — what would that look like, exactly?"

SIX

Mia

OKAY, SO APPARENTLY I'd just said that. *Aloud.* I licked my lips, aware that my choices basically consisted of bolting from the couch and making a run for the front door, after which I'd need to have extensive cosmetic surgery and change my hair color in preparation for moving to New Zealand.

Or, alternately, I could brazen it out.

"What would it look like?" Luca echoed blankly. "Um… well… I guess you'd go up to Byron's room and have sex with him?"

He looked faintly shell-shocked, which was fair—but his tone lacked the kind of jealous omega rage that one might normally expect in such a situation. Feeling like I'd fallen through a hole into a pitch-black cave system that I would now have to traverse blindly, I forged ahead, feeling my way.

"Just… with him?" I hazarded. "Not with both of you?"

Because, yeah, that was a totally normal question to ask someone you barely knew. Wasn't it?

Luca made a soft, choked noise.

"It's only that you kind of made it sound like the bar was a… *mutual*… pick-up expedition," I blundered onward, because that felt marginally less terrifying than trying to back-track, at this point.

"Oh, my god," Luca mumbled. "This is a *deeply* weird conversation to try and have from the opposite direction."

Abruptly, I hit the outer limits of my pop-corn and Dr. Pepper-boosted courage. I started to scramble up from the sofa and found its squishy, well-worn cushions surprisingly diffi-cult to escape.

"Sorry… sorry," I babbled. "Don't mind me, it's late, I should probably be leav—"

Slender artist's fingers grasped my fore-arm.

"No, stop," Luca said, sounding some-where between tired and mortified. "It's a totally reasonable question. Sit down. I'm the one who's sorry." He paused, frowning. "Huh. We both apologize too much. Thought that was just me."

Reluctantly, I sank back into the sofa's quicksand-like embrace.

"Omega thing?" I offered sheepishly, to fill the sudden silence.

"Maybe." Luca released his light grip on my arm. He turned his body to face me, swing-ing his feet up on the cushions and hugging his knees to his chest… making himself small. "To answer your question—yes, the singles bar would have been a mutual pick-up, if I'd found anyone suitable. Which I didn't."

"Okay," I said, not sure what else would be appropriate. Especially when I now had a deeply distracting mental picture of Luca and Byron tag-teaming some naked stranger who absolutely did *not* look like me.

The sharp bite of Byron's pheromones still permeated the room. I squirmed a bit, cursing my own betraying scent.

"Look," Luca said, drawing my gaze back to his expressive green eyes. "If you want to get revenge on your husband by having your own hookup, Byron is an A-plus candidate for that. He won't care that you're using him as much as he's using you, and he'll show you one hell of a good time, no strings attached."

I swallowed hard.

Luca sighed and continued. "But—and I don't mean to sound like an asshole, here—that's a bit too complicated for me. Especially since I already kind of like you. I'm definitely more of a C-minus or D-plus candidate for marital revenge sex."

It was such an honest answer that it succeeded in jolting me out of my mental porno reel, thank goodness.

Do not tell him how hot you think he is, I coached myself in firm tones. *Do not, under any circumstances, say anything to make it sound like you were using his friendly invitation for a movie night to get at his hot alphas. Because for one thing, that would make you an asshole, and for another, it's not even true.*

"You know what?" I said. "I think I need a friend more than I need another nail in the coffin of my marriage."

Luca looked relieved, though it might just have been because it meant he could change the subject to something less awkward.

"Cool. In my experience, relationship drama is more entertaining in movies than it is in real life." He seemed to waver for a moment, then he pulled out his phone and started thumb-typing. "I'm texting you Byron's number anyway, though. That way, you'll have it if you ever need to bring out the big coffin-nailing guns. You can bypass me completely and do whatever you need to do."

My phone was still turned off to thwart any pissy texts from Nat that might be coming my way. I resisted the urge to pull it out and check my messages. I *didn't* manage to resist my body's small, internal shiver of… what? Anticipation? Excitement?

When the hell had my brain decided it was excited by the prospect of cheating on Nat?

It's not cheating, I reminded myself. *We have an open marriage. Apparently.*

"Okay, thanks," I said. "I think." Narrowing my eyes, I examined him for any subtle signs of jealousy that I might have missed earlier. "And… you're really okay with that? I know you said at the bar that you and Zalen weren't together. But aren't you and Byron together? I mean, if you're bringing home people to, um… *share*."

Not your business, not your business, my conscience chanted.

Except… if Luca was setting me up with Byron, it kind of *was* my business.

Green eyes slid away from mine. Luca let his phone fall onto the sofa cushion next to his hip.

"It's not what you're thinking," he said, sounding tired. "Byron and Zalen help with my heats sometimes, that's all. The rest is… stress relief, I guess you'd say? It doesn't really mean anything. I'm not exactly mating material."

Once again, I stifled the urge to unpack someone else's baggage. Fortunately, the little voice in my head that occasionally steered me toward good life choices screamed *'danger, danger, do not proceed!'*

I actually listened to it, for once.

"Got it," I said. "But promise me that if I accidentally step on your toes in any way, you'll tell me? I wasn't kidding earlier when I said I needed a friend more than I need a bit of action on the side."

Even when the action was hotness in a three-piece suit.

Luca waved the words away. "I don't own Byron's dick. You're not stepping on anyone's toes."

I tried not to read anything into the fact that he didn't add, *'and Byron doesn't own mine.'* He probably thought it went without saying.

I couldn't stop the small, nervous laugh that escaped. "Well, for what it's worth, I'm not really *'action-on-the-side'* material. I think I just have a slight weakness for tattoos and rumpled three-piece suits."

To my relief, Luca only snorted. "Don't we all."

<hr>

I'd half-expected an interrogation from Nat the following morning. But when I finally checked my phone after pulling into the driveway, there had been no angry, butt-hurt texts waiting for me. Nat's office door was still firmly shut, and I gathered he was sleeping on his futon. By the time I woke up, he was already gone, presumably to the gym.

I couldn't decide if the icy cold shoulder was better or worse than another fight would have been. In the end, I went back to sleep until it was time to shower and go to the restaurant. Nat was already there, and the walk-in was freshly stocked with asparagus, at least. What minimal amount of conversation we exchanged was clipped and businesslike.

Only later that night, when we were back at the house, did he finally acknowledge that I'd left and gotten back well after one a.m.

"You've clearly got your own thing going on, Mia. Maybe it would be best if we focused on the restaurant. The rest of this isn't working, and it hasn't been for a long time."

"Yeah, I'd noticed," I told him, hating the way my inner omega wanted to cringe and grovel in the face of his emotional distance.

And then, he left.

Was he running to the arms of a lover? Staying at a hotel because he couldn't stand the sight of me? Sleeping on a bench in the changing room at his twenty-four-hour gym?

Unless I stooped to monitoring his credit card, I had no idea. And that assumed he only had the card that I knew about.

The next couple of weeks fell into an uncomfortable pattern where we interacted the bare minimum necessary. I texted with Luca a few times and met him for a morning coffee once, but I resolutely didn't use the number he'd given me for Byron. Things were plenty complicated already without adding *that* particular wrinkle.

Service at the Elderflower Inn continued to suffer. The staff was, understandably, on edge. There was nothing quite as catastrophic as that terrible dinner service on the night I'd visited Luca, but the quality of the food was suffering, and so was the front-of-house atmosphere.

Worst of all, the entire time it felt as though a guillotine was hanging over my head in the form of a Michelin star review. It took many positive visits for the inspectors to grant a star, but only one or two bad ones to take that star away.

If the forum gossip had been right... if an inspector had *happened* to show up on our worst night, and they *happened* to be one of the customers whose order was incorrect...

If a different inspector *happened* to follow up while Nat and I were dragging our marital shitshow into the kitchen…

———◆———

I wasn't kept waiting very long. The letter came twenty-two days after that first, terrible dinner service.

'We regret to inform you that after multiple anonymous inspections, our inspectors have found a sharp decline in the quality of fine dining at the Elderflower Inn. In fairness to our readers, we are considering removing your one-star status from the Michelin Guidebook. Rest assured that future inspections may eventually result in reinstatement, should the quality return to previous standards…'

I stared at the words for long minutes, uncomprehending. They blurred and shifted on the page, which rested on the chipped Formica of my kitchen table next to the torn envelope.

Nat wasn't here. As usual, I didn't know where he was.

A drop of clear liquid landed on the letter's formal closing. *Sincerely yours…*

In the next moment, I was sobbing—collapsing into a worn dining room chair like a puppet with cut strings. I couldn't breathe. Snot ran from my nose in a river. My eyes felt hot and tight in their sockets.

I wanted to scream, to throw things, to smash furniture.

But all I could do was weep, until my head pounded with pain, and my chest hurt like it was being constricted by a steel band.

Afterward, I lay with my head in my arms on the table for what must have been half an hour at least. Eventually, I peeled myself out of my chair and stumbled to the bathroom to splash icy water on my face. I stared at my reflection in the mirror for more long minutes, not truly recognizing the pasty gray woman with the bloodshot eyes gazing back at me.

Blankly, I pulled out my phone. The text with Byron's phone number was buried beneath random back and forth with Luca about whatever came into our heads that we'd wanted to share during the last three weeks.

I pulled it up and opened a new text window.

Hi, it's Mia, I typed. *Is that offer of no-strings attached sex still open?*

I hesitated, then hit send.

A minute passed, then another.

Just when I was about to turn the phone off in abject humiliation, dots marched across the screen.

Hot rom-com girl? Yeah, sure thing. Meet at a hotel? Where will you be coming from?

Jennings, I texted back, floating inside a gray, fluffy cloud of surreality.

Another pause, then more dots.

I'll be at the Super 7 North on Broadway in an hour. Ask for a key at the desk under my name.

Then, hard on the heels of that message…

Oh, right. I know you said there wasn't going to be a spelling test, but text me your last name so I can have that keycard waiting for you.

Dimitriadis, I sent.

See you there, he replied.

I turned the phone off and returned it to my pocket robotically.

"Well," I told the empty house. "That was a lot easier than I assumed it would be."

SEVEN

Mia

THE MOTEL WAS clean and pleasant, but nothing to write home about. I'd have liked to be able to say that I agonized over driving there... that I nearly turned around at every intersection.

It would have been a lie.

The woman at the front desk gave me a surreptitious once-over, which really drove home the fact that I was showing up for a one-night stand smelling like cooking grease and with eyes red-rimmed from crying. Fortunately, she didn't feel the need to comment. I had no doubt she'd seen way worse walk through the glass double doors into her lobby.

"Mia Dimitriadis," I said. "There should be a key waiting for me under the name Byron Harper."

"May I see some I.D., please?" she asked in a neutral tone.

I passed over my driver's license, telling myself it was good that they didn't let anyone walk in and claim to be someone they weren't. It wasn't as though she was going to post it to social media with the caption '*Look who showed up at the local Super 7 for a hook-up!*' followed by a bunch of shocked face emojis.

The receptionist made a noncommittal noise and handed the license back to me. She rummaged behind the desk for a few moments—just enough to make me irrationally nervous—and came up with a key card.

"Room 208," she said. "Checkout is at eleven a.m., and the wi-fi password is on the card sleeve."

I glanced down at the open cardboard sleeve as she placed it on the desk. Beneath the words '*Complimentary Wi-Fi in all rooms,*' someone had handwritten the password '*pRetty_fLy_4_a_WiFi!*'.

I was guessing motel reception work got boring sometimes.

"Thank you," I told her, trying not to sound like an unhappily married person getting ready to screw a virtual stranger after crying her eyes out over a lost Michelin star. I wasn't sure how well I succeeded.

I headed toward the elevators and suddenly realized that I didn't have a bag with me. Should I have packed a bag? Were you *supposed* to pack a bag for casual revenge sex? If so, what did people put in it?

I hesitated, stuck on this one small but ridiculous aspect of what I was doing. As I stood there gaping like a fool, a gray-haired couple hauling wheeled suitcases approached the elevator bank from the other direction, talking earnestly to each other. I wrenched myself free of my paralysis. Closing the final few steps, I pushed the elevator '*up*' button.

The doors closest to me dinged immediately and slid open. I stepped inside.

"Ooh, hold that for us, would you, love?" called the elderly woman.

I slapped a hand on the edge of the door to keep the elevator car open for them, and the pair hurried inside.

The woman smiled. "Thank you! Fourth floor for us, please." Her expression fell as I pushed the buttons for the second floor and the fourth floor. "Oh, dear. Is everything all right, sweetheart? Have you been crying?"

"Rosie!" said the man, sounding mortified. "Don't be rude!"

Rosie scowled at him. "It's not rude to ask if someone's all right, Jeff!" she shot back.

Thankfully, the elevator had already started its journey upward, and it barely took any time to reach the second floor. It settled to a stop and dinged at us, breaking the moment.

"I'm fine," I said, slipping out as soon as the doors parted. "Thanks for asking. Have a lovely evening."

I power-walked down the hall, the sound of the two betas arguing growing fainter behind me as I put distance between us. Unfortunately, based on the room numbers, I'd power-walked in the wrong direction. I waited until I could be sure the elevator had moved on before back-tracking.

Room 208 was about halfway along the hall on the right side. Only when I stopped in front of it did I realize that my heart was pounding like a sledgehammer in my chest, the vibration echoing throughout my body. My hand shook as I plucked the keycard out of its sleeve and stuck it in the slot. I pulled it out briskly, but the little light on the handle stayed red.

Feeling like I was trapped in one of those dreams where everything conspires to keep you from completing even the simplest of tasks, I turned it a hundred and eighty degrees and jammed it in the slot again.

Still red.

Was the universe trying to give me a message? Was fate trying to stop me from making a mistake I'd regret for the rest of my life, or—

The handle turned, the latch clicking open a moment before the door swung inward. I stood frozen in the hallway, staring at a broad chest covered with a partially unbuttoned light green tailored shirt and a dark, emerald-colored vest.

"Hello," said a faintly amused voice— deep, but smooth... like the purr of a lazy housecat.

I craned up to meet Byron Harper's gaze and swallowed hard. Had he always been so tall?

"Um... hi?" I said.

The expression of amusement deepened as Byron stepped back, giving me space to enter. "Hi. Why don't you come in, rom-com girl."

I went in, ignoring the sense that I should be taking this last chance to run back home and pretend this whole thing never happened.

The room appeared untouched except for an emerald-green suit jacket flung carelessly over the back of a chair, and a laptop open on the desk in front of it. Had he brought work to do while he was waiting, or in case I stood him up?

Behind me, the door clicked closed. I turned to see the blond alpha walking toward me, brushing past my frozen form in the room's cramped entryway. The sharp, delicious scent of aniseed and fennel wrapped around me, prickling its way along my nerves like tiny needles.

I cleared my throat. "So..." I began, with no idea what words came after that.

"So," he echoed, with the same crooked half-smile that had first made me realize I might be in trouble, back at his and Luca's house in Ladue. "You have the look of someone who's never done this before. Put your handbag on the dresser and have a seat on the bed."

I complied before realizing I was doing it, watching wide-eyed and silent as he leaned a hip against the heavy desk and started deftly removing his cufflinks.

"Is there anything I should know about before we start?" he asked casually, as though he had this kind of conversation every day.

Maybe he did.

"Like... what, exactly?" I asked. My mouth was dry. I licked my lips, trying to work up some moisture. Unhelpfully, my lady parts chose that moment to release a little pulse of dampness.

He tilted his head, considering me. "The usual. Likes, dislikes. Known venereal diseases. Whether that wedding ring on your finger plays into this scenario in a way I need to know about."

The blood drained from my face fast enough to make me dizzy. Like an idiot, I looked down at my left hand, where... *yup.*

Wedding ring.

I'd forgotten to take it off... not that you couldn't still tell I usually wore one. Zalen had figured it out quickly enough that night at the bar.

I squared my shoulders and tried to rally. "Didn't Luca tell you everything about me?" My tone came out more aggressive than I'd intended, but I forced myself to hold that pale alpha gaze defiantly. His eyes were gray, I noted. No hint of blue.

"Luca wants to be *friends* with you," Byron said, placing a faint, ironic emphasis on the word. "He hasn't told me a thing; not since warning me off, that first night when you came to the house."

"Well, it's pretty simple," I nearly spat the words. "My husband demanded an open marriage. So, I'm giving him one."

Byron nodded, as though to himself. "Fair. I can work with that."

For some reason, the urge to push boundaries made me keep talking. "Aren't you going to ask me why I've been crying?"

He tossed his cufflinks onto the desk. "Not your therapist, pet. Unless you want me to ask if you're a big girl who can make her own decisions about who she fucks."

Some kind of large, scary emotion was rising up in my chest, even as the scent of rich alpha pheromones frayed my control.

"I can make my own decisions," I grated out. "And no, I don't have any goddamned venereal diseases."

That was *one* positive aspect of never getting laid, anyway.

"Glad to hear it." He still sounded amused, the fucker. "Now tell me what you want out of tonight. Other than revenge, I mean."

A dozen answers swirled around, trapped behind my lips. None of them felt right, though. None of them felt *true*.

I took a hitching breath and whispered, "I want to forget. Just… just for tonight."

"Forget what?" he asked.

"Everything," I told him. "I want to forget *everything*."

He nodded again, as though he'd already known what I was going to say.

"That, I can definitely do." He lifted his chin, looking down at me with an assessing eye. "Now, strip and kneel on the bed, rom-com girl. You and I are going to be here for a while."

EIGHT

Mia

I GAPED AT the alpha still propping up the hotel room desk as he rolled his shirtsleeves up with slow deliberation. I wasn't quite sure what I'd expected out of this, but it was definitely something other than *'strip and kneel on the bed.'*

I didn't like the way my body seemed to be responding to his brusque, almost dismissive tone. The little needy throb in my gut didn't line up with the image I had of myself... of the competent, take-charge person I thought I was supposed to be.

The swirling scents of spicy alpha musk and my own lighter floral perfume were making it hard to think. I rose from where I'd been perched on the edge of the bed, straightening to my full—if not very impressive—five-foot-two inches as I tried to summon my head-chef mojo.

"Strip?" I asked in disbelief. "What, just like that?"

Why had I *come here*? Why did I feel the need to act like a bratty teenager with this alpha, when the smart thing to do would be to turn around and march straight out of this hotel room before anything irrevocable happened?

As if he'd seen straight through my skull and read my thoughts, Byron lifted an eyebrow. "Door's over there," he said, indicating the room's exit with a small jerk of his chin. "And your bag's right there. You're the one who initiated this hookup, rom-com girl." His gray eyes took on a calculating air. "*Stay or go.*"

A low alpha bark underlined the final three words, and a gasp escaped my lips—completely outside my control. My mind went abruptly, blissfully blank for the space of three heartbeats.

Then it penetrated that he'd ordered me to make a decision about… something?

Oh.

Right.

I was supposed to decide if I was leaving.

If you leave, you'll have to pick up all that heavy weight again and carry it, a small voice whispered. *If you stay here, you can put it down for a little while.*

I wasn't aware that my shaking fingers had started unbuttoning my shirt until it gaped open, baring skin and the cups of my bra.

"Keep going," Byron said. The bark was gone, but the threat of it was still there.

"Make me," I whispered, not sure if it was a plea or a dare. Already, the pleasant blankness was lifting, and that wasn't what the little omega voice that lived in my hindbrain wanted.

Byron made a low sound like a purr.

"Clearly, your husband is an idiot." His voice lowered to a murmur. "There's a lot of that going around these days, for some reason." Then the bark came back with a snap. "Shirt and bra *off.*"

I struggled out of the open shirt as though it had suddenly become red hot. My blood buzzed beneath my skin as I craned awkwardly behind me to undo my bra clasp. The constriction of the band around my ribcage released, and I let the straps slide down my arms. Cool air caressed my nipples, which had hardened to painful points.

"*Keep going.*" The words were half growl, half purr.

It felt like cliff-diving… like taking that first big jump into the unknown during my honeymoon in Costa Rica. The promise of cool relief from the heat waited far below, if only I could overcome the deep-seated phobia of leaping into danger.

I unhooked and unzipped, grasping work slacks and underwear together and pushing them down. The lips of my sex were slick and wet. My perfume rose around me in a cloud, darker and heavier than before.

Byron's nostrils flared. "Delectable. Now, kneel on the bed. Face the headboard and grab it with both hands. *Move.*"

The air in the room that had felt chilly against my skin a few minutes ago had somehow become thick and steamy. I practically had to swim through it, my consciousness floating through the murk of instinct. Byron's gaze felt like a physical touch. I imagined I could feel it traveling over my body.

The heavy wooden headboard was a grounding point of solidity as my knees wobbled on the shifting pillowtop mattress. I stared at the nondescript floral artwork hanging above the bed, afraid to look over my shoulder at the alpha prowling around the room. Was he getting undressed? The faint sound of fabric swishing against fabric reached my straining ears.

My whole body was trembling by the time a heavy weight dipped the mattress next to me. A whimper tried to escape my throat as a callused hand swept loose hair back from my face.

A silky strip of fabric appeared in my vision, and I jerked my head back, startled.

"Ah, *ah*," Byron tutted, waiting until I stilled before lifting it to cover my eyes.

My breathing quickened. The scent of fennel and anise imbued the cloth—a dark green necktie. *Byron's* necktie. I hadn't seen him wear one on either occasion I'd been in the same room with him, but this tie had hugged his throat at some point, close to his scent glands. The spicy aroma soaked into the cloth had the unmistakable richness of pheromones direct from the source.

The tremor in my muscles eased as I breathed it in. I let out a low moan as he snugged it around my head and tied it, blindfolding me.

"Good girl." The pads of his fingers were rough as he stroked down the length of my spine possessively.

The position should have been humiliating… perhaps even frightening. My sex pulsed, a dribble of slick dripping down my inner thigh.

My nipples ached, throbbing in time with my pounding heartbeat.

"Such a hot little omega," Byron murmured. "No one's taken care of you in a very long time, have they?" His work-roughened fingers trailed over my ass, kneading the firm globe. "Now... *don't move. Don't make a sound.*" The alpha bark was back, spiking through my brain, playing on the deeply buried instincts that demanded I submit.

The breath punched out of me, but soundlessly; my mouth open wide.

He could do *anything* to me like this. I'd given up control—the whole thing was out of my hands now. Only my memory of Luca's words kept this situation from being completely insane.

If you want to get revenge on your husband by having your own hookup, Byron is an A-plus candidate for that, he'd said. *He won't care that you're using him as much as he's using you, and he'll show you one hell of a good time, no strings attached.*

Luca wouldn't have hooked me up with some kind of crazy serial killer. This was exactly what it seemed like—an alpha who, for whatever reason, liked screwing random omegas for recreation without getting attached.

He was *exactly* what I needed, and I—

My thoughts fled like a flock of startled geese. The hand that had been stroking over my back and ass returned up the length of my spine. Byron circled a thumb over my virgin mating gland.

Nat had always been weirded out by this part of my omega biology. His appalled reaction when I'd shyly asked if he wanted to bite me on our wedding night had been my first clue that my marriage to a beta might not end up being as idyllic as I'd dreamed.

Byron's firm touch might as well have had a direct connection to my clit. Every muscle in my body locked solid. Only his earlier barked command not to move kept me from levitating off the damned mattress.

His large, warm hand covered the juncture of my neck and shoulder, urging my upper body down until my back was parallel to the bed and my ass was in the air. I held onto the headboard for dear life, and nearly bit my own tongue in half when the fingers of his other hand brushed my folds, sliding through slippery moisture.

I swallowed the noise that tried to escape as two slick digits pressed inside me, while his thumb swiped some of my honey further back, teasing a place that Nat had never even gone near.

Dizziness made my head spin, my eyes tightly closed behind the silken barrier of the blindfold.

"Such a sweet little omega," Byron crooned. "This is what you were made for, isn't it? Not some damned fool who doesn't appreciate what he's got."

My chest hitched on a silent, choked sob— every bit of my awareness focused on the fingers teasing me… the hand covering my mating gland.

My nipples and clit pulsed and throbbed with the need to be touched. But the slide and stretch of the fingers inside me was enough. It slowly urged my body higher, until everything felt warm and heavy and liquid.

When my climax rocked me, it came as a total surprise. The hand grasping my shoulder slid up to cover my mouth, holding in the low keening noise that had been building in my throat before it could escape. Slick gushed around Byron's fingers as I came silently, shaking like a palsy victim.

Before I could clamp down on him, he pulled out of me and attacked my oversensitive clit. I almost collapsed, only my shaking grip on the headboard keeping me up. Byron tormented me with slow, teasing circles around my nub, his other hand still muffling my mouth as he drove me to a second, stronger orgasm.

Beads of sweat popped out on my chest, my lungs heaving as I sucked in whistling breaths through my nose. Only when the last jerking spasms had subsided did Byron release me. He reached forward, unclenching my hands from their white-knuckled grip a finger at a time. Then he eased me down to lie on my front.

"You're doing so well, beautiful," he said. "Housekeeping's going to see the puddle on these sheets and know *exactly* what happened in here."

The words sent a shudder through me, but before I could decide whether to be mortified or hopelessly turned on, strong hands lifted my hips until I was kneeling again.

Presenting.

A whuffle of hot breath was all the warning I had before an agile tongue rasped up the length of my slit. I made a tiny, wounded-bird noise; unable to stifle it.

Byron either didn't notice or didn't care that I'd broken the rules, too involved in lapping up the mess I'd made of myself. His tongue curled inside me, setting off sparks behind the blindfold.

"More," I begged, beyond shame as my need to be filled up and knotted swamped my higher brain functions. "Please… *please,* alpha!"

A low hum of male satisfaction vibrated against my folds, thrumming up the length of my spine and making my scalp tingle. The lips and tongue disappeared, and my heightened senses tracked the sound of a zipper, followed by the sound of crinkling plastic.

A condom? *God,* I hadn't even thought to bring one.

Was he still fully dressed? My brain whited out at the mental picture, and only came back online when something large and blunt pressed at my entrance and slid inside, inch by agonizing inch. I moaned, trying and failing to stifle the sound.

"That's all right, beautiful. Let me hear you. Let's see if you can get us thrown out of this hotel for public indecency."

His hands urged me upright until my back was plastered against his front, my thighs spread wide around his as he thrust into me. As predicted, I yelped so loudly it probably woke whoever was unlucky enough to be in an adjoining room.

It was *so good*. It was everything I'd needed, and that was *before* Byron reached around me to cup and torment my breasts. One hand slid down my stomach to tease my clit, and I was gone, crying out in time with his deep, rolling thrusts.

I let out an honest-to-god shriek as my third climax hit, my body clamping around Byron's cock like a vise. He let out a low groan, his dick pulsing as he came. A moment later, I felt the swell of his growing knot inside me, tying us together.

A heavy, warm feeling spread outward from the connection, turning my muscles to jelly and my brain to goo. There was absolutely nothing wrong in the *entire world* as he eased us carefully down to lie spooned on the bed, pillowing my head on a well-muscled, cotton-clad bicep.

Nothing hurt. Everything was fuzzy blankets and rainbows as my consciousness settled into the absolute peace and contentment of a knotting fugue, cradled in the arms of a stranger.

NINE

Mia

I WOKE AFTER several hours of coma-like sleep interspersed with smoking hot sex — which had involved at least three rounds and included enough orgasms that I'd lost count. Three things jostled for my groggy attention, each one sending a shock along my nerves, but for totally different reasons.

First, there was a mostly soft cock nestled inside me. Byron's warm, muscular body was curled around and over me from behind, which had become a familiar sensation during the night. His weight pressed me into the pillowy soft mattress, and it had no business feeling nearly as good as it did. His knot was deflated, and I wasn't clamping down on him. He just... hadn't slipped out yet.

Second, and somehow considerably more jolting, teeth and lips were wrapped around the juncture of my neck and left shoulder, softly suckling at the tender skin there. My mating gland was on the other side — like most omegas, I was right-glanded. None of which did anything to stop the flood of melting pleasure spreading sluggishly through my veins in response to the symbolism of an alpha putting his mouth there.

I would have devoted more brainpower to freaking out over this and panicking about the best way to extricate myself. Except, *third*—the heavy drapes drawn across the hotel room's window were utterly failing to block the bright morning sun shining outside.

Morning.

Sun.

And not *early morning* sun from the looks of it. I yelped in dismay, my muscles jerking before I could control them. Byron startled awake, his dick sliding out of my body even as his teeth tightened convulsively on my skin.

I felt the moment he regained enough awareness to realize what he was doing to my neck. This wasn't difficult, since it involved him letting out an audible gasp while simultaneously shoving away from me as though my body had become red hot.

Meanwhile, I lay motionless as a statue, my omega freeze response in full force. *Thank you so much, limbic system. Really helpful. No, seriously. This is great.*

"Um," I managed, since that seemed to be my default verbal response around this alpha.

Silence fell.

The room was choked with stale sex pheromones, but behind me, Byron's spicy aniseed scent was doing something complicated that my nose couldn't interpret. The bed shifted as he rose, putting more space between us. I finally grasped some control of my muscles and rolled onto my back, tugging the cotton sheet up to cover my breasts as I moved.

This allowed me to see him properly in the diffuse morning light. And... *huh.* Apparently, not even Mr. Cool could make *'naked and freaked out with a used condom slowly sliding off his limp dick'* look anything other than painfully awkward.

His face resembled the human version of a PC rebooting. He stared at me blankly for several excruciating seconds before blinking twice. With what looked like conscious effort, he smoothed his expression and rescued the slipping condom before it could fall all the way off, tying a knot in it and tossing it in the trash. I tried, without success, to remember at what point in the proceedings he'd lost all his clothes.

My eyes slipped down, drawn to a deep, puckered scar in his side, a few inches below his ribcage. An attempt had been made to incorporate it into a large tattoo of jungle flowers and thorny vines, but it wasn't really the sort of scar that could be hidden.

He must have seen me looking, because there was a brittle edge to his voice when he spoke.

"Sorry, rom-com girl. I didn't mean to fall asleep on you. Not sure what happened—just tired, I guess."

He cleared his throat. "I have to go now, but you should help yourself to the shower or whatever. Checkout is at eleven. There's probably, uh, some kind of a breakfast buffet downstairs if you're hungry."

Without waiting for a reply—which was good, since I didn't have one—he scooped up his discarded clothing from the floor, the back of the chair, and a few other random surfaces, then disappeared into the bathroom.

I lay there, still mired in omega instincts screaming *stay still don't move* from the depths of my amygdala. Less than five minutes later, Byron emerged dressed, but otherwise looking exactly like someone who'd just had a wild, hours-long sexfest in an unremarkable two-star hotel.

He gathered up his laptop without a word. At first, it seemed like he'd flee the room without so much as acknowledging me, but as his hand fell on the doorknob, he paused.

"You know, life's too short to spend it harnessed to people who don't treat you right," he said over his shoulder. "Thanks for the evening, beautiful."

The door opened. The door closed.

I lay there for several more minutes, staring at it. Eventually, my panic over how late it was overpowered my panic over how good it had felt to let an alpha fuck me and then fall asleep with his teeth teasing my neck. I stumbled into the plastic shower enclosure and scrubbed the scent of sex from my skin with something like desperation, flinching as various intimate aches made themselves known.

Clearly, my body wasn't going to let me forget what I'd done anytime soon.

I dropped off the keycard at the front desk and drove back to Jennings on autopilot, dread sitting hot and heavy in the pit of my stomach. Nat already had suspicions about what I'd been up to lately, even if they'd been infuriatingly incorrect before last night.

I reminded myself firmly that all of this was *his* doing. *He* was the one who couldn't keep it in his pants. Somehow, that didn't make me any more excited about the prospect of walking into the house at nine-thirty a.m. while wearing yesterday's rumpled clothes.

The driveway was empty when I pulled in. On the one hand, it was a relief. On the other hand, it was only a delay of the inevitable. Maybe he'd been out all night, too.

I let myself into the modest home that seemed less like a haven and more like a battleground these days. It was silent except for the rumble of the ancient gas furnace and the rattle of the icemaker. I wandered into the kitchen, having been too rushed and freaked out to consider taking advantage of the free continental breakfast at the hotel.

My eyes fell on the table. Abruptly, sick queasiness flip-flopped my stomach.

The letter. How in the *hell* had I forgotten about the letter?

'*I want to forget everything.*' The ghost of my own voice floated through my hazy memory, followed by Byron saying, '*That, I can definitely do.*'

The warning from the Michelin review board was gone from the tabletop. Unless we'd fallen victim to an oddly specific burglar, Nat had been in at some point last night and found it. At a guess, it was probably sitting in his office now.

Not that it mattered.

The heavy weight of failure crashed down on my shoulders, one of which bore a faint bruise from being sucked on like an omega-flavored lollipop. My Michelin star… my precious and hard-won reward for creating something exceptional. I'd fucked up, and now they were going to take it away. I fumbled for a chair and fell into it, staring at the place where the letter had been.

God *damnit*.

Every single aspect of my life was in a fucking shambles, and I had no idea where to start when it came to fixing any of it. Worse, all it had taken was a fat knot in my pussy and a soothing cloud of alpha pheromones tickling my nose for me to completely forget my responsibilities.

Was *this* the siren song that lured perfectly capable and intelligent omegas into mating bonds with alphas? This desire to let someone else bark at you until you stopped caring about your troubles… until they became someone *else's* troubles?

I shook my head sharply, my bruised neck giving an accusatory twinge in protest of the sudden movement.

I was the head chef of a restaurant. Whether it had a Michelin star or not, I had responsibilities to my staff, to my customers... to the banks that held the liens on the building. I shoved away from the table and stood up, heading to the bathroom for another, longer shower in hopes that it would wash away the remaining dregs of last night.

It didn't help much. As I was dressing for work, my phone pinged from its wireless charger on the bedside table. I checked it with a degree of trepidation, only to find a text from Luca.

Did you break Byron last night?

I stared at the words without comprehension. After a few minutes, I typed '*No...?*' and sent it. Then I followed up with '*Why?*'

Dots marched across the screen.

He was late to work and he's acting really...

I waited. When no new message appeared, I sent '*acting really what?*'

Strange, Luca texted.

Somehow, responding with '*That's odd, he seemed fine when he fled the hotel room like a cat with its tail on fire*' didn't seem like the thing to do.

Before I could come up with anything reasonable to say, the dots appeared again.

So, how was it?

I swallowed hard. Was I really having this conversation over text at ten o'clock in the morning with Byron's housemate and occasional lover?

Complicated? I sent. *I got some bad news last night, and my decision making maybe wasn't the best. I have to go to work now, but we could get coffee tomorrow morning and talk then?*

Was it weird that I wanted to see Luca so soon after hooking up with his alpha? Yeah, that was probably weird. God help me, I was turning into a weirdo.

Sure, sounds good, he texted. *Usual time and place? See you there.*

See you there, I agreed.

<hr>

Nat was already at the restaurant when I arrived. He had dark smudges under his eyes, and new stress lines framed the corners of his eyes and mouth. A result of the contents of the letter, I wondered—or of my absence last night?

"Isaiah put in his two weeks' notice," he said, by way of greeting.

It took a second for my brain to refocus on this new piece of information. Then, my heart sank. Isaiah had been my sous-chef for just shy of eighteen months, and he was a talented kid. Him leaving was the last thing I needed.

"Did you try to talk him out of it?" I demanded. "We can't afford to lose him right now!"

"Yes, I tried to talk him out of it," Nat said. "But in case you haven't noticed, working conditions in the kitchens have been kind of shitty lately."

My temper rose; I shoved it back down. Because what was I going to say? No, you're wrong, everything's peachy?

"We need to fill that vacancy as soon as possible," I said instead. "Get a job listing posted. Get me some interviewees."

"Thank you," Nat said coldly. "Believe it or not, I am actually familiar with how staffing works."

Apparently, we weren't going to talk about the letter. Or anything else that had happened last night. Which was probably for the best.

"Sorry," I said. "I know you do. I'm just stressed. We all are."

Exhaustion bowed his shoulders for a moment. "Yeah," he agreed, and went off to do whatever he'd been doing before I got there. Posting the job opening, probably.

I found Isaiah and took him aside before the lunch service started, to see if there was anything I could do to make him stay.

"I would, chef," he said quietly, not meeting my eyes. "Honestly, I would. But it's my mom. She's got early onset dementia. I'm moving back to Philly to help my dad look after her."

I squeezed his shoulder, my heart aching for him. "I'm so sorry. Of course you have to go. She needs you more than we do. If we can write you a reference or help in any way, let us know."

He nodded, pressing his lips together to keep them from trembling, and mumbled a quiet thank-you before heading off to continue his pre-shift prep work.

The lunch crowd was a bit lighter than usual, which was both a relief and a worry. Had word started spreading that the Elderflower Inn wasn't as good as it used to be? I tried not to dwell on it—one lunch service wasn't statistically significant in the grand scheme of things.

I was deep in the rhythm of taking orders, organizing the line, and making sure everything that went out was the kind of quality customers expected from a nationally recognized restaurant. A couple of hours in, Nat poked his head into the kitchen and indicated he needed a word.

It didn't bode well for our relationship that my body's instinctive reaction was to dump a spike of adrenaline into my bloodstream, but I checked that everything was under control and stepped into the hallway that ran behind the staff areas.

"What is it?" I asked, careful to keep my tone neutral.

Nat looked like he'd swallowed a lemon after gargling with razorblades.

"Your alpha fuck-toy is out there," he said from between clenched teeth, the words dripping poison. "Apparently he wants to thank the chef *personally*."

I had a moment's incomprehension—how could Nat possibly know about Byron? He'd never even *seen* him! Feeling like the floor was dropping out from beneath my feet with every step, I turned wordlessly and moved in a daze toward the pass-through, where I could peek out and scan the dining room for a blond head and piercing gray eyes.

TEN

Mia

I SEARCHED THE modestly sized seating area for Byron, my heart in my throat. None of this made any *sense*—wasn't Byron supposed to be at the youth center in East St. Louis? Luca said he'd come in late and was acting strange. Had he left and come back across the river in the middle of the workday?

Even if he had, that still didn't explain why he'd be *here*, of all places. Unless… Luca had told him where I worked? He was the only one in Byron's orbit who knew the name of the restaurant, and for some reason the idea that he might have sent Byron here to talk to me felt like a betrayal.

I *knew* that was irrational. Why shouldn't Luca tell the others that I was the head chef at the Elderflower Inn? It wasn't as though I'd sworn him to secrecy. At most, I'd exhibited a bit of reticence about strangers finding out, because sometimes people got weird about it.

There was no sign of Byron at any of the tables. I was just about to round on Nat and demand to know what he thought he was playing at when my attention caught on long dreadlocks gathered up in a half-bun. The dreadlocks' owner had his back to me, but realization immediately clicked into place with a nearly audible *snap*.

It wasn't *Byron* crossing the invisible demilitarized zone between my fucked-up private life and my equally fucked-up professional life. It was Zalen.

And… not only Zalen. Next to him sat a very tall, very broad alpha with a shaved skull. *Emiel.* They were both wearing smart, well-tailored business suits, and were sharing the table with a pair of older white guys—betas, I was pretty sure—who were also dressed professionally.

My panic began to abate, though this unexpected plot twist did nothing to clear my confusion about why the hell they were here. I turned on Nat.

"For gods' sake," I hissed. "I *told* you—I met the man in a bar *once*, and we talked about neutral subjects for *maybe* ten minutes. That's the sum-total of my lifetime interaction with him!"

"Interesting," Nat said in a monotone. "Because you sure did seem excited when I told you he was out there."

I drew breath to snap at him, before realizing with a lurch that my only defense would be blurting out that I hadn't been excited, I'd been panicking—because I thought he'd been talking about the guy I screwed three times last night in a hotel room.

My inability to defend myself made anger flare in my chest, and the creeping sense of shame that came along with it made the anger even worse. Goddamn it, why was *I* always the one on the back foot, when Nat was the one who'd started us down this road?

"You know what?" I said, low and vicious. "You can go fuck yourself, Nat."

Turning my back on him, I untied my apron with sharp, angry movements and set it aside, revealing my pristine chef's whites beneath. Then I wiped my hands on a clean towel, checked that no stray hair was escaping my toque, and headed out of the kitchen to try and determine why on earth Zalen and Emiel were in my restaurant, asking to see me.

God. I was supposed to meet Luca in the morning for coffee. I'd have to talk to him about this, wouldn't I? What was I going to say, though? *'I'm upset because you told your house-mates something about me, even though I didn't make a point of asking you not to tell them?'*

When had I become such an emotional dumpster fire? Luca wasn't psychic. He hadn't done anything inappropriate. If I gave him a hard time about it, *I'd* be the one in the wrong. At this point, walking toward the table with my heart thudding double-time, I wasn't even one hundred percent sure why I was so upset that Zalen and Emiel were here.

Because their presence had set Nat off? What the hell kind of reason was *that*?

A really unhealthy one, my subconscious whispered helpfully. *Like, 'serious emotional abuse victim' levels of unhealthy. What the fuck, Mia?*

I was *not* an emotional abuse victim, god-damn it. I straightened my spine, squared my shoulders, and pasted a public-facing employee smile on my face as I reached the table.

"Hello," I said pleasantly to the four men as they looked up at me. "I'm Mia Dimitriadis, the head chef. I trust your meal was enjoyable?"

Zalen blinked at me. The two white beta guys greeted me and immediately started enthusing about the parmesan-crusted sea bass and vegetarian lasagna they'd just eaten. Both Zalen and Emiel looked surprised, and I realized with a tiny, internal flinch that I might have been blaming Luca for a situation that had absolutely nothing to do with him.

"Ah," Zalen said after a moment. "Hello. When you said you were a chef, I didn't realize you were the chef *here*. Small world."

"Hi, Mia," Emiel said. "I liked the food. It was really good."

"You three know each other?" asked one of the other men. "Well, that's an interesting coincidence."

I smiled with a bit more real warmth, reminding myself that the Elderflower Inn was one of the premier restaurants in the region, and sometimes random people simply *came here* for special occasions or when they wanted to impress someone.

"We're acquaintances," I said. "We share a mutual friend. Small world, as you say. I'm glad to hear the meal was up to par."

"More than," Zalen said, offering me his own smile.

It was… a truly *devastating* smile. How had I not noticed that before, at the bar? Combined with his clean lime and vanilla scent, I was vaguely horrified to realize that it had awakened a yearning deep in my belly.

One that should have been sated—if not completely comatose—after the night I'd just spent with Byron.

Zalen, thankfully oblivious to my growing embarrassment, gestured to his and Emiel's companions. "Mr. Kettlewell and Mr. Johanssen are here from Chicago. They run the largest private non-profit in Illinois supporting local youth shelters. We wanted to offer them a memorable meal during their visit."

A-*ha*. So, this visit fell on the 'wanting to impress someone' end of the spectrum, it seemed. Well, my irrational behind-the-scenes freakout aside, I hoped they'd succeeded in wooing their potential supporters with food. In fact, maybe there was something else I could do to ensure that they did—beyond providing a decent vegetarian entrée and a plate of perfectly cooked fish.

"That's wonderful," I said, dialing up my smile for the two betas. "From what I hear, the Hope Project is doing some amazing work in a place that really needs it."

I'd taken Zalen by surprise again. Meanwhile, a sweet grin at odds with his 'scary tough guy' appearance spread over Emiel's face for a fleeting moment before self-consciousness seemed to overcome him. Out of nowhere, the absurd desire to know what he smelled like when he wasn't using suppressors washed over me.

"Thank you for that," Zalen said quietly, breaking the moment. "And thank you for the meal, as well. It truly was wonderful."

"That it was," said Mr. Johanssen. "And everyone knows, the way to a donor's heart is through his stomach."

Mr. Kettlewell laughed jovially at this, and I hoped that was a good sign for whatever Zalen and Emiel needed from the pair.

From the corner of my eye, I caught Nat striding in our direction with a pinched look on his face and my patience just… *snapped*. I extricated myself as quickly and smoothly as I could, citing the demands of the kitchen, and headed toward him on an intercept course before he could get within speaking range of the table.

"Do. *Not*," I said through gritted teeth, grabbing him by the upper arm and turning him around to retreat to the kitchen. "Nat, I swear to god — whatever it is that you think you need to interject into this situation, you *fucking don't*."

I was mildly surprised that he let himself be manhandled. Nat was a strong guy even when he *wasn't* practically living at the gym during his off hours. I dragged him back to the empty corridor behind the kitchen and turned on him.

"As I may have already mentioned *several times*, Zalen runs a youth center," I snapped. "He's courting a pair of high-value donors, and in case you've forgotten, we run the only Michelin-star restaurant in the region. He brought the donors here to impress them, and he had no idea I was the head chef—because we've only ever talked for *ten freaking minutes!*"

I glared up at my husband, watching mulish stubbornness war with dawning self-awareness that he might've been acting like a douche canoe for no rational reason whatsoever. My curiosity at which direction he'd try to take this almost outweighed my general state of being *over it*.

"Well," Nat said, his tone giving nothing away. "He clearly knows you work here *now*."

"Yes, he does," I replied, because what the hell else was I supposed to say to that? "And if you have a point to make with that jab, don't bother clarifying. Because I really don't give a shit."

Without another word, I turned and stalked back to the kitchen, trying not to think about how homey and welcoming the big house in Ladue had been, or how my body had gone soft and liquid in response to the alphas' warm smiles.

ELEVEN

Luca

"LUCA?" THE VOICE—Zalen, I identified—sounded like this might not be the first attempt to get my attention.

I surfaced from the multi-page form I'd been filling out, blinking as the familiar dim lighting of my office swam into focus.

"Sorry," I said, the obsessive need to apologize coming helpfully to the fore.

For a big chunk of my life, getting so involved in something that I lost touch with my surroundings had been physically dangerous. That wasn't so much of an issue these days, but it was still disconcerting to realize that someone had been standing outside my office door calling my name, and I'd had no idea.

Two someones, and not the sort of someones it was easy to miss.

Emiel and Zalen stood patiently, just outside the defined boundary of my space, waiting for me to get my shit together enough to interact with them.

"You're back," I said stupidly. "Sorry, come in. I was working on the Johnston-Park Foundation grant. How'd things go with the Chicago people?"

Zalen smiled as he and Emiel came inside and closed the door. Immediately, the air sharpened with the scent of lime and vanilla, covering up the blank space where Emiel's pheromones should have been.

"I think we're in with a chance," Zalen said. "They seemed impressed, and they're cognizant of the unmet need for services in this area."

East St. Louis was an 'area' where Zalen would stand out like a sore thumb for using words like 'cognizant' and 'unmet needs' in casual conversation. He was St. Louis born and bred, but unlike the rest of us, he and his family had gotten out when he was young. His corporate-speak vocabulary was a holdover from the high-powered career he'd had in New York finance, before he'd chucked it all in to move back to his home city.

He'd given up a life of penthouse suites and exclusive cocktail parties in favor of trying to rescue kids like me from their own self-destructive life choices.

He still knew how to wear the uniform, though—even if a well-cut business suit hit a bit different when paired with long dreadlocks. Not, I reflected, that it was a *bad* kind of different.

Nope, not at all.

Nor was Emiel's dangerous, 'barely leashed crime family bodyguard' vibe... although that one tweaked a few more alarm buttons in my fucked-up psyche.

"Where'd you end up taking them?" I asked, knowing Zalen had planned to pull out all the stops.

Grants like the one I was currently working on helped cover the Hope Project's operating expenses, but accreditation and support from non-profits like Jason's Lighthouse in Chicago could pay for expansion and help launch programs like the college initiative Zalen and Emiel had been scheming for months now.

"We ended up at that place across the river with the Michelin star—the Elderflower Inn," Zalen said, looking at me with interest.

"It was good," Emiel said, surprising me by offering unprompted conversation. "Did you know your friend worked there?"

"She doesn't just *work* there. She's the owner," I replied, correcting him automatically. "Well, the co-owner, anyway."

It wasn't a big deal, sure… but something about the assumption that an omega couldn't own a highly successful business rankled.

"She's clearly living the dream," Zalen said. "The place was packed, and the food lived up to the hype."

There was something wistful behind his earthy brown gaze when he mentioned her, and it made a complicated knot twist tighter in my stomach. It wasn't jealousy… at least, not quite. Whatever it was, I didn't like it, though.

Emiel wrinkled his nose. "He had *tofu*. Who has tofu when there's steak on the menu?"

The moment broke.

"Vegetarians?" I offered, amused despite myself. "Hmm. Maybe I should hoard my pennies for a few weeks and go try out this place for myself."

"If Kettlewell cuts us a check for the new addition, I'll treat everyone to a celebration dinner there," Zalen said.

Wait, he wanted to go back? Did that mean he wanted to see her again?

I shook off the intrusive thoughts.

"What, you're going to ask Emiel to do social, people-y stuff twice in one month?" I teased, shooting the larger man a wink to make sure he knew I was kidding. "He'll need a cage match or two first, just to recover from today."

"Got one in a couple of days," Emiel said serenely. "Didn't want to risk showing up to lunch today with a black eye."

"Probably wise," Zalen agreed wryly.

"Want me to come cheer you on?" I asked Emiel, quashing my disquiet over the prospect of him going back to the fights. It was something we joked about, but not something any of us were really all that happy about.

Byron, in particular, seemed to hate the idea.

I'd seen a handful of Emiel's matches over the years. On the one hand, I liked watching him do something he was undeniably good at, especially since he was so self-conscious so much of the time. On the other hand, the unrestrained violence brought back some memories that were better left buried.

"You shouldn't go to those places, Luca," Emiel said, his heavy brow furrowing. "The people there aren't good people."

"*You* go there," I replied mildly.

"Yeah, I do," he said, as though it was an answer.

Zalen sighed. "He has a point, Em." Emiel drew breath to say something, but Zalen put a hand up to forestall him. "No, I get it. There's a reason we teach the kids here boxing and martial arts. I know it helps with… everything."

"Gotta keep my skills sharp," Emiel said. "Otherwise, one of these little punks'll take me down some day during sparring, and then where will we be?"

It was a fair point, even if there objectively wasn't much danger of that happening. On a daily basis, the alphas dealt with a building full of teenagers who'd grown up with guns, knives, and brass knuckles while other kids were playing with dolls and toy trucks. Not to mention, some of those teenagers were also alphas, and hormonal as hell on top of it.

Zalen, Emiel, and Byron were all capable of whipping out the dominance when it was needed, and it was needed with a fair amount of regularity inside the walls of this place.

"Don't worry," Zalen said. "I'll just keep pretending I don't know that one of my instructors pummels people in a semi-legal gambling venue for fun."

I winced. There was nothing *remotely* legal about the places where Emiel fought.

"You should try it some time," Emiel muttered. "'S good stress relief."

◆

I met Mia bright and early the following morning at a hole-in-the-wall coffee shop we'd visited a few times before. She came in with heavy bags under her eyes and her hair pulled up in a messy don't-give-a-shit ponytail. Not for the first time, I wondered if the woman ever slept. Restaurant hours didn't seem like they'd mesh well with meeting for coffee at six thirty in the morning... and yet, here we were.

The triple espresso she was currently eyeing like she wanted to have its delicious, highly caffeinated babies lent support to the idea that she was surviving more on stimulants than sleep. She took a sip, then closed her eyes and let out a nearly sexual moan before setting the cup down on the table in front of her.

I drank a few swallows of my own caramel macchiato, watching her intently.

"God, I needed this," she said. "So, how've you been doing?"

"Good," I told her, not untruthfully. Things had been quiet, except for an abused kid Zalen was currently trying to keep out of the court system, and Byron stalking around the place like someone had kicked his pet puppy. "Zalen and Emiel really liked the restaurant, by the way. They don't usually go on about food like that."

Instead of looking pleased, she flushed and looked down at her drink, turning it around and around in her hands.

"Oh," she said. "That's good."

I frowned, ducking down a bit to catch her eye. "Um… I'm not really getting 'proud restauranteur' vibes here. Were they not supposed to enjoy it?"

She shook her head rapidly and met my gaze with clear reluctance. "No! *No*, that's good to hear. Some of the services lately have been a bit rough. I'm glad they had a good meal."

"Only… you don't sound glad?" I pressed, unsure why I always seemed to feel the need to push Mia when she obviously didn't want to talk about a subject.

She appeared to steel herself, taking a deep breath and squaring her shoulders. "Sorry. This is embarrassing. When Nat told me Zalen was in the dining area and asking to speak to me — well, to the head chef — I thought maybe you'd told him where I worked and… sent him there, for some reason?"

I sat there for a moment, trying to untangle the subtext. Before I could speak, Mia barreled on.

"Then I realized it was just a coincidence, and they had no idea I was there until I came out to the table. So, I felt pretty stupid about that part. But, also…"

She trailed off, catching her lower lip between her teeth.

"Also, what?" I asked, because I definitely felt like I was missing something here.

I could tell she didn't want to answer, and that she was going to do it anyway.

"Like I said, it was Nat who came and told me Zalen wanted to see me. Except… the way he said it, I thought he must be talking about Byron. And I had no idea how Nat could possibly have found out about him so fast, when it was only the previous night when we'd—"

She cut herself off again and broke eye contact, pretending to look at the people standing in line for coffee.

The unpleasant twisty feeling that didn't *quite* feel like jealousy reared its ugly head again. For god's sake—I was the one who'd thrown her at him. Of *course* she'd had sex with him. Everyone who got a look at Byron wanted to have sex with him. *Mailboxes* wanted to have sex with him.

"So, how'd things go with him, anyway?" I asked, oh-so-casually. "Did you manage to scratch the itch? And if so, why are you worried if your good-for-nothing husband knows about it? Wasn't that the point?"

She looked up at me with an expression that could only be called tortured. And I wondered, not for the first time, what kind of Gordian knot I was getting myself tangled up in with this girl.

TWELVE

Luca

"I MEAN, it was really good," Mia said, too quickly. "Best sex I've had in, well… a long time."

Maybe I was imagining things, but it sounded like she'd been about to say 'ever.' If so, it would be a sad thing to admit, especially for someone who was married. Still not surprising, though. Byron was good at sex. He'd had a lot of practice, after all.

Before I could decide on an appropriate response, Mia plowed onward.

"You know how I said in my text that I'd just gotten some bad news, and my decision making wasn't very good in the aftermath?"

I nodded. "Yes…?"

"Yes." She waved a frustrated hand. "So… all of that. I wasn't thinking clearly, and the whole thing was probably a mistake."

I sat back, regarding her intently. "I get the feeling you haven't made a lot of bad life choices, historically speaking."

Her dark brows drew together. "What do you mean?"

I shook my head, trying to find the right words. "I'm just saying… getting upset about something and fucking a hot alpha so you don't have to think about it for a few hours is pretty common. People—omegas—do that kind of thing all the time, right?"

"Do they?" she asked blankly.

"In my experience, yeah," I told her, aware that my experience maybe wasn't the healthiest—or most normal—template for reasonable behavior. "Your husband declared open season in the marriage, so why shouldn't you? As long as you're safe about it, what's the problem?"

She opened her mouth, thought about it for an instant, and then closed it again. I watched her mentally trying out and discarding different responses before finally settling on one.

"I don't think I was very good at it."

I hesitated, still lost in the tangled depths of this conversation. "At sex?"

"At one-night stands." She started fiddling with her half-finished triple espresso again. "It's so... *awkward*, you know?" Her brown eyes sought mine, begging for understanding. "It's like—there you are, waking up in the morning with this complete stranger, and he's all, 'Well, that was fun, gotta scoot, but help yourself to the shower and the continental breakfast—bye now!' And you're still stark naked in the bed with your hair plastered down with dried sweat, wondering what the hell just happened."

I stared at her, lost in that desperate gaze as the sense of the words penetrated.

"Wait," I said. "He *slept* with you?"

Confusion sculled across her delicate features. "Three times."

I hesitated on a breath before shaking my head in frustration. "No, I mean he *fell asleep with you* in the bed and stayed all night? He didn't leave until morning?"

Because, this was *Byron* we were talking about, wasn't it? Had he been taken over by a pod person or something?

She winced. "I think we were both pretty tired. This is what I mean about being bad at one-night stands. Should I have left first? He seemed surprised I was still there when he woke up."

I continued to gape at her, unable to look away as my brain raced in confused circles. There was a *pod person* living in the bedroom down the hall from me. An alien creature had burrowed into Byron's stomach and taken over his brain.

At least that explained why he'd been such a basket case at work yesterday. Which government agency dealt with alien pod person invasions? Was it the CIA? Or maybe the NSA?

"I wouldn't worry too much about it," I told Mia. "Just let it be what it is. As long as you had a good time, it's fine, right? If your husband can do whatever he wants, so can you." My brain finally latched onto an important point it had skimmed over earlier. "What was the bad news? Sorry, I should've asked earlier."

She scraped a hand down her face, pulling at the skin. Her eyes slid away from mine again. "I got a letter. Or, rather, the restaurant did."

"What kind of letter?"

Her voice lowered to a barely audible mumble. "They're taking our Michelin star away."

And... *ouch*.

"Oh, Mia," I said, all too aware of how much of her self-image seemed to be tied up in the success of the Elderflower Inn. "I'm so sorry. That *sucks*."

She nodded, still not looking at me. "Nat and I let our marriage problems bubble over into the business. There was a stretch of time when things in the kitchen were... not good. Apparently, that just so happened to be when the undercover Michelin inspectors were there to check on us."

Christ, what a shitty piece of luck.

"I'm so sorry," I said again. "How does that work, though? They take it away, just like that, and write you a letter to let you know?"

"Not exactly." She grabbed a napkin and started shredding the corner into tiny pieces. "The Michelin guide publishes their US version in January. Assuming they don't reverse their decision, when the new one comes out, we won't be in it anymore."

"So, they might change their minds?" I asked, grasping for a silver lining.

She shrugged a shoulder, still focused on reducing the napkin to its constituent cellulose fibers. "It's very easy to lose a star. Much more difficult to gain one."

"You already did it once, though," I said, striving for optimism. "That means you can do it again."

"Doing it once destroyed my marriage," she replied darkly. "I don't know if I've got another Michelin star left in me at this point."

We finished our coffees in unhappy silence before parting with a promise to do something fun and low stress soon. Neither of our hearts were really in it.

———◆———

In the coffee shop parking lot, I saw that someone had stuck flyers under the windshield wipers of every single vehicle. It was a pet peeve of mine, partly due to the waste of paper and the inevitable litter when flyers blew away or people crumpled them up and tossed them on the ground.

Still, I glanced at the sheet—drawn by the well-designed layout and tasteful graphics. *GRAND OPENING*, it said. *Join us at St. Louis's hottest new restaurant, Bella Vita—conveniently located in historic Soulard.*

I winced, knowing Mia had probably found an identical flyer on her windshield. I doubted that an announcement about a new competitor would make her morning any better. With a sigh, I tossed the flyer onto my passenger seat and headed out.

Rolling into the Hope Project ten minutes early, I saw that Zalen's Bronco and Byron's

Audi were already parked in their usual spots. This wasn't unusual for either of them, especially when there was something out of the ordinary going on.

Zalen's current focus was a fifteen-year-old beta kid whose stepfather liked his victims young and male. I'd interacted with the boy a few times. He was messed up in the head in a way that I recognized all too well, even if the circumstances were a little bit different. In fact, I recognized it *so* well that I made a point of avoiding him as much as possible.

I wasn't shirking my job. It wasn't my responsibility to fix the kids. I was here to help make sure enough money flowed in to keep the place running—because otherwise, Zalen would fund it out of his own pockets until he eventually went bankrupt.

What he and the others were doing was an uphill battle—and didn't I know it. Seriously, the quickest path to burnout in this avocation was to look at the success rates. They weren't good, to put it mildly. Most of the teens who came to the Hope Project ended up right back in the gangs… addicted to drugs, in jail, or dead in an alley somewhere.

But some of us survived.

That had to make everything else worth it, or else what was the point? You needed to tell yourself that what you were doing was making a positive difference in the world. It was the truth, at least from a certain point of view. A low success rate was better than no success rate at all.

Anyway, Zalen was trying to keep his current project away from the abusive stepdad while also keeping him out of the foster system. The kid was *so close* to an age where he might be able to claim emancipated minor status. We just had to get him there in one piece, with the skills he'd need to make it on his own.

All three of the alphas were getting dangerously invested in the teen. I knew better, because I knew the steep uphill trek he faced. Mind you, the others knew better, too. It just never seemed to stop them.

I hauled my backpack up to my second-floor office and went back to work on the Johnston-Park Foundation grant, hoping that their next request wouldn't involve blood and urine samples or pledging someone's firstborn child.

Concentration wouldn't come. My thoughts kept drifting to Mia, and the puzzle of why I felt so drawn to her when omega biology should have insisted that she was a dangerous rival.

Neither reaction made sense. I'd decided long ago that the only way to be safe was to keep distance between myself and other people. *Emotional* distance, anyway. Zalen and the others had taught me that I could have the things I needed — a home, a job, safe partners to help out with my heats and... other things — while avoiding the complicated and dangerous shit that went along with alphas thinking they controlled me, just because I was an omega.

Mia was an outlier. A growing exception to my emotional distance rule.

She'd tempted me closer by having problems I thought I could solve for her. That was my weakness, and I knew it. Fixing someone else's problems meant I was too busy to focus on my own.

Stuck with an emotionally abusive beta husband? Play him at his own game and win. Better yet, divorce his cheating ass. A good enough lawyer could probably get Mia complete control of the restaurant as part of the settlement.

But this was more than my normal displacement activity. It was getting *personal*. I was treating her like a friend… except I didn't *have* friends. I had acquaintances. Well, acquaintances and whatever the alphas were. Housemates with occasional benefits?

Argh.

The grant paperwork stared accusingly up at me from the screen. Where was my brain today? Hell, what *time* was it?

Answer—almost lunch time. *Christ.*

I managed to finish the page I was on and start the next one. Then I went down the hall to the employee break room to get something from the vending machine. Byron was there, leaning forward with both hands braced on the countertop next to the sink, staring at nothing.

"Hi. You okay?" I asked, my tone cautious.

He straightened abruptly, as though he'd only just noticed I was there. "Yeah." Gray eyes swept me up and down. "You?"

I shrugged. "Distracted today."

His nostrils flared, scenting the air. "You were with rom-com girl this morning. Is that why you're distracted?"

I wasn't sure why the question made me feel so off balance. "Dunno. Maybe."

He nodded, as though I'd given a meaningful answer. "Right. You. Me. In my room. Meet me there at nine p.m. tonight."

The sense of relief that washed over me wasn't something I was proud of. "Just the two of us?" I asked, because that was unusual. Like, *really* unusual.

"Yeah," he confirmed. "Just the two of us."

The rest of the day dragged, my brain caught between its earlier distraction and anticipation of what was to come—pulled so thin between ruminating on the past and future that there was no bandwidth left for the present. I finished the workday, drove home to Ladue on autopilot, ate food that I didn't taste, and watched TV that I didn't pay attention to.

As nine p.m. finally rolled around, some of the tension drained from my shoulders as the promise of quieting my ugly inner voice, at least for a little while, beckoned. Byron's room was almost a caricature of a manly man's retreat—

all mahogany and dark leather; thick rugs and expensive oak. A massive flat screen TV dominated one wall.

By nine-fifteen, I was kneeling naked and bound on one of those luxurious rugs. A baseball game played on the screen behind me — Cards versus Cubs, not that I cared. My arms were strapped behind me, wrist to opposite elbow… my legs bent double, ankle strapped to thigh, so I was sitting on my heels.

In front of me, Byron slouched down on his leather couch until his hips were at the edge of the seat cushion. He unzipped his pants, his spicy scent growing stronger as he pulled his soft cock free of his boxers.

I knew he'd gotten himself off before I'd showed up, probably using a sleeve to keep his knot warm after he came. Chances were, he wouldn't get hard again at all tonight. If he did, he'd take care of it himself later, after I left.

A hand gripped my hair and guided me forward until Byron could feed his cock into my mouth. Even soft, it was all I could take, making it completely impossible to focus on anything else.

I closed my eyes and groaned in relief, unable to stifle the noise as all my troubles and worries fled.

"Shh," Byron said. "I'm trying to watch the game."

My mind went soft and blank. The TV buzzed meaningless nonsense behind me. A hand stroked through my hair like someone absently petting a lapdog. My cock grew heavy, half-hard with a sort of distant, gentle arousal. I couldn't do anything about it with my arms bound... and I didn't particularly want to, anyway.

No one was going to fuck me, or demand anything at all of me except to keep the dick in my mouth warm. I rolled my head to the side a bit, so I could rest against Byron's thigh, his open zipper pressing a zigzag pattern into my left cheek.

———————◆———————

Afterward, when we were finished, I pulled my joggers over my hips and reached for my T-shirt, a question pressing at the back of my teeth.

I shouldn't ask. I'd already decided it would be too complicated. Asking was pointless since I'd said right up front that I didn't want to do it.

I shouldn't...

"Have you considered bringing Mia here as our third?" I blurted.

Byron looked up at me, surprised.

"No," he said.

I wasn't sure what to feel about the fact that I could tell he was lying.

THIRTEEN

Emiel

IT WAS WAY TOO late in the day for this, and I was out of patience. I sat in a conference room at the Hope Project with Zalen, trying to decide if the woman across the table from us was stupid, evil, or both.

Tony, the kid Zalen and I were trying to help, wasn't here for our interview with his mother. The way things were going, that was just as well. After only a few minutes of dealing with her, my blood pressure was already through the roof.

She was very Italian, very Catholic, and very obviously trying to hide a black eye with makeup. She was also either in complete denial, or completely clueless about her second husband, Tony's stepfather.

"What are you implying?" Her angry voice was shrill. "My David isn't like that! You think I married some kind of a… what? A *faggot*?"

My blood pressure inched higher. A vein in my temple started to throb, promising a bombshell of a tension headache coming on.

Zalen, who could be made of marble when he needed to be, was doing that quiet alpha thing he sometimes did when a situation was really pissing him off.

"Your son Tony has leveled accusations of sexual molestation against his stepfather stretching back several years," he said, in such an even tone that I seriously wondered how he managed it.

"My son's name is *Antony*," said the woman, as though the poor kid's legal name had any goddamn thing to do with this conversation. "Antony Scalise, like the Supreme Court judge!"

That was enough to make even *Zalen* stumble for a moment. "You mean... Antonin Scalia?"

"That's what I said!" Tony's mother scowled at us, crossing her arms defensively.

Zalen opened his mouth, paused as he thought better of whatever he'd been about to say, and shook his head sharply, as though dislodging a fly.

"The point is," he said, steering the conversation back on track, "your son has declined to file a police report. However, it's imperative that he be removed from the situation to prevent further abuse. We need to discuss—"

Mrs. Scalise shot to her feet, her chair's legs screeching across the floor. "There is no *abuse*! He... he's just making up stories to get attention! I refuse to listen to this *slander* any longer!"

My temper boiled over in a red froth the color of blood. I pushed to my feet as well, looming over the table, and felt a surge of gratification when the woman cringed backward.

"You think a kid would *make something like that up*?" I ground out, the words feeling like rocks grating against each other in my chest. I slapped my palms against the tabletop, leaning forward. "You're his *mother*. You're supposed to *protect him*! Do you have *any idea* what kind of hell that boy is—"

A hand landed on my forearm, the suggestion of alpha power crackling through the contact. My teeth clacked together as my jaw clenched shut, cutting off the words.

"Why don't you step outside for a few minutes, Emiel," Zalen said, still in that eerily even tone of voice.

For a frightening instant, the knowledge that I was larger and stronger than Zalen burned in my stomach. I had more real-world fighting experience than he did, and I was fuckin' sure *angrier* than he was right now.

Immediately on the heels of that thought came the familiar queasiness.

Loss of control. I was losing control—the thing that I could never, ever do outside of the fighting ring. My anger was still there, every bit as red and bubbling as it had been a moment before. But I still had to shove it down. I had to jam it back into its box, deep inside my chest, where it couldn't get loose and hurt people the way I'd been hurt.

I gave a single, sharp nod, tasting bile as I pivoted on my heel and forced my legs to take one step after another—propelling me out of the room and down the hallway. Behind me, I heard Zalen's oh-so-calm voice, but I couldn't make out the words over the rushing of blood in my ears.

It wasn't quite five o'clock yet. There were still other people in the building, which meant I needed *not* to be in the building. My feet followed a familiar path down a set of back stairs, along a service corridor, and out a small side entrance into the stinking alley between the Hope Project and the building next door.

There was nothing much back here. A few metal trash cans that never got emptied, as far as I could tell. A pan of water. A second pan of cat food that I set out every morning for the local strays. It was about half empty. Sometimes I wasn't sure if the cats got more nutrition from the kibble, or from catching the mice and rats that came to steal it.

"*Mrrrow*," came a soft, trilling cry from behind the trash cans.

After checking that there wasn't any fresh piss on the step in front of the door, I sank down to sit on it and scrubbed a hand over my face. A few moments later, a slender gray form slipped out from its cover and padded toward me.

"Hello, Princess," I greeted with a sigh, stretching out a hand as the cat hopped up on the step next to me.

She was a gawky adolescent streak of a feline, stuck partway between kitten and adult. She was also way too fine for this alley. For this *city*. Somehow, she always managed to be clean and shiny, sleek as mercury. After a moment's consideration, she jumped onto my lap and submitted to my petting with a low, rumbling purr.

As it always did, her presence helped me stuff my rage back down where it belonged; out of sight until it had a safe target. I only had to hold on for a few more hours until my match tonight. Then I could get everything out of my system.

The doorknob turned behind me, the door creaking open on rusting hinges. A jolt of adrenaline cut through my hard-won calm. Princess twitched, digging claws into my thighs, but she didn't leave her perch on my lap.

The scent of cut grass and honeysuckle tickled my nose, out of place among the alley's stench of garbage and urine. I craned around to find Luca frozen in place, looking down at me with large green eyes. Beneath his own scent, the faintest hint of Byron's spice clung to him, hanging on despite evidence of the shower he'd taken this morning.

Sometimes I really hated the sensitivity of my nose.

I was always careful to suppress my own scent. I took blocker pills religiously. I'd toyed with the idea of having my scent glands removed surgically. Something always held me back, but someday, I'd do it.

Unfortunately, none of that did a damned thing for my sense of smell. There were dampeners you could take to dull the scent of others, but you couldn't take them all the time, or they lost effectiveness.

Those, I saved for Luca's heats.

"Hi," Luca said. "Sorry. I came out to clear my head for a few minutes; didn't realize you were here."

"'S'okay," I said. "I was about to go back in."

His gaze narrowed, his angular face screwing up in concern.

"Is everything all right?" he asked. "You look a little…" He trailed off.

"I'm fine," I said, not liking the feeling that maybe my mask wasn't covering the things it should be covering. I started to get up, realized I still had a cat velcroed to my trousers with her claws, and paused, stuck in place.

"You know," Luca said, gesturing at Princess, "you could bring her to live at the house if you wanted. She doesn't really belong in a place like this."

I looked at the cat. Glanced back at Luca.

He looked like hell, especially considering he must've got laid last night. In some corner of my brain, I knew I should turn his own question back on him… ask him if *he* was all right. But the idea felt overwhelming.

"Yeah, maybe," I said, detaching the cat from my clothing and gently setting her down on the pavement.

It would be nice to rescue something and have it *stay* rescued. Maybe I'd mention it to Zalen. It was his house, after all.

Luca was still examining me like he had X-ray vision that could see through my bullshit. I stood up, dusted myself down, and cleared my throat.

"Guess I'll go back in and take care of some paperwork until it's time to leave," I said.

An eyebrow rose. "You hate paperwork."

"Yeah," I agreed. "I do."

Luca stepped back and let me get past him, his sweet scent brushing across my skin like a physical touch. I moved quickly by him and headed for my office, not looking back. Only a few more hours until I could climb into a cage with another alpha and stop feeling like this for a little bit.

Only a few more hours.

FOURTEEN

Mia

"IT'S SO EMPTY in here tonight," Candace said, sounding bewildered. "Is it because of that new restaurant opening on Menard Street?"

As I cast an eye over the unoccupied tables in the dining area, I was wondering that, too. Candace was one of the newer servers, and she'd never known the Elderflower Inn to be anything other than busy. This was the first time since the previous Michelin guide had come out that we were running at barely half of capacity.

Isaiah took advantage of the lull to stick his head around the edge of the pass-through. He gave a low whistle. "You know, boss—we could send a spy over to the Bella Vita and see if it's busy. It'd be like—what do they call it? Corporate espionage."

"We are not sending a spy to the Bella Vita," I said firmly, ignoring the temptation to do exactly that. "Our job is to make sure the customers who come here get an amazing meal that will bring them back, preferably with friends in tow. What other restaurants in the area do isn't our concern."

Isaiah sighed. "Yes, chef."

"Candy, go check on table four, please," I told the server.

"On it," she said, but some of her usual bubbliness seemed noticeably subdued.

Nat chose that moment to walk in from his rounds in the front of house. "This is bad," he said. "We can't run the place with these kinds of numbers."

"It's only one night," I told him. "There's a new restaurant having a grand opening a couple of streets away. They've been wallpapering half the city with flyers."

His worried frown deepened. "We need a new social media campaign. Something to remind people we're here."

"That's a good idea," I said, keeping my tone neutral and professional. "When it comes to the quality of the food, if we can get people through the door, I'm confident we can beat any other kitchen in the city."

"I'll put something together tonight," Nat promised, and I wasn't sure what it said about us that this was the most civil conversation we'd had in days.

"Sounds like a plan," I told him. "There's a lull in orders, so I'm taking five. I'll be in the back."

After making sure the staff was on top of the handful of dessert orders in the queue, I wiped a towel over my sweaty face and went outside to cool off for a few minutes. One night wasn't make or break for a restaurant, but I'd be lying if I said I wasn't worried.

Hell, maybe Isaiah was onto something, and I *should* send someone over to Bella Vita to scope things out on the downlow.

To distract myself, I pulled my phone out and powered it on so I could check messages. There was one from a vendor about an upcoming change in the delivery schedule, which I forwarded to Nat. The other was from Luca. I frowned and opened it, surprised to hear from him so soon after our coffee date.

Hi, it began. *When do you get off shift tonight? And would you come to a late night underground fight venue with me?*

I tilted my head at the phone like a confused dog. I recognized all of those words individually, but I was struggling to get my brain around them collectively.

Why? I typed the word out and hit send.

Dots marched across the screen, then paused. It was a long enough pause that the pull to go back inside and start working again tugged at my awareness.

Then, *Emiel is fighting there tonight. I'm worried about him. He was acting off this afternoon.*

I thought about the big alpha with his scent suppressors and his unexpectedly sweet grin. I tried to picture him beating the shit out of someone else in a boxing ring. The image superficially made sense, but it also twisted something in my chest unpleasantly.

Did I want to go to an underground fight club? It definitely wasn't something I'd have done if left to my own devices... but Luca was worried. If we were going to be friends, that meant helping him out when he asked.

I still had questions, though.

Not saying no, but wouldn't it make more sense to ask Zalen or Byron?

My heart gave a little lurch as I typed Byron's name, but I hit send anyway and waited.

More dots.

Zalen needs plausible deniability since Em's an employee of the non-profit. And Byron doesn't like violence.

That gave me pause. The bad boy with tattoos all over his body was squeamish about a boxing ring? Then I remembered the bullet scar, its ugly pucker incorporated into a design of jungle flowers. There was a lot I didn't know about hiding beneath the surface, but I could see how getting shot might put a person off violence in general.

So… was there any reason I *couldn't* go watch Emiel's fight?

The most obvious answer was lack of sleep, but it wasn't as though I slept more than a few hours a night in the normal course of things.

Sure, I texted. *I get off at ten. Should I meet you at this place, or what?*

I'll pick you up, he replied. *10 p.m. sharp.*

◆

The Luca who showed up in a white Nissan Leaf was not the same Luca I was used to seeing. This wasn't 'sharply dressed omega ingenue' Luca, or even 'soft, rumpled watching-a-movie' Luca.

Tonight, he was dressed in clothing calculated to conceal. Baggy, faded jeans were topped with a dark hoodie so big he practically swam in it. The oversized clothes hid the elegant lines of his lithe body. The hood covered his perpetual rumpled bedhead, its laces pulled tight around his angular face.

On the positive side, it meant I'd fit in okay with the vibe wherever we were going, since I'd thrown a similarly shapeless hoodie on over my work clothes. On the negative side, I didn't like how pale and hunted Luca looked.

"Hi," he said tersely. "Thanks for doing this."

I didn't comment on his clothing, even though the change from what I was used to had freaked me out a bit. Or… maybe that was just the situation in general.

"Hi," I said back. "I didn't realize visiting an underground fight club was on my bingo card this month, but at least I can cross it off early. Or, um, whatever you do with bingo cards. I've never actually played bingo."

"I don't think you're missing much," Luca said as I got in.

We drove north, crossing the river on the Stan Musial Veterans Memorial Bridge rather than the Poplar Street Bridge. Luca exited onto St. Claire Avenue, then turned onto a smaller road leading into the old derelict meat packing district in National City.

I'd been *past* National City a couple of times, but it wasn't the kind of place you purposely went to.

The abandoned factories loomed like crooked, decaying teeth in the moonlight. Partially collapsed smokestacks rose drunkenly from partially collapsed buildings. The overall effect was eerie and foreboding. I couldn't help my shiver of reaction.

Luca must've smelled my misgivings in my scent. "Yeah, it's creepy as hell, I know. I think that's part of the reason the organizers chose it? That, and the cops don't give a shit what goes on back here."

We ended up having to drive around for a while before a glimpse of way too many cars through a gap in the trees led us to an overgrown parking area. Weeds didn't so much *sprout* from the crazy network of cracks in the pavement as launch a full-on ground invasion. There were no lights, no road signs, no signs of life at all… except for about a hundred cars and trucks mysteriously parked by an abandoned factory.

Luca chose a spot at the periphery, where the car was unlikely to be hemmed in by other vehicles. Only when we got out did I notice the rumble of a generator and see lights inside the structure, flickering through the patchwork of gaping, empty window frames that hadn't been boarded over.

"Stay close to me and keep your head down," Luca muttered.

He'd hunched in on himself, losing a couple inches of height and a couple inches of breadth… making himself small. Nerves thrumming, I pulled my hood up to cover my hair, hoping to make it less obvious that I was female.

We approached a pair of burly alphas on door duty, and this seemed like a bad time to ask Luca what the hell he was getting me into. The bouncers eyed us up and down, nostrils flaring, and waved us inside. Once my back was to them, my hand wandered into the large front pocket of my hoodie, where I'd stashed the little handbag that I used to carry my ID and cash.

And my pepper gel.

I popped open the handbag clasp and felt around for the small keychain cylinder inside, easing it free and thumbing the safety catch to the spray position by feel. Having it within easy reach and ready to use made me feel better. Reassured, I turned more of my attention outward.

The factory was a massive steel and concrete skeleton. It smelled of age and decay, and its belly was littered with the corpses of rusting machinery—hooks and chains and conveyors with the blown-out remains of old motors scattered about like disturbing industrial art exhibits.

Past the aging detritus of meat production, we reached a central open area. It was dominated by a large chain-link cage and surrounded by a milling, rumbling crowd of onlookers. Harsh lights had been set up overhead, glaring down on the cage like spotlights. A man in a white shirt and black trousers conversed with two men in suits.

"They're about to get started," Luca said tightly, just as a sound system fired up, pumping a pounding bass beat through the echoing space. "Emiel's in the second match."

Around us, bookies waved pieces of paper in the air, people shouting and jostling as insults flew and money changed hands. My sum total of experience regarding sanctioned fights revolved around watching boxing matches with my father on pay-per-view when I was young.

I hadn't had any particular like or dislike of the carefully staged spectacles set in venues like Madison Square Garden and the Vegas strip. It was just a thing happening on a screen. In this heaving, turbulent crowd, however, I couldn't imagine *anyone* feeling neutral about what was happening. Alpha pheromones and beta body odor choked the area around the cage. The occasional lighter scent of omega perfume led my eye to some simpering, scantily clad arm candy clinging to a hulking guy's bicep.

The jury-rigged lights positioned over the cage flashed on and off twice. Luca led me deeper into the crowd, pushing through tightly packed bodies like a flying wedge — ignoring the occasional irritated cursing flung at him as he elbowed past someone.

I felt unpleasantly on edge, my nerves jangling with pointless fight or flight response.

One of the men in suits lifted a microphone and spoke in a booming voice, introducing the first two fighters. They entered the cage—two large, wiry alphas with hard eyes and battered faces. They were wearing brightly colored trunks and nothing else—no boxing gloves anywhere in evidence.

The cage door closed behind them, locking them inside.

"Isn't there a referee?" I asked Luca, pitching my voice to be heard over the excited crowd.

"This isn't that kind of fight," Luca said grimly. "Wins are by submission or knockout only."

A bell sounded. The two fighters crouched, circling each other with wary movements. One feinted and then charged low, slamming into his opponent with crushing force. There was no fancy martial arts shit on display here. Just two alphas beating the crap out of each other, until one collapsed choking under the force of a roundhouse punch to the throat.

Clammy sweat had broken out on my forehead, and I clutched Luca's cold fingers with enough force to bruise. *Emiel* was going to do this? The guy who'd meekly vacated the TV room so Luca and I could watch a movie, and who'd told me how much he'd liked my food at the restaurant?

Abruptly, I understood why Luca had come here, even though the place clearly made him uncomfortable. What the hell was Emiel *thinking*?

In the cage, the alpha who'd been hit flopped around on the mat and eventually went limp. The bell clanged several times, and a cheer went up from sections of the crowd, overwhelming the disgusted groans from the people who'd lost money on the fight.

My heart thudded loudly in my ears as the unconscious alpha was dragged away. The announcer took up his microphone again and confirmed the winner, who punched a fist in the air in celebration. Sweat glistened in trails on his chest and back.

"Next up," the announcer boomed, "we have a special treat for you all. Undefeated crowd favorite Hamilton, versus newcomer The Iceman!"

A fresh flurry of betting erupted around us, while two more figures made their way toward the cage. I recognized Emiel with a jolt—but even if I hadn't, Luca's convulsive hand-squeeze would've clued me in. Then my gaze fell on the largest alpha I'd ever seen, and my heart leapt into my throat. Seriously, the dude must have been pushing seven feet, with broad shoulders, bulging biceps, and tree-trunk legs to match.

"Holy shit," I muttered hoarsely, as both men stripped off their robes and tossed them aside before climbing into the cage.

The walking alpha mountain *loomed* over Emiel. A slow smile twisted the bruiser's broad face as he ground one fist into the opposite palm. Emiel's back was to us; I couldn't see his expression. Before I could properly panic, the bell sounded.

Still grinning, the giant musclebound alpha darted forward with a kind of speed no human being that large should possess. His left fist pulled back and let fly, aimed directly at Emiel's face.

FIFTEEN

Mia

NAUSEA FLOODED MY gut as the huge alpha slammed a vicious punch into Emiel's jaw, staggering him. The crowd around us roared with excitement and bloodlust as flecks of red sprayed from Emiel's mouth.

My knuckles ground together painfully beneath the force of Luca's grip on my hand. He was shaking... violent, full-body tremors that transmitted to me through the contact.

In the cage, Emiel got his feet under him, setting himself in a fighting stance only to get hit again—this time with a punishing body blow that doubled him over. Clammy panic rushed through my veins, as abrupt and shocking as a plunge into icy water. What was I doing in this place, surrounded by rough alphas and betas working themselves into a frenzy over a display of mindless violence?

Why in god's name had Luca thought that us being here would be safe, or remotely *sane*?

I knew the answer, though. He was here because he was frightened for Emiel, and I was here because he hadn't felt like there was anyone else he could ask.

I was frightened for Emiel, too—and I'd barely met the man. He was getting beaten to a pulp, staggering around the cage with a dead-eyed expression. I couldn't tell if he wasn't landing any blows of his own because he was overmatched and disoriented, or because he wasn't *trying*.

What the hell was going on with this crazy pack I'd stumbled into?

I grabbed Luca's tightly clenched hand between both of mine, crowding close against him in a subconscious need for physical comfort as my omega instincts screamed that this place was *dangerous*... that we needed to somehow get Emiel and get away before something terrible happened.

My head swam beneath the force of the churning pheromone cocktail around us. I felt like I might throw up.

In the cage, Emiel blocked a punch only to go down beneath a brutal kick to the side of the knee, and my heart skipped a beat. Luca flinched as though he'd physically felt the blow.

Rather than take advantage of his opponent's fall, the massive alpha turned to play to the crowd—letting out a roar and thumping his fists against his chest, muscles bulging and slick with sweat. Emiel rolled to his feet. Blood spattered his temple and chin. His left eye looked swollen and red.

But something had changed. His blank, dead expression had shifted into something more focused. There was anger in the set of his jaw... in the glint of his dark gaze.

His opponent strutted around the cage perimeter until they were facing each other once more. Emiel's lips pulled back in a sharp, predatory grin as the other alpha sneered at him, arrogantly gesturing at him to attack.

Emiel just stood there, not moving even as the crowd howled its displeasure at the lull in the fight. His opponent's sneer turned to a look of irritation. With that same unlikely speed as before, he lunged forward and caught Emiel in the ribs, taking a jab to the jaw in the process. I was pretty sure it was the first real hit Emiel had managed.

Again and again, the big alpha came after Emiel, dealing punches and kicks while taking minimal damage in return.

I was shaking as badly as Luca. How much punishment could Emiel absorb before he went down and stayed down? The memory of the unconscious loser from the first fight being dragged out of the cage made me shudder with dread. Were there medics here? Would ambulances even *come* to a place like this if someone called 911?

Beside me, Luca drew in a sharp breath. I forced myself to refocus on what was happening in the cage. Emiel's opponent had gone for him again, but his movements had grown noticeably slower than before.

Emiel dodged the kick and spun past the other alpha, managing to land a punch to his kidney before putting distance between them. His opponent snarled and followed him, trying to trap Emiel in the corner.

I hadn't imagined things. The larger alpha was slowing down, his movements growing cumbersome as Emiel lured him into lunge after lunge. Bruises were blooming across Emiel's torso and face, but he was landing more blows as his opponent tired.

Enraged, the huge alpha bellowed like a bull and charged, shoulder down. I gasped as both of them crashed to the mat, with Emiel pinned on the bottom. His opponent continued to roar out his anger, driving blows into Emiel's head and chest.

I was shouting now, too — wordless cries of denial as the punches rained down.

Emiel heaved and twisted. It was too fast for me to see exactly how he did it, but suddenly his legs were tangled around the larger alpha's thigh and torso, and instead of being pinned beneath him, Emiel was snaking around his upper body.

Luca made a sharp noise of surprise, our fingernails digging into each other's hands. Emiel got fully behind his opponent and flung a muscular arm around his neck, bracing his forearm against his opposite bicep to lock the chokehold in place. The larger alpha howled, slapping ineffectually behind himself with both hands — trying to dislodge Emiel from his back.

The look on Emiel's face was frightening in its single-minded, vicious intensity. Something about that expression of righteous vengeance burrowed into my gut, calling to deeply buried instincts that dreamed of punishing every person who had ever wronged me.

I physically staggered back a step in reaction, bumping into the people pressed up behind me and drawing a curse and an irritable shove. By the time I'd recovered myself, steadying my legs, Emiel's opponent had gone limp in his grasp. The crowd went wild as the bell clanged, marking the end of the fight, and several people clambered into the cage.

They descended on Emiel as though they expected to have to pull him off the other man by force, but he'd already let go and was rising to unsteady feet.

The announcer's voice cut across the crowd's cheering and booing. *"And the winner – still undefeated – is… Hamilton!"*

One of the men in white shirts who'd hurried in to make sure Emiel didn't kill his opponent grabbed his wrist instead, raising his arm over his head in victory. Emiel's expression was already sliding back into blankness as the man held his arm aloft…but then his listless gaze slid over Luca and me and stuck there. Shocked surprise colored his bruised and battered features.

"Time to go," Luca said, speaking directly into my ear to be heard over the noise. He still sounded shaky, but his grip on my hand was firm as he tugged me deeper into the crowd, heading back the way we'd come in.

I felt like I was experiencing emotional whiplash. We weren't going to stay and make sure Emiel was all right? Because he sure as hell hadn't *looked* all right.

The jostling was twice as bad as when we'd first arrived and pushed ourselves to the front of the crowd so we could see. From the snippets of conversation I caught around us, a lot of people weren't happy that they'd bet on the big guy and lost all their money.

The crowd thinned out at the edges, the noise gradually dying down as we reached the derelict factory floor with its abandoned, rusting machinery.

"He can't keep doing this," Luca was muttering, as though to himself. "*Jesus fuck*, he's going to get himself *killed*."

I was hopelessly disoriented in the confusing space, still mired in the stale remnants of the adrenaline dump from the fight, but I vaguely recognized the dingy corridor we turned into as the one leading to the entrance.

We'd just turned another corner when two alphas stepped away from the walls, blocking our progress. Luca jolted to a halt, his scent spiking with an unpleasant miasma of fear. He whirled around as though to retreat, tugging me with him—but two more men had stepped out to block our way, hemming us in.

My pulse galloped into triple-time as Luca froze, paralyzed into immobility. One of the alphas stepped forward, grabbing him by the chin. The man was tall, dark haired, and olive skinned, with a cruel hook of a nose and a scar running down his cheek. The scent of diesel and hot steel rolled off of him, sharp and choking.

"So, it *is* you," the alpha said. "Thought I recognized you, you good-for-nothing little whore."

"*Don't touch me.*" Luca jerked backward, breaking the contact and retreating until his back hit the mildewed concrete wall. I followed, instinctively wanting as much distance separating us from these people as possible. Of course, all we accomplished was to trap ourselves further as they gathered around us in a half circle.

The alpha snorted, and a couple of the others laughed. Luca steeled himself and took a step forward, herding me behind him so his body was between me and the four men. Heart pounding, I jammed my hands in the front pocket of my hoodie and huddled against the wall, tense and watchful.

"Aww, don't be like that, baby." The alpha mock-pouted at him. Then his expression hardened. "Blaze still wants you back, you know."

"Blaze can go fuck himself," Luca spat, the vicious words doing nothing to hide the terror leaking into his sweet, summer-meadow scent.

"Getting away from your crew isn't as easy as you seem to think it is, *cunt*." Abruptly, all the mock gentleness left the alpha's voice. He grabbed for Luca's arm.

With panic clawing at my throat, I pulled out the pepper spray I'd been holding hidden in my pocket and ducked out from behind Luca, spraying it directly in the alpha's eyes.

He let out an angry shout, stumbling back and wiping frantically at his face. The stinging nip of capsaicin in the air prickled at my nose and lips, but the other three men were already lunging for us. Frantically, I whipped the little canister around toward the closest one and thumbed the trigger.

It sputtered, refusing to spray—a few weak droplets of the virulent orange liquid splattering onto the floor before the nozzle clogged completely. Luca shouted something, trying once again to get me behind him—even as heavy hands landed on both of us.

SIXTEEN

Mia

I SCREAMED AND kicked, aiming a knee at the groin of the beta who'd grabbed me. He cursed and lashed out with a closed fist. Pain exploded across my left cheekbone, setting off flashbulbs in my vision.

His grip on my hoodie dragged me off balance. I couldn't see Luca… couldn't hear him.

"Nice try, bitch," snarled the man holding me.

He gave me a rough shake, like a dog with a floppy rope toy. It felt like my brain was sloshing around inside my skull. I couldn't seem to get my bearings; couldn't get my feet underneath me to steady myself. I drew breath to scream for help again, with no idea if anyone in this terrible place would have the slightest interest in intervening.

"Help!" I shrieked. *"Someone help!"*

My captor shoved me hard against the wall where I'd been cowering moments before, the impact jarring through my back and knocking the breath from my lungs.

"Ain't no one coming to help your skinny ass, you ugly omega ho." The beta's breath was foul as it wafted into my face, gagging me.

A grunt came from nearby. Was that Luca? I tried to set myself and deliver another knee to the balls, but my legs felt like jelly. My vision wavered as I struggled for breath.

Out of nowhere, a heavy weight slammed into the man pinning me to the wall. He cried out, his grip on my hoodie yanking so hard before he lost purchase that I tumbled sideways, my body crashing to the cracked concrete floor.

Unexpectedly freed, I looked up, wheezing, and saw a dark blur pummeling a lighter blur. After blinking my vision into better focus, the dark blur resolved into Emiel—still barefoot, but with a blue satin boxing robe thrown over his trunks as he rage-beat my attacker to a bloody pulp.

I gaped up at him as he let the beta fall limply from his grasp in favor of grabbing the two alphas who were manhandling Luca. Emiel tore them away from the omega, spinning them around to face him.

Luca staggered back, gasping. But instead of running, he pulled something out of his pocket and hauled off, slamming it into the back of the nearest alpha's skull. The man went down without a sound, just as Emiel fell on the remaining alpha like a wild animal.

The ugly sound of flesh thumping against flesh echoed in the corridor, until the last attacker slumped to the ground, joining his fellows. Emiel turned to the alpha I'd pepper sprayed earlier and delivered a brutal kick to his ribs, curling him into a whimpering fetal position.

For the first time since we'd been accosted, my attention expanded beyond my immediate surroundings. A handful of other people were in the hallway, hanging back uncertainly as though they weren't sure if they were supposed to jump into the fight or stay the hell out of it.

Strong fingers wrapped around my bicep, pulling me to my feet.

"*Move*," Emiel said, the barked word jolting along my overstretched nerves.

I moved, staggering after the alpha who held my arm in one large hand and Luca's in the other. The men who'd been stationed at the entrance when we came in were nowhere to be seen. Emiel shoved the door open with his foot and tugged us outside.

The cool night air hit me like a slap, the skin beneath my left eye throbbing painfully.

"Where's your car?" Emiel growled.

I craned around to catch a glance of Luca. His face was so pale that it glowed like a beacon in the dim moonlight. His eyes had a dazed and absent look that said he wasn't going to be giving anyone directions, much less driving us out of here.

I tried to hammer my neurons into some kind of functioning order, thinking back to our arrival. "Over there," I quavered, pointing toward the edge of the overgrown parking area. "Emiel, Luca can't drive right now."

Emiel followed my gesture and gave a grunt in response. There was another problem, though—I didn't think *I* could drive us safely either. My head was pounding, and I felt like I might pass out.

Emiel led us to the white Nissan Leaf and let me go, propping me against the passenger side as he turned to Luca.

"*Keys*," he said, and Luca fumbled dumbly in his pocket, pulling out his keyring and handing it over without seeming to be aware of his surroundings at all.

Emiel took the keys and unlocked the car. He urged me into the back seat and pushed Luca in after me. With the doors safely closed on us, he climbed into the driver's seat with a hiss of discomfort. A moment later, the front seat slid back, nearly knocking me in the knees.

"Sorry," he mumbled.

The car chimed cheerfully at us as he started it up, then rolled silently out of its parking spot and turned, heading for the distant lights of St. Claire Avenue. I realized, with a sort of fuzzy surprise, that we were safe.

"What about *your* car?" I rasped, not at all sure that any vehicle left behind outside the factory would still be there in the morning.

"Took a cab to get there," Emiel muttered.

I let that sink in, my brain ticking off any remaining threats before apparently deciding that it was done for the night, thank you very much, and it planned to throw in the towel. Beside me, Luca sat silent and shaking.

Our shoulders brushed in the cramped backseat. Instinct had my body turning further into his even as he turned toward me.

Somehow, without really intending it, I found myself clinging to him, my throbbing face pressed into the crook of his neck. He buried his nose in my hair, breathing unsteadily against me.

We stayed like that as the car merged onto the highway, heading back across the river. Gradually, an unfamiliar scent threaded through the unpleasant haze of sweat and terrified omega. It was sweet and tart and complex, tickling my nose until my chef's mind reluctantly coughed up the words *bergamot* and *cinnamon* to describe it.

Something about that scent wove its way into my hindbrain, wrapping reassurance around the dregs of sick panic. I shifted to a slightly more comfortable position, aware that my muscles would be screaming their displeasure in a few hours. Something hard jabbed me in the hip. I freed a hand from its grip on Luca's hoodie and grasped the unfamiliar object—about eight inches long, with a leather-wrapped handle and a heavily weighted round end.

It looked like something a mafia enforcer would carry in a movie. A *blackjack*... was that the word? I remembered Luca swinging something at one of our attackers' heads right after Emiel had arrived, and a convulsive shiver wracked me.

I'd had my pepper spray. Apparently, Luca had *this*. I let it drop into the footwell and clutched at him again, closing my eyes. What would have happened to us if Emiel hadn't showed up?

The smooth ribbon of the highway gave way to start and stop traffic with more frequent turns. I let the complicated scent of spicy bergamot and the warmth of Luca's body lull me into a fugue, even as the memory of what had happened played over and over in a continuous loop inside my skull.

Eventually, the car slowed to a crawl and turned into a long, winding driveway. It pulled to a stop, and I dragged my eyes open. The left one felt so swollen that it barely opened a crack. Outside stood a familiar two-story Neo-Georgian mansion, coach lights illuminating the entryway with a warm and welcoming yellow glow.

"We're home." Emiel's voice sounded strained. "Sorry. Stay here a minute. I'll get Zalen."

Luca didn't react. It took me a few seconds to realize that Emiel didn't think we could get to the front door without help… and a moment more to realize that he was probably right.

"Okay," I said hoarsely, trying not to examine the relief I felt that he'd brought me here, and not to the restaurant in Soulard where my car was parked. Or worse yet, to my *house*.

The driver's door creaked open, and Emiel paused for a second before heaving himself out of the vehicle. He staggered a bit, catching himself against the side of the car. The suspension rocked under his weight. With an unpleasant lurch, I remembered that he'd had the shit beaten out of him in that cage tonight—and that was *before* he'd tackled three men and knocked out two of them singlehandedly.

He trudged up the cobblestone walkway with slow steps, still barefoot and wearing only his satin boxing robe and trunks. I wondered, with a brief and unpleasant twinge, what would have happened if the police had pulled us over on the way back.

Emiel reached the door and leaned against the frame as he fumbled Luca's key into the lock and opened it. He disappeared inside, leaving it standing open in the cool night breeze.

"Luca?" I whispered, hoping he was in better shape than I was when it came to things like needing to walk thirty feet from the car to the house. His only response was to grip me tighter against his body.

Zalen came jogging out of the house, hurrying toward us. He, too, was barefoot—wearing low-slung sleep pants and a gray T-shirt. He wrenched open the rear passenger door and leaned in. Luca flinched hard, only to relax when the scent of lime and vanilla wafted inside.

"*Christ,*" Zalen said. "Are you two hurt?" He had the groggy look of someone who'd been unexpectedly dragged from a sound sleep. His dreadlocks fell loose around his worried features. "Oh, god, Mia. Your *face*. Come on, let's get you both inside."

He helped Luca out of the car, slinging one of the smaller man's arms over his broad shoulders. Then he reached in, offering his free hand to me. I took it, letting him support some of my weight as I carefully stood up on trembling legs.

"Easy," Zalen said as I clutched his bicep, leaning on him as the three of us began to hobble slowly toward the door.

Emiel, also moving at a snail's pace, met us partway and reached out an arm as though to take Luca off Zalen's hands. Zalen came to an abrupt halt, his muscles stiffening. His clean alpha scent sharpened with anger.

"What the *fuck*, Emiel?" he snapped. "I've looked the other way for years when it came to this cage fighting shit! But involving *omegas*? Letting them get *hurt*? Seriously, what the *actual fuck!*"

Luca and I both cringed inward at the sound of an angry alpha's bark. A small whimper escaped me, completely against my will.

Derailed, Zalen flinched and glanced down at us, his expression stricken.

SEVENTEEN

Mia

"SORRY," ZALEN SAID. "I'm sorry, you two. No one's angry at you, and everything's going to be all right. We're going inside now."

His voice lowered to a soothing rumble, calming my jangling nerves. After a second's hesitation, he allowed Emiel to take Luca from him. The pair headed toward the front door with slow, hitching steps. Zalen carefully wrapped an arm around me and supported me as we followed.

I knew I should be protesting that I was okay, that I could walk—but the magnetic pull to lean against Zalen's solid frame and let his rumbly voice and clean, reassuring scent settle my whirling thoughts was inescapable.

Except for our brief interaction in the restaurant when Zalen and Emiel had brought their prospective donors in for a meal, I hadn't had any contact with Zalen since that very first night in the singles bar. Even then, his aura of calm tranquility paired with implacable protectiveness had made an impression on me.

This was an alpha who had experience taking care of distraught omegas. I supposed that made sense for someone who ran a center for troubled teens. Maybe that was where he'd learned the skill.

I let him guide me inside, more of the tension easing from my shoulders as I stepped into the welcoming foyer.

"Guest bathroom," he called to Emiel, who grunted a wordless response.

The four of us followed the main ground floor hallway past the elegant living room, to a closed door across from the family room where Luca and I had watched a movie together. The bathroom was large and clean, with a shower but no bathtub.

Emiel set Luca down to sit on the toilet seat, and the look of absent blankness on both their faces made a chill run down my spine. Zalen plucked a houseplant off the seat of a spindly chair sitting in the corner next to the marble vanity and eased me onto it. I had a feeling the chair was only meant to be decorative, but I was still grateful not to have to stay upright under my own power.

"Emiel," Zalen said, his tone carefully level. "You and I need to talk, but I'm fuckin' pissed at you right now. I can't deal with their injuries and yours as well."

"Didn't ask you to," Emiel muttered, with no particular emotion behind the words. He turned and left, closing the door softly behind him—but his final glance at Luca and me looked haunted.

When the sound of his shuffling footsteps disappeared down the hall, Zalen took a deep breath and let it out slowly, his shoulders sagging. When he turned to me, he, too, was wearing an unreadable expression.

"Mia, are you hurt anyplace else besides your black eye?" he asked.

I startled a bit at that. Black eye? Why hadn't I made the connection between the hot, swollen feeling and the idea that I might have a shiner?

My lips parted, but I had to work hard to call up words. "No, I'm okay."

It wasn't the complete truth—I was going to have a hell of a bruise on my hip where I'd hit the concrete floor. But I assumed he meant, like, broken bones or stab wounds, or that kind of thing. *Serious* injuries.

"All right, that's good," he said. "Give me just a minute and I'll get you some frozen peas or something for the swelling." He crossed to the toilet and crouched in front of Luca, looking up at him. "Hey. Luca. Are you with us?"

Luca closed his eyes and turned his face away.

I swallowed, wetting my cracked lips. "Two alphas grabbed him, but I didn't see anyone hit him. He seemed to be walking okay, but he hasn't spoken."

"Omegas sometimes shut down for a bit after undergoing a traumatic event," Zalen said absently. "It's a normal response."

"He fought back," I said quickly, not sure why I felt the urge to leap to Luca's defense.

"I'm guessing you both did," said the alpha, his tone growing dry. "Hence the black eye."

Blood rushed to my cheeks, which of course resulted in the black eye in question throbbing even hotter and achier.

"Okay." Zalen rose, frowning down at Luca for a second before moving to the nearest sink. "I'll be back as quick as I can. In the meantime—" He grabbed a washcloth and ran it under the tap until it was soaked, then wrung it out. "—hold this over your eye."

He folded up the damp washcloth and handed it to me.

I took it, gingerly pressing it to the painful bruising. It was cool, but not cold, and the damp terrycloth felt surprisingly soothing.

"Thanks," I whispered.

He nodded and ducked out of the bathroom, leaving me alone with Luca. I wanted to help him, but the few steps separating us felt insurmountable. All I could think of was how soon I'd be able to get horizontal and sleep for a week. How on earth was I going to get back to Soulard to pick up my car and drive home, when I could barely sit upright in a chair?

Good *god*, how was I going to get through my restaurant shift tomorrow?

Luca wrapped his arms around his torso, hugging himself as though he were freezing. I was pretty sure the bathroom was warm, but I was shivering, too.

Zalen hurried back in with a bag of frozen corn in one hand and a fleecy blanket wadded up beneath his arm. He set the blanket on the vanity a bit sheepishly.

"Right, let me wrap this bag in a dry towel and trade you for the washcloth." He rummaged for a clean hand towel and suited action to word.

It took a moment for the cold to permeate through the towel when I pressed it to my tender skin, but once it did, I groaned in relief. The sharp chill felt *divine*.

"Keep it there for fifteen minutes," Zalen said. "I need to make sure Luca isn't physically hurt. After that, you both need sleep. Do you need to call anyone and let them know where you are? Or have me call for you?"

It took a minute for the sense of the words to make its way through to my brain. When it did, my relief that no one expected me to show up at my house tonight warred with a faintly queasy feeling. Nat—assuming he was even home—would figure I was off screwing an alpha. *This* alpha.

There was literally no one who'd think it was odd if I was gone all night. If I'd been kidnapped or murdered at the old factory, I wouldn't have been missed until I failed to show up at the restaurant tomorrow.

"No, it's fine," I said hoarsely.

"I can make up a guest room for you," Zalen began, "but if you're comfortable sharing a nest with Luca, that might be better for both of you. I'd really rather he wasn't alone in his room when he's like this..." He hesitated. "But... uh, it probably shouldn't be an alpha with him."

I was missing subtext here, and I didn't have the brainpower to try and figure it out right now. "Okay," I said. *God*, I just wanted to sleep.

I braced my elbow on the edge of the vanity to keep the frozen corn pressed to my eye, as I let my head fall back against the wall, my good eye closing. I could hear Zalen speaking to Luca in that low, soothing tone of his, talking him through pulling off his shapeless hoodie and lifting his arms one at a time to be checked.

At some point, I must've dozed off. A hand on my shoulder brought me back to awareness, with my jaw hanging slack and the towel-wrapped corn sitting in my lap. Luca was gone from the room, and I blinked up at Zalen in confusion.

"He's in his nest," Zalen said, as though reading my unspoken question. "Come on, you need sleep."

I wasn't sure how I was going to get from here to there, especially if Luca's bedroom was on the second floor. That question was answered a moment later when Zalen leaned down and scooped me off the chair as though I weighed nothing.

I squeaked in surprise, clutching the frozen corn in one hand. The bruise on my hip throbbed in discontent, but Zalen shifted me into a more comfortable position, and then we were off. It was a testament to how far gone I was that the gentle rocking motion of being carried nearly sent me right back to sleep.

It seemed as though no time at all had passed when Zalen squeezed us sideways into a cozy room, dimly lit with red and orange fairy lights. There were cushions and pieces of soft furniture everywhere—the sort of nest every teenage omega dreamed of having. Zalen set me down on a pile of cushions next to Luca, who was curled on his side, making himself small.

The alpha cleared his throat and grabbed a blanket off the back of a nearby chair. It was the same one he'd brought into the bathroom earlier.

"I, uh, thought this might help," he said awkwardly. "But just kick it aside if you don't want it."

He shook out the fleecy throw and settled it over the two of us. Immediately, the scent of lime and vanilla surrounded me.

"Thank you," I managed, resisting the urge to bury my face in the soft fleece while Zalen was here to see it.

"Don't mention it," he said. "Yell if you need anything. I'd keep watch outside the door tonight… but I'm pretty sure Emiel's got a concussion and at least one cracked rib. I'm pissed off at him, but I can't actually leave him alone with those injuries. I'll hear if you call out, though."

I bit my lower lip, not sure how to respond to that.

With a strained smile, he turned on his heel and waded out of the sea of pillows, closing the door gently as he left. I wanted to try and check on Luca again, but it was too late. Sleep was already pulling me under.

<hr>

When I woke from a hazy nightmare sometime later, it felt like hours had passed, but also no time at all. I was disoriented. My swollen eye hurt. I sucked in a gasping breath, and was immediately wreathed in vanilla and lime, cut grass and honeysuckle.

Luca's nest.

Zalen's blanket.

The cage fight, and everything that had come after.

A stifled, choked noise came from somewhere on my right. I rolled onto my side and saw Luca, still curled into a tense comma shape as he shook with nearly silent tears.

"Luca," I rasped, not sure if I should reach out and touch him. "It's okay. We're okay now."

Wet green eyes met mine in the warm, womblike lighting of the nest.

"It's not," Luca said in an unsteady voice. "It's *not*. I'm so sorry, Mia. I should never have asked you to come to that place last night. *Christ.* You were almost—"

He cut himself off and shook his head sharply, a tortured expression twisting his fine-boned, angular features.

EIGHTEEN

Luca

"HEY." MIA'S SOFT VOICE cut through my spiraling panic, at least enough for me to focus on her battered face as she reached a tentative hand between us to cup my cheek. The delicate scent of elderflower and sumac wrapped around me like Zalen's fleecy blanket.

I blinked, trying not to stare at her black eye. The black eye that my screwed-up past had reached forward through time to give her. *Fuck,* I couldn't think about what had happened at the old factory. If I did, I'd come apart at the seams.

Blaze and his lieutenants *could not* still be after me, all these years later. My old life wasn't allowed to break through the fragile walls surrounding my new life.

"Hey," Mia said again, stroking a callused thumb over the tender skin beneath my eye. I shivered; I couldn't help it. The gentle touch, intended only to comfort, tore through my remaining defenses like they were made of wet toilet paper.

"Sorry, I'm all right," I whispered, sounding anything but.

"What happened wasn't your fault." Her voice was quiet and sleep-raspy. "You were worried about Emiel, and I think you were right to be. He looked like he was sleepwalking through the first part of that fight. Is he always like that?"

"No," I said, looking down so I wouldn't have to see the livid bruising on her face. "No, he's not."

It wasn't the first time I'd gone to watch Emiel fight. I'd gotten Byron to go with me once, but seeing the gray, queasy cast to his complexion as the fighters pummeled each other had convinced me not to repeat the request.

The underground fighting ring used to be a lot smaller and a lot less focused on high-stakes gambling. It hadn't felt like a big deal to pull on shapeless, concealing clothing and avoid making eye contact with anyone. I'd never felt particularly unsafe on my own… no more so than any other time an unclaimed omega went out in public alone, anyway.

But the fights had changed since the last time I'd gone. The gangs had moved in, just like they moved in on every goddamned thing that they thought could make them money.

"I used to enjoy watching him fight," I murmured, still unable to look at Mia directly. "I mean, it was scary, even then. But he's a good fighter and I guess…"

I trailed off.

"There's something about alphas doing, well, *alpha things*," she finished awkwardly.

"Yeah," I agreed on a sigh.

Alpha things.

Unbidden, the memory of Blaze's goons cornering us, putting their hands on us, blotted out the safe, familiar surroundings of my nest. I could still smell Zalen's secondhand pheromones and Mia's summery floral perfume, but now it was somehow tangled up in the memory of my old life.

Of what had been done to me, over and over, without my consent.

The idea that Mia might have been dragged away to suffer that same fate felt like insects crawling beneath my skin. It was all I could do not to start tearing into my forearms with my own fingernails in hopes of rooting out that terrible itch.

"They almost got you," I grated, not recognizing my own voice. "They almost—"

"Stop," Mia begged.

I didn't want to look at her injured face to gauge her expression, but something in her tone told me that I wasn't doing a very good job of hiding my thrumming panic. *Fuck*, I was making everything worse—

The hand that had been cradling my cheek slid around to the nape of my neck, and Mia's other arm came around my shoulders. Instinct had me curling into her, just as I'd done in the backseat of the car—an omega seeking the comfort of pack.

Even though I didn't have a pack.

Didn't *want* a pack.

Packs were for omegas who still knew how to trust.

"Just breathe for me, all right?" Mia's voice was worried, but her embrace was sure.

Christ, was that awful, uneven gasping noise coming from *me*?

I dragged in a ragged breath, held it for a count of four. Let it out, held it for another count of four. Lather, rinse, repeat. Again and again, until the band around my lungs eased.

Familiar as... well... *breathing*.

"Okay." Mia sounded less freaked out now, thank goodness. "Like I said, we're okay. Everything's okay. Just a couple of bruises and a bad scare."

She loosened her grip on me and pulled back, but only far enough that we could see each other's faces. The swelling around her eye had gone down a bit since last night, I was pretty sure. Zalen probably made her ice it while I was out of things.

She gave me a tremulous smile and leaned in. She must have been aiming for a kiss to the cheek—but I turned my head, startled, and her lips touched the corner of my mouth instead.

We both froze. The brush of her lips felt like a butterfly landing. Gentle... gentle. Nonthreatening. Her light perfume and Zalen's heavier pheromones filled my nose, sweet and tart and rich against the back of my throat. Promising safety, or at least the illusion of it.

I groaned roughly and turned my head another inch, returning the innocent kiss with... whatever the opposite of innocent was. *Ruined,* like a heroine in a Regency novel? *Sullied? Defiled?*

In my heart of hearts, I expected her to jerk away in distaste. She'd seen the real me now, not the polished marble omega who never let anything touch him — nothing penetrating more than skin deep.

Instead, she gasped against my mouth, her hand tightening around my nape. Tingles raced down my spine in reaction — and then we were kissing wildly, devouring each other like a pair of starving waifs. With a flood of desperate relief, I stopped thinking and started *feeling*.

All the reasons why I'd decided this was a bad idea — too complicated, too emotionally fraught — disappeared in a flurry of frantic hands tugging at clothing. Suddenly, I couldn't wait another second to feel her soft skin against mine.

We were omegas, high on secondhand alpha pheromones from a borrowed blanket. I might not be able to get her off… she might not be able to get *me* off. But I was harder right now than I'd been since my last natural heat, and as I finally dragged her underwear over her ankles and settled between her spread thighs, sinking into her, getting off didn't feel like the point.

Wet heat enclosed my cock like clenching, slippery silk. Our skin, sweat damp in the warmth of the nest, slid together in a dance as old as the stars. Sparks zipped along my nerves.

"We're safe," Mia said, sounding almost defiant about it — as though some ghostly presence inside her mind had whispered otherwise. She clutched my body tight to hers, wriggling her back and shoulders restlessly against the blanket beneath us. A fresh wave of vanilla and lime rose around us, heady and forbidden.

I couldn't quite bring myself to echo the words. I *wasn't* safe. Right now, it felt like I might never truly be safe again. But at least while Mia and I were fucking, I didn't have to face that bleak future.

My empty passage clenched, silently begging to be filled. I ignored it, because my body was an idiot. *This* was what I needed — rocking into Mia's welcoming warmth in a slow rhythm that might not lead us anywhere, but that still felt *goddamned amazing*.

"Wanted this," Mia gasped, her hips rolling to meet my slow thrusts. "Wanted you."

I remembered that long-ago awkward conversation on the couch in the TV room, with *Red, White, and Royal Blue* paused on the screen. It felt like centuries ago.

Out of curiosity… if I had been a singles bar pick-up, and I was here because I wanted to have sex — what would that look like, exactly?

It wouldn't have looked like this, that was for sure. She'd been talking about a threesome with Byron, not a post-traumatic desperation fuck with another omega. But she had wanted me. She *did* want this. She'd said so.

The part of my brain that wasn't doused in sex endorphins distantly registered the sound of the front door opening and closing, of footsteps moving through the huge house. Muffled voices exchanged unintelligible words, growing louder as the conversation continued.

One set of footsteps broke away, approaching up the stairs to the second floor. *Byron*, my instincts assured me. Finally getting home at whatever godforsaken hour it currently was. His room was down the hall from mine. No threat... no need to stop what we were doing.

I buried my face against Mia's rich brown hair, stifling a moan as her inner muscles milked and massaged my dick. *So good.*

The footsteps halted at my door, and an angry rap pounded against the wood. Mia and I both froze in place as though turned to stone.

Byron's voice called out, equal parts fear and frustration. "God*damn* it, Luca—what Zalen just told me had better not be fucking true!"

An instant later, the door swung sharply open, silhouetting Byron against the brighter lights of the hallway. He was breathing heavily; I could see his shoulders rising and falling. Our eyes met and locked across the distance separating us, even as Mia drew in a sharp, shocked breath beneath me and came hard around my aching cock.

NINETEEN

Mia

OH, *FUCK*... I was coming and I couldn't stop it, my muscles clenching hard around Luca's dick. That gruff bark from the doorway; the sudden, unexpected hit of Byron's aniseed scent. My back arched, and Luca made a cut-off, choked noise, shuddering above me.

Had he come, too? God, how was this so hot and so horrifically mortifying at the same time?

Sweet, sweet sex endorphins rushed through my veins and arteries, washing away the throbbing aches from my various injuries. I felt oddly clear-headed, as though my orgasm had been an icy splash of water to the face.

"*Jesus Christ.*" The bark was gone from Byron's voice, replaced with something else that I couldn't quite identify.

He took a step back from the door... then another, until he was no longer in silhouette, and I could see his face properly beneath the overhead hall lighting. His expression was frozen in a blank façade, but his gaze was focused unblinkingly on me.

My black eye, I thought. *He's staring at my black eye.*

"Byron—" Luca said, sounding half pleading, half wrecked.

Byron shook his head slowly back and forth, his unreadable expression set in stone. His scent, though… it was shouting a dozen different messages, and I couldn't untangle a single one of them.

Lust?

Anger?

Guilt?

Fear?

Or was I just imagining those things?

"*Byron*," Luca whispered again.

"We'll talk about this in the morning," Byron said, throwing the words down like an upset diner throwing down a wad of bills on the table before fleeing the restaurant. And sure enough, with that, he pivoted on his heel and disappeared down the hall like someone being pursued by demons.

As his footsteps retreated, followed a moment later by a door opening and closing, the reality of what had just happened slapped me in the face.

Holy shit. What had we done?

I'd had sex with Luca, who'd told me—flat out and early in our acquaintance—that he didn't think of me that way. That I was *too complicated*. But if that was the case, why had this been so easy? Why had it felt so right?

Luca was still frozen above me, resting his weight on one hand and one elbow as he stared at the place where Byron had been. He was an omega—he couldn't knot me any more than Nat could. But he was still inside me, still half-hard, and my body was doing its best to keep him there.

After a tense moment, his shoulders slumped. Green eyes slid closed, and he let his head fall until our foreheads bumped gently together. I let my eyes slip shut as well.

Jesus fuck.

With more strength than I might have given him credit for, Luca slipped one arm beneath my torso and used it as leverage to roll both of us over among the nest's cushions. The movement was smooth enough that he didn't even slip out of my body. We came to rest with him lying on his back and me straddling him. I pushed up until I was looking down at him, my hands braced on his shoulders.

"Well, that was painfully awkward," he said after a pause. His gaze darted to the doorway. "I wish he'd closed the door when he left, though."

I tried to quell the pulse of guilty heat in my gut at the idea that Zalen or Emiel might walk by and see us. *Not helpful.*

"Are you okay?" I asked instead… because Luca had been decidedly *not* okay when we'd started this. And frankly, I hadn't been much better off.

"Yeah," he sighed. "Oddly enough, I do feel better now."

I debated flicking him in the temple and teasing him for the offhand insult to my sexual healing abilities, but I decided against it.

Apparently, I wasn't the only one who'd needed an orgasm to reboot my brain.

I hesitated. "Luca... those men who cornered us. They knew you. Who were they?"

It wasn't fair of me to ask the question when we were in this position. But frankly, I figured he was less likely to bolt this way.

I was right, too. He twitched hard beneath me, and it was clear that if I hadn't been straddling him, my body clamped around his softening cock, he would have been on his feet and out the door in no time.

"You can tell me it's not my business," I added quickly, "but I'd argue that it *became* my business when one of them punched me in the face."

Luca quivered with tension beneath me for a long moment. Then all the fight went out of him at once. We both winced as his dick slipped out of me, leaving my passage clamping around nothing.

I swung my leg over to get off him, my bruised hip giving a helpful twinge of pain as I went. Settling myself on my unbruised side next to him, I propped my head on my hand so I could watch his face in the dim light.

A heavy sigh broke the silence. It sounded like it originated down around his ankles somewhere.

"I grew up in a gang," he said slowly. "Which you've probably already guessed. Except for Zalen, we all did."

I nodded. It made sense—who would be more passionate about helping teenagers escape gang life than people who'd escaped it themselves?

"My mother and father... weren't exactly in the running for any parent of the year awards," he went on. "I mistook the gang for stability. It's not hard to do when you've never known anything but chaos at home. Since I was small and quiet, they used me as a lookout, mostly. I was good at it, and I liked being good at something."

He paused and licked his lips, his eyes going far away.

"But?" I prompted, when the silence stretched for too long.

"My parents were betas." His voice had grown hoarse. "No one ever told me about my own body. I had no clue. I presented as an omega at age fourteen." He gave a rusty laugh with no humor behind it. "Late bloomer."

A queasy feeling took up residence in my stomach, and I fought the urge to tell him to stop... not to say anymore.

"I was the only omega in a pack of feral alpha and beta males. They used me as a fuck-toy. Pumped me full of synthetic heat stimulators so often that I was gagging for it half the time."

My breath caught in my lungs and stuck fast. I didn't want to picture this delicate, ethereal creature—barely more than a child at the time—being used and abused by people like the ones at the factory. Maybe by those *very same men*.

No wonder he'd been nearly catatonic with fear afterward.

"Luca," I breathed.

He went on in a monotone, as though I hadn't spoken. "Anyway, it took me four years before I finally managed to get away. Zalen took me in. Helped me earn my G.E.D. and acquire some marketable skills. Grant writing. Bookkeeping. Project management. That kind of stuff. And here I am."

The queasiness continued to grow. I knew I had to ask the next question even though I didn't want to.

"Luca… did I pressure you into having sex just now? Oh my god, I am *so sorry—*"

His bark of rusty laughter was unexpected, not to mention jarring. But Luca shook his head, his gaze coming into focus as he stopped staring at the ceiling and rolled onto his side to face me instead.

"No, Mia," he said, taking my hand in one of his. "You didn't assault me in my own nest. I *like* this kind of sex. The kind where I can feel in control."

I blinked at him, trying to reshuffle my thoughts around this new information. Sex where he was the one doing the penetrating, I supposed he meant. Which… made sense, I guess. As much as I desperately didn't want to think about the details, I doubted he was the one doing the fucking when he'd been in the gang.

"Okay," I said in relief. "Good. That's good."

Now he was the one looking worried. "Do you regret it? I know I said I thought of you as a friend, and then I just—"

"No," I said quickly, squeezing his hand. "I wasn't *expecting* it, exactly. But..." Heat suffused my face, making my bruised eye throb in time with my pulse. "I've kind of been nursing a thing for you since that night we met at the bar."

I couldn't see well enough to tell if an answering blush tinted his cheeks, but his scent deepened noticeably.

"I asked Byron if he'd considered bringing you in as a third," he blurted.

It took me a minute to untangle the meaning behind the words. Then I realized what he meant, and my empty passage gave a hopeful pulse.

"Oh," I managed. I wanted to ask what Byron had said in reply. But I also didn't want to know, because I wasn't sure what kind of answer I could live with.

Seeming to pick up on my awkwardness, Luca cleared his throat. "Sorry, I probably shouldn't have told you that. Look... um, I don't know what time it is, but I think it might be best if we snuck out of here early, before Byron or Zalen manages to corner me and start telling me how stupid I acted last night. I could drive you home?"

Home. Dear god, I was going to have to get back to the house, clean myself up, and figure out if I owned enough makeup to disguise my bruised face when I went in for my shift at the restaurant. The very *idea* exhausted me.

"Actually, if you could take me back to Soulard where my car is parked, that would be great," I said wearily. "You sure you're okay to drive?"

He nodded, looking as drained as I felt. "Sure, it's no problem. I'm fine."

Somehow, I doubted that, but it was true that he seemed more himself now. His horrific tale of abuse had blindsided me, but he'd already had years to learn how to cope with it.

"Then I guess I'd better get back," I said, dreading the next few hours.

***

Luca drove me to the parking lot, where I picked up my car. Thankfully, the little red Kia hadn't been molested overnight. After an awkward farewell, I got in and turned on the engine. Luca waited until I'd pulled out of my spot before heading out of the lot and disappearing into early morning traffic.

I felt like week-old dog vomit as I made the drive back to Jennings. All the lovely pain-killing properties of a good orgasm had fled into the gray light of predawn. I arrived at the house, my heart sinking as I pulled into the driveway next to Nat's Jeep.

Of course he would choose *now* to be home, damn him.

It was early, though. He was probably asleep. If I was quiet, maybe I could sneak into the bathroom with a gallon or two of foundation and concealer.

I let myself in as silently as I could — which wasn't very.

Jesus, I thought as the door squealed. *Did WD-40 work on door hinges? Or did you need actual oil for that?*

I tiptoed in, only to find the light on in the kitchen. No way past without being seen, then. Not unless I wanted to go right back out the front door and try to sneak in through the back like a burglar in my own damned house.

Girding myself, I straightened my shoulders and strode down the hall.

"Mia?" Nat asked, getting up from the kitchen table with a cup of coffee in hand.

Indecision almost made me stumble. I could ignore him. Walk past as though he hadn't spoken. But was that really what my life had come to?

I paused outside the kitchen, not turning my head to look at him. "Yes, Nat?"

My heart thudded as he came up to me, frowning in my peripheral vision.

"Mia, look at me." His voice held an urgent note.

Something inside me responded to the command before I could stop myself. I turned and heard his sharp intake of breath as he took in the state of my face.

TWENTY

Mia

"WHO DID THIS to you?" There was a tremor behind Nat's words, although I couldn't tell for sure if it was down to fear or anger on my behalf. "Was it that alpha you're seeing? Give me a name. We'll go to the police. I'll back you up."

He reached a hand toward me, as though he might touch my chin to tilt my head so he could see the bruising better. Then he seemed to catch himself, his fingers clenching into a fist as he lowered it to hang at his side.

"*Mia.*"

The pain in his voice was unmistakable. I hated myself just a little bit for how much that one word made me want to tumble forward into his arms and confess everything. We'd loved each other once. He'd had my back, and I'd had his. We'd been partners in more than a restaurant.

What the hell had happened to us?

I choked down the unhealthy urge and took a step back. "It's not what you're thinking. I went out for the evening with a friend. An omega." The memory of Luca's cock sliding into me, of his lips on mine, threatened to flood my cheeks with red. "Some guys tried to mug us. I had pepper spray, and then a Good Samaritan waded in to help. We got away. It's fine."

From his expression, I couldn't tell if Nat believed me or not. That was probably fair since it was partly truth and partly lies. How guilty should I be feeling right now?

"Did you go to the police afterward?" Nat asked cautiously.

I wondered if he was feeling me out. If I'd filed a police report, that would lend weight to my story, I supposed.

"No," I said, exhaustion creeping into my tone. "I couldn't even give a decent description of them, it all happened so fast. And Lu—" I caught myself. "And my friend was nearly catatonic once reaction set in. We went back to his place. I stayed with him until he recovered a bit, and I was sure he'd be okay."

All technically true.

"You could still file a report," Nat said. "I can drive you to the nearest station right now. Where did this happen?"

"I'm not filing a report, Nat." I went to rub my eyes and stopped myself just in time. I'd made that mistake earlier, and it *fucking hurt*. "We were stupid. We ended up in a bad area and nearly paid the price for it. Lesson learned."

Had it been learned, though? I wasn't so sure, in Luca and Emiel's case.

I got the distinct sense that all I'd accomplished with my denial was to make Nat even more convinced that I was screwing Zalen, and that he'd gone all 'alpha caveman' on me and punched me in the face. The irony was palpable, since I'd never even gotten a hint that Zalen had the first bit of interest in me. Or, at least, the first bit of *sexual* interest in me.

There was no doubt I was on his radar. Especially now that Luca had called me in to act as backup at Emiel's fight, rather than going to Zalen himself.

Nat looked like a ship lost at sea. As much as it pained me to admit it, I knew exactly what this must sound like from his perspective. The cliché about domestic violence victims bending over backward to protect their abusers was a cliché for a reason. Of *course* he thought my mugging story was bullshit.

A good chunk of it actually *was* bullshit.

I'd put him in a difficult position, and despite my best efforts, I felt bad about it. Should he call me a liar to my face if that's what it took — in his mind, at least — to keep me safe? Or should he let my paper-thin story slide, while believing I might go back to someone who was hurting me?

I hated the position we'd put each other in with a sudden, sick intensity. From his expression, so did he. His face had gone paler than I could ever remember seeing it.

"Mia," he began, pasty and grim. "This... this is my fault. Our marriage... hasn't been good, these last couple of years. But it was never my intention to drive you to a place where you feel like you have to put yourself in dangerous situations."

He paused and swallowed hard, his Adam's apple bobbing.

"I know you probably won't believe this," he continued, "but I honestly thought we could both get what we wanted. I was angry and resentful, yes. But I thought, okay, I'll get my needs met with casual hookups, and you won't be pressured into sex that you obviously didn't want."

If I hadn't been so exhausted, I might have choked on a bitter laugh.

"Right," I said. "So, how's that whole thing been working out?"

He hesitated.

"I… don't know. Because we don't actually communicate about anything except gross customer receipts and asparagus shipments."

A breath of tired laughter did manage to escape this time. "And whose fault is that?"

His dark brows furrowed. "Mine, to start with. But at this point, I'm pretty sure the highway is closed in both directions." He swallowed again. "Maybe all of this was a terrible mistake. If I stop seeing other people, will you stop putting yourself in danger?"

There was a haunted look behind his deepset brown eyes, and for the first time, I really stopped to wonder if there was another person out there who'd become important to him for more than just sex. What—or who—would he be giving up by making me this offer?

This is it, whispered a voice in the back of my head. *This is what you wanted, right? To turn back the clock? Pretend none of this open marriage stuff ever happened?*

It was so tempting.

So. Very. Tempting.

And it would be an even worse mistake than the one Nat had made when he'd first sprung all this on me. It was too late now for backtracking.

I drew breath, choosing my words with care. "I appreciate what you're offering. I truly do. But, Nat, pretending this never happened won't fix the underlying issues in our marriage."

"I won't stand by and see you hurt," Nat said hoarsely.

I closed the space between us and cupped Nat's jaw, trying to remember the last time we'd touched each other skin to skin.

"I know you don't believe me about the mugging," I said, overcoming my omega instincts in order to meet his gaze and hold it without blinking. "But I give you my solemn word that no one I'm seeing is hitting me. I really *was* with another omega, and we really *were* attacked by a group of strangers."

Strangers to me, at any rate.

I could see Nat struggling with his own instincts over whether or not to believe me — and maybe that shouldn't have hurt. Yet, somehow, it still did.

After a few moments, his expression cleared, and he nodded. "All right. Just so you know that no matter what else happens between us, you can always come to me if you're in trouble."

And, despite everything else happening in our lives, I knew that much was true. That knowledge curled in my stomach—uncomfortable, yet also strangely warming.

"I know," I whispered.

Something that looked like grief lurked behind his eyes, and I could tell he'd felt the same shift between us that I had. I also knew that I would have to be the one to say it aloud.

"Nat... I... think we should do a trial separation." The words burned more than I expected them to. I licked my lips, trying to moisten them. "Maybe it would be best if we focused on running the restaurant together. We're *good* at that—at least when we're not bringing our marriage problems to work with us."

Nat looked like a man who'd seen this coming. He also looked like someone who'd been slammed upside the head with a two-by-four.

"I'll move out," he said quietly. "Give me a week or two to find a cheap studio apartment or something. You know what the household finances are like these days."

I placed a hand on his arm. "No. Don't do that. Stay here. I might have a place I could crash for a bit. And if not, I can always go live with my parents until you and I figure out what we're doing. Which is something that's one hundred and ten percent *not an option* for you."

"Oh god, no," he agreed, a small shudder running through him at the thought of returning to his Bible-thumping fundie adoptive parents. He straightened his shoulders and looked down at me. "Will you at least let me take you to urgent care for that eye?"

But I shook my head. "I think it's okay. I just need to slap enough makeup over it to keep every person I meet from demanding to know what happened."

With an internal cringe, I realized that if I didn't do a good enough job, a certain percentage of those people would assume the bruise had been Nat's doing. Our marriage troubles weren't exactly well-hidden these days.

I couldn't do that to him. I *couldn't*.

"It'll be fine," I said gamely, swallowing down my queasiness.

"If you're sure," Nat replied after a moment. "If you change your mind, just say so."

I forced a wan smile and nodded my agreement. Then I resumed my trek to retrieve my makeup case so I could hole up in the bathroom. I managed to get the bathroom door closed behind me and cross the small room to the vanity before the tears came.

TWENTY-ONE

Byron

SO, THIS WAS apparently what whiplash to the dick felt like. Also, I was going to throttle Luca when I eventually caught up to him.

I'd never gotten hard so fast in my fucking life as when I'd opened that door and scented Luca and rom-com girl going at it like bunnies in Luca's nest. And I'd never gone limp so fast as when Mia had turned her head, the light from the hallway falling on her bruised face.

Zalen didn't tell me they'd been *hurt*. Probably because he knew I'd lose my shit worse than I already had.

And now Luca and Mia had managed to sneak out of the house at oh-dark-thirty without me so much as hearing a door close—alpha senses or no. It was my own damned fault. I'd figured they'd be out cold for hours, between the adrenaline let-down and the sex.

This is what you get for barging into an omega's private nest without an invitation, the truncated remains of my conscience snarked.

Was I supposed to feel guilty about it? Because *fuck that,* when Luca had done something so monumentally *stupid.* Why had he taken Mia into that snake pit? Why hadn't he asked Zalen instead? Why hadn't he asked *me?*

Why in god's name had he gone at all?

But that was dumb. I knew why the little idiot had gone. And there, come to think of it, was someone whose head I could bite off *right now*, as opposed to having to wait several hours to do it.

I stalked toward the central staircase and jogged up to the top, entering the attic bedroom. There wasn't a door; the stairway simply terminated in the middle of the converted space. Even if there had been, I would have barged in anyway, because *screw* Emiel and his self-destructive bullshit.

Someone had left a desk lamp turned on, angled away from the sleeping area but still bright enough to cast a dim glow over the room. Zalen's work, probably. The old myth about waking someone with a concussion every hour or two had been debunked years ago, but he still would have been up here several times to check on Emiel's breathing and make sure the self-centered fuckin' asshole wasn't in distress.

"You self-centered fuckin' asshole," I said aloud, and clicked on both switches controlling the overhead lights.

Emiel snarled, clawing awake at the sudden intrusion into his space... blinking at me owlishly with the eye that wasn't swollen shut. At least he'd been hurt worse than rom-com girl.

Good.

"Get out," he rasped, wrapping an arm around his ribs. His knuckles looked like someone had run them through a meat grinder.

"I'm not going anywhere until I get a god-damned explanation," I snarled back.

An unfamiliar scent tickled the edges of my awareness, like someone had left an unfinished cup of that weird hippy tea Zalen insisted on drinking sitting out in the room. It seemed out of place, since I was pretty sure Emiel would rather drink his own piss than drink anything that came in a teabag.

"I don't owe you nothin', asshole," Emiel said.

God, he looked like shit. I couldn't ever remember seeing him beat to hell like this—not after any of his fights.

"Yeah?" I shot back, goading. "And what do you owe Luca and Mia?"

An absolutely blank expression fell over his battered features—frightening in its utter *absence*. It was the kind of blankness I imagined a serial killer wearing… or a prisoner of war.

It was definitely the kind of blankness that had every hair on the back of my neck standing up in alarm, because alpha or no, I'd just invaded the room of someone who could snap me in two like a twig. Only the knowledge that I could run down a flight of stairs a hell of a lot faster than he could in his current condition kept me in place.

The silence drew out for much longer than I liked.

We continued to stare each other down—me with combined anger and fear. Him with… *nothing.*

"I got them out," he said eventually, his gravelly voice a monotone.

"You got them *injured*," I growled. "*You did that*, because of whatever sick, selfish need you have to slide back into the sewer we all crawled out of!"

I hadn't thought it was possible for Emiel's expression to get any emptier than it already was. I'd been wrong.

"*Byron*." Zalen's *calm-but-holding-onto-his-temper-by-a-thread* tone filtered up from below us. Heavy footsteps on the wooden treads of the staircase announced his approach. "We're not doing this right now."

"Then when the hell *are* we doing it?" I demanded, resisting the urge to throw my hands up in disgust like a sulky kid in a temper.

"Preferably when you haven't just woken someone with a concussion out of a sound sleep."

My eyes were still glued to Emiel. I could feel a vein throbbing in my temple. When he turned without a word and lay down on his side with his back facing me, the throbbing intensified.

"Turn off the lights, Byron," Zalen said.

Exhaustion laced his tone. He probably hadn't slept any more than I had, and he'd been practically living at the Hope Project for the last few days, dealing with his latest teenage rescue attempt.

He'd rescued all of us, damn him. Sometimes it was hard not to resent him for that. My blood pressure felt like it was about to burst something inside my skull, but I turned off the lights. Swallowing the verbal parting shot at Emiel that wanted to escape was considerably more difficult.

Zalen's footsteps headed back down the stairs. It was a few seconds before I could force my feet to follow him. He was waiting for me on the second-floor landing.

"Why are you okay with this?" I hissed, squaring up to him.

"Who says I am?" he shot back—still with that tired tone and those soft brown eyes of his.

I wanted to hurl something at him—some piece of eviscerating vitriol that would make him see that he had to *shut this shit down*. Instead, I turned on my heel and stalked down the hall toward my room.

Emiel was out for the count today, but Luca wouldn't bail on work no matter how much he wanted to avoid me. If I couldn't pound sense into one of them, I'd pound sense into the other.

◆

I was waiting in Luca's office for him when he arrived. Yes, his office door had been locked when I got here. No, standard door locks weren't much of a deterrent in a place like the Hope Project, full of people like me who'd been well-versed in breaking and entering since we were tall enough to reach doorknobs.

And, okay, relocking the door once I was inside had probably been an asshole move. The lock clicked, the doorknob turned, and Luca slunk through the door like *he* was the criminal in this scene. Then he turned around, saw me sitting behind his desk with my feet up, and bit off a startled scream—his shoulders thumping against the wall as he backpedaled.

"*Christ*, Byron!" he yelped, an angry flush staining his pale cheeks.

"Told you I'd talk to you about this in the morning," I said, not bothering to take my feet off his desk. "It was your choice to do it here instead of at the house."

The two patchy spots of red still highlighted his perfect cheekbones as he stomped over, shoved my feet out of his way, and slapped his work bag down with more force than was probably wise for the laptop stored inside.

"You want to read someone the riot act, read it to Emiel," he said through gritted teeth. "Unless this is about what you saw between me and Mia, in which case *fuck you*."

"Why the hell would I care whether you and rom-com girl screw?" I asked, to hide the fact that my dick apparently cared *very much* about this subject. "And who do you *think* I yelled at this morning, since you weren't around to yell at?"

Luca scoffed. "*Sure* you did. Because Zalen is gonna let you tear Emiel a new asshole while he's hurt."

Okay. He'd scored a point there, not that I'd admit it.

"Right," I shot back. "And meanwhile, I can see that you're not feeling guilty *at all* for dragging rom-com girl into Emiel's shit and getting her hurt."

For a fraction of a second, Luca looked like he might throw up on his cluttered desk.

"She's got a name," he whispered.

"Yeah," I agreed. "She's got a name… she's got a husband… and now she's got a shiner like she went five rounds with Mike Tyson."

I only realized how vicious a shot that was when I saw the unshed tears pooling in Luca's eyes. "No one there was supposed to recognize me," he said, the words hoarse. "It should've been safe."

A chill skittered through me, prickling every protective instinct in my body as it went. I sat up straight in Luca's chair, leaning forward to peer at him intently. "What the hell is that supposed to mean? *Who recognized you?*"

I hadn't intended for the alpha bark to creep into my words, but Luca flinched.

"People from my old gang," he said, in a voice like sandpaper. "They said… Blaze is still looking for me. They said he wants me back."

I was out of the chair before I even realized I was moving. My hands closed on Luca's shoulders, turning him to face me. He'd curled in on himself, becoming small, but he didn't shake off my grip.

"That's bullshit," I said. "No one's taking you anywhere you don't want to go. Just... don't go back to that cesspit. *Ever.* Problem solved."

Huge green eyes met mine—dry of threatening tears now, but red-rimmed with exhaustion and stress. "Emiel will go back there," he said, as though Emiel being an idiot had anything to do with his own safety.

In his mind, I guess it did.

"He won't if I have anything to fuckin' say about it," I growled, wondering if that was the kind of promise I had the power to keep.

TWENTY-TWO

Mia

OF COURSE, THIS ended up being a day when I had to conduct a couple of hiring interviews at the restaurant — black eye, pancake stage makeup, and all. In addition to my sous-chef leaving, we were also down a waiter after Chloe transferred to a college in Ohio to finish up her pre-vet degree.

The applicant for the waitstaff job had been a beta kid named Joe. He seemed like a pleasant enough guy, and he had a bit more than six months' experience as a server at a national sit-down chain restaurant. Not exactly fine dining, but it meant he knew how to handle himself in a fast-paced environment, as the corporate types liked to call it.

I'd hired him, and when he'd stuck his arm out to shake hands, I'd noticed the bottom half of a forearm tattoo poking out from beneath his jacket sleeve. I couldn't make out the details — it looked like the letters "I.O.S." in some kind of a fancy gothic font.

The fact that he might not be as clean-cut as he'd appeared didn't bother me. These days, I was spending a fair amount of time around tattoos, it seemed. An unwanted image of Byron's vibrant jungle flowers twining down his scarred torso intruded on my thoughts, and I firmly set it aside.

Unsurprisingly, I felt like complete crap today—between the physical aches, too little sleep, and my lingering crying headache, it was honestly a miracle that I was functioning well enough to get through a shift.

I would be singlehandedly keeping makeup companies in business for the next few days, and I'd come to work armed with a backup tube of concealer in case the heat of the kitchen started to melt off my flesh-colored armor before the day ended.

Zalen's package of frozen corn had probably been the reason I was able to pull off the ruse that everything was okay. I looked a bit puffy, but more in a 'hey, are your allergies bothering you' way than a 'hey, did someone punch you in the face' way. At least, no one had commented on it so far. I was taking that as a win.

My three o'clock interview showed up at ten minutes till—a middle aged omega woman with skin a couple of shades darker than Zalen's. Merry brown eyes shone out of a broad, pleasant face.

"Ms. Jones," I greeted, standing to meet her as Trinn showed her to the table in the corner where I'd been waiting for her. "Thank you for coming. Please have a seat."

According to her application, Shaniqua Jones had just graduated from culinary school. It was a good one—Escoffier, in Boulder—but she would have been at least twenty years older than most of her classmates from the look of things.

"I'm excited to be here," she said with a warm smile that crinkled the well-worn laugh lines at the corners of her eyes. "It's not every day an opportunity like this one comes up — especially right in my hometown. I imagine you've got people knocking down the door to get the job, so I'll try not to take up more than my fair share of time."

I found myself smiling, despite the terrible day I was having. It was something about her aura, I thought. Shaniqua Jones radiated a kind of calm easiness. I had a feeling that very little ruffled this woman.

"Let's get started, then," I told her. "Tell me a little about yourself. What inspired you to go into the food service industry?"

Her resumé hadn't sugar-coated anything. Before culinary school, her career was listed as 'homemaker.'

Ms. Jones leaned forward with quiet enthusiasm, resting her forearms on the table and lacing her fingers together.

"What inspired me?" She gave a pleasant little laugh. "Oh, dear. This is a bit embarrassing to tell a Michelin-star chef, but I fell in love with cooking for pack get-togethers. I have a fairly large family — six co-mates, twelve pups, and now two grand-pups. They're a social bunch, to put it mildly."

"Good grief," I said, unable to help myself. "I'm amazed you found time for any kind of cooking that didn't involve plastic trays and a microwave."

She snorted. "One of the benefits of a large pack is that you can usually shuffle the pups onto someone else when you need to work. Or, in my case, to cook. Anyway, with the last of the youngsters out of the house and off to college, I decided to pursue a culinary career professionally. Now, I just need to find someone willing to take on a forty-four-year-old graduate, fresh out of school and with no fine dining experience."

It wasn't an idle concern. Ageism was a real thing, and this industry was worse about it than many.

"Do you have a favorite style of cuisine?" I asked.

Her face lit up. "I'm a nose-to-tail kind of girl, as it happens. That, and local farm-to-table produce. The pack used to buy beef by the side from a woman down in Cedar Hill. She was producing grass-fed cattle with an intensive grazing program. Regenerative agriculture. It's *fascinating* stuff. Anyway, a lot of her customers didn't want the organ meat from their purchases... or the tripe... or the bones. I always paid to have her throw in some of the extras she had leftover."

I sat back, letting her wax lyrical about osso buco and kidney pie... soaking in the uncomplicated passion of someone who hadn't been ground down into cynicism by years in the industry. I was daydreaming about possible menu additions involving beef heart when she seemed to catch herself.

"Ah, I'm rambling on—sorry about that," she said with a smile. "Long story short, I'm probably the least qualified candidate for this job that you'll be interviewing. But I couldn't let the opportunity slide by without throwing my hat into the ring, because what you're doing here is amazing. I'd love to be a part of it."

From there, I steered the interview through the requisite cliché territory. *What do you think is your greatest strength? What about your greatest weakness?* But through it all, I found myself riding the high of someone else's enthusiasm for food and cooking.

At the end, I thanked her again and shook hands, letting her soothing omega scent of cherries and warm, baking bread surround me.

After she left, Nat approached the table. He looked as brittle as I felt, but he only asked, "What do you think? We'll need to make a decision on this hire within the next few days."

I nodded. "On paper, some of the others are a better fit. She's had a non-traditional approach to the industry, and zero work experience."

Nat raised an eyebrow. "But?"

He knew me too well, and the reminder of that fact ached on this day, of all days.

"But… I've got a feeling about her," I said.

"Then hire her," Nat told me. "Sometimes the right person isn't the obvious person."

"Yeah," I said softly, picturing what the addition of that kind of combined enthusiasm and calm serenity could do for my kitchen. "Actually, I think I will."

The rest of the shift felt brutal, even though it was another surprisingly light evening. I knew I needed to start worrying more about the amount of business the Bella Vita seemed to be taking away from us — but tonight, the lack of a dinner rush was a blessing.

My day still wasn't over, though. There was one more thing I needed to do.

I got in my car, pulled out my phone, and texted Luca.

Hi. Nat and I are separating. Is there a time we can get together and talk?

The idea of asking Luca what I was about to ask him made my guts squirm, and I wasn't sure why. But I was visiting my parents in a couple of days, and I needed an answer from him before then.

Right on cue, three dots marched across the screen.

How are you doing? Do you want to come over now? I've got ice cream.

I couldn't help the wet laugh that escaped me. A part of me cringed at being so needy. I'd spent most of last night at Luca's place, curled up with him in his nest. Now I was going to show up on his doorstep again, so I could cry on his shoulder about my shitty marriage?

But the larger part of me succumbed to a wave of longing at the idea of returning to that big house in Ladue. I'd never claimed not to be weak.

You had me at ice cream, I texted. *Be there in thirty.*

The twisting road lined with spectacular houses was becoming more familiar, even at night. I barely needed to rely on my phone's directions. Soon enough, I was pulling into the long driveway and parking in the circle drive. The coach lights flanking the front door threw off a welcoming glow.

"Hi," Luca greeted, opening the door for me. "So, you finally did it, huh? I'm glad."

My teariness from earlier had disappeared at some point, replaced with numbness. "Yeah. It seemed like the right time."

I followed Luca to the elegant kitchen, presumably in pursuit of the promised ice cream.

"Did he make a fuss about leaving the house?" Luca asked, rummaging for spoons.

I chewed on my lower lip.

"I didn't ask him to leave," I said. "I told him I'd go instead."

Luca went still.

"I can stay with my parents," I hurried on. "I'm having dinner with them on Monday… it's my day off because the restaurant is closed. Not that I'm looking forward to having this conversation with them…"

I was babbling. I snapped my mouth shut, trying not to cringe at the sudden silence.

Luca looked conflicted for long moments. Then, his expression smoothed.

"Well… I'd have to talk to Zalen and the others, but you could maybe—"

He cut himself off abruptly, his eyes snapping to something over my right shoulder. I turned and followed his gaze to find Emiel standing arrested in the kitchen doorway — staring at us both with the one eye that wasn't swollen shut.

TWENTY-THREE

Mia

EMIEL LOOKED *TERRIBLE*. There was no other word for it. Either I'd been too out of it last night to really register the extent of his injuries, or else the swelling had gotten worse since the fight; I didn't know which.

I'd *seen* the amount of abuse he'd taken in the cage fight. I'd just managed to convince myself that since he was an alpha, and he'd been upright and functioning afterward, he'd be okay.

And, to be fair… he probably *would* be okay. Even if Zalen was angry with him, I was sure the soft-hearted alpha would've dragged Emiel to a hospital if his injuries seemed truly dangerous.

"Hi," Luca greeted cautiously. "I'm guessing you heard all of that?"

"Some." Emiel rested a hand on the doorframe, his upper body hunched inward like his ribs were hurting him.

I imagined they *were*—Zalen had mentioned one or more possible cracked ribs.

Luca's eyes flicked to mine and then back, as though seeking permission to share what was going on. I swallowed and nodded.

"Okay, so… long story short," he said, "Mia's married to a dickwad, and she's finally leaving him."

"It's only a trial separation," I protested weakly.

"A trial separation during which you'll be leaving him," Luca retorted. He hesitated, clearing his throat, and turned his attention back to Emiel. "I was about to tell her that we've got loads of room in this place, and maybe she could crash here until she gets things figured out… if you and the others are okay with it."

Even after my various brief interactions with Emiel, I didn't feel like I had a read on the big alpha at all. It didn't help that—except for the brief hint of bergamot and spice in Luca's car last night—I couldn't scent his pheromones to gauge his mood.

Now, the silence as he contemplated Luca's words stretched uncomfortably. I had to fight the urge to fill it with more babbling… to repeat that I could stay with my parents if necessary, or to try and reassure him that I wouldn't intrude on his space if they decided to let me stay here.

Was he silently judging me for my failing marriage? Was he wishing he could escape this conversation and go grab a bottle of ibuprofen from the bathroom? I had no idea. His battered features might not have held quite the same scary blankness that they had in the fighting ring, but there was still no obvious expression to interpret.

"If you're staying here, will you show Zalen how to cook pasta so it doesn't come out mushy?" he asked, a second before I would have broken and started dumping random word-vomit into the silence.

"… Yes?" I replied carefully.

"Okay," he said, and limped away without another word.

Luca blinked after him. "I might've mentioned before that Emiel doesn't really do social interaction."

"You did," I agreed. "Thanks, by the way. I wanted to ask you about staying here. But then I got here, and it felt like asking would make things weird."

Luca retrieved the spoons and the ice cream. "I can't promise that it *won't* make things weird, after everything that's happened. Also, I really *do* have to talk to the others first." His smile looked strained. "It's not my house. I just crash here."

I nodded rapidly. "No, I understand. Like I said, I'm visiting my parents Monday evening. If you have an answer by then, that would be great. But if you don't, or if the answer is no, that is absolutely, one-hundred percent fine."

"I'll get you an answer," Luca said. "Promise. Now, let's go eat strawberry chocolate-chip ripple and watch a stupid sitcom or something."

"Yes, please," I said meekly, and followed him out of the kitchen.

Sunday at the restaurant wasn't much more pleasant than Saturday had been. Everything still hurt. I was still sleep-deprived. My eye looked, if it was possible, even worse than before.

The only high point in the day was my brief call to Shaniqua Jones, letting her know that Nat and I felt she would be a good fit for the restaurant and asking when she could start work. I could practically feel her elation over the phone. Even better, she said she could start on Tuesday, meaning Isaiah would still be around to help train her for the first few days.

I muddled through the brunch, lunch, and dinner services without fucking anything up too badly, and fell into bed that night without having heard anything from Luca. I was alone in the house when I woke up around nine a.m. on Monday, feeling slightly more human than I had the day before.

Omegas didn't heal as fast as alphas, but we still healed quicker than most betas. The ugly green and yellow bruising on my face and hip was going to take awhile to fade, but a lot of the puffiness around my eye was gone, thank heavens.

I wondered idly where Nat was, and if he'd been home at all last night. Then I realized with a startled jolt that if we were formally separating, his whereabouts weren't really my concern anymore. Pausing in my liberal application of foundation and concealer, I stared in the bathroom mirror and let that sink in for a minute.

Why did I feel like crying again?

I blinked rapidly and stared up toward the ceiling, unwilling to sacrifice the work I'd already put in on my makeup. Christ, I needed to *keep it together* if I was seeing my parents today. Trying to sneak the facial bruising past my mom was going to be bad enough. If I showed up with eyes red from crying, it would be lights out for any kind of calm discussion regarding what was happening with Nat.

Bottling everything up, I went and made myself a very non-gourmet late breakfast consisting of grapefruit, toast, and stale Froot Loops with almond milk. Such was the glamorous life of a Michelin-star chef.

It was early afternoon, and I was catching up on some paperwork for the new hires when Luca texted.

Hi. The others are okay with you staying here for a few weeks. But Zalen says anything longer than that will require a more in-depth discussion with all of us present.

A strange combination of relief and trepidation squirmed inside my stomach. It was true that I wasn't at all enthusiastic about the idea of moving in with my parents again at the ripe old age of twenty-seven. But the prospect of shacking up with not one, but *two* guys I'd recently had sex with was also pretty daunting. Not least because I didn't know for sure if those encounters had been one-offs.

Would they assume sex was on the table? Would they assume it *wasn't*?

Thank everyone for me, I texted back. *And tell Zalen to schedule a thirty-minute block of time for Pasta 101 at his earliest convenience. Mushy pasta is an affront against the natural order.*

LOL, Luca replied.

My parents lived in a modest mid-century split level in Florissant. Dad's family had moved here from Greece when he was five, and he met my mom when they were in high school.

They were both betas, and neither of them had ever expected to have an omega daughter. They'd been the most loving and supportive family anyone could ask for. But as the years passed, I was coming to understand that they had raised me more or less as a beta child — simply because they didn't know how else to do it.

"Hello, sweetheart!" Mom greeted, wrapping me in a hug as I smiled and entered the house.

"It's good to see you, *koukla mou,*" my father boomed, taking his turn to embrace me. "You are too busy and successful these days. You need to visit us more often."

"Sorry, Dad," I told him, accepting a kiss on the cheek and trying not to wince as the half-healed bruise there throbbed.

"You're here now, darling," Mom said. "Come in, come in. It may not be haute cuisine, but I'll have dinner on the table in a few minutes."

"Don't say that," I teased. "You taught me everything I know about food."

She scoffed and bustled off to get our meal ready. When we were alone, Dad gave me a critical once-over, tilting his head as though to get a better look at me.

"You look very glamorous tonight," he observed. "Do you have a hot date with that husband of yours after you escape our clutches?"

I winced internally. "No, nothing like that. I'm, uh… just trying out a new look. Got tired of staring at the fine lines and dark circles under my eyes."

"What nonsense," my father said, waving me toward the comfortable old couch in the living room. "You are beautiful, and you will always be beautiful—even when you are old and gray. You shouldn't fall for all that Instagram nonsense about makeup and Botox!"

I laughed, although it felt strained. "All right. No Botox, I promise."

"Come on in and load up your plates," my mother called from the dining room.

Relieved for the escape from my father's focused attention, I led the way to the familiar, kitschy dining room, with its antique hutch full of fine china and ceramic roosters. The table was set for three, and laden with a hodge-podge of American and Greek comfort food.

My stomach rumbled, Froot Loops long forgotten.

"Dig in!" my mother said cheerfully, and the three of us applied ourselves to the food for a pleasant few minutes.

Once my initial hunger was sated, my nerves had me pushing the remaining food around my plate as I picked at it, stomach churning. It didn't take long for my mother to pick up on it.

"What's the matter, dear?" she asked, frowning. "You look like someone contemplating a walk to the gallows. Has something happened?"

I set my fork down, steeling myself.

"Sorry," I said. "Yes, I'm afraid I've got some bad news, and there's no good way to sugar-coat it. Nat and I... we're, um... we're separating."

TWENTY-FOUR

Mia

"YOU'RE GETTING A *DIVORCE*?" my father asked, sounding appalled. And this was what I'd been afraid of. My parents weren't remotely like Nat's when it came to religion or morals—but my father had grown up in a devout Catholic family of Greek immigrants, and sometimes it still showed.

"No, it's a trial separation," I told him patiently. "Not a divorce. We're just... giving each other a bit of space for now, that's all."

My mother's expression was pinched. "If that's what you both think is best, dear," she said, giving me a clear-as-day *'we'll talk later'* look as she did. "But good heavens... what about the restaurant? That place means everything to you."

"It shouldn't affect the restaurant." Even as I said it, a little voice whispered, *'won't it, though?'*

"I see." Mom still sounded skeptical. "So, you've asked him to move out? Does he have someplace else to stay? Besides his parents' place, I mean."

We all knew what a dumpster fire *that* would be.

My throat felt dry. "I thought it would be simpler if *I* moved out, actually."

My father frowned, worry clear in his brown eyes. "How is that simpler?"

"Do you need a place to land?" Mom asked. "We could make up your old room for you. We're only using it for storage—it wouldn't be any trouble."

"Thanks, but..." I grabbed my water glass and took a sip, desperate to get some moisture in my mouth. "I, um... I'm going to crash with an omega friend of mine for now. They've got plenty of room, and it's closer to work."

"Oh, I see." My mother sounded somewhere between disappointed and worried. "An omega friend? Do we know her?"

Argh.

There was no getting around this. "He's a he, not a she. And no, you don't. His name's Luca—he works as a grant writer at a center for at-risk youth."

My father's frown was deepening. "You're separating from Nat in order to live with another man? That doesn't sound very proper."

It was in no way *'proper.'*

"He's another omega, dear," my mother said. "It's different. Besides, it's the twenty-first century, not the nineteenth. If Mia says there's nothing untoward going on, then I'm sure it's fine."

I absolutely refused to think about curling up in Luca's warm nest... about his lips on mine, or climaxing with him inside me.

"Ah, this generation," my father muttered. "So many radical ideas. We trust you, Mia—but please take a moment to think how you would feel if Nat left, and said he was going to stay with a woman friend. Because that's probably how he will feel about *this*."

Yikes. I guess irony could be pretty ironic sometimes.

"I'm pretty sure he'll understand why I'm doing it," I managed, and I felt proud of myself for not injecting too much sarcasm or bitterness into the words.

"Well, I hope you two can work things out," Dad went on. "Nat is a good man. Maybe you should try that couples counseling I'm always reading about in magazines."

Mom shot me a look laced with sympathy at being subjected to my father's ideas on relationship dynamics. "It's not a terrible idea, sweetheart. You're both under a lot of stress with your restaurant, and that can have an impact on a couple's home life."

"I'll keep it in mind," I promised. "Not sure Nat would go for it, though."

My father nodded. "It's harder for men. To talk about feelings, I mean."

Maybe it was. I didn't know. Luca and Zalen seemed to do all right at it… though to be fair, Emiel and Byron were locked up tighter than Fort Knox. And god knew it felt like having my insides scraped out whenever I had to talk about this kind of shit.

"I'll suggest it," I promised.

The rest of the meal was a bit strained, but I gave my parents points for letting it go while we ate. It was only when the food was finished, and they had filled me in on all their recent news that my mother caught my eye with a significant look.

"Come help me get the dishes rinsed and in the washer, sweetie," she said. "Michalis — why don't you pull out those photos you took when we went to Miami. I'm sure Mia would love to see them. We'll be done in a few minutes and join you."

Dad mumbled vague assent and headed out of the dining room. Bracing myself, I rose and started gathering up the plates and silverware. Mom did the same, and we settled into the old, familiar rhythm of her rinsing dishes in the sink and handing them to me to arrange in the dishwasher.

"What did he do?" she asked quietly, as I straightened from slotting a pan into the upper rack.

"What do you mean?" I asked, deflecting for all I was worth.

She made a chiding 'tsk' sound. "Nat. He did something to make you leave him. You don't have to tell me if you don't want to, love… but I wish you would."

It was a good thing I hadn't picked up another dish, because I probably would have dropped it when all the pain and confusion and anger and resentment crashed over me at once, and I collapsed abruptly into tears.

"Mia!" My mother hurriedly rubbed her hands on a towel and stepped close, wrapping me up in her arms.

I sobbed—great, hiccupping spasms that stole my words for long minutes as I pressed my face against her neck. She shushed me and made reassuring noises, rubbing my back until the tears subsided into ragged, uneven breathing and finally, stillness.

She eased me back so she could see my face, and only when her look of horror registered did I realize what a bad mistake I'd just made.

"Oh, my god," she breathed. "Mia—is that a black eye? He's *hitting* you?"

"No!" I said quickly, scrubbing at my snotty nose with my sleeve and taking a step back. "Mom, no. That wasn't Nat! I got mugged on Friday night. They didn't get anything—I pepper sprayed one guy, and the people I was with managed to run the others off. I didn't want to worry you—that's why I hid it."

Her expression held the same skepticism Nat's had held when I told him my concocted story, and somehow that realization felt like cactus spines jabbing my heart.

"Then what?" she demanded. "If he's not abusing you, why are you separating?"

Abruptly, I was so tired I could barely stand it. My shoulders slumped.

"He demanded an open marriage because he wasn't happy with our sex life," I said, defeated.

She went very still. "Oh."

214

"Yeah," I agreed weakly.

"So… you refused, and now you're separating?" she asked.

"Not… exactly." I hesitated. "I'm sorry, Mom. But it's really hard to talk about the details right now."

She gave a slow nod. "Of course. You're not obligated, sweetheart. But… why separation and not divorce him right away? You've got grounds for it. I suspect even your father would agree."

"Oh, god—don't tell him," I blurted, picturing nightmare scenarios of Dad storming into the restaurant to confront Nat.

Those same visions must have been playing across my mother's thoughts as well, because she said, "No. Definitely not."

Unfortunately, I didn't *know* why I'd told Nat we were separating instead of telling him I wanted a divorce. Maybe it was the way he'd freaked out when he saw my eye. Maybe it was our years of history, or my worry about the restaurant.

"It's complicated," was all I could come up with.

Mom nodded again. "I understand." Then she paused, as though unsure of her next words. "Sometimes I worry that we didn't raise you the way an omega child should be raised. Back then, I didn't know anything about packs, or bonding, or how alphomic relationships worked. No one talked about it openly to betas."

It was easy to forget sometimes that it had only been about forty years since the Alphomic Accords that granted equal rights to alphas and omegas. The distrust had lasted long beyond that.

"There's no way you could have done anything different, Mom," I said. "You were great parents. You still are. But, yeah, I'm not sure either Nat or I really understood what we were getting into when we married beta-style."

She reached out and hugged me again. "That's no excuse for what he did, though. He hurt you. Just so you know that your dad and I only want you to be happy. It doesn't matter what that looks like... or even if we understand it. You do know that, right?"

I did. Deep down, I really did.

"Thank you," I murmured against my mother's hair. "I love you both."

This was something Nat didn't have, and never would, I reflected. It occurred to me for the first time that he must be navigating this mess completely on his own. And despite the fact that his problems were ninety-nine percent of his own making, in that moment, I felt for him.

TWENTY-FIVE

Zalen

"WHAT ARE YOU going to do about this shit, Zalen?" Byron demanded, cornering me in the kitchen as I dropped my work bag on the counter and turned to rummage in the refrigerator for a beer. Frankly, I could have used something stronger—but nothing good ever came of that.

"What am I going to do about *what* shit?" I shot back, mostly just wishing I could slink off and get a decent night's sleep. It was after ten p.m., and even now I felt guilty about leaving the Hope Project rather than just crashing on a couch there or something.

"Any of it," Byron said sharply. "*All* of it. Did Luca talk to you?"

I stilled. "You mean about Mia staying here? You know he did. I said yes, didn't I?"

"Not that." He made a frustrated gesture with one hand. "About what happened at the fight. About his old gang."

Disquiet tingled along my nerves.

"*What*?" I asked dumbly. Luca hadn't let a single damned word slip about the details of whatever had happened to blacken Mia's eye and send him into a state of near dissociation. Between him and Emiel, it was like trying to communicate with a pair of clams—both of them shut up tight against the world.

Had he talked to Byron? "What did he tell you?"

Byron looked angry, and on edge, and maybe a little bit frightened. "He told me that some members of his old gang were there. They recognized him, and they let him know in no uncertain terms that the leader wants him back. I'm guessing they tried to snatch him, and that's when Mia got hurt."

Ice water flooded my veins, driving away my exhaustion and replacing it with useless adrenaline. Ghosts from the past stirred restlessly in their graves.

"No," I managed. "He didn't talk to me about any of that."

"He's not safe. Anyone with half-decent internet search skills could figure out he works at the Project," Byron went on doggedly. "He's on LinkedIn, for Christ's sake."

"Under the name he took after he got out of the gang," I retorted, glad beyond measure that he'd agreed to let me help him change his name legally. "Not the one on his birth certificate."

Byron's shoulders relaxed a bit at that. "True. A name change is still in the public record, though."

I felt this new worry pile onto my shoulders with all the other worries... and stiffened my spine to bear the added weight. "I'll talk to him. If he'll allow it, we can start walking him to and from his car at the Project. That should be enough. It's not like gang members from the

SSG are going to cross the river and storm a neighborhood in Ladue with guns blazing."

Byron flinched at the mention of guns, the movement barely detectable—and I immediately felt like an asshole. Drawing attention to the lapse would only make things worse, though. So, I pretended I hadn't noticed, or smelled the faint spike in his scent.

"Probably not," he agreed grudgingly. "Next question—how do you plan to keep him from diving headfirst into that snake pit the next time Emiel goes back there to get the shit beat out of him? Because I've got a *suggestion* for that one."

There was real vitriol in the last sentence; enough to let me know that my longstanding policy of looking the other way when it came to Emiel's cage fights was coming to an ignominious end. The weight on my shoulders grew heavier.

A faint rustle of clothing had both of us turning sharply toward the arched kitchen entrance. Emiel had materialized there, silent as a ghost. The swelling on his face was mostly down, though the fading bruises still lingered, and his ribs would take time to mend even with accelerated alpha healing.

He stared at us impassively, with that blank expression of his that had always disconcerted me.

"I didn't ask Luca to come," he said. "Told him not to, actually."

Byron rounded on him, obviously ready for the fight I'd denied him before.

"And you thought that'd keep him from doing it?" he demanded. "You have actually *met* Luca, right?"

"M'not his keeper," Emiel said, still dead calm. "Neither are you."

"I don't suppose you were eavesdropping for the part where his old gang leader is trying to get him back?"

The tone of Byron's question was vicious, but I didn't step in to intervene this time.

Emiel's blank façade shivered, cracks forming in an icy pond.

"What?" he breathed.

"You heard me, goddamn it," Byron shot back, relentless. "That's on you. He wouldn't have been in that shithole if not for *you*."

"I told him not to come," Emiel repeated, but now those spreading cracks of uncertainty extended into the words.

"You're not responsible for someone else's choices," I told him. "But it's also true that Luca and Mia wouldn't have been at a gang-run illegal fighting venue if *you* hadn't been there. It's time to find a different way to deal with your demons, Emiel."

The ice hardened again. "Sure. I could start screwing everything with a pulse. I hear that works."

There was no question where *that* particular shot had been aimed. But Byron only offered him a smile that reflected his ice like a mirror.

"Let's put it this way, champ. I've managed to avoid causing any physical injuries so far... or receiving any. From where I'm standing, that puts me ahead of *you*."

"Fight in legal matches," I told Emiel, resisting the urge to add, '*and find a decent therapist so you can figure out who you're really trying to punish.*'

"Or else?" Emiel asked, tone once more flat.

The list of possible consequences played through my mind.

Or you won't be employed at the Hope Project anymore.

Or you won't be welcome under my roof.

"Or you'll be making my life more complicated than it already is," I said aloud.

Emiel and Byron both drew breath to speak, but the sound of the front door opening interrupted them. Low voices reached us, along with the faint sound of someone thudding around. By unspoken agreement, Byron and Emiel both shut up as two omegas' footsteps approached along the hall.

"Coming through," Luca said airily.

Emiel stepped out of the way as Luca and Mia appeared in the hallway carrying boxes.

"Hi," Mia said uncertainly, peering at us through the archway.

"We're getting a start on moving Mia's stuff out of her house," Luca said.

"Hello, you two," I told them. "If you run out of space in the guest bedroom, there's plenty of room for storage downstairs, Mia."

She gave me an uncertain smile. "Thanks," she said, and followed Luca toward the back staircase at the end of the hall.

"I'm going to bed," Emiel said, once they'd left. His eyes were fixed on the place where the omegas had been. A haunted look passed over his bruised features, but it was laced with longing. He stalked off without another word, leaving me alone with Byron in the kitchen.

"Do you have the faintest idea what you're getting us into with these two omegas?" Byron asked, as though he was genuinely curious.

"It's only temporary," I told him absently, the scent of honeysuckle and elderberries tickling my nose. After a moment, I turned my full attention on the other alpha. "Besides, she's good for Luca. She got past his walls. Not many people do."

Byron snorted. "Past his walls? Yeah... that's one way to put it, I guess." His expression hardened. "So, are you actually going to enforce what you told Emiel just now?"

"Yes," I told him, aware that I probably should have shut that shit down a long time ago. And equally aware that my pack dominance over the hulking, angry alpha was strictly psychological, if it even existed at all.

"Good," Byron said, and walked out.

Alone, I let the sounds of the house tease the edges of my awareness — the omegas speaking in low, conspiratorial tones as doors opened and closed, boxes thumping as they were stacked. Having Luca here was already sweet torture, after all the things I'd lost in my previous life. Having Mia here would be worse.

I knew better than most what it felt like to have the best parts of yourself ripped away. The truncated scar tissue of my broken mate bond still throbbed and ached at the smallest reminder of the loss, even all these years later.

But I'd built this pack-that-wasn't-a-pack on top of the wreckage of my former existence, and its founding tenet was that anyone who needed shelter would find it here. No matter how broken they were… no matter where they came from.

I might not have been picturing a successful Michelin-star chef who smelled like summertime when I'd made that decision—but she'd befriended Luca, and that was enough for me. Now it just remained to be seen whether we'd end up chasing her off with our sharp edges, once she really got to know us.

TWENTY-SIX

Mia

I HADN'T INTENDED to stay overnight in Ladue. Unfortunately, after the stressful dinner with my parents and the less stressful—but still tiring—couple of hours spent hauling boxes around, I made the mistake of crashing on the comfortable sofa to watch TV with Luca.

Just to decompress, I'd said.

Just for thirty minutes, then I really have to go, I'd said.

And, of course, I'd woken up seven hours later in a comfortable tangle, drooling all over Luca's sage green button-down shirt.

I'd packed all sorts of crap in that first load of boxes—but not an overnight bag, since I hadn't been planning to stay overnight. So, after a polite refusal of breakfast and an awkward goodbye to Luca, I stumbled out to my car in yesterday's sweaty clothes and made my bleary way back to Jennings.

When I saw a familiar maroon Dodge Caravan parked in our driveway, I came perilously close to blowing straight past the house and not stopping until I was somewhere safely out of range of the imminent nuclear detonation.

Canada, maybe.

Nat's mom and dad had descended. I assumed it was both of them, anyway. They usually came as a set.

My foot hovered between the brake and accelerator pedals for a split second before my conscience — along with my completely legitimate need to get cleaned up and dressed for work — took control. Jaw clenching, I pulled into the driveway, squeezing carefully past the van to park next to Nat's Jeep.

Apparently, despite everything, I retained just enough loyalty to Nat that I couldn't stomach the thought of throwing him to the jackals alone. Tom and Martha Bell were the most toxic of toxic born-again Christians, and they had been ever since I'd known them. They never missed a chance to remind Nat of the sacrifices they'd made in adopting a half-Chinese orphan, or pointing out all the ways he'd disappointed them.

For the first time, it occurred to me to wonder how much of Nat's *I demand an open marriage'* bullshit had been subconscious rebellion against thirty solid years of being moralized at. Too bad this wasn't a good time for a psychological eureka moment.

I had a feeling this confrontation was going to be brutal unless we both straight-up lied about our marriage being on the rocks — which I, for one, had no intention of doing.

I got out of the car, locked it, and girded myself for spiritual battle. When I cracked open the front door, the sound of a gruff male voice shouting about the evils of divorce greeted me through the gap.

Question answered, then. Clearly, we weren't trying to cover it up.

"Good morning," I greeted cheerfully as I stepped into the small entryway at the edge of the living room.

Three sets of eyes fell on me—two scandalized and one desperate. It was surprisingly easy not to quail under those stares. None of them were alphas, for one thing, and I also felt a strange sense of lightness upon realizing that I no longer had any reason to walk on eggshells around my prickly in-laws.

"Mia!" Martha gasped, with as much offense as if I'd strolled through the door naked. "Your eye!"

"Hello, Martha," I said, still in my best annoyingly chirpy voice. "Hello, Tom." I touched the slowly fading bruise over my cheekbone. "Yeah, about that. I got mugged the other day. Nothing to worry about. Bit early in the morning for an unannounced visit, isn't it?"

Martha immediately fell into an aggrieved stance. "Nat here can't be bothered to call or visit—"

Hmm, wonder why?

"—so, what *choice* do we have?" she finished, her tone bordering on a whine. "And now this talk of divorce!"

"Were you out all night?" Tom demanded aggressively, as though some universe existed where that was remotely an appropriate question.

Omega instinct tried to shy away from the prospect of a large, angry man turning his poorly regulated emotions in my direction. But I'd recently been beaten up by professionals, and while I'd always suspected Thomas Bell had been a proponent of *'spare the rod, spoil the child'* when Nat was young, he wasn't going to physically attack an adult woman in front of witnesses.

Nat bristled, angling himself to step part-way in front of me. "That's an inappropriate question, Father. You will speak civilly to my wife, or you will not be welcome in this house."

I couldn't help the small frisson of goose-bumps that rose and fell in response to that calm, deadly quiet tone. Nor could I help the faint thrum of satisfaction I felt at watching Tom realize that his gym-addicted adoptive son might be more than a match for his own middle-aged, paunchy physique.

"Not going to be your wife for much longer, is she?" he grumbled.

"We're undergoing a trial separation while we try to figure out our issues," I said, stepping out from behind Nat's shoulder. "I was moving boxes to the place where I'll be staying last night, and I ended up too tired to drive home safely."

"What kind of issues?" Martha asked, still in that whiny, put-upon voice.

Nat went very stiff, no doubt wondering if I was going to take this chance at revenge by spilling the details of what he'd done.

"Sexual incompatibility," I said, not willing to let him off the hook completely. Besides, it was satisfying to watch the blotchy red color rise in Tom's cheeks, while Martha made high-pitched, squeaky noises of shock.

Surprisingly, Martha recovered first. "You mustn't let... *unfortunate personal issues* ruin God's plan for your marriage, Mia! I know the perfect thing—there's a Christian marriage retreat that worked *wonders* for my friend Betty! I'll send you the website link on Facebook—"

Nat, I couldn't help noticing, looked like he wanted to die on the spot.

Understandable.

I couldn't have said why I decided to take pity on him. Maybe because I felt genuinely bad for him... or maybe because there was something mildly addictive about baiting his parents, now that I had the chance.

"I'm not sure Christian marriage counseling would be a good fit, under the circumstances," I said. "You see, I think I might be a lesbian. So, mostly, I just need to take some time to find myself."

Nat made a cut-off choked noise, so soft I barely heard it.

"A *what*?" Martha nearly shrieked. "Mia, you can't go down that sinful path!"

"This is some kind of omega nonsense, isn't it!" Tom put in. "Nat, we warned you about marrying across designation boundaries! But would you listen?"

I blinked. Had they, now? Interesting… though maybe not a complete surprise.

Nat, who'd been looking like passing out was a real possibility, rallied. "Mother, Father — I think it would be best if you left now. This is *our* private business. Not to mention the fact that we need to get ready for work."

He managed to herd them out of the front door.

"So good to see you both!" I called after them before it closed.

When Nat returned, he was physically shaking. He sat down on the battered couch and leaned forward, his elbows resting on his knees.

"You didn't have to do that," he said, not looking up at me. "Taking the heat, I mean."

"I know," I told him, letting some steel creep into my voice. Then, I softened. "You do understand how toxic they are, right?"

He gave a listless, one-shouldered shrug.

I sighed. "I don't want you to take this the wrong way, Nat. But you should really get into therapy to deal with some of that shit."

At that, he looked up. "Do you… think we should do couple's counseling? *Real* counseling, I mean. Not whatever horrific fundie reeducation camp my mother was talking about."

I froze, caught completely by surprise.

"No." It came out before my brain made even a half-hearted attempt at engaging. "I… uh… maybe you should just start with solo counseling for now." I fumbled over the words.

The faint light of hope that had kindled in his deep brown eyes flickered and died. "Yes. You're probably right. Maybe I'll look into it."

My pulse had skyrocketed, and I didn't know why. On that awkward note, I escaped to the bathroom for a shower... where I immediately started second-guessing my knee-jerk negative response to the proposal. Shouldn't I *want* marriage counseling? *Especially* since Nat was the one to bring it up.

I stepped into the spray of hot water, turning my face into it. What the hell was wrong with me, anyway? First Nat had offered to stop seeing other people, and I'd thrown it back in his face by moving out. Now he was asking for couple's counseling, and I'd shut that down as well.

All of this would be so much easier if I hated him. But he was still the guy who'd had my back without question when he thought someone was abusing me. He was still the guy who'd physically stepped between me and his asshole of a father, even though deep down, Nat was terrified of the man.

No matter how badly he'd screwed up the marriage, I couldn't hate him. And that made everything else a hundred times more complicated. I thumped my forehead gently against the clammy tile wall, a growl rumbling up from my throat.

"Fuck."

TWENTY-SEVEN

Mia

IT TOOK NEARLY a week to get all my stuff packed up and either moved to the Ladue house or put in storage in my parents' basement. I knew I could have taken everything to Zalen's house, but even though he'd said it was all right, it still felt presumptuous, somehow.

So, I'd stuck to moving in with only the stuff I was actually likely to need over the next few weeks. Luca had helped me get the guest bedroom ready, his omega nesting instincts triggered as much or more than my own, it seemed.

Tonight was the night. It was Sunday, which meant tomorrow was my day off. I had my overnight case full of toiletries and sleep-wear in the back of my car. Once this shift was over, I would be driving to Ladue not because I was visiting, but because I lived there — tempo-rarily, at least.

I wasn't sure whether I was supposed to feel excited because I was finally moving for-ward, or sad because I was leaving the home I'd made with Nat… or maybe something else en-tirely? Mostly, I just felt numb. That, and busy, because the Elderflower Inn was *packed* tonight.

"Whatever social media voodoo you did, it obviously worked," I told Nat when he poked his head in to see how things were going on the line.

He tried to smile, but it was strained at the edges. I might not have figured out how *I* was supposed to feel about tonight, but *he* definitely had. Still, he only nodded.

"Online scavenger hunt with a hundred-dollar gift voucher up for grabs," he said. "The final clue is on a special hidden menu page on the website, only accessible via the new QR codes taped to the tables."

"I understood some of those words," I told him. "Which is why marketing is your job and slinging hash is my job."

"We don't serve hash," Nat said, trying for humor.

"We could serve hash," Shaniqua Jones called from her station at the grill. "I make *amazing* hash."

A couple of the line cooks chuckled, and I felt a smile tug at my lips. Even Nat's tense face relaxed a bit.

"Maybe we'll start opening for breakfast," I called back, and the chuckles turned to groans. It seemed no one was in a hurry to add an early morning shift to the roster, and I couldn't blame them.

Candace poked her head into the kitchen from the front of house, interrupting the moment of levity. Her eyes were wide as she beckoned Nat and me over.

"What is it?" I asked. "Something wrong up front?"

"Not... really?" she said. "Only, there are a couple of guys from the Bella Vita checking out the place, and I thought you'd want to know. They're at table six."

Frowning, I followed her out with Nat at my back. A couple of alphas in dress slacks and button-downs sat at table six, chatting pleasantly with the new waiter, Joe.

"Okay, I'll bite," I told Candy. "How do you know they're from the Bella Vita?"

Her cheeks reddened, and her eyes darted to the side as she cleared her throat. "So... you know how Isaiah was talking about maybe going over there to scope out the competition? I kind of... did that last week."

"We're doing corporate espionage now?" Nat asked. "Huh. Okay. How was it?"

"It was, y'know, good," Candy said, still looking like she wasn't sure if she was in trouble or not. She jerked her chin toward the table. "One of those guys was doing the rounds in the dining room, making sure the customers were happy. I saw the other guy behind the bar, talking to the bartender."

"Well," I said, "I guess we can't get too upset about them coming here to spy on us, since we've already spied on *them*."

Candy opened her mouth to say something, but she was interrupted by a loud clatter and an ominous thud from the back of house. I winced, knowing a sound like that from the back of a restaurant could herald anything from *'no big deal'* to *'oops, there's a few thousand dollars down the drain.'*

Nat and I lunged for the double doors as one. Toby, one of the line cooks, was standing at the top of the stairway leading down to the walk-in cooler, both his hands clamped over his mouth in horror as he stared down at whatever carnage lay below.

Instinct propelled me to rush forward, find out what happened, and immediately start doing damage control. I tamped it down and placed a restraining hand on Nat's arm when I saw that my new sous chef had beaten us to the scene of destruction.

"What are you—" Nat began, looking down at my hand.

"Shh," I said, pulling him back a step with me, so we were out of their line of sight. "I need to see how she handles a crisis. I'll step in if I need to."

Nat gave a reluctant nod, though his arm was tense under my grip.

"What happened?" Shaniqua asked. "Are you okay? Not hurt or anything?"

Toby shook his head, still looking panicked. "I'm so sorry, chef! I was trying to grab the door, and I don't know what happened. I slipped on something and dropped the tub. It fell down the stairs, and now everything's ruined! I didn't mean to do it—"

"Of course you didn't," Shaniqua told him. "Was it the lamb?"

I cringed, since that probably meant we were on the *'oops, there's a few hundred dollars in expensive meat down the drain'* section of the spectrum. At my side, Nat made a low, visceral noise of financial pain.

Toby nodded miserably. "I'm so sorry! There are four orders in for the lamb already — that's why I was bringing it up! What should we do?"

Shaniqua hesitated for a moment, and I held my breath. This was the first really challenging service we'd had since Isaiah left, and I needed to see if her lack of real-world restaurant experience was going to be an issue when things got tough.

After a slight pause, she nodded with the air of a woman who'd successfully wrangled six co-mates and twelve pups for the better part of two decades.

"All right. Grab all the waitstaff and warn them that lamb is off the menu," she said. "Then find Nat and ask him to let the customers who've already ordered know what's happening."

At that, Nat strode forward. "I'm here. What *did* happen? I heard a crash," he said, playing along with my plan.

Shaniqua calmly recounted events, while Toby looked like he wanted to sink straight through the floor. Pleased with what I'd seen — except for the unexpected hit to the pocketbook, obviously — I headed for the kitchen to take over there. Behind me, Nat's gruff voice was telling

Toby that accidents happen, and to be more careful from now on.

The rest of the service went as well as could be expected. Nat sent the four disappointed diners off with gift cards for future visits, and awkwardly told me he'd see me on Tuesday after we closed for the night. I still hadn't decided what emotions I was supposed to be having, but I agreed and told him to have a good rest of the weekend.

I found Shaniqua smoking a cigarette behind the restaurant as I left, locking the back door behind me.

"Hey," I greeted. "Good job tonight. I really appreciate how you handled things with Toby. You've got a good, calming presence in the kitchen."

She smiled, stubbing out the cigarette a bit sheepishly. "Thanks. That means a lot, coming from you. And for the record, I stopped officially smoking a couple years ago. I only carry this pack for emergencies, and tonight was pretty intense."

I snorted. "Your secret's safe with me. Right, I'm out. See you on Tuesday, Shaniqua."

"G'night, boss," she said. "Oh, and feel free to call me Shani. Most people do. One thing, before I forget it—there was a patch of oil or grease at the top of the stairs going down to the cooler. I cleaned it up as best I could, but Toby's accident could have been a lot worse. We need to make sure that doesn't happen again."

Christ. That could have been serious.

"Definitely," I agreed. "I'll talk to everyone first thing on Tuesday about cleaning up any spills as soon as they happen. Good night, Shani. And thank you again."

She smiled, and I rummaged for my keys, heading for the lot where I'd parked.

It was time to go home, for my new definition of 'home.'

———◆———

The commute to Ladue was actually quite a bit shorter than the commute to Jennings. Luca greeted me when I let myself in, hauling my overnight case with me.

"Welcome home," he said warmly, and something inside me relaxed.

"Hi," I said, dredging up a grin for him. "Do you think everyone would be okay with me putting on a late sit-down dinner tomorrow to say thank you for letting me stay here?"

Luca smirked, taking my case from me, and leading the way into the house. "I think you'd better be careful about cooking for us, or you're likely to find yourself chained in the kitchen with an ankle shackle," he said over his shoulder.

Honestly, there were days when that didn't sound like too bad of a deal... but boundaries were important.

"Nuh-uh. Once a week, tops. Besides, once I teach Zalen how to make pasta without mangling it, you won't even need me."

"See, you say that now," Luca shot back. "You haven't seen how badly we eat around this place. Speaking of which, there's some left-over takeout curry in the fridge if you're hungry."

"Not hungry," I said, having grabbed a salad earlier at the restaurant. "I could murder a can of Pepsi, though."

I'd just pulled one out of the fridge and cracked it open when Zalen came in. He was carrying a box under one arm, and he looked pretty rough—exhausted, and with dark circles under his kind eyes.

"Hello, you two," he greeted, setting the box down in front of me. "Welcome to the house, Mia."

I put the soda can down on the counter.

"Hi," I said, surprised. "Is this for me?"

"It is," he told me. "Sorry I didn't manage to get it wrapped. Go ahead and open it if you like."

TWENTY-EIGHT

Mia

I LOOKED FROM Zalen to the box, and back to Zalen again. "You didn't have to do that," I said, surprised that he would have bothered with a welcome gift for me.

Luca raised an eyebrow. "You don't *have* to play chef for us tomorrow, either," he pointed out. "But apparently you're not letting that stop you." He glared at Zalen. "Which means you need to be home by nine p.m. tomorrow, by the way."

I wondered if that meant Zalen had been at the Hope Project tonight, even though it was a Sunday. From what Luca had told me, the center was closed on Sundays.

Now, though, I tore my attention away from the exchange in favor of opening Zalen's mystery box. It was about eight inches square and unmarked, not particularly heavy or particularly light. Something inside it shifted and rustled when I tilted it. I picked at an edge of the tape with a fingernail until I could peel it away and lift the top flaps open.

Inside, a black bag with gold foil accents lay nestled among the shredded paper packing material. The faint scent of coffee beans tickled my nose—arabica, I was pretty sure, but it had an intriguing fruity, floral note. 'Pacamara Limited Edition,' read the label.

"Oh, *wow*," I said. "Zalen, you shouldn't have!"

He mustered a smile for me. "Luca said you were a coffee fiend. I usually go for tea myself, but I'll make an exception for this stuff. There's a grinder in the cabinet under the cutting board, and the coffee machine's over there." He pointed. "Hopefully it'll go some way toward making up for our odd hours of coming and going."

"*Thank you*," I said, opening the top of the bag and inhaling the scent like a junkie taking a hit. "Sorry, Luca, but Zalen's my favorite now."

Luca snorted, and Zalen chuckled.

I made myself stop mainlining the smell of coffee beans and straightened. "Right. Like Luca said, I'm making dinner for everyone tomorrow. Nine p.m. sharp. You're vegetarian. Anything else I need to know? Food allergies or intolerances? Other preferences?"

"No, I'm the only snowflake in the bunch," Zalen said. "And I'm sure anything you make will be wonderful. We all work tomorrow, but if you need to buy anything, it can go on the joint household expenses."

"Thank you again," I said, cradling the coffee to my chest like a treasure. "For everything, I mean — not just the fancy caffeine delivery system."

He offered another one of those weak smiles that didn't manage to chase away the shadows lurking behind his eyes. "You're welcome. Thanks in advance for feeding us tomorrow."

Luca leaned his elbows on the counter. "You look like someone who got bad news today. Why are you working until almost ten o'clock on a Sunday?"

Zalen took in a slow breath and let it out. "It's Tony." He glanced at me, adding, "Kid stuck in a terrible home situation. We're trying to help him, but…"

"Wasn't the judge supposed to rule on making an age exception for emancipated minor status on Friday?" Luca asked, his voice sounding carefully neutral.

"Yeah," Zalen replied heavily. "No joy there. He'll have to wait until he's sixteen. Which we'd pretty much expected."

Luca frowned. "But…?"

"But he ran away from home last night. His mother called the project this afternoon to accuse me of harboring him."

"Which you aren't?" Luca asked.

"No, Luca. I'm not harboring an underage runaway at the Hope Project." Zalen's tone was dry, but he didn't sound angry that Luca had asked.

"Just checking," Luca said. "I'm sorry, Zalen. That really sucks. I know this kid's case is personal for you and the others."

"They're *all* personal." Zalen straightened his shoulders, visibly shaking off the heaviness. "Anyway, make yourself at home, Mia. Our house is your house. If you need anything, just ask."

"Thank you, Zalen," I said. "I'm sorry to hear about this kid Tony. But I hope you know how important the work that you and the others are doing is to the community."

"We do what we can," he said, but his expression held a haunted air.

———◆———

I finished my Pepsi and chatted with Luca, resisting the urge to add a cup of expensive imported coffee to the caffeine and sugar I'd just imbibed.

"It's getting late," he said reluctantly, after I'd crushed the empty soda can and put it in the recycling bin under the sink. "I should probably call it a night."

I nodded. "Are the others already in bed?" Not that I'd expected a full welcoming committee or anything, but I was a bit surprised not to have seen Byron or Emiel at all.

"Emiel's upstairs—he's got the attic bedroom," Luca said. "It's kind of an unwritten rule that no one bothers him up there. Byron's out tonight, which is pretty much par for the course. He's usually quiet when he comes in, so hopefully he won't wake you."

"Gotcha." I wondered, a bit uncharitably, if Byron was in some anonymous hotel room with a stranger at this very minute. I was disturbed by how much the idea bothered me.

Apparently, blatant hypocrisy and I were going to be spending some quality time together for the foreseeable future.

I grabbed the strap of the overnight bag and hefted it over my shoulder.

"Goodnight, Mia," Luca said.

"Goodnight," I told him, having absolutely no idea what was appropriate with a friend you'd fucked once during a post-traumatic fever dream, who was now your roommate.

He might have been dealing with the same issue, because we parted with a supreme level of awkwardness that had heat rising to my face. I took my bag to the guest bedroom tucked at the back of the main floor, while Luca disappeared up the staircase to the second floor.

Someone had left the lamp on the bedside table turned on for me. It was draped with a length of red chiffon—one of Luca's contributions. The effect was a low, warm glow that immediately soothed something buried deep in my hindbrain.

I'd been prepared to make the bare minimum of changes to the room during my stay. I was used to beta bedrooms—they were all I'd ever known. But Luca had vetoed that plan, instead digging up mountains of cushions and blankets from the depths of the huge house. A few of them smelled like him—honeysuckle and fresh mown grass. Most were neutral and would pick up my own scent as time went on.

I hadn't let him talk me into getting rid of the nice double bed altogether. I was sure Zalen would have been fine with it—he seemed surprisingly laid back for an alpha. Yet moving furniture around when I was only likely to be here for a few weeks felt like taking advantage. Like I was taking liberties when I didn't have the right.

So, Luca had huffed and helped me arrange far too many pillows against the headboard. He'd also dragged in the biggest beanbag chair I'd ever seen, grunting and mumbling curse words as he pushed and shoved the thing through the doorway.

The room had a large window, but it was hung with heavy blackout drapes that sheltered me from the outside. That had been a minor bone of contention between Nat and me early in our marriage. I'd wanted blinds and thick curtains kept closed all the time. He'd said that not being able to see out the window made him feel claustrophobic.

I'd won that one eventually. And then it had become moot, when he'd started sleeping in his office rather than in our bedroom.

Unexpectedly, my throat grew tight and heavy. I swallowed hard, refusing to get maudlin on my very first night away from the marriage.

I hadn't redecorated our master bedroom into a nest after Nat quit using it. I wasn't sure what had stopped me, to be honest. It seemed ridiculous now, not to have done it as soon as I had the chance. Had I been worried that he'd think it meant I wasn't invested in our marriage anymore?

I shook my head sharply, trying to dislodge the unwanted introspection. Luca was right — it was late. I cleaned up and got ready for bed in the guest room's en suite bathroom, then I came back in and regarded the bed full of pillows and folded blankets. Instinct made me want to pull everything into a chaotic heap and burrow into it. Habits instilled in a childhood spent with beta parents balked at making an unnecessary mess that I'd just have to clean up in the morning.

In the end, upbringing won. I shook out two blankets and turned back the comforter, crawling in and grabbing a single pillow to hug to my chest.

It was one of the ones that smelled faintly of Luca's summery scent. I turned off the chiffon-covered lamp, plunging the room into darkness. The caffeine and sugar from the Pepsi churned through my bloodstream, while unwanted thoughts churned through my mind.

I'd turned down Nat's heartfelt offer to stop seeing other people... to get into couple's counseling and try to fix our broken marriage. Instead, I'd chosen to move out and stay with people I'd only known for a few weeks — at least one of whom was involved in an illegal fighting ring with dangerous gang ties.

I'd slept with two of them, and I had absolutely no clue where I stood now with either of them. Did Luca assume we'd go back to being platonic friends? Did Byron have any interest in a repeat performance, or did he only do one-night stands? Was he okay with me being here, or did he find it hopelessly awkward? He'd certainly made a point of being elsewhere tonight.

God. What the hell was I doing? How did I think this was going to help my situation in the long run? The gaping maw of uncertainty stretching out beneath my feet suddenly felt insurmountable. Would my restaurant be okay? Would Nat and I be able to act as business partners while our marriage unraveled?

Sudden panic at the idea of the Elderflower Inn failing grabbed me by the throat with choking intensity. Tears gathered behind my eyes, hot and stinging. In the dark of the unfamiliar bedroom, surrounded by a mountain of pillows I was too timid to use as a proper nest, I let them fall.

I tried to keep my hitching sobs quiet, and hopefully I succeeded in this house full of sharp-eared alphas and omegas. Eventually, the tears stopped. I lay staring into the impenetrable dark, knowing I needed to fall asleep and unable to do it.

I hadn't unpacked my alarm clock, and my phone was plugged into the charger on the dresser, out of reach. I didn't know what time it was, but I was sure at least a couple of hours had passed when a faint knock tapped on the closed door.

"Mia?" Luca's voice was pitched low enough not to wake a sleeper. "I can't sleep. Are you awake?"

I turned on the bedside lamp and padded to the door in my T-shirt and loose shorts. Opening it, I met Luca's red-rimmed gaze with my own.

"Yeah," I said. "I'm awake."

"Can I come in?" he asked, uncharacteristic hesitancy in his tone.

A flood of relief I didn't want to examine too closely washed away some of the tension in my shoulders.

"Sure," I said, and opened the door wider to let him in.

TWENTY-NINE

Mia

I FELT MY CHEEKS heat as I ushered Luca into the guest bedroom in his own house. Even more so when he glanced at the undisturbed pillows on the bed and frowned, like he was wondering why I hadn't used them to make a proper nest for myself.

"What's keeping you awake tonight?" I asked before he could say anything about it.

He hesitated. "I feel bad dumping this on you after…" He swallowed hard. "After Emiel's fight."

I waved him toward the ridiculous bean-bag chair and hopped up to sit cross-legged on the bed, hugging the summer-smelling pillow to my stomach. "Nah, go on. I'd rather worry about someone else's problems than my own right now."

He let out a soft huff of laughter, though the sound didn't have much humor behind it. "You sound like me," he said, picking at a seam on the beanbag. "Okay. It's the kid. Tony. The runaway. I told myself I wouldn't get invested in his case. Not like the others have."

I nodded. "Sure. And how's that working out for you?"

A wry snort. "About as well as you'd expect."

Zalen had said the teenager had a bad home life, and Luca had mentioned an unsuccessful hearing to become an emancipated minor.

"If his home life is so messed up, maybe it's just as well he got away," I suggested carefully.

"His stepdad has been sexually molesting him for years," Luca said in a flat voice. "And I'd love to think that he's crashing on someone's couch, getting help and support from a school friend's family."

A wash of queasiness roiled my stomach at the revelation. "But you *don't* think that."

"No." The word was a whisper. Luca cleared his throat and continued, "I think he's going to end up with a gang, exactly like what happened to me. It'll seem like a safer situation; but in reality, it'll be like dangling fresh bait in a shark tank."

My heart ached.

"Is he an omega?" I asked.

Luca shook his head. "A beta. I'm not sure if that's better or worse."

"Equally bad," I suggested. "I'm sorry. This must be bringing a lot of things back for you."

Silence fell for a long moment, as Luca continued to worry at the threads holding the beanbag closed.

"It's just frustrating," he said at last. "Nothing changes, no matter how hard the others work to *make* it change."

"The others?" I asked. "You're doing that work, too, you know."

"I sit in a cushy office and write grants," he said, not looking at me.

"Grants that pay the bills so the others can keep doing what they're doing," I shot back.

He shrugged.

I regarded him in the low light—a slender figure with wild bed-head and dark circles under his eyes. "Do you want to do more hands-on stuff with the kids at the project?"

That startled him into meeting my eyes. "No," he said quickly. "*God*, no. I'm a walking PTSD case looking for a trigger in a warehouse full of triggers. This is what I can do to help that doesn't end up in me melting down." He quirked a sardonic eyebrow. "Well, most of the time, anyway."

"Then you're doing what you need to be doing," I told him. "Maybe things will still work out with Tony."

"Maybe." He didn't sound convinced. "Or maybe he'll surface in a few weeks as an overdose case… or with a bullet in his head." He took in a shuddering breath. "Damn. Now *I* need someone else's problems to focus on. Why can't *you* sleep?"

I chewed my lower lip for a moment, rolling the plump flesh between my teeth.

Luca glanced at me from under dark lashes. "Sorry… you don't have to answer that question if you don't want to."

I shook my head. "No, it's just, um, too much change in too short a time, I think. Too much uncertainty."

As soon as the words left my mouth, I felt stupid. I was talking to a guy who'd lost everything he'd ever known at least twice in his life, and he'd undergone the kind of horrific abuse I couldn't even imagine along the way. By contrast, I had a supportive family and a successful business. Who the hell was I to complain about my life?

But all he said was, "This can't be easy for you. And I guess Byron and I aren't exactly making it any easier."

I looked away, caught out. "I'm not sure what the rules are supposed to be, here," I admitted. "And even worse, I'm not sure what I'd *want* them to be, if it were my call."

"Dunno if they make a rulebook for this kind of situation," Luca said wryly. "But I should warn you, I'm probably going to be shit at this." He rubbed the back of his neck, a nervous movement. "I haven't had a lot of practice having sex with people I actually *like*."

I frowned. "What about Byron?"

He looked discomfited. "That's different. It's not—" Another pause. "Him and me... it's not like that."

I was living with these guys, and I still didn't have the faintest clue what was going on with them. "Okay," I said. "That's fair."

He made a frustrated noise. "It's not fair to you that I can't explain what I feel. I mean... I definitely didn't come down here tonight to try and get in your pants or anything. But... I really like you, Mia. Being with you feels easy."

A warm flush suffused me. "I know what you mean."

He leaned forward, resting his elbows on his knees. "What about you? Do you want more? Than just friendship, I mean."

Yes, I thought.

"I don't know," I said aloud. "It would be kind of complicated right now. But I'd like it if you stayed tonight. I'm not doing so good on my own."

I had no doubt it was blatantly obvious that I'd been crying, both from my scent and my swollen, bloodshot eyes.

"Same," he said, rising and stretching with a yawn. "But I am *not* sleeping on that bed until you use those fucking pillows for their god-given intended purpose. Seriously, why did I even drag them out of storage if you're not going to *use* them?"

I let out a startled laugh. "I don't know; you tell *me*." But I reached back and began dragging everything into a messy pile, shoving blankets around until the whole mess formed a soft depression surrounded by cushy luxury.

"That's more like it," Luca said, mock officious, and tugged me into the middle with him. "If I achieve nothing else, I *will* teach you to make a proper nest like a normal person."

I almost asked him if he didn't think it was a lot of unnecessary work to tidy and fold everything in the morning. But I'd seen Luca's nest. Apparently, 'normal people' didn't bother with that, which certainly held its own appeal.

So, rather than protest, I snuggled down with him in the space I'd made for us. On a hunch, I urged him to turn around with his back to me and curled up behind him as the big spoon. Or, more accurately, as the somewhat shorter spoon who still happened to be in back.

He went very still, and for a moment I worried I'd done something wrong… but then he let out a shuddering breath and melted into my embrace. He wriggled his top arm free, laying it over mine to keep me in place. With that motion of acceptance, something inside me loosened from its tense tangle.

I buried my nose in the wild hair at the base of Luca's neck and breathed in. Within moments, I felt his muscles grow lax in sleep. I was only able to enjoy it for a few minutes before I followed him, my brain floating downward into the nest of soft warmth.

<hr>

When I woke up, I was alone. The heavy curtains held the light outside at bay, but my phone informed me it was ten-thirty. A quickly scrawled note tucked under the case said that the others were all at work and to text or call if I needed anything.

Luca had signed it with his name and a line of x's and o's.

I wasn't used to sleeping so deeply, or for so long at a stretch. My head felt like it had been lined with cotton wool. I stared at the confusion of pillows and blankets covering the bed, wavered for a moment, and left everything as it was.

This was my one precious day off per week, but I felt oddly at loose ends. I took a shower, checked the smear of blueish bruising that was the only remaining reminder of my black eye, and found it pretty much gone. My hair went into a messy day-off ponytail, and I threw on some comfortable sweats.

Two cups of Zalen's amazing gourmet coffee swept the remaining cobwebs from my brain. A quick inventory of the cupboards and pantry confirmed that my new roommates weren't making proper use of their gorgeous kitchen. I most definitely needed to go shopping before attempting a sit-down dinner for five.

I made cinnamon toast for my late breakfast, glad to see that they at least had a fully stocked spice rack—even if the bottles were worryingly dusty from lack of use. Then I tore a page from the little notebook sitting at the end of the counter and sat on a stool by the breakfast bar, composing a shopping list.

A glance at my phone showed it was eleven-thirty already. I should probably leave soon since I might have to go hunting for things in an unfamiliar grocery store, and I didn't want to feel rushed today.

After retrieving my keys and wallet, I was debating whether I needed to go around and make sure all the doors were locked when the sound of the front door opening and closing startled me. For an instant, adrenaline surged through my veins… but then the spicy smell of aniseed and sweet fennel reached me.

"Hi," I said stupidly, as Byron Harper walked into the kitchen.

He raised a dusky gold eyebrow at me, as relaxed and at ease as a freshly fed jaguar.

"Hi yourself," he said, a hint of irony lacing his tone. "Luca sent me to check on you. But I see you haven't managed to get lost in the house or fall down the basement stairs in his absence."

"Not yet, anyway," I told him, feeling off-balance in the presence of the sinfully hot alpha. "I was just about to go buy some food for tonight's dinner."

"Grocery shopping? How very domestic," he said. His head tilted, as though he was assessing me. "Come on, then. I'll take a long lunch and play chauffeur for you."

THIRTY

Byron

MIA DIMITRIADIS HAD no idea what she was doing with her life, and I wasn't sure why that fact niggled under my skin like an itch that couldn't be scratched. An unhappy female omega barreling toward a nasty divorce was in no way my problem… except for the part where she was crashing in the same house I lived in for the next few weeks.

Well, that and the fact that she somehow had Luca tied up in knots. More tied up in knots than *usual*, that was to say.

I watched her trying to decide whether or not to take my offer of driving her to the grocery store at face value. Speaking of faces, hers was an open book, reflecting every emotion and reaction in real time, along with her flowery scent. She hadn't learned to wear a mask. Not the way Luca had. Not the way the rest of us had.

"Okay," she said after a slight pause. "I, um… I was going to hit the Schnucks market off Ladue Road. Do you guys have any reusable shopping bags? I couldn't find them in the kitchen."

"Not that I know of," I told her, since apparently, she had a highly inflated view of both how serious we were about grocery shopping and how much effort we put into saving the environment.

"No problem," she said. "I've probably got some jammed into a moving box somewhere, but that'll have to wait for another day."

I made an agreeable noise and herded her out the front door. I hadn't bothered to park the car in the garage since I'd only been checking in on her. She gave a little squeak and stopped dead on the front porch, staring at the red two-door coupé in the circle drive.

"Is that what I think it is?" Her voice and scent conveyed sudden excitement.

My dick began to sit up and take notice, because sudden girlish excitement suited Mia a lot better than uncertainty and nervousness.

"If you think it's a 1985 Audi Quattro, then yes," I said, unable to keep the hint of smugness out of my tone.

What can I say? Chicks dig the car.

"*You drive a classic Audi Quattro?*" she asked, breathless. "Oh, my god! Where did you even *find* it?"

Some chicks dug the car more than others, it seemed. She led the way to the car, wide-eyed.

"I got it at an estate auction," I said. "Some guy in Illinois had it parked in his barn with a tarp thrown over it for thirty years. When he died, his heirs found the thing sitting there and had no idea how to value it. I picked it up for about the same price as a slightly used Hyundai and spent a few thousand restoring it."

"It's *gorgeous*," she said, reaching out a hand toward the flared quarter panel over a wheel well. Then she froze, glancing at me.

I couldn't help the swell of uncomplicated amusement and pride that splashed up against the wall of my customary cynicism. "You can touch it if you want. It isn't a museum piece."

She wrinkled her nose at me before running gentle fingers over the distinctive lines and angles of the forty-year-old sports car.

"This is *so cool*," she said. "Is this seriously your daily driver?"

"It seriously is," I assured her, a smile tugging at one corner of my lips despite my best efforts. I unlocked the doors and opened hers for her, watching her settle into the rally-style leather seat.

"Thanks," she said, with the air of an omega who wasn't used to people opening car doors for her.

I got in and started the engine, which rumbled into life with the distinctive rough purr of an inline-five.

"Mmm," she said, closing her eyes and snuggling into the creamy leather of the seat in a way that wasn't doing a damn thing for my trouser situation.

I depressed the clutch and put the car in first, pulling away from the house. "So, where did you develop your lust for classic cars?" I asked. "I didn't realize there was much crossover between gearheads and gourmet chefs."

She let out a soft noise of self-deprecation. "You'll laugh at me."

Intrigued, I pulled onto the road and accelerated smoothly through second gear and into third. "Promise I won't."

"I'm not a gearhead," she admitted. "It's just this car specifically. My mother is a British TV addict."

I took a moment to try and puzzle that out.

"Okay. Not sure I'm seeing the connection...?" I prompted.

I caught her shaking her head at herself in my peripheral vision.

"Sorry. She used to watch BBC America all the time when I was a kid, and sometimes I watched with her. There was a car like this in *Ashes to Ashes*. British crime drama," she explained in response to my blank look. "Set in the eighties. Starred Philip Glenister and Keeley Hawes?"

"Never heard of it," I admitted.

"I really loved that show," she said, nostalgia overtaking her tone. "Mostly for the music, but also for this car. Apparently, they're *great* for car chases."

"I wouldn't know." I was losing the battle against my smile. "I'm afraid my car-chase days were over well before I picked up this beauty."

Ladue was too rich to have any food deserts, and the drive to the store was a short one. I spent the last part of it silently reciting baseball statistics until my dick finally got the memo that we were shopping for food, not pussy.

Christ, why did she have to smell so good?

I trailed in her wake, watching the professional chef navigate her natural habitat of the produce section.

"How does everyone feel about spice?" she asked, pausing by a display of what seemed like a wholly unnecessary number of fresh pepper varieties.

"I'm fine with it, I've seen Luca pack away some fairly eye-watering curry, and Zalen has been known to substitute habanero sauce for ketchup," I told her. "Not sure about Emiel."

Even now, thinking about the big alpha brought a surge of frustration. I put it aside with some difficulty.

She nodded. "Got it. Sauce on the side, just in case."

"What's on the menu tonight, anyway?" I asked, trying not to picture two omegas in my bedroom for dessert.

She shot me a sidelong glance. "If you can't figure it out from the shopping list, I really *am* going to worry about how you four manage to feed yourselves."

I snorted, silently accepting the challenge. Three kinds of peppers went in the cart, followed by a selection of tomatoes, onions, avocados, limes, lettuce, cheese, spices, artisan tortillas, rice, frozen shrimp, and a box of something that claimed to be vegan chorizo.

"So, lasagna, then?" I asked innocently.

She snort-laughed and threw a bag of red beans at my chest.

After returning Mia and her haul of ingredients to the house, I resisted the urge to linger. There was work to be done, and the temptation to do something reckless like suggesting a repeat of our night at the hotel was too strong.

I didn't like the way it had felt to wake up next to her on that sterile pillowtop mattress. Or rather, I *had* liked it. *A lot*. That was the problem.

One thing Luca and I firmly agreed on was that both of us had no business getting within a hundred yards of a *relationship*. You could only be so broken inside before it just wasn't fair to other people to impose your baggage on them.

That was why Luca and I worked together, to the extent that we did. The two of us knew enough to keep emotions out of it. All the benefits of a relationship, with none of the risks. I knew the shape of his sharp edges. He knew the shape of mine.

No unreasonable expectations.

I sat in the Quattro, preparing to head back to East St. Louis and my job. Unbidden, my fingers traced the ugly divot of a long-healed bullet wound, surrounded by an expensive and intricate tattoo that totally failed to hide the damned thing.

Pressing on the scar didn't hurt. Scars didn't denote the presence of pain, so much as the absence of feeling.

My flashbacks were rare these days. But as I sat in the driveway with the engine idling, fragments of images rose before my eyes, obscuring the familiar trees and pavement of the driveway.

It was dark, the streetlights on the main road barely penetrating the wide alley between an abandoned shoe factory and a run-down warehouse. The sound of gunshots echoed off the brick walls with an almost physical force, the deafening blasts stabbing through my skull.

I'd had a headache to start with—caught between one drunken, drug-fueled bender and the next. The nine-millimeter Sig felt heavy and cold in my hand.

I was a nobody in this gang. Before, it had usually been enough to flip up the hem of my T-shirt, displaying the pistol grip sticking up from my waistband. On a handful of occasions, I'd pulled it out and brandished it, just to prove I wasn't dicking around, and that I wouldn't be an easy mark.

Now bullets were flying back and forth in the enclosed space, pinging off walls, sending chips of brick dust flying.

It's war now, fuckers, G had said, checking the magazine on his Glock.

I'd strutted and trash-talked with the rest of them, secure in the knowledge that no rival gang trying to move in on our territory would get away with it.

Screams sounded in the alley in front of me. Several familiar silhouettes went down, falling with limp, wet thuds. I pointed the Sig in the general direction of the alley mouth, frozen in place and unable to pull the trigger.

"Shoot, you useless little cunt!" G snarled from beside me, firing off half a dozen rounds.

I opened my mouth, desperate to say something... to tell him we needed to retreat, to *run*. Before I could find the words, a heavy impact slammed into my left side. I staggered and went down under the force. It felt like a punch to the gut, but it didn't hurt.

Why didn't it *hurt*?

Dazed, I lifted a hand to the side of my torso. My shirt felt warm and wet. My vision swam as I lifted the hand and stared at it in the uncertain light from the streetlamp filtering in. The palm and fingers were dark and shiny, like I'd spilled ink over them. A rich, metallic tang filled the air.

I blinked stupidly at my hand, trying to bring my surroundings into focus. More shouts and cries sounded from all around me as the walls of the alley began to spin in slow, dizzying circles.

And then, the pain hit.

I inhaled sharply, heart thudding as the serene surroundings of a sun-drenched, tree-lined property in Ladue blotted out the memory of an East St. Louis alley at night. My hands sat at ten o'clock and two o'clock on the worn vinyl of a forty-year-old steering wheel.

What the hell had brought *that* on?

With a sharp shake of my head, I slowed my breathing and let the adrenaline shakes drain away. Still feeling faintly nauseous, I put the car into gear, heading away from the house and the sweet-smelling omega inside.

Luca was falling for Mia, and that realization filled me with a different kind of disquiet. Luca and I were a known quantity. We had an *understanding*. But now Luca was making noises about bringing Mia in as our third… and I had no idea what that would mean for me.

For *us*.

I turned onto the main road that led to the interstate, putting my foot down harder than I needed to. The car growled its approval, leaping forward into traffic.

THIRTY-ONE

Mia

BYRON WAS LONG gone, leaving me rattling around alone in the huge house. But even a couple of hours later, my body still buzzed with the memory of his nearness… of the scent of aniseed and old leather inside his car.

His sexy, *sexy* car.

Goddamn it, why did he have to drive my childhood pinup car? It was so *random*. Like, it wasn't enough that he was handsome and dangerous and smelled like the best Italian cooking and fucked like a stallion. He also had to drive a perfectly restored red Audi Quattro.

"*Argh,*" I said to the ceiling of my empty bedroom.

There was nothing to do until an hour or so before my planned nine p.m. dinner. It wasn't as though a serve-yourself taco bar required huge amounts of pre-prep.

Did omegas who lived with alphas feel this way *all the time*? If I was an actual beta woman instead of just playing one inside my doomed marriage, I'd have a trusty vibrator hidden away in my belongings. But I was an unbonded omega married to a beta man — one who'd probably have felt threatened by the idea of me using bottled alpha pheromones and getting myself off without him.

I sprawled among my hoard of borrowed pillows and blankets. They were already starting to smell like a combination of me and Luca after only one night. Like the last week before school break, when the air was full of the scent of flowers and mown grass, full to bursting with the endless possibilities of summer vacation.

The alphas' scents weren't obvious in this seldom-used guest bedroom. Yet my nose still knew they were there. Fennel and aniseed. Lime and vanilla. My brain even conjured the memory of rich bergamot laced with cinnamon, despite the house holding no trace of Emiel's dampened pheromones that I'd been able to detect.

My hand stroked down my front, detouring over one breast. My skin tingled, even through the worn cotton of my 'day off' T-shirt. Feeling ridiculous, I continued my trek downward, delving beneath the elastic waistband of my sweats and burrowing into my practical black panties.

I was wet, but I knew within seconds that my body wanted something more than my own fingers. With what was probably an overly dramatic sigh, I pulled my hand free and stared at the ceiling some more. What was I doing, lying here in the middle of the afternoon and frigging myself to thoughts of the people who were letting me stay in their house?

"Mia Dimitriadis, you are an idiot," I said, and got up to wash the fragrant slick off my hand.

I spent the next few hours logged into the cloud account where Nat backed up all the restaurant's business records, stressing out about the dip in revenue we'd seen ever since the Bella Vita opened nearby. It was a relief when the front door opened a few minutes before six.

Closing down my laptop, I wandered out and found Luca in the front hall.

"Heya," I greeted. "How was work?"

He met my eyes with a smile, but it was strained. "Hi. Not great, actually. There's still no sign of the kid, Tony. The cops showed up a couple of hours ago to interview Zalen and search the place. I guess his mother sent them over to harass us."

"What?" My eyes widened. "Can they do that? Zalen hasn't done anything wrong!"

Luca shook his head wearily. "I don't think they had a warrant. Zalen offered to take them around the building—since, as you say, he hasn't done anything wrong. No one there has even *seen* Tony since he disappeared."

My heart ached, both for the teenager and the alphas who'd been trying to help him. "What a mess," I said. "Look, it's still a couple of hours until I need to start the meal prep, but do you want a drink first? I've got tequila and limes for the sauce."

"Sold," Luca agreed. "It's been a tequila kind of day, now that you mention it."

I found a couple of shot glasses and dipped the rims in salt while he dumped his work bag and changed clothes. We perched on stools at the breakfast bar and saluted each other with our drinks, downing them and chasing the alcohol with wedges of lime.

"Better," Luca said with a sigh.

I nodded. "Good. Hey, did you know that Byron came back here at lunch and drove me to the grocery store?"

Luca peered at me as though he was waiting for a punchline. When there wasn't one, he said, "Really?"

"Really. Love the car, by the way."

He shrugged. "It's pretty cool for something that old, I guess."

I scoffed. "*Pretty cool*, he says. There's a TV show I have to introduce you to. Byron as well, if he's willing. And, well, the others too, if they're interested. I just have to figure out if it's streaming anywhere. I don't think it ever came out on DVD on this side of the pond."

"What's it called?" Luca asked. "I'll track it down for you."

I told him, and he dragged me back to his room with him while he googled it. The only option was an obscure streaming service I'd never heard of that specialized in old British shows.

"Do you guys have this one?" I asked skeptically.

Luca was busy tapping in payment details. "We do now," he said.

It was such a silly little thing—a subscription with a free trial that he could cancel as soon as I left. But I still found myself getting teary. I blinked back the burn in my eyes, trying to convince myself it was the fault of the single shot of tequila.

"Thank you," I said, succumbing to the urge to wrap my arms around him from behind.

He gave a weak laugh and patted my hand. "It's no big deal, seriously. But I reserve the right to jeer at the television if this series is terrible."

"What… you don't trust ten-year-old me's taste in TV shows?" I demanded, mock offended.

"Ask me again after I've seen this one," he said, and this time his smile reached his eyes.

The others trailed in over the next hour or so, Byron first, then Emiel, and finally Zalen, who looked positively haggard. Since there was no reason to wait, I started dinner, chopping and measuring while Emiel and Luca sat around watching me work. Emiel looked almost as bad as Zalen did. I guessed that Tony's disappearance was weighing heavily on him as well.

"Are you a fan of spicy food?" I asked him. "Byron wasn't sure."

"It's okay," Emiel said, as communicative as ever.

"I'm doing the salsa on the side, but it's going to pack a kick," I warned him.

There was something deeply satisfying about throwing fresh ingredients in a blender and ending up with a velvety, fragrant sauce a minute or two later. I sauteed the vegan chorizo, chopped up the various garnish options, seared the shrimp, and started crisping up the first few tortillas while Luca went to round up the others.

"You didn't have to do this, you know," Emiel said from his perch on one of the stools.

I glanced over my shoulder, surprised. His dark eyes were on me, like he wasn't sure what to make of me.

The feeling was mutual.

"I know," I said. "It's not a problem, though. I wanted to. I'm a chef. I *like* cooking for people."

His face still bore faint impressions of the beating he'd taken—so much worse than my own black eye had been. "You didn't have to come to my fight, either."

I stilled, only just remembering to flip the tortilla I was crisping before I gave him my full attention. "Luca asked me to. He's my friend, so I said yes. He was worried about you."

I had the sudden sense of having wandered into quicksand, but this had been bothering me... and now I lived here, with these four complicated men. For the moment, at least.

"He shouldn't." Emiel's face was taking on a hint of that disconcerting blankness I'd seen in the fighting ring.

"Shouldn't worry?" I asked carefully. "Emiel, Luca cares about you. I think he's going to worry about something like you getting the crap beaten out of you in a cage fight."

"He shouldn't," Emiel repeated, still in a monotone.

I hesitated, then plunged deeper into the mire. "Why do you do it? Fight, I mean?"

For a long moment, I thought Emiel wouldn't answer.

"It helps to have an enemy you can hit," he said, after an interminable pause.

There were bright red *Do Not Proceed* signs plastered all over that sentence. I'd just drawn breath to barge past them when footsteps in the hallway announced the arrival of the others.

Emiel's eyes met mine. I held them, trapped in their rich brown depths. "The food smells really good. Thanks for making it. No one here can cook for shit."

I wrenched my attention away to rescue the tortilla before my taco became a tostada. "Like I said, I enjoy feeding people," I told him, trying to inject an air of lightness. "And don't worry, I'll school Zalen on the finer points of pasta as soon as I get the chance."

THIRTY-TWO

Byron

I HEARD VOICES coming from the kitchen as Zalen, Luca, and I approached. Emiel and Mia were... *chatting*. Which was obviously impossible, because Emiel didn't *chat* with people. What the actual fuck?

"... I'll school Zalen on the finer points of pasta as soon as I get the chance," Mia was saying as we came in. She looked up, gracing us with a sunny smile. "Oh, hi." Her gaze landed on me, a twinkle of humor appearing in her brown eyes. "The lasagna's ready!"

The others peered at her in confusion as the scents of the spicy Southwest wafted out to us.

"Is this some kind of *avant garde* fusion cuisine?" Zalen asked lightly.

"Nope, just a private joke," she said. "It's tacos. Build your own—the chorizo is vegan."

"And the salsa is spicy," Luca added. "Also, there's probably some tequila left for later."

God help me. At this rate, I was going to need it.

"It smells wonderful," Zalen said, making the first move for a plate. "Thanks for the spread. I think I can safely say this meal will be the highlight of an otherwise unpleasant day."

He looked a little bit lighter already, like some of the weight had fallen away from his shoulders.

"Luca told me about the police showing up at the Hope Project," Mia said, grabbing her own plate and sliding a steaming tortilla onto it.

"They were blocking the front door when I got back from lunch," I said dryly, handing Luca a plate with a tortilla before taking one for myself. "Honestly, it felt just like old times."

Emiel waited until we were all out of the way before joining the end of the taco line. "At least they're trying to find the kid," he muttered.

"My thoughts exactly," Zalen agreed. "They're welcome to search the place, if it means they can narrow down the number of places where he might be."

I snorted, spooning guac over the too-large pile of shrimp, pico, lettuce, and cheese covering my tortilla. "Sure. Now they can narrow it down to everyplace except a single three-story brick building."

Luca kicked me in the shin with his bare heel.

"I'm sure they're checking his friends' houses, and his extended family, too," Mia said, giving me a warning scowl as she headed toward the dining room with her plate. "I bet he'll turn up soon."

"I wouldn't count on it," I muttered. As far as I was concerned, if Tony was smart, he'd keep his head down until that all-important sixteenth birthday rolled around.

The ensuing uncomfortable silence held until we were all seated, setting our plates next to the silverware that had been laid out alongside tall glasses of pale orange aqua fresca that smelled like fresh cantaloupe.

"You should come visit the Hope Project next Monday on your day off, Mia," Luca said, clearly trying to steer things toward a more neutral subject.

She looked startled, as though she hadn't expected the invitation. "I'd like that," she said hesitantly. Her gaze turned to Zalen. "If I wouldn't be underfoot, I mean."

"You're welcome to visit anytime," Zalen said, and I was damned if our fearless leader wasn't sweet on her, too—in his reserved, gratingly gentle and understated way. "I'm proud of what we do there... even if it isn't always happy endings."

"You *should* be proud." Mia's tone was earnest—almost painfully so. "I'd love to come and meet the kids. I don't suppose any of them are interested in cooking or food service careers? I could put together some resources."

More of the weight visibly lifted from Zalen's bowed shoulders. "That would actually be amazing. We do quite a bit with vocational training, but we have youngsters there with *so much talent* that's going to waste."

Her smile lit up the room. "I'll see what I can come up with. Seriously, half the scholarships out there go unclaimed, just because people don't know how to apply for them."

Emiel swallowed a mouthful of taco. "I'll introduce you to Princess while you're there."

I couldn't help the startled quirk of my eyebrow, and I bit into my taco to keep from commenting on his sudden use of words as a medium for communicating thoughts and ideas. The taste of bold spice, creamy guac, and perfectly cooked shrimp exploded across my palate.

"Is Princess one of the kids?" Mia asked, understandably confused.

"She's a cat," Luca explained.

"Oh," Mia said, her face clearing. "So, sort of an unofficial mascot, then? That's really cool."

"She's just an alley cat," Emiel said, directing the words to his plate. "I feed her sometimes."

"A couple of the kids are allergic," Zalen said. "Otherwise, I wouldn't mind having her inside the place."

Luca looked back and forth between them with the air of someone who was about to stick his oar in where it wasn't necessarily wanted. "I was telling Emiel the other day that he should bring her here, to live with us. She's too sweet natured to live on the streets."

And if *that* wasn't the voice of experience speaking, I didn't know what was.

Emiel glanced up sharply, his gaze landing on Zalen.

"I've no objections," Zalen said easily. "There's plenty of room for a litter box in the laundry room."

"They make these *automated* ones now," Luca said, with the enthusiasm of someone who'd spent too much time researching the subject of kitty litter recently. "It senses when the cat leaves and rakes up the mess into a bag at the back. All you have to do is tie it off and dump it in the trash every few days."

"O brave new world, that has such technology in it," I said, unable to help myself. Several glares came my way. I shrugged and went back to the frankly delicious taco, which had started dripping chili-scented grease onto my hand.

"You should definitely bring her here, Emiel," Mia said. "With a name like Princess, she deserves to live in a palace like this place instead of an alley."

"Maybe I will," Emiel said.

"You'll need to get her vaccinated and dewormed," Luca put in. "And spayed, of course. I'll research the reviews of local vets and see who's best."

He and Mia immediately fell into a discussion of the vet her parents had used before their elderly dog died a few years back. I excused myself to get another taco, and Zalen followed me into the kitchen. I glanced at him sidelong as I turned on the burner beneath a skillet and tossed a tortilla into it.

"Things getting domestic enough for you yet?" I asked innocently.

The urge to needle Zalen about his broody tendencies was always present, even though it was probably cruel, given his background. In my defense, it wasn't like the needling ever succeeded in getting a rise out of him. Whatever bitterness Zalen held about his dead mate and their lost future, it was buried so deep I wasn't sure it would ever see the light of day.

His expression was as calm as a still lake when he replied, "Why? Are things getting too domestic for *you*?"

I scoffed. "What do I care? It's nothing to do with me. I just live here."

"Hmm," he agreed wordlessly.

"It's only a cat," I said, aware even as the words left my mouth that I was protesting too much.

"Exactly." Zalen gestured to the skillet, where my tortilla was sending up the first hints of a charred smell. I cursed under my breath and tipped it onto my plate. He just smiled and shouldered me aside to warm his own tortilla.

⁂

Luca and I offered to clean up the dishes after the last taco was eaten—we weren't *complete* heathens, after all. Zalen acquiesced to Mia's gentle suggestion that he looked like he could use a good night's sleep, and Emiel disappeared up to his room without prompting shortly afterward.

Mia stuck around, sitting on a stool at the kitchen island to supervise our dishwasher-loading and counter-wiping efforts.

"This may be a new record when it comes to the number of bowls and pans utilized for a single meal in this house," I observed, scrubbing greasy bits of chorizo from a pan that looked too far gone for Cascade's patented sheeting action.

"Go on—don't lie," Mia teased, one leg swinging idly beneath her. "That was the best lasagna you've ever had in your life."

Luca straightened from the overburdened dishwasher, eyeing us from beneath a fringe of unruly black hair. "Are you two going to explain the joke at some point?"

"Nope," Mia said, popping the 'p.' "You kind of had to be there."

He rolled his eyes heavenward. "Fine, keep your secrets. Byron, we need your TV tonight."

I narrowed my eyes, beset on both sides by the sweet scent of omegas. "What's wrong with the TV in the family room?"

"Nothing as such." Luca added soap and rinse aid to the dishwasher. He closed it, pressing the start button.

That wasn't particularly enlightening. "What are you planning to watch? Hentai tentacle porn?"

"*We,*" Mia began firmly, "are watching the show that spawned my love of red Audi

Quattros, because you need to learn about your car's British heritage."

"Uh…" I said.

Luca picked up the half-finished tequila bottle and sloshed the contents back and forth suggestively. "C'mon. Look, there's even booze."

"Fine, you've talked me into it," I told him, hanging the dish towel I was holding through its kitschy little wooden hoop by the sink. "Are there any limes left?"

Thankfully, there were.

With salt, limes, tequila, and shot glasses in hand, we went up to my room. I closed the door to keep the TV noise from carrying while Zalen was trying to sleep; trying not to remember all the times I'd had Luca and some nameless third person naked and writhing in this room.

Have you considered bringing Mia here as our third? Luca had asked, after the last time I'd had him in here with me… just the two of us.

A better question would be, had I ever managed to *stop* considering it.

"Nice," Mia said, looking around at all the hardwood and leather. "I like it."

It probably didn't hurt that my TV was about twice the size of the one downstairs. Luca set down the bottle he was carrying and pounced on the remote, programming in some new streaming service I'd never heard of. Mia started salting the rims of the glasses and pouring shots.

Feeling thoroughly surplus to requirements—and increasingly lightheaded as my blood flowed steadily south in response to all the pheromones flying around—I flopped down on the couch. Luca sat down a moment later, leaving a Mia-shaped space separating us.

She handed out shots and lime wedges before hesitating. I downed my drink, sucked on the lime, and smiled up at her, showing teeth.

"Sit down. I don't bite unless I'm asked," I said. "But then, you already knew that."

Her lips set in a stubborn line. She threw back her tequila, set the glass down on the end table, and squeezed in between us.

"Here we go," Luca said, clicking on episode one of something named after a David Bowie song.

He set the remote down and tossed back his shot, then curled up with his bare feet tucked under him. On the screen, opening credits rolled—a disorienting upside-down view of what was probably London. I stretched an arm along the back of the sofa and willed my dick not to rise to the occasion too obviously. The three of us watched as a female British cop got sucked into a hostage crisis with her daughter, was shot in the head, and woke up in the nineteen eighties to the melancholy strains of Ultravox singing "Vienna."

I clenched my jaw and tried to focus on the television, as sweet pheromones and tequila wrapped around me like the scent of temptation. *"This means nothing to me..."* Midge Ure crooned from the speakers, and I made a concerted effort to convince myself that he knew what he was talking about.

THIRTY-THREE

Mia

I COVERED MY FACE with one hand, stifling a laugh as Luca groaned and reached for the tequila bottle.

"That's it," he said. "I'm declaring a drinking game where we have to take a shot whenever the main character has a flashback and passes out."

I dropped my hand. "Luca, I have work tomorrow!"

"So do I." He brandished a shot glass at me, and I took it despite my protests. "And I'm supposed to be at work *way* earlier than you are."

"I think the episode's nearly over anyway," I muttered, reasonably confident that there wouldn't be too many more fainting spells for the unlucky Detective Alex Drake.

How old were you when you first watched this?" Byron asked, accepting his shot from Luca.

"Ten," I admitted. "But the car, though!" I tipped back my drink, coughing a bit as it burned its way down, then gestured at the screen. The Quattro roared onto the scene and skidded to a halt next to the docks where the bad guys were about to get away with their hostage and a few hundred pounds of cocaine.

"It's a nice car," Byron admitted. "Too bad he's always driving it on the wrong side of the road."

"*Dude*." Luca downed his shot, his slender throat bared to my gaze. "It's *England*. Driving on the wrong side of the road is the *law*."

I choked on a laugh, startled to realize that I was having more fun than I'd had in ages. The first two shots had drained away the stress that was a constant companion these days, and with the third, I was sliding toward tipsiness. I wasn't sure if Luca was a lightweight, or if he simply felt relaxed while curling against my side on Byron's couch.

It was hard not to wonder about the details of their relationship, sitting here with the scent of their growing arousal mingling with my own. Two men I'd had sex with separately... but sometimes they shared a partner. And Luca had invited me—had practically *dragged* me— to Byron's room.

Stress relief, he'd called it once. I wriggled a bit awkwardly on the rich leather of the sofa, trying to ease the growing ache between my legs.

On the screen, Detective Drake reeled after receiving a mysterious message from the future delivered through her 1980s TV—but she didn't pass out. After a soliloquy about how she wouldn't give up on getting back to her daughter in the year 2008, the credits rolled.

"Well, that was certainly... a thing," Luca said, making no effort to stop lounging against me. "The male lead's surprisingly sexy, considering he's not all that handsome. Is the actor an alpha?"

"I'd always assumed so," I said. "Betas can't get away with being that much of an asshole and still be likeable."

"*Oy*," Byron said, shooting me a narrow-eyed glance.

It struck me—abruptly and viscerally—that I was more or less tucked under his arm, which lay along the back of the sofa behind my shoulders.

"No, she's *absolutely right*, though," Luca said, with the passion of the borderline drunk. "If a beta or an omega was that much of an ass to people, you'd just want to smack him. You wouldn't secretly want to fuck him."

Byron turned his full attention to the two of us as the next episode started playing automatically in the background. The atmosphere in the room changed between one heartbeat and the next, suddenly becoming charged.

"Hmm… so, you want Detective Asshole's cock in you, Luca?" His lazy gray gaze met mine. "Is that what I'm hearing here? Check for me, will you, romcom girl? See if he's hard."

My breath caught, my lips parting on a soundless gasp. This only succeeded in drawing in the thick, intoxicating scent of Byron on one side of me and Luca on the other. I hesitated, unsure what to do—until Luca's small, needy moan overcame whatever rational second thoughts I might've had.

That moan spoke to a deeply buried part of me that longed to ravish and be ravished. Bolstered by three shots of tequila, I reached over and boldly cupped my palm between Luca's legs. He flexed his hips mindlessly, pressing a hard length into my loose grip. A patch of dampness stained the worn denim of his jeans further back, at my fingertips.

"Oh, *fuck*," I said hoarsely, knowing my sweats were sporting an even larger wet patch.

"That's a yes, then," Byron said dryly.

If I was going to blame the tequila anyway, I might as well throw caution to the wind, right? I stretched out my other hand and pressed it against Byron's altogether more impressive bulge. He hissed out a startled breath between his teeth, and my lust surged like a caged animal finally gaining its freedom.

Heat and aching need flooded me, turning my surroundings hazy beyond the confines of the couch and the two male bodies bracketing mine. I licked my lips, hunger overtaking me.

Byron caught my wrist, lifting it away from his cock and forcing my eyes to focus on his face.

"Just so we're clear, Luca and I don't do relationships," he said, his voice going gravelly. "We'll take you to heaven tonight if you want, but don't go picturing mating bonds and picket fences."

I pummeled a few brain cells into life. "I'm married," I reminded him, and kneaded Luca's erection through his jeans until he arched and whimpered.

"So I keep hearing," Byron said. The arm that had been resting behind me flexed, fingers catching my hair and using the grip to tilt my head back. "New game, in that case. Instead of a drink, Luca's going to give you an orgasm every time the hottie on the TV screen faints."

My entire body twitched, as though I'd touched a live wire. A pulse of slick turned the damp patch on my sweats into a soaking wet patch.

"On your knees, Luca," Byron said, sounding faintly amused. "Detective Drake's looking a bit woozy already."

Luca made a soft, surrendering noise and slithered down from the comfortable sofa. Before I could decide if this was real or a tequila-fueled dream, his fingers hooked in the waistband of my sweats and panties, tugging them down and off. Then he grasped me behind the knees and pulled me forward until I was slumped with my hips balanced on the edge of the seat cushion. Heated breath tickled my soaked folds, and then Luca was devouring me, sucking and licking like a starving man who hadn't just eaten a hearty, home-cooked meal.

A half-stifled, high-pitched cry tore its way free of my throat as Byron, still holding me in place with a firm grip on my ponytail, settled in to watch the television show as though nothing at all was happening.

I had no fucking clue if Detective Drake fainted again or not. I only knew that Luca was playing me like a fine instrument, holding me on the edge for endless minutes before pushing me over, only to immediately start again. I trembled and shook, sweat and pheromones seeping from my pores until the room smelled like an orgy in a summer meadow.

My passage clenched rhythmically, begging for something to fill it. Eventually, Luca obliged, sliding three long fingers inside me as he focused on tonguing my clit. It was too much and somehow also not enough, and by the time my fifth or sixth orgasm crested over me, I just *couldn't*.

"Please," I begged hoarsely. "Please... I can't... I need..."

Luca didn't stop. He *did* curl his fingers in a way that sent fresh trickles of sweat rolling down my chest and back. I keened, and Byron gave a little warning tug on my hair.

"Shh," he said, his tone still laced with smug amusement. "The show's just getting to the good part."

I swallowed a high-pitched sob, my body vibrating like a violin string. Luca's teeth just barely grazed my clit, and I shuddered apart. My mind subsided into a delicious sort of blank helplessness, giving up on controlling anything about the encounter.

My body gave in to Luca's merciless mouth, even as it tried to clamp around his fingers as though they were a knot. The storm of pleasure and desperation raged through me, and I was as powerless as a leaf tossed in a hurricane.

Sometime later, Byron's voice reached me. "You think she's ready now, Luca?"

Luca made some sort of vague affirmative noise without lifting his head. I felt it vibrate along my stripped nerves.

"You want the sea monster tonight?" Byron asked nonsensically.

At that, Luca pulled away. After a brief hesitation, he whispered, "Yes."

"Go get it," Byron said. "Strip and put it in while Mia watches."

Luca's fingers slid free of my body, and Byron urged me to sit up on the couch properly. His grip on my hair still controlled my head, forcing me to watch through heavy-lidded eyes as Luca efficiently shucked off his clothing, revealing his lean, pale frame to our gaze.

He went to a drawer and retrieved something out of it, not meeting our eyes as he returned.

"Sit down and slide it inside you," Byron said. "I'm fucking her over the arm of the sofa. While that's happening, you're going to choke her on your cock until you come down her throat."

Luca's ragged breathing joined mine, but he sat down next to me without a word. He lifted one leg, resting his heel on the edge of the seat, exposing the soft pink folds behind his erection. Byron let my ponytail go, and I watched, open-mouthed, as Luca worked the biggest knotting dildo I'd ever seen into his passage.

It was blue-green; shaped like a sinuous alien tentacle with a bulging head and a much larger bulge near the base. A groan escaped me as it disappeared into his body, inch by inch, his rim stretching obscenely around the knot. He let out a choked noise when it popped inside, leaving only the flared base of the toy visible.

His cock twitched restlessly against his stomach, fluid dripping from the tip to smear on his belly. "*Christ,*" he rasped.

"Good boy," Byron said. "Now, get her T-shirt and bra off while I find a condom."

I was still a drunken marionette, none of my limbs working properly after an hour of Luca's merciless oral torture. Somehow, he helped me raise my arms and peel the worn T-shirt over my head. The bra was more difficult, but it slid off a moment later and tumbled to the floor, forgotten.

I heard rustling and looked up to find Byron unbuttoning his shirt, but not removing it.

"Up you get, romcom girl," he said, crossing to me and grabbing the condom packet between his teeth to free both hands.

I was pulled onto wobbly legs and led around to the side of the sofa where Luca was sitting. The padded leather armrest hit me at mid-thigh, and I yelped as Byron nudged my legs wide and pushed my upper body down. Luca helped me catch myself before I headbutted him ignominiously in the groin, but I still ended up eye-to-eye with his dripping cock.

It smelled like dessert. My mouth watered, and I licked my lips.

"Is this okay?" Luca asked quietly. His hand tangled in my half-loosened ponytail, just as Byron had done earlier.

"Please," I begged again. "Please, I'll do anything, just fill me up!"

I didn't recognize this pathetic, sexually ravenous female omega. She couldn't be me, could she?

"Oh, sweetheart," Byron said, a low growl rumbling beneath the words. "You've *never* been filled up like this before."

The sound of a zipper lowering followed by the crinkling tear of a foil packet reached me. That huge, blunt alpha cock that I'd felt once before pressed insistently against my folds, sliding in with a delicious stretch and burn. I panted rapidly through my nose, not prepared for how perfect it felt—even though I should have known better the second time around.

"Now, open wide," Byron said, his big hands gripping my hips. "I'm about to take both of you on the ride of your lives."

It hadn't been a bark, but my lips opened instinctively, my tongue straining toward the clear fluid gathering at the tip of Luca's cock. I didn't resist as he lowered me onto his length, my scalp tingling as the hair pulled. Sweet hardness slid past my lips and over my tongue, filling my mouth until I could barely think.

One of my arms was trapped beneath me, and I had a death grip on Luca's hard thigh with my other hand. Luca gave a shuddering sigh as I bottomed out, my nose pressed against crinkly dark hair and his tip rubbing against my hard palate.

"Fuck, your mouth feels *so good*, Mia," Luca said, his hand shaking against the back of my head.

"Hold her where you want her," Byron said, and that was all the warning I got before he pulled back and thrust in sharply, driving Luca into my throat. The fingers tangled in my hair clenched convulsively, and every single thought in my head circled the drain, disappearing never to be seen again.

THIRTY-FOUR

Mia

BEING SPIT-ROASTED helplessly on two cocks was a little bit terrifying, yet somehow the uncertainty and loss of control wasn't doing a thing to stop my passage from dripping slick and clenching convulsively with every rough thrust from Byron.

I should have been gagging whenever Luca's dick hit the back of my throat… and I did, the first couple of times. But my body felt like it was made of Jell-O after all the orgasms I'd had already. It *needed* to be taken, adjusting quickly to the feel of penetration from both directions.

Byron was doing all the work. I just had to take it. I *wanted* to take it.

Gradually, my death grip on Luca's thigh relaxed. A deeply buried part of my brain uncoiled, and somehow it didn't matter that I had tears in my eyes and drool on my chin. I was pleasing my mates and being pleased in return—taking sweet revenge on Luca for the heights he'd driven me to earlier… reveling in the strong hands pressing finger-shaped bruises into my hips from behind.

Beneath me, Luca was coming apart at the seams. I couldn't imagine what it must feel like to have someone go down on you while also clamping around a knot the size of that insane dildo.

Apparently, it felt pretty good. Luca's breathing had grown ragged, the sound perilously close to dry sobs. Byron's hips snapped forward, a barely audible growl rumbling in his chest in counterpoint to my choked moans.

Every thrust drove me higher. The sensation building inside me felt completely different than what Luca had wrung from me with his fingers and mouth. It grew and grew, burrowing deeper into me instead of exploding outward. My mating gland ached with unexpected ferocity, throbbing its unrequited yearning along my nerves.

My moans grew high-pitched and desperate around Luca's hard flesh. The thigh muscles under my hand trembled.

"Mia," Luca's voice was barely recognizable past the buzzing in my ears. "I—I'm going to—"

One of the hands holding my hips let go, sliding up the length of my spine to grasp me by the nape of the neck. Byron pushed me down until Luca was as deep as he could go.

"Suck him hard, pet," Byron ordered, a bark creeping into his voice.

I held my breath and hollowed my cheeks as the alpha rocked into me with a devastating roll of his hips. Luca cried out and convulsed, little spurts of salty fluid rolling over the back of my tongue and sliding down my throat as

Byron pumped into me with fast, ragged strokes.

As though Luca's climax had completed some kind of circuit within me, the pressure that had been building in my deepest hidden places erupted. I could feel myself squirting slick around Byron's cock... hear myself making some kind of awful, broken noise around Luca's softening erection in my mouth.

It was so *all-encompassing*. I didn't know what to do with the feelings that ricocheted through my body—not just physical feelings, but emotional ones as well. I'd never felt this way during sex. Not *ever*.

My core knew what to do with those feelings, though. As Byron groaned and jerked out his release inside me, it clamped down, trapping his growing knot like a vise. Luca shuddered, oversensitive, and lifted my mouth away from his spent cock. He shifted around on the couch with a quiet hiss until I could rest my upper body more comfortably in his lap.

Honestly, my bones felt like they had liquefied at some point. I could have been lying on a bed of nails and it still would have felt comfortable. I spared a second's thought for Byron, who was more or less stuck in place, standing at the end of the couch until our bodies released each other. Then Luca's hands tugged the hair tie off of my ruined ponytail and started idly stroking his fingers through the freed strands.

At which point, I fell fast asleep, floating on a cloud of bliss.

I woke an unknown amount of time later to the sound of low voices.

"You two should go back to her room and get some sleep." That was Byron. "Or your room. Whichever."

"Right. 'Cuz she can totally walk after that." Luca sounded tired.

"Can *you* walk?" Byron asked.

"Dunno. Why would I want to?" A pause. "I can maybe make it across the room to your bed."

A longer pause.

"This is a terrible idea," Byron muttered.

"I'm drunk, and she's passed out from endorphin overload." Luca didn't sound amused. "Pick her up and put her in the damned bed, Byron. We all have work in a few hours."

And that was how I found myself being carried across the room to Byron's sleeping alcove like a very relaxed sack of potatoes. Somehow, I ended up spooning Luca from behind while Byron lay at my back, a few careful inches separating us. At which point, I fell asleep again.

I only woke up once more during the night. But when I did, Byron had rolled over in his sleep and was pressing himself along my body like a second skin. His nose was buried in my neck, inches from my mating gland. I must have twitched in surprise—because he snorted awake, froze for an instant, and quickly rolled away from me.

I extricated myself from Luca with awkward movements and wriggled around to lie facing Byron instead. Luca snored on, dead to the world. The alpha's gray eyes were luminous in the early morning darkness. He stared at me warily, probably hoping I'd fall asleep again so he wouldn't have to acknowledge that he'd been blatantly cuddling me.

Maybe my brain hadn't come back online yet, because a question that had been quietly burning in the back of my mind slipped past my lips.

"How did you get shot?"

It was none of my business. The question was incredibly personal, and probably traumatic as well. For a long moment, I thought he wouldn't answer. After all, he hadn't even wanted me staying in his room tonight. He *definitely* wouldn't want me grilling him about his past.

"It doesn't take a genius to figure out that all of us except Zalen came from gangs," he said slowly.

I nodded. "Yes, I'd gathered that much."

The silence stretched for a few more seconds.

"I was running with a crew up in Newport. A rival gang from Madison tried to move in on our territory. There was a firefight, but we ended up getting pinned down in a dead-end alley."

I tried to imagine Byron in a gang… Byron with a gun, shooting at other people.

"Everyone else died," he said quietly. "I didn't. End of story."

"Oh," I said after a moment — the stupidest, most useless reaction imaginable to learning something like that about another person.

His shoulder moved in a half shrug, a darker silhouette against the gray of the room. "Play stupid games, win stupid prizes," he said in a monotone.

I reached out and put a hand on his shoulder. He stiffened for a moment, but he didn't shake the gesture off.

"I'm glad you're still here," I told him.

<hr>

The next time I woke up, it was mid-morning, and I was alone. I blinked blearily in the cheerful light filtering through the blinds, feeling out the shape of my headache.

The bedclothes were such a tangle that the queen-sized mattress might as well have been a nest, even though nests weren't really an alpha thing. A post-it note was stuck to Luca's pillow, off-kilter and hanging on by a single corner after I must've disturbed it in my sleep.

Ugh, it read in spidery, slanted handwriting. *Tequila, am I right? Byron left you some aspirin and a glass of water on the bedside table. We should probably talk tonight, sorry.*

-Luca

xoxox

That was… ambiguous, to put it mildly. Between the ominous *'we should talk'* and the *'xoxox'* at the end, I wasn't sure if my sudden queasiness had more to do with the shots last night—or the prospect of having fucked up a new set of relationships before the dust had settled from my *last* fucked-up relationship.

I rolled over. Sure enough, aspirin and a tall glass of water with the tiny remains of melted ice cubes sat on the little table beneath the lamp. The fact that Byron had put them there felt… significant, somehow? I shook my head sharply, aware that I was acting like a teenager—trying to manifest telepathy so I could crawl inside other people's heads and divine what they were feeling, rather than having to ask.

My head protested the sudden movement, but honestly, I wasn't that badly off. I hadn't drunk *that* much, after all. Indeed, when I rolled into a sitting position, my head wasn't the source of the worst ache.

I winced at the tackiness between my legs, abruptly aware of how very badly I needed a shower.

After popping a couple of pills and washing them down, I went to transform myself back into a functioning member of society. The house was, as expected, empty except for me. I cleaned myself up, dressed, made whatever meal involved eating buttered toast at ten a.m., and reflected that it might be kind of nice to have a friendly cat around for company in this huge place.

I was oddly excited about visiting the Hope Project next Monday and meeting Princess the cat, who'd somehow managed to wriggle her way past Emiel's ten-foot-thick emotional walls. The nasty voice that whispered self-destructive things in my ear murmured, '*Sure, if they still want you to come… if Luca and Byron don't decide you should leave after what happened last night.*'

I stomped the voice down. '*We should talk*' signed with hugs and kisses did not equate with summary eviction from my new living arrangements. If anything, the conversation might be more along the lines of '*hey, having sex was a mistake, maybe we shouldn't do that again.*'

Given everything else going on in my life, it probably *had* been a mistake. For that reason, I couldn't exactly protest, if that was what Luca wanted. My mind chose that instant to flash back to crashing pleasure and warm bodies tangled together in the dark — which was the polar opposite of helpful.

So, rather than dwell on things, I left for the restaurant a bit early. Nat had already beat me there. He tipped his chin up in greeting when I poked my head into the back office, but he didn't look up from the pile of papers he was shuffling. He still looked like he hadn't slept properly in a week.

I left him to it, heading off to check inventory and start the day's prep. The other employees trickled in, getting everything ready in the familiar dance between front and back of house.

I was relieved to find that we were rocking a pretty decent lunch crowd after the first couple of hours. I'd just managed to convince myself that maybe the slow days were finally behind us when the sturdy, overhead metal rack we used to hang pots and pans in the center of the kitchen area collapsed on Shani's head as she was reaching for a clean skillet.

THIRTY-FIVE

Mia

ADRENALINE POURED INTO my veins as Shani's startled shriek joined the deafening clatter of falling pots and pans, making everyone in the kitchen whirl around to see what had happened.

The industrial-grade stainless steel overhead rack hung cockeyed from two of its four chains, all but three of its pots strewn across the floor. Shani stood in the midst of the destruction, one hand clutching her other shoulder, staring with a slack-jawed expression at the collapsed contraption.

Her chef's hat was askew, a tiny trickle of blood visible at her hairline.

"Shani!" I cried.

Her wide brown eyes turned to me. "I... I'm all right," she said, with the calm certainty of someone who might or might not be going into shock after a knock to the head.

"Everyone else, stay where you are!" I snapped, heading off the people who'd already started toward her. "Attend your stations. Do *not* let anything burn or boil over!"

"What's happening?" Candy appeared on the other side of the pass-through, quickly joined by the other waitstaff. She froze at the scene of destruction. "Oh."

"Watch my grill," I told the line cook next to me, abandoning two ribeyes and a burger to pick my way around a labyrinth of scattered pots. Nat appeared at a near-run, sliding to a stop inside the double doors. "Nat, call an ambulance. There's been an accident."

"*Christ*," Nat cursed, digging in a pocket for his phone.

"No," Shani said quickly. "Seriously, I'm okay. But I don't know what I did wrong... I was just reaching for a skillet."

I got to her, gently taking her by the arm that she wasn't clutching. "Shani, you're bleeding." I made a valiant effort to keep my tone gentle, trying to modulate the stress markers in my scent. "And your arm's hurt."

She blinked at me and looked down at her shoulder as though she hadn't been aware she was clenching it. Moving it gingerly, she let go in favor of reaching up to touch her temple. Her fingertips came away stained with blood, but not very much.

"Oh," she said blankly. "Honestly, I don't think it's bad. Can I go check it in the employee restroom?"

I met Nat's eyes. My instinct was still to call an ambulance. But as long as she was conscious and rational, Shani had the right to refuse treatment.

"Of course you can," Nat said. "I'd like Mia to go with you, assuming you're comfortable with that. Mia, I'll get the first aid kit from the break room for you, okay?"

"Thanks," I said, keeping a supportive hand on Shani's arm, just in case. "Is that all right, Shani?"

"Sure," she said, seeming to realize that we'd become the focus of attention of basically the entire restaurant. Sheepishly, she added, "Promise I'm not about to swoon, everyone. Only tough-as-nails omegas in this restaurant!"

A couple of worried customers had joined the press of employees at the pass-through. Reassured that Shani wasn't too seriously injured, I forced myself to take stock.

"Candy, please get the customers back to their tables and apologize for the scare. I think we can get the current meals out to them, but warn Diane that we're closing to new customers for the afternoon."

Nat hurried back in with the first aid kit. He eyed the destruction. "Can you work around this thing safely without disturbing it? I don't want anyone touching the rack until we've investigated the... uh... the *incident*."

For a split second, I wondered what on earth he thought there was to investigate. Then I remembered that we ran a business with employees who probably expected to get through a shift without heavy objects falling on them, and that things like *OSHA* and *paperwork* existed.

"As long as we can clean up the pots and pans, I think so," I said cautiously. "Toby, get someone else to cover your station and gather up anything that's fallen in the traffic areas, please. If it touched the floor, it needs to be washed. Make a note of anything cracked or dented and stack those in the back."

"Yes, chef," Toby said. He looked unpleasantly pale—probably remembering his own recent close call with the grease spill by the stairs.

With a final look around the kitchen to reassure myself that nothing was about to explode or catch on fire, I urged Shani carefully past the mess and toward the employee areas.

"I'm really sorry," she said, once we were out of earshot of the kitchen. "I have no idea what happened."

Alarm made me stop her in the hallway by Nat's office and the breakroom. "Hang on. No idea, like you can't remember what happened?"

She gave a short, self-conscious laugh. "No, no. I mean, I just put my hand on the skillet handle to lift it off the hook. I swear I didn't pull on it or anything."

My sudden fears of concussion and short-term memory loss eased. "It wasn't you. That thing should be able to support a person hanging off each corner—not that I recommend that from a safety perspective. But there's no way it should have just come down like that. All I can think of is that it's a pretty old building. Like, maybe the joists in the ceiling have dry rot or something."

We entered the employee restroom. Shani extricated herself from my grip, seeming steady enough on her feet as she crossed to the mirror over the sink. The fluorescent lights weren't doing her any favors when it came to the grayish undercast to her dark skin, but she poked at the bloody spot on her hairline matter-of-factly.

"It'll bruise a bit, but it's just a graze, promise," she said, with the air of a pack mother who'd dealt with a scrape or two in her time.

"What about your shoulder?" I asked. "I can go stand outside if—"

She waved off the words and started unbuttoning her white chef's coat. "You're fine, boss. Feels like that one's going to be a bigger bruise. But shit—I mean, *stuff*—happens. I'd really rather not make a big deal about it, if that's all right."

She shrugged off the coat, revealing the tank top she was wearing underneath. Angling her shoulder toward the mirror, she frowned at the spreading patch of blue and black, then carefully moved her arm through its range of motion.

"Yeah, no big deal," she concluded.

A bit more of my tension drained away as she pulled her white coat back on. "Okay," I told her. "Thank goodness for that. Nat's still going to need to file an incident report for insurance purposes, and you should be aware that refusing medical treatment now doesn't waive your right to make a worker's compensation claim, should it become necessary in the future."

She shot me an amused, slightly fond look through the medium of the mirror. "I'll keep it in mind, boss. Have you two got a reliable contractor to get that thing fixed and check the, what was it? The joists?"

"That's Nat's responsibility, but I expect so," I replied, handing her a gauze pad and some antiseptic to clean up her temple.

She took it and nodded, leaning forward to dab at the little cut. "Let me know if not. Three of my co-mates are in the construction industry."

She slapped an adhesive bandage over the graze and straightened.

"I will," I promised. "Now, talk to Nat to see if he needs anything from you right now in terms of paperwork, and then head on home. I don't know yet if we'll be able to open up this evening for the dinner crowd, but I'd feel a lot better if you'd take the rest of the day off regardless."

"If you say so, boss," Shani said. "But I'll be in tomorrow as usual—don't you worry."

"I'm really sorry this happened," I told her. "We'll do whatever it takes to make sure it doesn't happen again."

◆

Once we got all the lunch customers fed and sent home the staff, it was just me and Nat, staring at a hunk of metal framing hanging half off its supports.

In the confusion, I'd been wrong about my assumption of what had happened. All four of the steel chains at the corners of the rectangular frame were still firmly attached to their large lag bolts installed in the ceiling.

"Wait," I said. "If the joists weren't rotten, how did this fall?"

The rack itself was welded — there were no bolts or nuts to come loose. The chains terminated in hooks that were every bit as thick and solid as the links they were attached to, and the hooks went through holes drilled directly through the corners of the rack's frame. Again, there was nothing to come loose or get unscrewed.

Nat was perched on a stepstool, holding the end of one of the loose chains. "I'm not entirely sure."

He plucked one of the S-shaped hooks from the end of its chain and handed it down to me. Rather, it *had* been S-shaped. It wasn't now. One of the curved ends had bent like it was on a hinge.

"Does that look like it has hacksaw marks in it to you?" he asked.

My head shot up. "*What?*"

"Mia." He removed the other bent hook and stepped down from the ladder. "You must have thought about it, too. First the grease spill, and now this?"

I stared at him, appalled. "You think someone *did this purposely?*"

He gave the hook in my hand a significant look. "Hacksaw marks?"

I returned my attention to the little hunk of twisted metal. "How should I know? What do hacksaw marks even look like?"

The idea that this might have been sabotage—that someone would do something like this knowing people could be seriously injured—roiled in my stomach like bile.

"I can't be certain." Nat examined his own hook. "But if someone sawed, say, halfway through both of these, and one of them randomly gave way, the sudden strain would take out the other one, too."

This couldn't be happening. Not in my restaurant. *Our* restaurant.

"What do we do?" I asked blankly.

"Quietly installing surveillance cameras in the kitchen is top of my list," Nat muttered. "Guess I should have done that a while ago."

"But… today?" I pressed. "What about the dinner service? What if there's more damage we don't know about? My god, Nat—there are gas lines to all the cooktops."

"I think we're going to have to go over the place inch by inch before we let anyone back in here," Nat said grimly, looking around the kitchen as though he half expected something else to crash down on us. He held up the metal hook. "On the positive side, S-hooks are cheap. I'll pick up replacements in the morning and get this thing fixed, anyway."

I nodded dumbly, aware of just how little we could afford to miss dinner services when we were barely making ends meet to start with.

I finally got back to the house in Ladue around one a.m., after having fired off a text to Luca to let him know I was going to be in late.

We hadn't found a single suspicious thing during our careful search of the restaurant. The remaining two hooks on the overhead rack had been fine, and neither of us could be one hundred percent sure that the other two hadn't simply had some kind of manufacturing defect. Nat planned to replace all four just in case.

I let myself in the front door as quietly as I could, not certain if anyone would still be up. Emiel always seemed to disappear up to his room early, while Luca and Byron had gotten way less sleep than I had last night. I tiptoed down the hall, only to pause when I saw a light coming from the kitchen.

When I peered around the doorway, it was to find Zalen slumped on a stool, staring morosely at an empty glass with the white remains of almond milk clinging to its sides. He glanced up at me, dredging a half-smile from somewhere.

"Hey. Luca said you'd be late tonight. Everything okay?"

Giving into the temptation for a sympathetic ear, I came in and dropped my bag on the counter, taking up another stool. "Let's just say that it's been a day." I sighed. "Workplace accident. No serious injuries, thank goodness... but

I've got an employee with bruises, and I *really don't like that.*"

Zalen's dark brows drew together. "I'm sorry to hear that. Paperwork?"

"Out the wazoo," I agreed. "Thankfully, most of that is Nat's department."

I debated telling him about Nat's suspicions of sabotage, but it was one in the morning, and I couldn't quite decide how paranoid that would sound.

Instead, I asked, "How about you? You were staring at that milk glass like it personally betrayed you."

He let out a breath. "Oh. Just… I got another visit from Tony's mother this afternoon. The cops told her they've checked all his known friends and relatives' addresses, and they haven't found him. In the absence of new information, they aren't pursuing it any further."

"You're kidding," I said, appalled.

He shook his head. "Honestly, I was a bit surprised they devoted as many resources to the case as they did. No one in St. Clair County cares about runaways when people are getting shot in the street every day."

My heart sank for these four men who'd devoted themselves to making a difference, despite being confronted every day with their failure to do so.

"I'm so sorry, Zalen," I told him. "Are you doing okay?"

"Not really," he admitted, gesturing at the clock on the wall. Its hands pointed accusingly at both of us—one-fifteen a.m. "Drink?"

"Sure," I said, resting my elbows on the table as he went to get us something stronger than almond milk.

THIRTY-SIX

Zalen

I HATED HOW familiar this feeling of exhaustion and inadequacy was becoming in my life. Either I was so tired that I fell asleep early, only to wake up at two in the morning in a state of existential dread… or else I couldn't get to sleep at all.

Tonight was one of the latter nights, and apparently, I was going to have Mia as an audience. I'd given up on sleep around midnight and come in here rather than staring at the ceiling in my room until morning. Grabbing the bottle of almond milk from the counter where it had been sitting, I stuck it back in the fridge and lifted a mostly empty box of red wine from the bottom shelf.

"Ooh, wine in a box?" Mia teased as I set it on the edge of the counter and went rummaging for glasses. "Classy."

As tired and demoralized as she seemed, she still dredged up a smile and a bit of humor for me. In that moment, she reminded me of Julie so much it hurt.

"Only the best boxed wine in this establishment," I told her solemnly, placing one glass down and filling the other from the super-classy plastic spout. I handed it to her and filled the second glass for myself.

"Thanks," she said. "Just the one for me tonight, by the way. I'm still recovering from too much tequila."

As soon as she said it, a blush darkened her olive-tinted cheeks and her scent deepened. I could only imagine what tequila plus Byron might have led to last night. Possibly I was happier not knowing, since I didn't really have the extra bandwidth to deal with any Byron-related drama at the moment.

"Smart," I said, painfully aware of the picture I made—a grown-ass alpha sitting alone in his own kitchen in the middle of the night, wearing pajama bottoms and a T-shirt with a worn terrycloth robe thrown over them. "And honestly, I do know better than to treat insomnia with wine."

She lifted her glass in an informal toast, raising an eyebrow. "Special circumstances. Besides, moderate intake of red wine has been shown to have a positive correlation with heart health and longevity."

She was still teasing… still going out of her way to lighten the mood.

I tapped the rim of my glass to hers. "Here's to moderation and cardiovascular health, in that case."

We sipped what was, in the end, a very mediocre grocery store red, each lost in our thoughts. Since my own head was just about the last place I wanted to spend time these days, I asked, "What happened to your employee today?"

She scowled and let out a very un-omega-like grunt of displeasure. I tried not to find it charming.

"Picture a great big, welded steel rack for storing pots and pans, hanging from the ceiling by heavy chains and hooks." Her tone was grim. "Now picture two of the hooks snapping when someone goes to reach for a skillet."

My eyes widened. "Good god. And you say they weren't hurt badly?"

Christ, I'd never thought of restaurant work as being a physically hazardous career.

"Bruised shoulder, graze to the temple," she said, still scowling at her glass of wine. "Omegas have good reflexes, fortunately."

It was stupid and patronizing, but knowing the employee who'd been banged up was an omega sent an extra little spark of distress through me. Then something else she'd said penetrated.

"Hang on—two hooks on this thing snapped at the same time?"

Her look of anger transformed into one of deep disquiet, her scent souring with distress. "It could have been a coincidence," she said, not sounding like she believed it. "Like, one of them had a manufacturing defect and when it failed, the sudden stress on the other corner snapped the second one."

I hesitated. "You don't sound too certain of that."

Her addictive floral scent sharpened further, and she took a deep draft of her wine. "Nat thinks it was sabotage."

Nat. The husband and co-owner. I remembered him barging into the singles bar that first night and making an ass of himself. From the tiny amount of contact I'd had with the man, I wouldn't immediately assume he knew what the hell he was talking about on any given subject. But I also hadn't been the one to marry him.

"Is that kind of sabotage common in the restaurant industry?" I asked, aware of the note of skepticism in my tone. Still, two pieces of industrial-grade hardware failing at once *did* seem awfully strange.

"Not common, no." Mia toyed with the stem of her wineglass, then lifted it and knocked back the rest of its contents. She set it down with too much care, as though she was fighting the urge to slam it onto the counter with frustration. "But then again, most restaurants don't have the only Michelin-star rating in the Midwest. Or, at least…"

She trailed off, and her already distressed pheromones flooded with the curdled-milk sourness of grief.

I recognized that scent far too well. I'd had more experience with it than I cared to dwell on.

"'At least'…?" I prompted, uncomfortably aware that she'd come home a bit upset after a hard day, but after only a few minutes' conversation with yours truly, she'd graduated from being 'a bit upset' to 'borderline distraught.'

"Sorry," I said quickly. "You don't have to—"

"We're losing our Michelin star," she said in a rush, cutting off my words. "The updated guide publishes in January, and it's pretty clear we're not going to be in it."

I paused, having no idea how the vagaries of restaurant stars worked. She, however, *did*— and I doubted she'd appreciate some kind of bullshit pep talk about how she might be wrong.

"I'm sorry," I told her. "Getting one in the first place was an amazing accomplishment. I can't imagine how difficult it must be to face the prospect of losing it."

She stared at the empty wine glass for a few more seconds. Then her face crumpled into an expression of emotional agony that tore at my heart like claws.

Idiot, I berated myself, jumping up from my barstool and stripping off my tatty robe. *She's already had a bad day, and you thought this was a good topic for conversation?*

"Mia." I approached her slowly and lifted the robe to cover her shoulders, giving her plenty of time to duck away or tell me to stop. It settled over her, too large and painfully plain. "Forgive me. I shouldn't have pushed the topic."

She hesitated, then shook her head sharply, grabbing the edges of the robe and pulling it tight around her body. I quashed the heady rush of satisfaction as she tucked her chin, burying her nose in the worn fabric of the lapels and breathing in my scent.

Rather than give in to the purr trying to rumble up from my chest, I reseated myself on my kitchen stool and let her regain her composure. It took several minutes, but she finally lifted red-rimmed eyes to mine.

"No," she whispered. Clearing her throat, she continued in a stronger tone. "I'm the one who's sorry. The restaurant stuff… it's all so stupid and *petty*, when you and the others are dealing with kids facing life and death every day."

I reached out and covered her hand with mine, ignoring the little voice in my head saying what a bad idea that was.

"It's not," I said firmly. "That restaurant is your life, and just because other people are facing different struggles, it doesn't mean your struggles are somehow less real."

For a moment, I thought she might start crying in earnest… which was very much the opposite of what I'd intended. But this was a woman who'd built an award-winning restaurant from the ground up, in a place she should never have been able to do it. She firmed her lips, lifted her chin, and nodded.

"I know," she said. "It's just…" A sigh. "Rough year, I guess."

"Rough year," I agreed, giving her hand a final squeeze before releasing it. I was a bit alarmed by how difficult it was to let go.

She licked her lips. "I should… uh…" She tilted her chin toward the door and the hallway beyond.

"Yeah," I managed. "Okay. Goodnight, Mia."

"Goodnight, Zalen," she said, and disappeared into the depths of the house.

I sat at the kitchen island, breathing in the scent of elderflowers and grief for a long time afterward.

———◆———

The following morning, Luca sidled into my office at the Hope Project as I was mainlining my third cup of coffee. Furtiveness was written all over his body language, which usually meant only one thing.

"Hey," he said awkwardly.

"Hey," I echoed. "What can I help you with, Luca?"

"Nothing." The reply was so quick it was nearly instantaneous. He coughed, not meeting my eyes. "I mean, I don't need help with anything. I just… thought you should know that I'll be using a heat suppressor again this quarter. In case you were, y'know… wondering."

I nodded, knowing the worst thing I could possibly do would be to make a big deal out of it. "Okay. I can get it for you if—"

"No." Luca bristled slightly. "I've been getting my own suppressors forever. I'm handling it."

I lifted my hands in a gesture of surrender. "All right. No problem. Thanks for telling me."

Luca still looked like a cornered animal. He lifted his chin defiantly. "It's your house. So, I figure you should know. I'll get back to work now, I guess."

He slipped out as quickly as he'd come in, not leaving me time to reply. I waited until he was out of earshot to sigh and rub at my gritty eyes.

This city was my home, even if I'd left it for years before returning. But there were times when I fantasized about living in a place where parts of the law weren't still mired in the times before the Alphomic Accords.

In most of the civilized world, getting suppressors was a matter of a quick visit to any doctor or clinic and a trip to the nearest pharmacy. Here, it was wrapped up in a fundamentalist culture war that insisted any interference with reproduction was an affront to the creator, or some fucking thing.

I was pretty sure the undeclared war on omegas' self-determination had been devised as a test case for going after beta birth control as a next step. But in practical terms, it meant that Luca—and any other omega who used blockers or suppressors, presumably including Mia— had to get their drugs on the black market.

It was one more way my little pack-that-wasn't remained tied to their murky pasts, and I hated it. Every time, I offered to get Luca what he needed so he wouldn't have to dip his toe back into that world. Every time, he refused.

If I wasn't so sure that Luca was too smart to get his supplies from anyone even remotely associated with his old gang, I would've put my foot down. Maybe I should have anyway. But Luca already dealt with enough trauma related to his heats. He didn't need me adding to it.

He'd said it himself, after all. He'd been getting his own suppressors since he'd escaped the gang. There was no reason this time should be any different.

THIRTY-SEVEN

Luca

"WHAT DO YOU mean, there's a supply shortage?" I asked in dismay. "How can there be a supply shortage of *heat blockers*?"

Leah shrugged her narrow shoulders, not looking any happier than I felt. "Sorry, Luca. I'm just the messenger. Most of that stuff comes in by mail from aid organizations in Scandinavia and the Netherlands. Rumor is that the feds busted a huge shipment in customs, and now the supply chain's screwed until they can smuggle more in somehow."

An unpleasant shiver of dread skittered up my back. I clenched my jaw, telling myself firmly that there was no reason to panic yet.

I was still two weeks out from my heat. The blockers had a pretty short shelf life unless you had access to a medical-grade deep-freeze, but I always gave myself as much lead time as I could get away with. You never knew when a dealer would get busted and disappear from the scene. If you needed to scramble to find someone else, it was best to have extra time to prepare.

This, though… it felt different, somehow. Bigger. Harder to work around. It was the first time I'd ever heard of an entire region losing its supply.

"How long until you get some?" I asked, trying not to let irrational fear creep into my voice.

Or maybe it *wasn't* so irrational, since Leah only shrugged again, looking sympathetic. "I dunno, man. It just depends. They're saying the Post Office has dogs that can sniff it out now. Maybe they're tightening things down on the supply side. You want a birth control syringe in the meantime? Just in case, I mean."

"No." The word was out of my mouth before my brain could register what a stupid decision it was. I swallowed, debating whether to take it back, but after a moment, I shook my head. There was still time to find a different supplier—someone who hadn't sold out yet, or who got their pills via different means. "I'm good, thanks. I'll figure something out. Do you know of anyone else in the area who's still got some?"

Leah's expression soured. "No one I could send you to in good conscience. Sorry, Luca." She consciously smoothed her features. "Don't worry. This'll be a one-off, I imagine. They'll find some way around the new restrictions before long. They always do."

"Yeah." I played along, trying not to project my own trauma responses all over the situation. "Okay, thanks anyway. Stay safe, Leah."

"You, too." She mustered a smile for me, forced though it was.

The drive back to Ladue gave me way too much time to think... a state of affairs made even worse by the fact that I had to stop at a public charging station north of Granite City to top up the Leaf for the rest of the drive home.

There were lots of dealers located closer to St. Louis—especially on the Illinois side of the river, where the sentences were lighter for possession with intent to distribute. But I was extremely paranoid about going to anyone close enough to East St. Louis or Washington Park that they might have ties to my old gang.

Then again, it wasn't paranoia if they really were out to get you. Wasn't that what they always said on TV?

God. Sometimes I hated my own brain. It wasn't as though I didn't do natural heats occasionally; meaning whenever my doctor bullied me into doing it 'for my health.' That ended up being once a year or so, usually.

It was the control thing that got to me.

If I *decided* to have a heat, then fine. It was something I chose for myself, because it was the lesser of two evils and better than ending up with multiple forms of cancer by the age of forty. I chose it, and I took a birth control shot, and that was that. Depending on what else was going on at the time, either Byron or Zalen took a dampener so they wouldn't end up going into rut, and they helped me get through it.

How interesting that alpha dampeners aren't regulated, I thought, unable to quell a pulse of irritation. The damn things didn't even require a prescription. You could walk in and get them over the counter.

My irritation over that was stupid, though. After all, the last thing I wanted was an alpha in my nest who *wasn't* on dampeners.

And that was right back to my control issues. I knew what it was like to get sucked into a heat you didn't want, with alphas you hadn't chosen, who didn't give a rolling shit for your wellbeing.

I guess I was lucky that Blaze killed any alpha underling in the gang who was stupid enough to bite one of 'his' omegas. No one had ever tried to go after my mating gland, though it had taken years for the scars of bite marks on other parts of my body to fade.

Lucky. Yeah… that was me, all right.

I had plenty of other scars. They were just on the inside, like the one that was throbbing a warning right now. I wasn't choosing this heat. I didn't *want* this heat. I'd already told Zalen I wasn't going to have it. And now the stupid universe was trying to make me a liar; trying to prove that I still didn't get to choose.

Well, screw that.

I had two weeks to get this figured out. I'd heard the unspoken words behind Leah's muttered *"no one I could send you to in good conscience."* The gangs were probably sitting on some of the stuff — and making crazy profits by selling into the shortage.

But A) god only knew how old the pills they were selling would be, much less whether they'd been stored properly. And B) I wasn't actually that stupid. *Or* that desperate.

I really, *really* didn't want to show up at Zalen's door again, this time to sheepishly explain that I couldn't find blockers after all, and could he please get me some by whatever means necessary. The good news was, I didn't need to go down that route yet. Or hopefully at all.

———◆———

Mia got home a few minutes before midnight. I was waiting up for her, aware that my lack of sleep was starting to catch up to me at work, but pretty sure I would have been awake and fretting regardless.

She looked tired, but she didn't smell distressed tonight. I hoped that meant nothing else bad had happened at the restaurant. Apparently, I couldn't make the same claim about my own perfume, because she stopped outside the TV room and peered inside.

"Luca?" she asked, coming in and plopping down next to me on the battered couch. "Everything okay?"

I sighed, and paused the episode of *Ashes to Ashes* on a frame with the Quattro half obscured by dust as it slewed around a corner, mid-chase.

"Not exactly," I said, hastening to add, "It's nothing serious, don't worry," when her brows creased in concern.

"What's up?" she asked. "Something wrong at the Hope Project? It's not about Tony, is it?"

"No, nothing like that," I told her. "Look… this is embarrassing, but I guess there was a big shipment of heat blockers stopped at the border, and now none of the local dealers around here can get them. My usual source is out, and she doesn't know when she'll get more."

Real alarm flashed over Mia's pretty face. "Shit! I'm due in three weeks! What about you?"

"Two," I replied grimly. "There's still time, but—"

She nodded, way ahead of me. "Let me run upstairs and grab my laptop. I'll see if my source is still good."

Some of the tension drained from my tight neck muscles. "Thanks."

She smiled, tipping her chin at the TV. "Restart that for me. I love this episode. Be right back."

I grabbed the remote and went back to the beginning, pausing it to wait for her. She returned a couple of minutes later and sat down next to me, our thighs pressing together warmly as she opened up the computer and powered it on. I set the episode to playing as background noise while she called up an internet browser.

"This source has been solid for a couple of years now," she said absently, navigating to a popular website for sellers of handmade and vintage items. "She's in Vermont—one of those people who sells blockers privately, disguised with code words and packed in with other legit items."

I'd heard of those sources, but I'd never tried to use one. It was probably the gang kid in me, but I'd always been more comfortable dealing face-to-face with people, so I could get a better read on them.

This was definitely a 'beggars can't be choosers' type of situation, though.

"Bless 'em all," I said. "If she's got what we need, she's my new hero."

"Right?" Mia said wryly. "Let's see… okay, here we go. Handblown glass vases… buy one, get a free packet of fifty 'flower food' tablets to keep your cut flowers looking fresh." She paused, punching the air in triumph. "In stock!"

I guessed the blockers came in the packet of flower tablets, which was actually fucking brilliant. It was easy enough for an omega to sniff out a hormone pill from among a bunch of sugar tablets. Much harder for any poor postal drone tasked with screening for controlled substances with a thirty-year-old X-ray machine.

"Quick, get some," I said with feeling. "In fact… does your restaurant have a freezer? Maybe we can stock up."

"Not a medical-grade deep freeze, sorry," she said. "I looked into that, actually — but those are much colder."

She quickly tapped in an order, and we both held our breath while the payment processed. When the success page popped up, we let it out with a whoosh in perfect unison.

"Crisis averted, hopefully," she said.

It wasn't a sure thing—the uncertainty of shipment and delivery was another reason I preferred to deal in person. Still, Mia had been using this source for a long time. I wrapped an arm around her shoulders and leaned over to kiss the top of her head, feeling much lighter than I had before.

"You're a lifesaver." Then I noticed the shipping address as Mia went to close the laptop—someplace in Jennings. "Hey, you can get that package delivered here, you know."

She shook her head and leaned into me, curling up comfortably. "Nah. It's fine. The downside of sources like this is that if the politicians ever decide to criminalize simple possession, the dealer has a nice, handy list of names and addresses for them if they get busted. No need to put Zalen on a list like that."

I looked down at her, one eyebrow raised. "Whereas it's not a problem putting Nat on that list?"

She sighed, her shoulders rising and falling beneath my arm. "I could be a bitch and say something like 'serves him right'... but the truth is, Nat and I are already on that list, and we have been for a long time."

It wasn't an issue at the moment. The culture warriors weren't interested in the optics of arresting individual omegas for possession. They were only after the distributors, for now.

"As long as it won't be a problem retrieving the package when it arrives," I said mildly.

"It won't," she replied. "As weird as it sounds, Nat and I are getting along better than we have in a very long time. There should be a tracking number tomorrow, and we can follow it from there. Now, let me watch the show. This part's good; you'll like it."

I settled back with an armful of warm, sweet-smelling omega cuddled against me, relieved to find that the day had gone from seriously bad to pretty damned good, in the end.

THIRTY-EIGHT

Mia

"I HOPE THIS gives you all an overview of the different career paths available within the restaurant industry," I said, looking out at the classroom full of teenage faces. They ran the gamut from innocent to world-weary; from interested to bored to antagonistic. "Or perhaps I should have said, a *taste* of the different career paths."

That garnered a few chuckles, at least.

I'd made good on my promise to put together an informational packet and a short presentation for my visit to the Hope Project. It wasn't my first foray into public speaking—not by a long shot. It was my first in quite a while, though. Not to mention my first time speaking in front of a room full of kids with rap sheets longer than my arm.

Zalen rose from the table he'd been leaning against, hipshot, and joined me at the front. "Ms. Dimitriadis has been kind enough to provide us with a list of available scholarships for anyone interested in pursuing a degree in the culinary arts. See me privately during regular office hours if you'd like to discuss it further."

A bit of chatter started up in the room, and Zalen raised his voice to be heard over it. "That's all for now. Tomorrow, we'll discuss budgeting and savings accounts."

A few groans reached us, but they sounded surprisingly good-natured given the subject matter.

"I'm with them," I said wryly, as my captive audience escaped toward the promise of freedom that lay beyond the classroom door. I didn't even want to *think* about the state of the savings account I shared with Nat after the past few months.

Zalen chuckled, gathering up the folder of papers and contacts I'd brought along. "Thanks for doing this, Mia."

I raised an eyebrow and made a noncommittal humming noise, stifling a smile. "Hey, I'm always ready to recruit for the restaurant industry. The pay isn't usually that great, but at least the hours are terrible."

Zalen let out a startled bark of laughter, and my smile broke free. Had I ever heard him laugh before? I wasn't sure, but I didn't think so. He was usually so controlled… so sober and self-contained. An unwanted thought floated through my awareness. Was he *always* so reserved? Or was he one of those repressed alphas who turned into a wild animal in the heat nest?

Cursing the little pulse of warmth in my belly, I quashed that thought hard and fast—*damn* the run-up to an omega estrous cycle. I was still two weeks out, but being around alpha pheromones was already enough to turn me into a shameless hussy.

When I'd checked the tracking on my illicit blocker shipment from Etsy this morning, the parcel had arrived in a facility in Indiana, with an expected delivery date in two days. It couldn't come fast enough, as far as I was concerned. The idle musing about what it might be like to have a natural heat with Byron, Zalen, and even Emiel had wormed its way into my brain all too easily. I needed a concrete reminder that it wouldn't be happening to keep myself from climbing the damned walls.

Maybe Luca would be up for a bit of *stress relief* tonight, as he insisted on calling it. He had to be even worse off than I was, with his heat due in a week.

Luca... or Luca and Byron together, whispered the little voice of my hormonal lust.

Nope. Nope, nope, *nope*.

We weren't going there. Byron had been the poster boy for running hot and cold, and I wasn't about to push him when he hadn't made another move on me since the tequila incident. Luca's ominous 'let's talk' note had come to nothing... so far, at least. The first day had passed, and then the second—and then there'd been the scare over the heat blocker shortage.

But Byron clearly had mixed feelings about what had happened in his room, and... wait. Why was I standing here in front of Zalen thinking about hot, three-way sex?

Crap.

"Sorry," I said. "I'm a thousand miles away."

He looked amused rather than offended, thank goodness. "No worries. Did Luca give you the full tour earlier?"

I nodded. "He did. What you've done here is really impressive, Zalen. I know it's not perfect, and you always feel like you should be doing more—but you're really making a difference with this place."

He offered me a tired smile. "I appreciate that. It's an uphill battle, but… I can't *not* do it, you know?"

I wondered, not for the first time, what had happened in his life to make this his calling. Because it *was* a calling. He hadn't fallen into it like the others had. He hadn't been in a gang.

Maybe I'd eventually get to know him well enough to feel right about asking. Until then, it wasn't my business.

"You know, I still haven't met Princess," I said lightly. "Can't miss that while I'm here."

Zalen glanced at the clock hanging on the back wall. "Definitely not. Emiel should be finishing up with his kids in a few minutes. I'll take you down to the gym, and he can handle the feline introductions."

I didn't protest that I could go alone. I'd known within thirty seconds of meeting him that Zalen had a chivalrous streak a mile wide. Besides, while he'd described the Hope Project's clients as being 'mostly good kids,' that didn't change the fact that they were kids who'd come from gang life of varying degrees of violence… and some of them had already presented as alphas.

I wasn't about to go traipsing around the place on my own when I was a total stranger to them.

"Thank you," I said, curious to see Emiel in his role as a teacher.

We went down to the basement level of the old brick building, where the alpha in question was overseeing a sparring match in the boxing ring. Two teenagers were circling each other warily, throwing the occasional jab.

They wore face guards and protective mouthpieces, along with fat red boxing gloves. The scene was about as far away from Emiel's illegal underground cage match as I could imagine. It still jarred me for a second, though.

But *this* Emiel wasn't the dead-faced Emiel who'd suffered a sadistic beating without a flinch, only to turn on his opponent and steamroll them at the last possible moment. No… *this* Emiel shadowed his two charges like a hawk, stepping in to offer advice and correct tiny imperfections of form.

Papa bear, I thought nonsensically, and my stupid hormones immediately jumped into the fray with opinions about how much they liked that mental picture.

Zalen and I watched from the edge of the room while the match wound down. Emiel spoke with both of the boys as they peeled off their gloves and protective equipment. He ruffled the hair of the one who'd seemed more intimidated by the idea of being hit, and the boy ducked his head, muttering something unintelligible.

When the boxers and the handful of onlookers had all left the gym, Zalen ushered me over to the ring. "Hey, Em. If you're all done here, you need to see a woman about a cat."

Emiel glanced up and nodded. "Okay. Just a minute, Mia. Let me put this gear away."

I smiled at him and went to sit on the edge of the raised boxing ring. "Dinner's at nine," I called after Zalen. "Don't be late."

"I wouldn't dare," Zalen said over his shoulder. "See you both then."

"What are we eating?" Emiel asked from the locker he was leaning over.

I grinned, though he couldn't see it. I'd decided to make dinner for everyone on Mondays since it was my day off.

"Lasagna," I told him.

"Sounds good," he said, closing the locker. "I'm going to go put Princess's food out now. She usually comes to say hi when I do."

"Lead the way," I told him, and followed him up the stairs to the first floor.

He stopped at a storage closet to retrieve a bag of cat food, then ducked into an office and emerged with a bottle of water tucked under his arm. He led me to what looked like a service corridor running along one edge of the building, and opened an unassuming door onto an alley that smelled overpoweringly of trash and urine.

"Sorry," he said. "I don't think anyone ever comes back here. Not to clean, at least."

"It's fine," I said gamely, even though my eyes were starting to water.

He set the bottle and the bag of food down. "Here. You can sit on the steps."

Before I could decide if I trusted the unidentified stains on those steps, he'd whisked off the navy blazer he was wearing over a blue button-down shirt and laid it on the concrete.

"Thank you," I said, taken aback that anyone would actually do that in real life. I sat gingerly on the off-the-rack wool blend, trying and failing to catch any hint of bergamot from the fabric. But Emiel was already busy with the food and water pans laid out next to the steps, cleaning them out and refilling them.

A soft meow emerged from behind a collection of trash cans, and a silver-gray form darted out. The little cat trotted over and immediately started winding between Emiel's ankles, clearly more interested in his presence than the food.

"Hi, Princess," Emiel said, more gentleness in his voice than I'd ever heard there. "This is Mia. She wants to meet you."

Princess paused in her rubbing to peer at me with yellow-green eyes. Then she plopped down and started licking one lithe gray shoulder, ignoring me completely.

"Her name suits her," I said, amused and charmed in equal measure.

"Yeah," Emiel agreed. "She's too good for this place."

He finished with the food and water and came to sit across from me on the steps. Princess rumbled a purr and immediately walked her front paws up his shin to knead at the wool of his dark trousers. He rubbed her head, and she pushed into the contact, purring louder.

"Emiel," I said seriously. "You need to bring this cat to live at the house."

He paused in his gentle petting. "You really think so? She's a feral cat. She might scratch up the furniture or pee on Zalen's floor."

I wanted so badly to scoot over and take his free hand… but instinct warned me that would be a mistake. I poured the feeling into my voice instead.

"I really think so. *Look* at her, Emiel. This cat is yours. She shouldn't live in an alley."

He didn't look up, but I could tell he was listening. Had this man ever had a pet of his own? Had he ever been allowed *anything* of his own while growing up, simply because he cared for it, and it cared for him?

"Zalen already said it was okay," I added, hoping to close the deal.

Emiel looked up then, from beneath lashes that were surprisingly long and dark. He drew breath, only to hesitate for a moment before finally speaking.

"I guess he did." He licked his lips. "Maybe you're right. But I still have to buy all the stuff she'll need. I didn't get anything yet."

I couldn't help the smile that stretched across my face. "Can you take a long lunch today? Let's go to the nearest pet store and get it right now. You can set everything up tonight and bring her home tomorrow."

THIRTY-NINE

Mia

EAST ST. LOUIS was short on retail stores in general, and pet stores in particular. After a quick map search, Emiel and I ended up going back across the river to a boutique pet shop located a few blocks north of my culinary stomping grounds in Soulard.

We drove separately, since he'd be going back to work afterward, while I'd be returning to the house to start preparing the evening meal I had planned. It was hard not to spend the drive speculating on what was going on in Emiel's head. He was so closed off… such an enigma.

But it would just be that—speculation. He couldn't make it any clearer that he wasn't seeking any emotional connections with me… or anyone else, with the possible exception of Princess. And that was his prerogative, even if it didn't stop me wondering about him.

PawPrintz was tucked behind a brick and glass storefront with on-street parking. At this time of day, I had to park half a block away. I fed money to the meter and wandered back to the shop, enjoying the cool breeze and sunshine. Emiel arrived a couple of minutes later, having lost the parking lottery and ended up even farther away.

I smiled at him as we approached the entrance. "Do you have a list?"

He opened the door and let me go in first. "Litterbox, litter, food, treats, new food and water bowls."

"Toys?" I suggested.

"Do you think she'll play with toys?" he asked, frowning. "She's an alley cat."

"Good day," greeted the grandmotherly figure behind the counter. "Welcome to PawPrintz. How can I help you?"

Emiel looked faintly startled, as though he hadn't expected random human beings to speak to him without prompting.

"Hi," I said. "We're bringing home a stray cat. So, we need all the usual cat… stuff."

"Oh, that's lovely!" said the woman. She rose from the stool and bustled around to join us. "This will be your first cat, then? Or do you have other pets?"

"No other pets. We're starting from scratch," I told her. "Huh… she'll need a scratching post, won't she?"

"Probably so," she said, including Emiel in her twinkling smile. "How exciting! Let's go pick out everything you'll need."

PawPrintz wasn't a large store, but it was well-stocked. Half an hour later, we walked out with six bulging bags full of cat-related items, and an eye-watering bill that Emiel paid without comment. In fact, he'd managed to get through the entire thing without speaking more than a few words.

I got the impression that was typical. I couldn't help wondering if he would have come here on his own, as opposed to simply ordering everything online. Did he function well day-to-day with things like this? He hadn't shown any difficulty when he'd been interacting with the kids under his guidance at the Hope Project...

Shaking myself free of the speculation, I smiled up at him. "Where did you park? I'll help you load all this stuff. Unless you'd like me to take it back to the house? My car's probably closer."

"I'll get it." The words came immediately, as though he felt strongly about being the one to set things up for Princess's arrival. "I'm parked around the corner."

I followed him one block down and half a block over to his old Ford Bronco. It was well-kept for its age, but where Byron's Audi was practically a show car, the Bronco's paint job exhibited signs of its many years of use. We loaded everything in the back.

"Thanks," he said. "I'll walk you back to your car."

The urge to say it was fine, that he didn't need to do that, hovered on the tip of my tongue. I consciously swallowed the words. Why shouldn't I let an alpha walk me back to my Kia?

Sure, the likelihood of anything bad happening was tiny. Sure, I was in favor of omegas being empowered and self-sufficient. But I'd been empowered and self-sufficient for most of my life… and look where it had gotten me in my relationships.

"Okay," I said. And then, on a whim, "Hey… do you have time for a quick lunch with me before you go back?"

Emiel went completely still.

I hurried onward. "Only, I'm kind of hungry, and we're not eating until nine this evening. There's this restaurant I've been meaning to check out. It's only a few blocks south of here, actually. So, I thought—"

"We can get lunch."

I snapped my mouth closed. Did he seem wary about the request? Was he humoring me? It was so difficult to judge his reaction with no scent to read. Even betas' scents changed with their emotions—a little bit, at least.

"Great," I told him. "Do you want to drive separately, or…?"

"Is it close enough to walk?" he asked.

I consulted my mental map of this part of the city. "About two-thirds of a mile? Maybe three-quarters."

"Let's walk." He rubbed a hand over his shaved head. "I like the fresh air."

'Fresh air' might've been a bit of a misnomer with the river so close, but it *was* a nice day. I watched the cars and people as we strolled south on Truman Parkway and turned left onto Lafayette, feeling oddly free without the need to stay alert for danger.

That lasted until the Bella Vita's discreet sign came into view. Coming here had been a spontaneous decision, and possibly not a very smart one. But the owners had eaten at the Elderflower Inn without announcing who they were, so it wasn't as though they could act offended if I did the same thing.

"Our new competition," I explained to Emiel—not that he'd asked. "I figure I should check them out in person since they've been taking so much business away from us."

"Just don't get the lasagna," Emiel said, and... had that been a joke?

I glanced at him sideways. "Oh, I don't know. You could get theirs for lunch, and then give me a comparative review with mine tonight."

"Yours'll be better," he mumbled.

We went inside, where we were greeted by a friendly beta hostess and a pleasant, if somewhat cliched, atmosphere. Chandeliers shed a low, warm glow over old-world furnishings. We were seated without a wait, although the place was doing a brisk business at the lunch hour.

"Smart of them to be open when your place is closed," Emiel said, picking up the lunch menu and examining it.

I made a noncommittal noise. "They're open seven days a week. That can be brutal on the staff unless they've got a lot of part-timers to cover shifts."

I ordered the risotto, since risotto was a good way to judge the kitchen's skill. Emiel ordered chicken parm.

"I'll get that right in for you," our waiter said, and left us alone with our bread sticks and marinara dipping sauce.

Emiel watched me watching the way the front of house ran. It was smooth enough. Professional, if nothing extraordinary. The biggest tipoff that whoever was running the show might lack vital experience was the pricing. It was too low.

But they'd figure that out soon enough, and it was easy enough to hike the prices and print new menus.

Aware that I wasn't being a particularly scintillating lunch companion, I dragged my attention back to Emiel and started chatting about things he might do for Princess, like installing a fully enclosed cat balcony on one of the second-floor windows at the back of the house.

"That way she could sit in it on nice days and survey her new domain," I finished.

"She'd probably like that," he agreed, glancing up as the waiter returned with our entrees.

"Here we go, folks." The waiter—Chance, as he'd introduced himself—set his tray down on a stand and placed my risotto in front of me. "Let me know if there's anything else I can get for you."

"This looks wonderful, thanks," I said, unwrapping my silverware.

Chance set Emiel's chicken parm down and smiled, not noticing how still Emiel went as he withdrew.

"Terrific," Chance said. "I'll come back and check on you in a few minutes. Enjoy!"

Emiel watched him leave, still not moving. A frisson of unease ran over me, although I couldn't have said exactly why.

"Everything okay?" I asked, trying to keep my tone light.

Emiel blinked, his attention returning from whatever had caught it. He looked down at his plate and took up his fork. "Yeah. We should eat."

I frowned, but I took his advice and started eating. The risotto was... fine. In fact, for the price, I suppose it was better than fine. From what I could see and smell, Emiel's dish was also pretty good.

He didn't seem to notice either way. His focus had turned outward, and he was watching the staff move around the dining room every bit as closely as I'd done earlier. I still couldn't tell what was off—but whatever it was, it put me on edge.

We ate in uncomfortable silence. Uncomfortable on my end, at least.

Toward the end of the meal, an alpha in a dark suit approached, surrounded by the scent of iron and sandalwood. With a faint jolt, I recognized him as one of the men who'd come into the Elderflower Inn to scope us out.

"Good afternoon," he said. "Chef Dimitriadis, isn't it? Welcome to the Bella Vita. We're honored to have you here. And Mister...?"

"Hamilton," Emiel said in a monotone. And then, he stuck out a hand for the other alpha to shake. "Pleasure to meet you."

I stared, struck by how out of character the move seemed, but our host didn't hesitate, stretching a hand out to return the greeting.

"Blake Berlusconi," he said. "I'm one of the owners. I hope you both enjoyed your meal?"

The back of my neck prickled unpleasantly, for absolutely no rational reason. I started to speak, and then had to clear my throat when my voice emerged high and unsteady. "Y-yes. It was lovely. My compliments to my counterpart in the kitchen."

Berlusconi gave a pleasant laugh. "I'll be sure to pass it on. I do hope you'll both drop by again."

Emiel remained stonily silent.

"Thank you," I said, the perfectly adequate risotto churning unpleasantly in my stomach.

The waiter brought us the check shortly after his boss excused himself, and Emiel grabbed it before I could. "Let me," he said, the first words he'd spoken since greeting Berlusconi.

I let him, feeling so freaked out by this point that all I could think about was getting away from here. As soon as Chance brought back the credit card receipt, Emiel signed it carelessly and ushered me toward the front door. It felt as though he'd gained six inches of height and twice that much in breadth as he loomed over me, bristling with alpha protective instincts.

I let him herd me along without touching me until we were a full block away from the restaurant, before I finally gathered myself and turned on him.

"What was all that about?" I demanded, cringing when I heard a quaver beneath the words.

Emiel turned to face me, looking down at me with a worried furrow in his brow.

"Don't go back there alone, Mia," he said. "Actually, don't go back there at all."

"Why?" I asked. "What did you see that I didn't?"

The worry lines on Emiel's face deepened. "That waiter. He had a gang tattoo. SSG. So did the owner."

"SSG?" I echoed stupidly.

"White supremacist trash," Emiel said, an edge of anger creeping into his tone. "You don't want nothing to do with them, trust me. They're Luca's old gang… the one he ran away from."

FORTY

Mia

I WAS IN shock as I drove back to the house in Ladue. After we'd left the restaurant, Emiel insisted on walking me back to my car like a bodyguard. He even waited, watching as I started the Kia's engine and pulled into traffic.

It was as though he expected some random white supremacist gang member to jump out from the shadows and try to assault me, which was frankly more alarming than the initial revelation about the Bella Vita had been.

Intellectually, I knew it was just alpha instincts kicking in. This was simply what alphas were *like*—even the ones who used pheromone suppressors and kept their emotions locked down tighter than Fort Knox, apparently. No one from the Bella Vita had secretly shadowed us out of the restaurant with an eye toward public mayhem in broad daylight.

It still took several minutes behind the wheel before my pulse stopped jumping like a startled rabbit confronted with a fox.

The Bella Vita was run by Luca's old gang. What the *hell* was I supposed to do with that information? Should I tell Luca? I was pretty sure I had to tell him. Not telling him felt too much like keeping something secret when it was directly related to his business.

I resolved to pull him aside as soon as he got home and relay what Emiel had said. I wasn't sure how much it would upset him, or if it would even upset him at all. But very few things pissed me off more than people who tried to wrap omegas in cotton wool as though they couldn't handle life's troubles. It would be the ultimate irony to let myself turn into one of those people, simply because I hated the thought of Luca's distress.

When I eventually pulled into the driveway and parked, I sat in the car for long moments, trying to get my head on straight. I would tell Luca what was going on, and then at dinner, I'd ask Zalen what he thought I should do, if anything. I had a resident expert on gangs at my fingertips—it made sense to use that resource.

Feeling a little better about things, I got out and locked my car, then let myself into the empty house. It would be nice to have Princess here for company when the guys were at work… even if she ended up giving me the feline cold shoulder like she had in the alley. Had that only happened this morning? God, this Monday felt like it had encompassed an age, and it was barely midafternoon.

With nothing much to do for the next few hours except fret, I settled in the TV room and binged a few episodes of *Life on Mars* on the British streaming service Luca had bought for me. Both he and I were developing an unhealthy obsession with the main character who appeared in both this show and *Ashes to Ashes*. I wasn't proud of the way my hormone-addled brain wanted to overlay Emiel's overwhelming physical presence and gruff demeanor over Detective Inspector Hunt's, but that was omega biology for you.

Apparently, my pre-heat libido was intent on acting like a magpie collecting shiny objects. Whichever alpha I'd been around most recently seemed to be the one that dominated my idle fantasies.

Mmm.

Dominated.

The front door opened, and I snapped back to myself. On the positive side, I'd certainly managed to turn off my brain. In fact, I'd managed to turn it off so successfully that when Luca's light summer scent wafted into the room, I had a sudden urge to ask if he wanted to go steal one of Byron's spice-smelling blankets and have a quickie before I needed to start work on dinner.

Then, the events of the day rushed back in, and my frustrated horniness crashed and burned against the proverbial mountainside of practicality. I dragged my attention away from the fiery wreckage with a sigh.

"Hi." Luca poked his head in, offering me a strained smile. "Any updates on the heat blockers?"

At least there was some good news on that front.

"Expected delivery on Wednesday," I told him. "Packages don't usually show up at our place until the afternoon, but I'll swing by after work and pick it up."

"We should seriously send that seller a card or something," Luca said. He cocked his head at me. "Everything else okay? You seem a bit…"

"Yeah." I sighed again. "I am a bit. Come in and join me for a sec?"

I turned off the TV as he dropped his bag by the sofa and sat down, half-facing me.

"Okay, now you're worrying me," he said.

I shook my head. "Sorry—I don't think it's anything that's genuinely going to cause a problem. I just thought you should know what Emiel and I found out at lunch."

Luca blinked. "Wait. You and Emiel went out to *lunch*? Like, *together*?"

"Yeah, after we went shopping to get supplies for Princess," I confirmed. "He's planning on bringing her home tomorrow, by the way." I waved that off. "Anyway, I dragged him to the Bella Vita so I could scope it out in person."

He frowned. "That's the place that popped up recently and started poaching your business, right? Any good?"

"It is, and the food seemed fine," I replied. "They've got everything priced way too cheap, though. Honestly, that's probably how they're drawing so much business, even if it's not sustainable."

"Okay," Luca said cautiously. "So, what exactly did you and Emiel find out while you were there?"

I took a deep breath and let it out slowly. "Emiel says the place is being run by members of your old gang. He recognized the tattoos, I guess."

I watched Luca's face carefully. His complexion paled for a moment, but then he swallowed and nodded.

"The bigger gangs get into all sorts of shit," he said lightly. "I mean… maybe don't go there again unless you want to indirectly support human trafficking and the drug trade. But I'm not, like, shocked or anything."

With what they were charging for food, I'd be surprised if the gross receipts at the Bella Vita were even funding their monthly payroll successfully. That wasn't the point, though.

"Believe me, I don't plan on making it a regular lunch spot," I assured him. "But I wanted you to know upfront, because I figured I'd ask Zalen if there was anything else I should do about it."

"The best thing to do is stay far, far away," Luca said sourly.

"That's definitely my first choice." I nudged his shoulder with mine. "Right. I need to get the lasagna started."

"Let me get changed. I'll come keep you company in the kitchen, assuming you don't mind me stealing bites." He nudged me back. "I'm absolutely *starving*. Stupid hormones."

"Tell me about it." I always ended up gaining ten pounds in the run-up to my heats, even when I blocked them. "See you in a bit."

———————◆———————

At dinner, Zalen took the news that gangs were getting into the restaurant business in Soulard with surprising equanimity.

"Not a surprise, I'm afraid," he said, pausing with a forkful of lasagna halfway to his lips. "And I wouldn't suggest taking it to the authorities. There isn't any solid proof of illegal activity, so there's not much they can do. Restaurants are actually a pretty common sideline for organized crime."

"But why?" I asked. "They're not exactly a quick path to untold riches, and I say this with some authority on the subject."

"Maybe not, but they do a fair amount of turnover in cash." At my blank look, he went on. "Money laundering. Car washes and laundromats work well, too. Any kind of business where banks don't look sideways at you when you bring in large cash deposits multiple times a week."

Byron, who'd looked grim-faced at the mention of Luca's old gang, had pity on me. "Drugs and prostitution generate loads of cash. But you can't just take it to a bank and stick it in a personal account. You'd get flagged and investigated within a week. So, instead you buy a business that has a steady influx of legitimate cash, and you pad it out with some of the illegal cash every time you make a deposit. Who's to say your car wash isn't really successful?"

Understanding clicked. "Or your restaurant. Wow."

"That's probably why the prices were so cheap," Emiel muttered.

"Because they don't really care if the restaurant is making a profit in its own right," I finished. A dark snort of laughter escaped me. "Must be nice for some."

"Not really," Luca said mildly.

I shot him an apologetic smile, though I was relieved he didn't seem too upset about the whole situation.

"Well, for what it's worth, I promise this eggplant lasagna is free-range and cruelty-free," I said. "I'm reasonably sure we're not supporting any illegal activity by eating it."

"It's better than that stupid chicken parm from lunch," Emiel said, his attention fixed firmly on his own plate.

"Best tacos I've ever had," Byron added. He saluted me with a forkful of sauced pasta and cheese, although his striking features were still drawn and unhappy.

Despite his seeming indifference toward the news about the Bella Vita, Luca wordlessly stepped back to let me into his nest when I showed up at his door at one a.m., unable to sleep. We didn't end up having sex, but somehow, lying tangled up with him among the profusion of sweet-scented pillows and blankets also fulfilled a need in me that I hadn't been aware existed before I came to this place.

As was becoming the norm, I woke alone the following morning, the others long gone for their jobs. A quick check on my phone showed that the heat blockers were out for delivery a day early. I let out a relieved breath, glad that something was going to plan.

With luck, I'd have them safely in hand when I returned here tonight after work. Between that and Princess's arrival this evening, today was shaping up to be an all-around good day.

I left a few minutes early for the Elderflower Inn, eager to catch up to Nat and give him the scandalous gossip about the Bella Vita. He was at his desk, running accounts, and he looked up with a hesitant smile as I walked in.

"Hi, Mia. You're early today. How is everything?"

I hitched a hip on the edge of the desk, suddenly missing the easy familiarity we'd once had. *Hormones*, I reminded myself. *Heats are the ultimate rose-colored glasses.*

"Things are good," I told him. "I've got some hot gossip about our new competitors, though."

I watched Nat's eyebrows climb as I relayed the news about the owner and the probable money-laundering scheme. When I was done, he sat back in his chair and blew out a breath.

"Holy shit," he said. "Do you think they could somehow be behind the sabotage of the hanging rack?"

"Uh…" I paused. "Did we decide for sure that it *was* sabotage?"

Nat leaned forward again, his elbows resting on the desk as he looked up at me. "You saw the hooks. Why would two of them fail at the same exact instant? It wasn't as though Shani was hanging off the thing like a trapeze artist. There was no more pressure on the chains than there ever is."

I really, *really* didn't want to think about someone having orchestrated that accident deliberately.

"Why would someone from another restaurant want to do anything like that?" I asked, my voice weak.

Nat's brows drew together. "I don't know. I mean… they've taken some market share in the area, sure. But they're never going to become the go-to option when they're located a couple of streets over from the only Michelin-star restaurant in the Midwest."

I huffed, looking away. "If that's their worry, they could just wait around until next January when the new Michelin guide comes out," I muttered.

Nat's warm hand covered mine where it lay on the desk, giving a brief squeeze before withdrawing. I glanced up at him.

"Hey. Nothing's certain until it's done," he said. "And besides, what we've built here is more important than a star in a pamphlet printed by a bunch of food snobs."

I mustered a smile for him. "Way to spin it, babe. I'm still planning on being super-upset about it, though. Just a heads up."

"Fair," he said. "Now, do you have a few minutes to go over some figures with me?"

I nodded and lost myself in the minutiae of business management until the rest of the staff started trickling in, only realizing after the lunch crowd had come and gone that I'd forgotten to tell Nat about the package.

I caught up to him after the midday rush thinned out. "Hey, I almost forgot. I've got an important package arriving at the house this afternoon. I'll need to swing by after close tonight and pick it up."

Nat's expression went suddenly blank. "Wait, it's being delivered to *our* house? Today?"

An unpleasant, tight sensation lodged in my throat. "Yes? Why?"

"How big is this package?" he asked. "I mean, is it too big for our P.O. box? And, when you say 'important'…"

He trailed off. I swallowed past the lump growing ever larger in my throat. "Nat. Talk to me. Why would there be a problem getting a package delivered to the house?"

FORTY-ONE

Mia

NAT BLINKED, SHAKING himself free of his momentary paralysis. "There may not be a problem. It's just that everything is getting forwarded to the post office box at the moment. Someone started stealing our mail last week. I assume it's just kids playing a prank or something, but—"

He shrugged helplessly, and I tried not to panic. The heat blockers weren't shipping via the Post Office. My seller had switched to private shipping since the last time I'd used her—probably hoping it would mean looser security checks for controlled substances and contraband. That meant the package wouldn't end up at the P.O. box.

"This is FedEx," I said. "They require a street address for delivery. Are you sure someone was stealing the mail? Is it possible we just didn't get anything for a couple of days?"

Even as I said it, I knew it was unlikely. The paperless revolution hadn't yet arrived for restaurant owners. Not completely, anyway.

Nat's expression hardened. "They weren't exactly subtle about it. All the envelopes were torn open and dumped in the front yard. It happened last Thursday, Friday, and Saturday while I was here at the restaurant. It was just pure luck that there wasn't anything too important or sensitive taken. I'm sorry—I should have told you. I was hoping it was just an isolated thing."

"Why would someone do that?" I asked, as though Nat would have any more idea than I did. "Isn't tampering with the mail kind of a big deal?"

"It's a federal offense… if they get caught," Nat said tiredly. "Which is the challenging part. Anyway, I went and filled out a form on Saturday morning to get everything sent to the post office box for now. They still got to Saturday's mail, but everything's safe starting yesterday. I put up a security camera Sunday morning to try and catch them if they come back."

An itchy sensation of worry had taken up residence beneath my skin. The restaurant was dotted with security cameras now, as well—a precaution after the two 'mysterious accidents' over the past couple of weeks. No doubt it was partly down to my fluctuating hormones as my heat cycle approached, but I couldn't help feeling like there was some sort of invisible target painted on our backs.

It was slightly after two p.m., and the thought that my vital package of blockers might be sitting unattended on the front porch at the house was unbearable. If it had just been for me, maybe I could have waited… but it wasn't. Luca was depending on those pills, and unlike me, he wouldn't have time to try and find another source before his heat.

I never did things like this. *Never.*

And yet, with the itchy prickle of dread crawling beneath my skin like insects, I looked up at Nat and said, "I need to go see if it's arrived. Shani and the kitchen staff will have to cover things for a bit without me."

Nat looked surprised, and I couldn't really blame him. But, to his credit, he only nodded. "It's the afternoon lull. They'll be fine for an hour. Just..." He hesitated. "Why did you have the package sent to our house, instead of where you're staying? Is everything okay there?"

I rubbed the bridge of my nose, squeezing my eyes shut. "Because I'm an idiot, apparently," I muttered. Letting my hand drop, I met his gaze and held it. "Yes, everything's fine. But I do appreciate you asking. And I promise that if it was anything like what you're worried about, I'd tell you. But right now, I have to go. I'll be as quick as I can."

After giving the kitchen a heads up, I jogged out to where my car was parked, feeling equal parts foolish and worried. It was raining—a steady shower that was too heavy for intermittent wipers, but too light for the low setting. The rubber wiper blades squeaked across the windshield, grating on my already overstretched nerves.

At least the traffic was relatively sparse, with a couple of hours left before rush hour hit.

The familiar drive felt oddly jarring. This route had worn tracks in my mind over the years, gradually becoming second nature. Yet, I hadn't driven it since moving in with Luca and the alphas. Normally, it took no conscious thought, my body making the turns on autopilot. This time, I kept getting jolted back to reality with every familiar landmark.

I told myself I was being ridiculous. The package would be safely under the cover of the porch, waiting for me. I'd grab it and go back to the restaurant with all my worries soothed. Any juvenile delinquents with nothing better to do than steal people's mail would have either lost interest or given up when everything started going to the post office box instead.

I set my turn signal and approached the little white house's driveway, just as the rain turned from a steady shower to a downpour. Through the sheets of water sliding over the windshield, I could just make out several chunks of torn and soaked cardboard on the cracked concrete. My tires crunched over broken glass as I pulled in, and my heart leapt into my throat.

No.

I set the car in park, not bothering to turn off the engine as I opened the door and was immediately pelted by huge, cold drops of rain. More glass crunched beneath my shoes. Two flower vases had been hurled against the pavement, a few large shards sitting near the wall of the house, while the smaller pieces of broken glass had washed halfway down the driveway beneath the force of the rain. Lengths of discarded bubble wrap lay forlornly nearby.

I hurried up to the area next to the front porch, water dripping from my eyelashes. My clothing was completely soaked through after only a few seconds.

The large box had been ripped into several pieces. Hoping against hope, I scoured the driveway for anything in a small plastic bag that might have somehow escaped notice. Only when I expanded my search to the grassy front yard did I finally find what I was looking for.

Two empty plastic Ziploc baggies floated at the edge of the expanding puddle of rainwater that always collected over the slight depression in the yard where our water meter sat. The water was cloudy white, and a couple of dozen tiny lumps sat at one edge of the muddy pool.

Pills, or rather the half-melted remains of them—dissolving away to nothing as I watched.

In a daze, I picked up a little square of heavy paper that lay nearby. Its bright colors had run, but the cheerful message printed in black was still legible.

"You Matter!" it said. *"Have a Wonderful, Flower-Fresh Day!"*

I sat in my car, still in the driveway, with the defroster making no inroads on the condensation obscuring the windows as my soaked clothing steamed its moisture into the air.

Feeling as though I was moving in slow motion, I rummaged in my bag for my phone and pulled it out. As quickly as I could, I navigated to one of the emails from the seller and clicked the link, opening it in a browser.

Maybe there was an option for overnight or two-day shipping that I hadn't seen the first time. I could get it delivered directly to the house in Ladue this time—

Out of stock.

The rectangular notice half-covered the photo of a flower vase, bold and unavoidable. Desperately, I scrolled through the rest of the seller's items, but there was nothing else that came with flower food tablets… nothing that could remotely be used to hide contraband pills.

I let the phone fall to my lap and covered my face, breathing deeply. I had two weeks until my heat. That would probably be enough time to find a different source and get it shipped to me. It wouldn't be in time for Luca, though. His heat was in a week, so he'd need the blocker within the next few days.

I desperately didn't want to have to tell him what had happened… but I needed to. Reluctantly, I lifted the phone again and pulled up a text window. My fingers felt like lead as I typed.

Luca, I am SO SORRY. The package was destroyed. The flower food tablets are gone. Seriously, I am SO SORRY about this.

I hit send, feeling like I was stabbing myself in the stomach with a rusty knife. Long moments passed before a series of dots started marching across the screen. It stopped, then started, then stopped again.

I rolled my lower lip between my teeth, feeling like the worst friend who had ever friended. Finally, a new text bubble popped up.

OK. Thx for letting me know.

My stomach cramped and turned over. I resisted the urge to text back with something inane and useless — more 'sorries,' or 'maybe there's still time'. I'd have to talk to him when I got home. Right now, I had a kitchen to run.

Because there wasn't another choice, I waited until the defroster won the battle against the vapor clinging to the car windows and drove carefully back to the restaurant in the pouring rain.

Waving away the various expressions of concern, I put on a clean chef's coat over my wet clothing and tied on an apron. Then I spent the next several hours working hard to keep my shit together, focusing on getting excellent food out to hungry customers in a timely and efficient manner.

After service was finished, Nat succeeded in cornering me.

"Careful, there's broken glass in the driveway at the house," I told him flatly. "Do me a favor and see if the camera caught anything this afternoon."

And then, I walked out.

It was stupid. Finding out who'd been playing porch pirate wouldn't help Luca, and

I'd have to be an idiot to press charges over a package that had contained contraband drugs.

Assuming there was even a way to identify the vandals.

The rain had stopped. The air held that chilly, late-night humidity peculiar to the aftermath of heavy downpours. Flashes of distant lightning illuminated the remnants of the storm along the eastern horizon, now dumping its contents somewhere over Illinois.

I drove back to Ladue, dreading having to talk to Luca face to face.

FORTY-TWO

Mia

THE HOUSE WAS quiet and largely dark when I got there, only a light in the attic bedroom and the light in the front hall—that Luca and the others always left on for me—illuminating the windows.

I went inside and turned off the porch light, locking up after myself. My hair and skin still felt clammy, even hours after getting soaked in the downpour. All I wanted was a hot shower, preferably followed by waking up to discover that this afternoon had been a bad dream.

Reluctantly, I put my work bag away and tiptoed up the stairs to the second floor, using my phone's flashlight. Everything was dark and quiet, the bedroom doors all closed and no sound of anyone stirring. I wavered, wanting to take the excuse to slink back to my borrowed bedroom and hide away until the others left in the morning. Knowing that if I did, I'd hate myself for it later.

I stopped in front of the door to Luca's nest, chewing on my lower lip. My light, tapping knock was probably quiet enough not to wake a sleeper. "Luca?" I whispered.

There was no response. Was it plausible that he'd be able to sleep after the news I'd texted him this afternoon? Some people reacted to stress with insomnia. Other people used sleep as a way to hide from whatever was going on. Luca demonstrated insomniac tendencies at the best of times, but that didn't mean he didn't flip the other direction when he got bad news.

I tapped on the door again. "Luca, it's me. I know we need to talk, but… I guess it can wait until morning?"

No reply. No sound of movement from inside.

I lowered my hand and stood there for a few more moments before giving up and back-tracking toward the stairs. I was halfway to the main floor when I realized that I'd seen no sign of Princess in the house.

That was weird.

She could have been hiding somewhere. Becoming a housecat must have been a big change for her after living on the streets her whole life. But I needed a distraction from beating myself up, and I really *did* want to make sure she'd arrived here safely.

Rather than head directly to my room, I kept going down the stairs to the basement. I hadn't been down here much at all—only to stash a handful of moving boxes that wouldn't fit in the guest bedroom. It was a huge space, partly finished near the stairs. By contrast, the back half was unfinished concrete with pipes and conduits running along the walls.

Emiel had decided to keep Princess's litter box, food and water bowls down here, where they'd be out of everyone's way. I felt around for the light switch at the bottom of the stairs and turned it on, blinking in the sudden illumination.

The litter box was laid out near the water heater, but the food and water bowls sat empty. Apparently, there'd been a change of plan—I really hoped everything was okay.

Feeling even more misgivings than before, I returned to the stairs and turned off the light switch before heading up.

When I got to the main floor landing, the prospect of going back to my own room and facing a night alone felt almost unbearable. Without consciously making the decision to move, I found my feet carrying me up instead of down, heading toward the attic bedroom and the light I'd seen through Emiel's window when I'd come home.

It was an unwritten rule that no one bothered Emiel in his room. I was about to trample all over that rule, because I was stressed out and guilty and worried about Princess. Had our lunch and shopping trip only been yesterday? At the time, it had felt like Emiel and I were gaining a rapport. I guess we were going to put that fragile emotional connection to the test.

I'd never been up here before. It turned out, there was no door, which made this feel like even more of an invasion of privacy. I hesitated before my head popped into the line of sight of the bedroom, my work sneakers giving a telltale squeak on the stair tread.

"Go away," came Emiel's voice, in that flat, dead tone I was coming to hate.

I licked my lips, summoning my courage. "Emiel? It's Mia. I'm worried about Princess. What happened?"

Silence fell for a couple of seconds, then Emiel appeared at the top of the staircase. He was wearing loose gray track pants and an old T-shirt that stretched across his broad chest. None of it did a damn thing to hide his mountains of muscle and overpowering maleness. The faintest shadow of stubble was visible across his shaved head.

I swallowed convulsively, cursing my oncoming heat for the hundredth time in the past few days.

"She didn't show up for her food today," he said.

"Can I come up?" I asked.

Another hesitation.

"Okay."

It wasn't exactly a warm welcome, but I mounted the last few stairs and stepped into the attic bedroom. The place was spartan. There was a desk and a chair in one corner, with a sleeping area taking up about a third of the space across from it. I didn't see any photos or artwork... nothing to put a personal stamp on the room.

Rather than intrude any further into Emiel's territory, I leaned against the sturdy stair railing. "Has she ever gone AWOL before?" I asked hesitantly.

Emiel went back to his bed and sat heavily on the edge of the mattress. "Sometimes," he said. "She's feral. She goes where she wants. Guess she didn't want to come to the alley today."

It sounded perfectly reasonable. Cats were notorious for not doing what you wanted them to do. I still didn't like the flatness that had crept into Emiel's expression since yesterday, though. It reminded me too much of how he'd looked during the cage fight.

"Guess you can bring her home tomorrow, then," I told him, trying to keep my voice light. "There's probably a joke in there somewhere about herding cats."

It sounded hollow to my own ears. It must have sounded hollow to Emiel's, too... or else my scent was giving me away. He frowned.

"Something's wrong. You didn't go back to the Bella Vita, did you?"

I shook my head. "No. Definitely not." Drawing breath, I started to speak and paused, suddenly unsure. This was Luca's private business, but it was also *my* business. Plus, there was a slight chance that Emiel might have a line on some heat blockers locally that Luca didn't know about. He used pheromone suppressors, after all.

"This is a bit awkward," I began. "But there's a shortage of heat blockers right now. I tried to get some shipped in from a seller in Vermont, but someone's been vandalizing the mail at our house in Jennings. When I went there to pick up the package, it had already been destroyed."

Emiel's frown deepened. "Luca's due next week."

"I know," I said. "I'm due the week after. Anyway, I feel terrible about it, because Luca was depending on me to get the pills. I wanted to talk to him tonight, but he's already asleep."

At the mention of my upcoming heat, Emiel's already closed-off body language grew even more closed off. I rushed onward into the verbal abyss, wondering if coming up here had been a mistake after all.

"I might be able to find another mail order source in time for my heat." The words came out in a tumble. "But Luca needs his blocker within days. I don't suppose... you know anyone in the area that might have a supply?"

Emiel's frown smoothed into that vacant mask I hated so much. "Ask Zalen in the morning," he said in a monotone. "You should probably go back downstairs now."

Disquiet churned in my stomach, even though asking Zalen for help sounded like good advice. I wasn't sure what I'd done to shut Emiel down so abruptly, but I didn't get the sense that pressing the issue would be a good idea.

"Okay," I said, trying not to feel hurt by the rejection. *Hormones. It's just the hormones messing with my emotions.* "I'm sorry to bother you. I'll talk to Luca and Zalen in the morning. I look forward to seeing Princess here tomorrow night."

Emiel gave a single, tight nod. I started down the stairs, leaving him to it.

***

When my phone alarm went off at stupid o'clock the next morning, I groaned and buried my face in the messy pile of pillows at the head of the bed.

As my brain came reluctantly online, the events of the previous day paraded across my memory like a particularly unwelcome marching band.

"Ugh," I said into the pillows, and dragged myself off the bed to catch the others before they left for work.

Pulling on a pair of yoga pants beneath my sleep shirt, I scraped my hair back into a messy ponytail and stumbled into the hallway. Low voices were coming from the kitchen.

"*I don't want this heat.*" Luca's voice was a growl.

I paused awkwardly a few steps from the doorway, listening.

"*I'm sorry, Luca.*" Zalen's tone, by contrast, was reasonableness personified. "*I know you told me you had it covered. But I saw a news story about the federal seizure of the blocker shipment. I asked around, just in case your usual source fell through. There's nothing available locally that I've been able to find. I can ask again. Maybe someone in the area got a line on a new supply in the past few days—*"

Steeling myself, I walked into the kitchen. Luca was perched on one of the bar stools with the air of a wild animal treed by hunting dogs, while Zalen stood on the other side of the breakfast bar.

"Hi," I said, clearing my throat when my voice cracked. "Luca, I feel awful about this whole thing…"

"I told you that you should have had them delivered here!" he snapped, and it was the first time I could remember him ever raising his voice to me.

The scent of aniseed and fennel tickled my senses. "Who should have had what delivered where?" Byron asked, strolling in.

Even at this hour, he had that alluring combination of being perfectly put together, while still somehow giving the impression of having been up to no good the previous night. It was an illusion, I was pretty sure. As far as I knew, he'd already been fast asleep in his room when I got in after work.

"There's a shortage of heat blockers," Zalen said. "Mia and Luca had some shipped, but the package was destroyed."

"The gangs might still be sitting on some," Luca said, desperation creeping into the words. "I could talk to—"

Byron stiffened. "*No, you fucking will not.*"

I gasped as the alpha bark slapped across us, freezing both of us in place. Luca let out an involuntary whimper, then shook it off and shot to his feet with an honest-to-god *snarl*, looking even more like a trapped animal than he had before.

Zalen looked back and forth between the three of us, rubbing at his temples with a sigh.

FORTY-THREE

Luca

"BYRON," ZALEN SAID, very purposely not using his own alpha bark. "Stow it."

Peripherally, I recognized that Byron looked faintly sheepish, but it was difficult to focus on that past the red haze of fury clouding my vision.

"Fuck you," I choked, aware on some level that I was having a full-blown meltdown in the middle of the damned kitchen, at six-thirty a.m. on a Wednesday. *"Go to hell,* Byron! You do *not* get to bark at me like I'm your pet fuck toy!"

The others were looking at me like I was a dangerous wild animal. The helpless feeling crawled higher up my throat, lodging there like a lump of lead.

"You are not going back to the gangs for this," Byron said, stowing the bark as Zalen had commanded, but not the sentiment behind it. "You're not *stupid,* Luca! Use your brain for just a damned minute—"

Zalen closed a hand around Byron's bicep. It wasn't a gentle gesture—I could see his fingers digging in. I hated the way my breathing was giving me away… frantic, shallow panting that made me feel dizzy and lightheaded. My hands started to shake.

"Luca," Zalen said. "There's absolutely no way to guarantee that anything you get from a gang source is going to be legit—or that it's been stored properly, even if it's the right hormones. I don't claim to understand what you go through when it comes to your heat cycles—"

"That's right! You don't!" I snapped, hating myself more with every second that ticked by.

"—but you were probably going to have the next one naturally, right?" Zalen continued, as though I hadn't spoken. "It's been almost a year."

"That's not the point!" I said. "I wasn't going to have *this* one!"

Byron jerked his arm free of Zalen's restraining grip. Zalen let him go.

"Yeah… I think you'll find that in the absence of heat blockers, you *are* going to have this one," Byron said.

If there'd been even the faintest trace of smugness in his tone, I might have taken a swing at him. Appalled by the impulse, I backed up until my hip knocked into the edge of the breakfast bar.

Through all of this, Mia had stood hunched in the corner of the kitchen like she was afraid if she drew attention to herself, she might come under verbal attack. My fault, of course. I pressed the heels of my hands into my eye sockets, trying to stuff the emerging headache back inside my throbbing skull.

God. Why hadn't she just had the damned blockers sent *here*?

"I'll check with my contacts again," Zalen was saying. "But, Luca, from what I was able to find out the first time, there simply aren't any blockers available in the area. If I can't source any in time, it's completely your choice whether you want to use us or lock yourself in your room and tough it out. Or hire a rent-a-pack, for that matter."

A hint of strain entered his voice on the last few words. Next to him, Byron gave a low, warning growl.

"I can't have this conversation right now," I managed, shoving away from the marble countertop—intent on escape.

"If you need to take a wellness day from work today—" Zalen began.

I cut him off. "No, I don't need a fucking wellness day, Zalen!"

I needed a damned blocker pill.

Trying not to look at Mia's pale, unhappy face as I passed her, I fled the kitchen, my juice and bagel forgotten. It wasn't like I'd be able to keep down food right now, anyway.

***

Sheer stubbornness propelled me through a morning of grant work—even though my head was pounding, and my eyeballs felt like someone was trying to inflate them with an air compressor.

That same stubbornness was at play when it came to ignoring Mia's tentative texts. I knew, on some level, that none of this was her fault. I hadn't even given her a chance to explain the details of what had happened to the package. It was moot, wasn't it? The pills were gone. Learning the reason why wouldn't magically bring them back.

Besides, she was in roughly the same boat as me now. Granted, she had a bit more time to try and find another source, but if Zalen was right, there might not *be* another source.

Would she go back to her asshole of a husband for her unexpected heat? Would they have to close the restaurant while the two of them were locked in their bedroom, banging non-stop?

Or would she ask Byron or Zalen to help her instead, whispered a niggling little voice in my head. I prodded at the thought like a broken tooth, trying to figure out what kind of feelings I had about it.

With a frustrated grunt, I pushed away from the desk and stood up to pace. My stomach was cramping and rumbling after skipping breakfast. It was past eleven, so I put my laptop to sleep and reluctantly ventured out of the safety of my office.

The kids didn't usually come up here, thank goodness. A couple of the older teens had already started throwing me speculative glances. My deepening scent might as well have been a flashing neon sign where alphas were concerned — even clueless alpha pups who had no idea what to do with their own knots yet.

Maybe Emiel was onto something with his pheromone suppressors.

For about the ten thousandth time in my life, I wished that I'd been born a beta so I wouldn't have to deal with *any* of this shit. How different would my life have been without all of the omega crap?

Shaking my head at myself, I braved the upstairs break room and randomly chose something from the vending machine. There was probably some irony around the concept of living with a Michelin-star chef and eating Funyuns as my first meal of the day. I grabbed a red Gatorade and headed toward the back stairs, needing to get out of the building for a bit.

The alley behind the Hope Project was the opposite of *fresh air*, but it wasn't like I was going to go hang out by the basketball hoops with the kids, or pop down to the cafeteria room. I opened the door and was immediately assaulted by the familiar stench of piss and garbage.

The olfactory landscape of my early life. Just like old times.

Emiel looked up sharply from his seat on a cleanish section of the concrete steps. I hesitated, fighting the scared-rabbit part of me that urged me to turn right back around and go inside.

Jesus, I hated that part of me.

Instead, I stepped fully outside and let the door close behind me. Glancing around, I took in the untouched bowl of cat food and the bowl of clean water sitting at the base of the stairs.

Pulling my head far enough out of my ass to focus on someone else's problems was harder than I liked to admit... but I'd been excited about Princess coming to live with us. Not as excited as Emiel had been, maybe. Even so, her continued absence from her usual haunting grounds was enough to pull my attention away from my own issues.

"Hi," I said. "Still no sign of her? Has she ever missed two days of feeding in a row before?"

"Couple of times," Emiel muttered. "Not for a while, though."

My brain whispered, *she's gone forever*, but I at least had the presence of mind not to say it aloud. "Maybe tomorrow, then." I frowned at the untouched cat food... the silence of the alley. "Surprised you don't have any other takers, though."

"There's been fewer cats around here lately," Emiel said. "Should've taken her home sooner."

The last part sounded like it was directed at himself, not me. It would have been hard to argue against the sentiment convincingly—I'd been one of the people arguing for him to do exactly that. So, I kept my mouth shut.

After a few moments, he angled a glance in my direction. "Heard you and the others barkin' at each other in the kitchen this morning."

I looked away, unable to meet his gaze.

"You're having a heat next week, I guess?" he asked.

I shrugged a shoulder, still not looking at him. "Not by choice." There was no mistaking the bitterness in my tone.

"You were gonna have to do the next one anyway," he said, a bit stiffly. "Does it matter so much if it's this one instead?"

"It matters to *me*." I fought to keep the words unemotional—hard enough at the best of times, when discussing this subject. Even harder now. "I should get to choose."

"Don't always have a choice about that kind of shit, do we?" Emiel asked, his voice tight. "At least you've got alphas who'll treat you right. Could be worse."

I was aware that he was trying to help, in his own slightly fucked-up way. I was also aware that Emiel would much rather get repeatedly kicked in the face inside a chain-link fighting cage than deal with anything related to omega heats.

Sometimes—like now, for instance—I wondered what had happened to put him off the subject so thoroughly. He was an alpha. What the hell did *he* have to be upset about when it came to estrous cycles?

I licked my lips, braving a sidelong glance at him. His shoulders were a tense line; his attention focused firmly on the cat food bowl. As we watched, a rat peeked out from behind the nearby trash cans, clearly assessing its chances of getting to the kibbles without getting caught.

"I know it could be worse," I said carefully, forcing myself to rise above my own trauma response for a moment. Moving to the far end of the steps from him, I sat down on a reasonably clean looking spot and tore open my plastic bag of Funyuns. "I just get so... *angry* about all of it sometimes."

"Yeah. I know," Emiel agreed, and I was pretty sure we weren't talking about *me* anymore.

FORTY-FOUR

Mia

I DIDN'T MANAGE to successfully corner Luca until Saturday morning. I'd spent the last three days very carefully not freaking out about the way he'd withdrawn from me, because, in the end, neither of us were twelve years old.

Sometimes omega instincts made it hard to remember in the moment, but I was a grown-ass adult, and I did, in fact, understand that people around me could be upset about something without it meaning they were angry with me personally.

Luca was upset, and who could blame him? Hell, *I* was upset. It wasn't as though I could waltz into Nat's office and say, "Oh, by the way, I completely fucked up acquiring my heat blockers this quarter, so I guess we'll have to close the restaurant for the better part of a week, sorry."

The only difference was that I had an extra week to figure something out, and Luca didn't. I'd been scouring the shadowy corners of the internet in every free moment, trying to reacquaint myself with the places where people discussed the black market for omega hormones in veiled terms.

So far, I'd gathered that the new trend was to smuggle heat blockers under the auspices of selling 'appetite suppressants,' which was either bitterly ironic or someone's idea of dark humor. I'd also learned that anyone needing blockers fast was going to have to look beyond the U.S. The short shelf-life of the pills outside of specialized medical storage meant it had taken little more than a week for the existing inventory stateside to disappear.

I'd spent a couple of hours late last night arguing with myself about the wisdom of using a scammy-looking website based in Mexico, which claimed to have the 'appetite suppression pills' everyone was looking for. For one thing, the price was eye-watering even before adding cross-border shipping. For another, the pills could be fentanyl laced with rat poison for all I knew.

I was leaning toward taking my chances and relying on my nose to decide if the pill smelled the same as I was used to. But my pocketbook was already limping around on metaphorical crutches and covered in bandages. It really didn't need to take another hit.

Luca was alone in the kitchen when I stumbled in for coffee after another night of poor sleep. I paused in the doorway, not entirely sure I was welcome in his space.

He looked up with bloodshot eyes.

"Zalen still hasn't been able to find any pills," he said, by way of greeting. "But he scored two syringes of birth control. They're in the fridge. *Just in case.*" Bitterness laced the final words.

I swallowed a useless *'I'm so sorry'* before it could escape. Luca already knew I was sorry. After my fourth apologetic text on Wednesday, I'd received a terse, *'I'm not angry at you... I'm just angry'* in return. He'd been avoiding me since then, it was true—but I had no reason to think he'd been lying.

So, instead of babbling out another unnecessary apology, I came over and rested my elbows on the edge of the breakfast bar, standing across from him.

"I'm paying a Mexican website for something that may or may not show up at all, and may or may not be a heat blocker if it does," I said. "If I end up tripping balls and jumping off the roof because I think I can fly, please engrave the words 'Here lies Mia Dimitriadis; she may have been a Michelin chef, but she was also dumb as a post' on my tombstone."

"That's a pretty long epitaph. Sounds expensive," Luca said.

"So's the pill," I told him, and earned a wan half-smile for a second before it faded.

Taking that for the victory it was, I sobered as well.

"Luca, please tell me you're going to stay here where it's safe. Let the alphas rock your world for a few days, instead of doing anything dangerous," I begged, hoping that he was finally in a place to hear it.

Luca's already pale face was even paler than usual this morning—his porcelain skin almost translucent except for the blue-gray smudges underlining his green eyes.

"I'm not actually an idiot, Mia," he said, without much heat behind the words. "No one around here has any blockers, including the gangs. And I'm not stupid enough to lock myself alone in my room for several days of agonizing cramps and mental torture."

I let out a slow breath of relief. "Okay. I still feel awful that this happened, but I'm really glad you're going to let the others help."

He didn't reply directly, but he didn't look away either. "What about you?"

The question was pointed, and I didn't like the squirming sensation of discomfort it raised in my stomach. I hesitated, chewing the inside of my cheek.

"I'm… not sure yet," I said. "Hopefully the Mexican drug cartels will end up doing me a solid."

"And if they don't? Will you go back to Nat?" Luca asked, not letting it go.

It was a reasonable question… probably. But I couldn't go crawling back to the husband who'd deep-sixed our marriage at least partly over my lack of natural heats.

"No." My voice cracked on the word, and I cleared my throat.

Luca didn't give an opinion… didn't grill me about my intentions toward his alphas a scant few days after they'd be leaving his heat nest. He only nodded, lifting his glass of juice in salute. "To the Mexican drug lords," he said, like someone proposing a toast.

"Here, here," I replied, with feeling.

On top of the heat-blocker debacle, there was also the Princess debacle — as though we needed more incredibly depressing crap in our lives to further bring us down.

I blamed my compulsive need to focus on something else besides the money I'd just thrown into a Spanish-speaking black hole. That was my excuse for spending almost two hours after work on Saturday night scouring adoption and found pet websites for young, gray female cats.

St. Clair County, where East St. Louis was located, wasn't exactly a beacon of modern infrastructure and governance. From what I could tell, they had an animal control division, but none of the website links on the page worked properly. Worse, a Google search for the stated name of the animal adoption arm of the department only brought up a couple of social media accounts that hadn't been active in almost six years.

Even so, I made up a document with links to all the gray cats listed on every private rescue site I could find in the Gateway metro area. When I made my way to the kitchen on Sunday morning, headachy and sleep-deprived, Emiel was there eating a bowl of cereal.

He looked up warily at my entrance.

"I couldn't sleep last night, so I went looking for Princess on local animal rescue sites," I said, in lieu of a 'good morning.' "I thought because she's so friendly, maybe someone picked her up. I made a list of gray cats that fit her description if you want to look at it later?"

Emiel's brows drew together. Apparently, I'd surprised him. Then his expression smoothed back into its blank mask.

"The private rescues only take pets, not feral cats," he said. "I've been checking the website for the adoption center that partners with county animal control every day. She ain't there."

My heart sank. "I'll give you the list I made anyway," I told him. "You can at least check; make sure none of them are her."

He shrugged listless agreement, his dark eyes already going distant and dead again.

"Did you call the adoption center and talk to someone directly?" I asked, following a hunch.

"No," he said.

Right. Of course he hadn't. The idea of calling and asking someone who worked there for help probably hadn't even occurred to him.

"We need to do that," I said. "In fact, we should do that right now."

"It's Sunday," he pointed out. "They're closed."

"Crap." I thought for a second. "What's the place called? I'll send an email. We'll phone them and follow up first thing in the morning."

Again, he shrugged—humoring me, but clearly without any hope that it would yield results. I got the impression that he didn't place much faith in random people being helpful for the sake of it. Or in happy endings, for that matter.

"First thing in the morning," I repeated sternly, and went to make toast.

<hr>

Work was thankfully uneventful, and one of the busier Sundays we'd had recently. There was no reply to my email when I got home, but I hadn't really expected there to be.

I slept poorly again, trying very hard not to think about the blissful nights I'd spent curled up with Luca... or with Luca and Byron together. My heart might have felt like those nights were the start of something, but my brain had understood that it was stolen time. And no one in the house was in a frame of mind for that kind of thing at the moment.

When I dragged my sorry carcass into the kitchen a few minutes before nine a.m., Zalen and Emiel were both already there. The smell of high-end coffee greeted me.

"Hi," I said blearily. "Let me get caffeine, and I'll call the adoption place as soon as they open."

Zalen tilted his head. "What adoption place?"

I jerked my chin in Emiel's direction. "It's the rescue that does all the adoptions for the county animal shelter. I thought maybe someone there might know about Princess, in case she was picked up and taken to the pound."

Zalen's expression morphed into understanding. "That makes sense. Good idea. Em—isn't that where you donate all the fight winnings I'm not supposed to know about?"

And… say *what*, now?

"Yeah," Emiel said.

I stared at him. "And you didn't think to call and talk to them in person?"

He blinked at me, bewildered. "She's not listed on the website."

Shaking myself free of my own bewilderment, I glanced at the clock. Nine-oh-one.

"Okay, then." I pulled out my phone and dialed the number I'd entered last night. "Hello? Yes, I can hold."

I ended up holding for quite a while before a harried woman picked up. I quickly put the phone on speaker so the others would be able to hear.

"Gateway East Animal Adoptions," she said. *"How can I help you?"*

I glanced at Emiel. "Hi. I'm looking for information about a small gray female cat that might have been picked up by animal control."

"Have you filed a lost pet report?" the woman asked.

"She's feral," I explained, not sure how much information would be too much information. "A friend of mine has been taming her. He was planning on bringing her home as a pet when she suddenly disappeared."

There was a short pause. *"I'm sorry. We don't generally deal with feral animals. Your friend should try putting food out for the cat—"*

"I understand he's a rather large donor to your organization," I said, interrupting her. "My friend, I mean."

Silence. It stretched for a couple of seconds. *"Hold, please."*

I waited, crossing my fingers.

A new female voice picked up—younger than the previous one.

"Hello. My name is Mandy. I'm the organization's liaison with St. Clair Animal Services. I hear you're looking for a feral cat that might have been picked up? Could you describe the animal, please? And also, the area where she was last seen."

I relayed the information a second time, reading off the address of the Hope Project that Zalen jotted down on a notepad for me.

"A gray female? No markings?" asked the woman.

"That's right," I said, fighting the urge to hold my breath.

"Okay. Please understand that I can't promise anything... but we did have a cat of that description come in last week. A gentleman has been trapping feral cats in that area recently, but he's refused to join the TNR program."

"TNR?" I asked, confused.

"Trap-neuter-release," said the woman. *"It's the preferred method for dealing with feral cat colonies. It's not mandatory in the city or county, though. And this person indicated that he wants the cats gone from the neighborhood permanently."*

I set that information aside, focusing on the important part. "But you have Princess there? The, uh, the gray female?"

I could feel Zalen and Emiel burning holes in me with their intent gazes.

"No," the woman said with evident regret. *"I'm so sorry. She was here for a couple of days, but I'm afraid she's no longer being held at this facility."*

FORTY-FIVE

Mia

"WHAT?" MY HEART sank. "You had Princess, but she's gone? Was she adopted?" The idea of some stranger taking Princess was better than thinking that she was just gone forever, but it was still a huge blow. I didn't think Emiel was even breathing.

"*No.*" Mandy-the-shelter-liaison sounded regretful, and I braced for more bad news. "*As I'm sure Louisa told you, we don't generally accept feral animals here. One of the volunteers at animal services made a special request, because the gray cat was young and looked as though someone had been taking care of her. He said she was having trouble adjusting to conditions at the center, but he thought she might calm down in a different environment.*"

"Someone *has* been taking care of her!" I said, unable to keep my voice from rising. "My friend, while he was taming her!"

"*Yes,*" Mandy said, maintaining her calm. "*I can see this is an unfortunate situation all around, but we had no way of knowing the circumstances. I agreed to have the cat transferred here in hopes that she would be adoptable. However, I'm afraid she became increasingly aggressive toward the staff. There were multiple biting incidents.*"

Sudden doubt assailed me. "Princess wouldn't do that," I said uncertainly. Maybe this wasn't the right cat?

"Yes, she would," Emiel said. He looked queasy... afraid in a way that he hadn't looked when confronted with an underground fighting ring, or even a group of aggressive alpha gang members.

My shoulders slumped. "Okay, sorry. My friend says she might behave aggressively. Does that mean you sent her back to the pound?"

"*We returned her to St. Clair Animal Services, yes.*" Mandy paused before continuing. "*Look... I won't lie to you. The county shelter is over capacity, and it has been for as long as I've held this job. We remanded her on Friday, late enough in the day that it's likely they kept her over the weekend. However, it's less likely that she'll still be there later today, if you take my meaning.*"

I looked up at Emiel, desperation tightening my throat. "If you tell us where to go, we can leave right now."

"*All right,*" Mandy said, as though making a decision. "*The situation isn't as straightforward as it might sound, simply because the county doesn't do animal adoptions directly. But once I get off the phone with you, I'm going to call the director and see if I can put a hold on... Princess, you said?*"

"Yes, that's her name," I replied, a glimmer of hope warring with the desperation.

"*Get to the shelter as quickly as you can without breaking any traffic laws. It's not technically open to the public without an appointment — but tell them you're meeting Dr. Mandy Kadakia about an emergency adoption. I'll bring all the necessary paperwork to transfer her back to Gateway East, so we can process the adoption on our end."*

Emiel was already on his feet.

"Thank you," I said, the words heartfelt. "What's the address? We'll leave immediately."

I wrote it down, gave her our full names in return, and disconnected the call.

Zalen looked between us. "Go. Take the day off, Emiel. We've got things covered at the Hope Project."

Emiel nodded. "I'll drive. C'mon."

I spared a half-second's thought for my ratty T-shirt, yoga pants, and sleep-tousled hair before mentally saying *fuck it*. Emiel, like Zalen, was dressed professionally—Zalen had mentioned on Friday that they had some kind of investor meeting at ten a.m. today. Emiel would have to be respectable enough for both of us.

"Let me grab some shoes and my bag," I said. "They may want to see I.D."

As I was jogging back to join him, I briefly considered offering to drive, on the assumption that he was almost certainly more freaked out about the situation than I was. Then I remembered his absolute control behind the wheel of Luca's Nissan while driving us to safety with a fresh concussion and cracked ribs.

I kept my mouth shut and followed him into the six-car garage, where his battered old-school Bronco sat parked and waiting. He opened the door for me without a word, then got behind the wheel and fired up the engine.

We… *might* have broken a few traffic laws after all, not that I was complaining.

My phone's map insisted it would be a thirty-eight-minute drive. We arrived at the address in Belleville twenty-nine minutes after pulling out of the driveway in Ladue. It was a nicer area than I'd been expecting. The sprawling one-story brick building facing the street appeared modern and inviting, but I could just make out an institutional concrete addition hidden in the back.

Emiel pulled sloppily into a parking spot, and we were both out of the gray Ford in a flash. The main entrance had steel double doors, with a small but functional reception room inside. The receptionist was locked behind a thick glass window with a small slot at the bottom for passing paperwork back and forth.

I jogged up, abruptly self-conscious about looking like a sleep-deprived wreck, while my professionally dressed companion barely spoke to strangers in the normal course of things. Possibly, not stopping to change had been a tactical mistake on my part.

"Good morning," I began gamely, preparing to brazen it out.

Emiel stepped up beside me, surprising me. "We're here to meet Dr. Kadakia about an emergency adoption. Is she here yet?"

The young man gave us a polite smile. "I don't believe so. Let me ask the day supervisor if he knows about this meeting. I'll just be a moment."

My fingers gripped the edge of the counter, because his response didn't exactly inspire confidence. Especially when he was still gone five minutes later, leaving us poised at the security window with suppressed nerves.

"It'll be okay," I said, not certain if I was trying to reassure Emiel or myself.

"You don't know that," Emiel said in a low voice.

He sounded like a man who was bracing himself for the worst. I wanted so badly to reach out to him... to wrap my arms around one of his tree-trunk biceps and lean against him for comfort. I restrained the impulse, knowing that it would be a terrible intrusion for someone like him — but it was hard.

One of the front doors opened, letting in a breath of cool wind from outside. I turned to see a curvy woman in her thirties with olive skin and dark, short-cropped hair, carrying a manilla folder stuffed messily with papers under her arm.

"Dr. Kadakia?" I asked, mentally crossing my fingers.

She smiled with the air of someone who had a gazillion other things on her to-do list, but who'd deemed the current item more important than anything else. "Yes, that's right. You must be Mr. Hamilton and Ms. Dimitriadis. Let's see if we can get you reunited with your cat."

I nodded with enthusiasm, hoping that meant she'd successfully put the brakes on

Princess's appointment with the feline executioner. "Yes, let's."

The receptionist chose that moment to come back with a gray-haired, stoop-shouldered man wearing a polo and khakis in tow.

"Here we go," said the younger man. "I believe Mr. Schneider can get you sorted out."

Mr. Schneider gave us a tired smile. "Morning, folks. Morning, Mandy. I got the call from the director just in time. It's CF-83425 you're after, right?"

"Morning, Bruce." Mandy opened the manilla folder and checked a paper. "Yes, that's right. Gray female, estimated nine months of age, no markings."

The supervisor nodded. "Right, you can come on back. I've got one of the volunteers retrieving her from her cage. We'll bring her to one of the introduction rooms so you can make sure it's the right cat."

Mandy led the way through the interior door leading into the depths of the building. Back here, the surroundings were cold and impersonal, like an old high school or a county jail. The smell of animal waste and disinfectant burned my sinuses. We went through a second door, and then a third.

"This way," Mr. Schneider said, gesturing toward a room with the front wall made of glass. 'Introduction Room #1' was painted in black over the doorway.

An instant later, a shrieking yowl followed by a startled human yelp echoed from deeper in the maze of hallways.

Emiel let out a low, nearly inaudible growl. He was off like a shot before the others could so much as react. Instinct propelled me after him, even as the supervisor called, "Sir! Ma'am! Visitors aren't allowed in the—"

I slipped through the door marked 'Feline Wing' that Emiel had thrown open, ducking in before it closed behind us. Somehow, Emiel was already halfway down the hall—not running, but eating up the distance in long strides. Another angry yowl reached me, louder now, and Emiel turned right at a junction, disappearing from view.

I charged after him, rounding the corner to find a startled teenage girl backed against the wall across from a line of dozens of cages. She was wearing heavy canvas gloves, and blood welled sluggishly from four parallel scratch marks on her cheek.

"Where is she?" Emiel demanded, the hint of an alpha bark in his tone making my skin tingle.

The young volunteer gaped at him for a moment. "She got away from me. I'm sorry, but who are you?"

Mandy and the supervisor hurried into view, taking in the scene.

"Mr. Schneider!" the volunteer said sheepishly. "I'm really sorry… I was reaching into her cage. Cats *never* get away from me, but she just freaked out and went for my face, and then—"

A low hiss came from the far end of the hall, where one of the ever-present doors formed a dead end.

"There she is," the volunteer said in relief. "Hang on, I can catch her…"

Another low growl rumbled up from Emiel's chest.

"No, let us do it," I said quickly. "I know it's irregular, but would the rest of you please just stay back?"

I glanced at Mandy and Mr. Schneider with a pleading look. Mandy hesitated, then nodded.

"Let them give it a try, Bruce," she said. "That cat's scared to death."

The supervisor let out a sigh. "Yes, go ahead. But no one here breathes a word of this to the higher-ups, got it? It's more than my job's worth."

The volunteer glanced between us and started taking off her heavy gloves. "Here, you'll need these," she began.

Emiel brushed past her without a word, heading for the far end of the hallway. "We're here, Princess," he said, dropping into a crouch. The gentleness in his voice brought tears to my eyes, and I had to bite my lip hard to hold them back. "Come on, beautiful. We're going home."

A slender gray shape detached from the shadowed corner. "*Mreow?*" Princess said—a tiny, tremulous noise that made my soul ache.

"It's me." There was an unaccustomed quaver beneath Emiel's voice. "It's all right. I've got you."

Princess launched herself forward, scampering across the twenty feet or so separating them as though the hounds of Hell were chasing her. She leapt into Emiel's arms, her claws digging into the shoulder of his suit jacket as she tried to hide her little body against his.

Emiel flopped backward under the impact, sitting down hard on his ass. His back was to us, but I saw his arms lift to cradle her close. A moment later, his head dropped forward, and his shoulders began to shake with silent tears as he nuzzled against Princess's sleek gray fur.

FORTY-SIX

Emiel

PRINCESS WAS SAFE. I thought I'd doomed her by deciding to take responsibility for her. The moment I'd agreed to take her home, she'd disappeared — because life was shit and nobody could keep anybody else safe, not *ever*.

But now she was here, curled in my arms in this awful piss-and-bleach-smelling concrete shithole of suffering and death, and she *wasn't gone forever*. I knew, on some level, that I was sitting on my ass in the middle of a hallway with Mia and a bunch of strangers watching me fuckin' crying over a *cat*. But I couldn't do a goddamned thing about it.

Mia was talking quietly with the shelter supervisor and the adoption liaison about *paperwork* and *postoperative care* and *home introduction*. And I was still sitting here with my face buried in Princess's fur, getting cat hair stuck to my wet cheeks.

She wasn't trying to squirm away, but she wasn't purring, either. Just rubbing her face over and over against my shoulder, making a soft little mewling noise every once in a while.

I knew by the scent of summer flowers that Mia was walking toward us. God, I really needed to get on pheromone dampeners, like, *yesterday*. Between her and Luca coming into heat soon, I was losing my damned mind. I braced in case she was gonna put her hand on my shoulder or something, but she just skirted around us and crouched in front of me.

"Hey." Her smile was watery. Probably not as watery as my face was.

"You saved her," I said hoarsely, because that was the least stupid thing I could think of to say.

"*We* saved her," she corrected. "Not sure this would have gone so well if you weren't helping pay the adoption center's bills with your donations. Anyway, they say she's been spayed already, when she went to the Gateway East facility last week. The vet used dissolving sutures, so she won't have to go back to have them removed."

"Okay," I said, trying to take in any details beyond *she's here, she's safe*.

"She'll need to go in for additional vaccinations and boosters," Mia continued, "and right now we need to go sign a bunch of stuff."

"I left the cat carrier at the Hope Project," I said stupidly.

She rolled her lower lip between her teeth, and my gut lurched with something hot and unwanted. "Yeah, I didn't even think about that when we were rushing over here. We'll figure something out, I'm sure. Are you two ready to get up? They said we can do the paperwork in that glass introduction room, so Princess can stay close by."

I wasn't ready, but I also didn't want to be stuck in this concrete box full of unhappy animals any longer. I lurched to my feet, cradling Princess against my chest. Nodding my willingness to go, I let Mia lead the way, heading back in the direction we'd come from when I'd first heard the yowling.

The next forty-five minutes was a blur, but eventually, we walked out of the front door, with me carrying Princess in a cat carrier borrowed from Dr. Kadakia. As soon as we reached the Bronco, Mia stopped and held out her hand to me, palm up.

"Keys," she said. "I'm driving, no arguments."

I didn't usually let other people drive my truck. But if I drove, Princess would have to be alone in her carrier, not knowing what was happening or where we were going. I dug out the keys and dropped them in her palm.

Riding in my own passenger seat was weird, and not all that comfortable with the carrier jammed crosswise on my lap. Mia drove extra-cautiously, I guess because she was used to a little tiny car. But she only fumbled the clutch once, while reversing out of the parking spot. After that, she shifted gears like she knew what she was doing.

"Do you need to stop at the Hope Project and pick anything up for her?" she asked, once we were on the highway out of Belleville.

I shook my head. "I'll get the carrier tomorrow and take this one back to the adoption place during lunch. Maybe give 'em some more money while I'm at it."

The soft smile she angled toward me made me feel uncomfortable. I stuck my fingers through the ventilation holes in the carrier. A soft cheek rubbed against my fingertips, and a moment later, Princess started gnawing gently on my ring finger — her sharp teeth not breaking the skin.

"Home it is, in that case," Mia said. She seemed to catch herself, shooting me a sidelong glance. I wondered when she'd started thinking of Zalen's house as 'home.' I kept quiet, though; playing with Princess through the carrier's air holes… trying to keep her distracted.

When I finally trudged down the basement stairs with my new cat and let her out of the carrier, it still didn't feel real. Fairytale endings were just that. Fairytales. But Princess was here, and she was mine now.

Mia had waved me off when we came inside the house, saying she'd just make Princess more nervous, and they could get to know each other after she'd settled in. Then she'd gone off to make sandwiches.

I sat alone on the bottom step, watching Princess explore the food and water bowls before giving the litter box a skeptical sniff. The feeling behind my ribs wasn't exactly good or exactly bad. Mostly, it was just *big*.

Contrary to what other people probably thought, I wasn't stupid. I knew this tight, too-big feeling was tied up with my own psychological shit. It was why I'd dragged my heels for so long about bringing Princess home in the first place.

Dragged them for *too* long, almost.

I'd been... really young when I learned that no one was coming to save you from the monsters. Like, *really* young. People who had more power did whatever the fuck they wanted to people with less power. People who were stronger did whatever they wanted to people — or animals — that were weaker.

Society had all these rules about what was allowed and what wasn't... what you could do to someone else's body without their permission and what you couldn't. Yet, in dark corners all across the world, people ignored those rules day in and day out. Mostly without ever facing any consequences.

I'd promised myself that I'd become big enough and strong enough and mean enough that no one would ever think they could hurt me again. But I'd also promised myself that I'd never become the monster. I just wanted to be left alone. Not being hurt, and not hurting others... not unless we'd both signed up for it inside a chain-link cage.

The cage fights let me keep my edge, so I knew I'd always be able to fight off another alpha whenever I needed to. They also let me thrash out the monster that lived inside of me, so it wouldn't escape when I didn't want it to. I'd always figured everyone in the world had a monster like that inside them, but lately, I wasn't so sure anymore.

Did Mia have a monster hidden away? Did Luca? Did Zalen? Byron did, but I was pretty sure his had been beaten down too far to ever come out again. I didn't know if that made him more or less broken than I was.

Princess let out a little chirp and wound her body back and forth through my legs. I didn't understand why she wasn't afraid of me. She probably should be. Most people seemed to be. And the rest just didn't know me well enough yet.

I didn't like the feeling that I might not be able to keep Princess safe for the rest of her life. What if she ran out the door and got hit by a car, or she got in a cabinet and ate something poisonous... or she got cancer... or chewed through an electrical cord and got electrocuted... or—

I shook my head sharply, knowing that the way my heart started racing in response to all the *what-ifs* wasn't normal.

Instead, I poked at the feeling I got when I thought about how someone had trapped Princess and dragged her to a big concrete building to get killed, and we'd saved her in the nick of time. No one had come to save *me*, but I'd helped save *her*.

A light knock sounded on the door at the top of the stairs. I twitched, startled, and Princess scampered away to hide in the shadows behind the water heater.

"Hey," Mia called down softly. "I've got those sandwiches. I'm coming down."

The door opened cautiously. With no sign of a cat trying to make a break for it, Mia came down with two stacked plates held in one hand and two cans of soda tucked under her arm, along with a couple of paper towels. I got up from the bottom step hastily, clearing her path.

"How's she doing?" she asked, handing me a Dr Pepper and a paper towel.

"Jumpy," I said.

"Can't really blame her, poor thing," she replied, sympathy heavy in her tone. "Here, take one of these sandwiches. They're tuna salad, and I saved some tuna for her on the side."

She slid one of the two sandwiches from the top plate to the bottom one and handed the top plate to me. Sure enough, there was a little pile of canned tuna sitting on one corner.

"Thanks," I said, swallowing the sandwich in a few bites and setting the plate down on the floor. "Guess this was a Michelin star tuna sandwich, huh?"

Mia had retreated to a perch about a third of the way up the staircase and was working more slowly on her own lunch. She snorted.

"Oh, *totally*." This, around a mouthful of food. She swallowed gracelessly and wiped her mouth with the back of her hand. "Only the best canned tuna and mayo-from-a-jar at this establishment. I did chop the celery, though."

I had to tear my eyes away as she licked traces of mayonnaise from her fingers, turning to look back at Princess's hiding place instead.

Fuck, I was taking those damned dampeners starting *today*.

"It was good," I mumbled.

Princess chose that moment to poke her head out, whiskers arched forward and nose twitching as she scented the air. After a suspicious look in Mia's direction, she prowled forward and started delicately eating the tuna from my abandoned plate.

"Smart girl," Mia said approvingly. "Always go for the human food when it's on offer." She set her empty plate on the stair tread next to her and leaned back on her elbows. "We did good today, Emiel. I'm really happy for both of you."

I prodded at the big ball of overwhelm still stuck behind my lungs. Was this happiness? I wasn't sure.

"I thought she was gone forever," I admitted, not sure why I'd said the words aloud.

Her expression sobered. "I know you did. Sometimes it feels like there aren't a lot of happy endings in the world. I guess we just have to celebrate the ones we *do* end up getting."

"I guess so," I said, looking down in wonder as Princess finished her tuna and started winding around my ankles again.

FORTY-SEVEN

Luca

WHEN I GOT HOME from an exhausting day at work on Monday, there was a gray cat sitting on the kitchen counter.

"You got her," I said, still able to muster some relief and happiness on behalf of a cat and the alpha who loved her.

"*Meow*," Princess said, lifting a front paw to lick at it delicately.

Emiel and Mia turned to face me, both wearing grins that could only be described as goofy. I'd never seen an expression even *close* to that on Emiel's face before. It suited him, I couldn't help but notice.

Or… possibly that was the hormones talking. This close to a heat, it was hard to tell.

"She was at the county shelter," Emiel said, offering six entire words to me without being prompted.

Mia set down the wooden spoon she'd been holding. "They tried to run her through the adoption program—but apparently, she kept biting and clawing the volunteers. Anyway, heroic nick of time rescue from the shelter, happy endings all around."

Her smile softened as she glanced at Emiel, and I tried not to resent her easy happiness. God, I was becoming such a self-centered asshole as my bitterness festered, year after year.

This abrupt insight into my own assholeishness probably should've been valuable, but instead it just made me feel even worse.

I shook my head in frustration and set all that aside. Dropping my work bag by the kitchen doorway, I came forward slowly, rubbing my fingers together and making the universal *pss-pss-pss* noise used to gain a cat's attention.

Princess burbled another meow at me and deigned to rub her cheek against my fingers when I got within arm's reach. I let the sleek fur slide across my knuckles, appreciating the temporary sense of calm that came with being accepted by a cat.

"Oh, *I* see how it is," Mia teased, from her station next to the stovetop. When I looked up, she winked at me… the gentle smile from earlier still playing around her full lips. "She won't so much as give me the time of day."

"Keep feeding her tuna," Emiel suggested.

The alpha seemed uncharacteristically okay with being in the same room as my incipient heat pheromones… and Mia's, for that matter. I gathered he must've taken dampeners a day early to block our scents' effect on his nervous system. Again, resentment bubbled up in my chest. I hated this feeling of being a burden. I hated the way alphas got to choose whether or not they'd be affected by a heat, and I didn't.

Princess purred and scooted her whole body against my hand. I stroked her, ears to tail, and tried to let her uncomplicated happiness seep into me via osmosis.

"I'm really happy for you," I told her, eye to eye. "You're about to become the most spoiled housecat in the St. Louis Metropolitan Area."

"As evidenced by the fact that she's only lived here for a few hours and she already has free run of the kitchen counters," Mia agreed, laughing. She turned to the stove and set a lid on the pot she'd been stirring, cutting off the source of the rich scent that had permeated the kitchen. "That is *such* a health code violation, you know."

"I'll teach her not to," Emiel mumbled.

"But maybe not today," Mia finished. "She's had a rough week. We all have. Now, this needs to simmer for a couple of hours. I'll have to check on it occasionally, but in between, I plan on vegging out in front of the TV. Anyone else?"

Predictably, Emiel shook his head. "I want to show Princess the upstairs rooms. Might put a second litter box in my bedroom so she doesn't have to go so far."

"I'm in," I told Mia. "The other's will be late, but they know to get home by nine. What's for dinner tonight, by the way?"

"Moroccan vegetable tagine with pita wedges," she said. "And you should eat as much as you can."

My nose wrinkled, but she was right. "I know."

This heat hadn't even started yet, but it was already acting like a royal bitch. I'd had that uncomfortable 'might-be-hunger, might-be-queasiness' feeling for more than a day. Once the hormones hit me properly, I wouldn't eat or drink *anything* for several days. It was important to be well-fed and well-hydrated going in.

Of course, my body wouldn't care one way or the other while I was in the throes, but it would make all the difference when it came to my recovery time afterward. I knew that from long and bitter experience with forced heats in the gang.

Clearly uncomfortable with the new topic of conversation, Emiel scooped up Princess and stood. The cat immediately started rubbing the top of her head against his chin, purring like an outboard motor as the two of them exited the kitchen.

Mia peeked under the pot lid, checking her stew. When the sound of retreating footsteps faded, she turned to me and let out a slow breath. "It was close today, Luca. With Princess, I mean. I'm not sure how he would have taken it if we'd been too late."

I imagined a cat that bit multiple volunteers wouldn't last long at the shelter.

"Badly," I said, picturing chain link and fists on flesh. "He would have taken it badly."

We went to watch TV in between Mia's occasional trips to the kitchen to babysit her tagine.

"How are you?" she asked, stroking my hair as I indulged myself by resting my head on her shoulder, breathing in her sweet scent.

"Horny," I said. "Pissed off. Did you get a delivery date on your scary Mexican cartel 'appetite suppressant pills' yet? I'm hoping at least one of us still gets to have bodily autonomy this quarter."

"It's supposed to arrive on Friday," she said unhappily.

I made a sympathetic noise. "Cutting it fine."

"Yeah," she said on a sigh.

I licked my lips. "Will you stay in my nest with me tonight? I know I've been an ass these last several days—"

Her hand stilled, then resumed its steady stroking. "I'd like that. If you really want me there, I mean. And I don't blame you for being pissed off. The whole situation just sucks, no matter how you look at it."

I wrapped an arm around her middle and squeezed, startled by how badly I needed her. Horn-dogging for another omega wasn't... a *deviation*, exactly. Lots of omegas played with other omegas sometimes. But normally, this close to a heat, the only thing my body could focus on was alphas. It felt good to think about sex where I was riding the edge of heat, but where I could still be in control.

My dick, which had been making a nuisance of itself for days now, twitched awake with fresh interest. I nuzzled against Mia's throat, and she hummed in approval, arching her neck to offer me more access.

Neither of us heard the front door open. We were both startled by an influx of lime, vanilla, and spices, coupled with Byron's muttered, "Gonna need those fuckin' dampeners early," as he and Zalen stopped in the doorway of the TV room.

Mia cleared her throat, straightening away from me self-consciously… although it did nothing to hide the richness of our mingled scents. "Hi," she squeaked. "Um. The food should be ready in five minutes. I'll, uh, just go get everything plated, shall I?"

"Thanks, Mia," Zalen said, at the same time Byron smirked and said, "Don't hurry on *our* account."

I flipped him off. Zalen elbowed him, herding him toward the kitchen and dining room. Mia covered her face with one hand for a moment, her cheeks bright red. When she dropped it, it was to point a finger in my face.

"You. Me. Nest. Tonight," she said.

Despite myself, I huffed a breath of laughter at her bossy tone. "Yes, *ma'am*."

Dinner was probably delicious. My taste buds were already whacked, but I was at least able to eat a decent-sized portion without tipping from 'maybe queasy about food' to 'definitely queasy about food.' Meanwhile, Princess only tried to get on the dining room table twice.

Mia and I shamelessly left the cleanup to the others, jogging up the stairs to the second floor, hand-in-hand like a pair of teenagers. I locked the door to my nest behind us and pushed her up against it, the scent of alphas still clinging to my nose.

"Have you ever used a strap before?" I asked breathlessly, pressing the words into the skin of her throat.

She pushed me back a few inches so we could see each other. "A strap? Is that, like, a bondage thing?"

"No, a strap-on," I clarified, already picturing the feel of a knotting dildo sliding into me, catching on my rim over and over until my body clamped down and trapped it inside. "A fake cock you can strap onto your hips with a harness to fuck someone."

She looked intrigued rather than shocked, which felt like a win. "You'd want me to do that?"

"God, yes," I said. "I bought one for you in case you ever wanted to use it, but it never really seemed like the right time to talk about it. Can I get it?"

She nodded, her pupils blown wide and dark in her large, brown eyes. "Okay."

I forced myself to pull away in favor of retrieving the unopened package from its drawer. She came and watched over my shoulder as I tore it open and sorted out the mess of straps.

"Why are there two dildos?" she asked, picking up one of the matched pair. Both were a reasonable size—unlike Byron's sea monster—with a generous knot near the base.

"The second one's for you," I said, attaching it to the ring set in the crotch area of the harness to demonstrate.

"Oh," she said faintly. "Wow. Okay—clothes off. *Now.*"

My inner omega slut rolled over happily in response to the command, so different than the helpless, terrified tension I felt if an alpha barked at me when I wasn't expecting it.

We both stripped, and I helped Mia get the harness fastened around her hips. Slick pulsed from my passage when her eyes rolled up, a moan slipping out of her as I eased the first dildo into her body and tightened all the buckles.

"Oh, holy... fuck," she groaned, leaning against my shoulders as her knees went unsteady. "God, *Luca.*"

"I am *so* wet for you right now," I told her.

She laughed, although it was breathless. "We're wet for each other. Who needs alphas?"

The answer was that *I* would need alphas, soon enough—but not tonight.

"This is going to be so good," I promised instead.

She hefted the second dildo in a cupped palm, looking down at it in fascination. "Do I just...?"

"Peg A, slot B," I said, stealing a hard kiss before turning and dropping to my hands and knees among the profusion of pillows on the floor. God, I needed this *so bad.*

I felt everything shift as she knelt behind me. Slender fingers grasped my hips. Knuckles slid over my soaking entrance.

"Fair warning, I have no idea what I'm doing," she said, as though this bore any relation to rocket science.

Before I could dredge up words to reassure her, the cool, blunt end of the fake cock pressed against my hole. I let out an embarrassing high-pitched groan and rocked back, at the same time Mia cautiously pressed forward. We both whined as she slid inside, the dildo's knot stopping her forward progress when it hit my rim.

Beads of sweat popped out all over my body. "Mia… please… I *need* it…"

"Oh god," she said, and rammed it in.

I bit down hard on a wail, not really wanting every alpha in the house to hear what was going on. "Move. Move!" I rasped, wriggling my hips.

The stretch and burn as Mia rolled her pelvis, pulling the knot partway out of my body before my passage sucked it back in, was everything I needed to drive unwelcome thoughts out of my brain. I hated what was going to happen to me over the coming days. I'd turn into a mewling, needy bitch in heat; begging the alphas for their knots, for their bites.

And somewhere deep down, I'd still know that I wasn't good enough for a real pack. I was too broken, too damaged. I hated those days where I wanted it anyway. Where I wasn't in control of my own thoughts. Where I wasn't in control of my own actions.

It was so much better to be here, with Mia, getting off with her because it was something we both wanted. Something we both *chose*.

"Touch me," I begged. "Mia, please, touch me. I'm gonna—"

Mia snarled an omega puppy growl and latched onto my shoulder with her teeth. The hand that wasn't digging fingernail-shaped marks into my hips snaked forward, closing around my dripping cock. I thrust forward into the circle of Mia's fist... backward onto the strap-on.

Once. Twice. Three times... and my orgasm crashed over me, driving a choked cry past my control.

"Luca! Luca... *fuck*..." Mia groaned against the nape of my neck, and a moment later, she was jerking out her release as well, her hips twitching even as my body clamped around the latex knot stretching me wide.

What felt like an age later, we tumbled sideways in a messy tangle, still connected, panting like we'd run a race. For this moment, in this warm, protected nest, I didn't feel so utterly alone inside my own head.

The next words slipped out before I even knew my lips were forming them. "Mia... stay with me during my heat? Please?"

Behind me, Mia went very still.

FORTY-EIGHT

Mia

MY BRAIN FROZE like a flower dipped in liquid nitrogen. It had just begun to slip into the soothing, warm molasses feeling of a really good orgasm, and apparently it was not prepared to deal with Luca's sex-drunk request.

I'd been living so deep in denial that it was embarrassing. I hadn't even warned Nat that I might be out of action next week if the extremely dodgy Mexican heat blocker didn't pan out. I hadn't talked to Zalen or Byron about it. In fact, I hadn't thought about it at *all* if I could avoid it.

When the Princess debacle had popped up, I'd jumped into it with both feet. As long as I was dealing with a life-or-death emergency, I had an excuse for not making contingency plans... for not thinking through the reality of what I was facing.

And now Luca wanted me with him during his heat, which might well start as soon as tomorrow. I was expected at work tomorrow. And the next day, and the next day, and the next. I'd given no one the slightest hint that I might need to be absent. What if I took off this week to stay with him, and then the heat blocker didn't show up on Friday like it was supposed to? Or it *did*, but it ended up being a fake?

I couldn't disappear off the face of the earth for two solid weeks with only a day or two of warning. But I couldn't abandon my friend to a heat that he obviously found traumatizing when he'd specifically asked for me to support him.

My breathing had grown fast and shallow. Why hadn't I made better plans? Why had I ignored what was coming for so long? Fuck, fuck, *fuck*... I was about to have the world's most awkward panic attack, stuck fast to another omega by two dildos and a faux-leather harness.

What should I tell him?

Christ, *what should I say?*

"S-sorry," Luca stammered, sounding mortified. He was shaking, a full-body tremor. "I shouldn't have asked that. You've got the restaurant to worry about, and your pill is coming on Friday, and you and Zalen aren't even *like* that with each other. Sorry, forget I—"

Unthinking, I wrapped my arms around his chest from behind and squeezed hard, cutting him off. The abrupt movement shifted the harness, sending a jolt of confusing pleasure outward from my core and driving a startled hiss from Luca.

"Not now, okay?" I asked unsteadily. "Not like this. We'll talk afterward, I promise."

He hesitated, then nodded—a final shudder running through his body before he went limp in my hold. And maybe this was why omegas didn't usually get involved with each other in the absence of alphas. Without an alpha, there was no one around to short-circuit the feedback loop of omega anxiety when it reared its ugly head.

This can wait twenty minutes, I told myself firmly. I rested my forehead between Luca's sharp shoulder blades and held onto him, even though the mood had been comprehensively ruined by this point.

Idly, I thought back to all the lurid alphomic romance novels I'd read in my teens, when I'd been trying to figure myself out as an omega born to beta parents. Back then, I'd been seriously freaked out by the cliched storyline of the omega protagonist helplessly going into heat and ending up mated, sometimes to as many as half a dozen animalistic alphas.

In this moment of mingled guilt, nervousness, and uncertainty, I began to see the appeal for the first time in my entire life.

Give up control.

Make it all someone else's responsibility.

Luca covered one of my hands with his, threading his fingers between mine and squeezing. We waited until our bodies finally released the knotted toys. It felt like an age, time ticking by in painfully slow increments. By unspoken agreement, we cleaned up and covered ourselves, Luca offering me an oversized tee from his dresser that hit me at mid-thigh.

The nest reeked of pre-heat sex hormones, but there was nothing much to be done about that part.

I sat on a handy beanbag chair, my elbows resting on my knees as I scrubbed at my face — half-hiding my expression from Luca, who lay flopped on his back among a pile of pillows.

"Seriously, I'm sorry," he told the ceiling. "That was heat-brain talking, but it was still a shitty thing to ask."

I made myself sit up straight, letting my hands drop. "It wasn't," I said.

"It was," he insisted. "You don't owe me anything, Mia."

I didn't like the way this conversation seemed to be heading.

"I'm not sure 'owing' comes into it," I told him. "Look... the truth is, I haven't made plans like I should have done, because this whole situation is seriously freaking me out. I've been mostly ignoring it and hoping it would go away, to be honest."

Now it was Luca's turn to drag a hand over his face, stretching the porcelain skin. "I don't think it's going to go away. What are you going to do if the Mexican pill is no good? Have you decided?"

The trapped, panicky feeling began to rise in my throat again. "I can't ask Zalen or Byron to help me so soon after your heat."

"Yes, you can," Luca said.

"They've got important jobs, too!" I protested. "A hell of a lot more important than mine, if we're being honest."

"Mia, they're *alphas*." Luca sounded tired. "Helping omegas in heat is kind of hardwired in."

Desperation—not to make a fuss, not to be a burden—pulled the next words from me. "I thought about asking Emiel?"

Luca stilled. "Do *not* ask Emiel. I'm serious, Mia. Don't."

"Why not?" I asked, my mouth still running ahead without input from my brain. "I think he likes me all right, especially after we saved Princess... and I know he's stand-offish, but it's *heat*! Instinct would kick in, wouldn't it?"

I was babbling. Luca sat up, giving me the full weight of his focus. "Mia, *no*. Emiel doesn't do heats. He doesn't do *talking* about them. He absolutely, one-hundred percent doesn't do *having* them."

"Why not?" I demanded, not sure when my stupid thoughts had galloped away down this path. I needed to shut up. I needed to *stop talking*, right the fuck now.

"I don't know," Luca said. "And, I mean, I guess it isn't my business, or anyone else's, really. But trust me on this. You do *not* want to ask Emiel. Talk to Zalen. Or Byron, if you don't mind dealing with non-stop innuendo. And if you're not going to do that, then get on one of the rent-a-pack websites and lock down the dates you need. I'm guessing there's been a spike in demand with the heat blockers getting cut off."

I was heading back toward panic-attack territory. Forcing myself to take slow, deep breaths, I closed my eyes until the dizziness started to recede and my thundering heart slowed down a bit. Luca, bless him, didn't push while I was trying to drag my shit together.

Finally, I was able to look at my choices with something approaching clarity. I couldn't go back to Nat with my tail between my legs. The humiliation would be unbearable. The idea of letting rent-a-pack alphas fuck me when I was out of my mind made me feel nauseated. It sounded like even mentioning my heat situation to Emiel would be a quick way to undo the fragile rapport I'd gained with him.

"I'll talk to Zalen," I said hoarsely, trying to ignore the fresh wave of guilt at the idea.

Luca nodded. "Good. Now, as much as I hate to say this, both of us should probably try to get a decent night's sleep."

He didn't look like there was much chance of that happening, in his case. He also didn't ask me to stay in his nest with him, which I could understand after what had just happened. The idea of lying alone on my borrowed bed in my borrowed room felt daunting, but I'd just done a spectacular job of making this whole evening about me. I knew how exhausting that kind of thing could be when you were stressed out and on the receiving end of it.

"Okay," I said. "I'll set an alarm and talk to Zalen first thing in the morning. Get as much sleep as you can. I'll make French toast when you get up, if you can stomach it."

"That sounds good," Luca said, his façade of being all right firmly back in place.

I slunk back to my room shortly afterward, my clothing rolled in a messy bundle beneath my arm. The next few hours were spent ricocheting between helpless horniness at the prospect of being tag-teamed by Byron and Zalen, and helpless panic at the idea of having to ask, out loud, to their faces, if they'd help me.

Not for the first time in the last few weeks, I had no idea how I was going to get through another exhausting day of work in the restaurant tomorrow.

FORTY-NINE

Mia

"ZALEN? CAN I talk to you?" It was six o'clock on the morning of the day when Luca's heat might reasonably be expected to start, and I'd had maybe three hours total of restless and broken sleep.

Now, I was about to bother Luca's alpha with something that I was one hundred percent sure he'd be happier not dealing with—especially given how haggard he looked these days. The dark circles and worry lines accenting his rich, brown eyes were totally understandable. It felt like it had been one thing after another these past several weeks, and the only bright spot had been the successful rescue of Princess.

"Morning, Mia," Zalen said. "You're up early. Is everything okay?"

Was it, hell.

"Nothing new has happened, if that's what you're asking," I told him, stepping fully into the kitchen in Luca's rumpled T-shirt and a pair of sleep shorts. Belatedly, I realized that the shirt was so big on me that it probably looked like I wasn't wearing anything underneath it.

Stellar.

Sure enough, Zalen's eyes flickered down to thigh level for the barest instant before his attention moved firmly back to my face.

"Is this about your heat?" His tone was admirably neutral. Inviting, without pressing. "Or… about Luca's?"

"Kind of both, actually," I admitted. "So, I ordered a blocker pill from a decidedly suspect-looking Mexican site. But I need to make plans in case it's not the real deal… and I know I should have done this ages ago, but—"

"We've all had a lot on our plates," Zalen finished for me. "Plus, it's not as though you've had a lot of time to line up contingency plans."

"Yeah," I said on a shaky exhale.

Zalen got up and grabbed a mug from the cabinet over the coffee maker, filling it up for me. The rich, floral fruitiness of Pacamara Limited Edition wafted toward me, overpowering the alpha's scent of lime and vanilla mixed with my own nervous perfume.

I remembered, with a sudden pang, Zalen's thoughtful housewarming gift to me when I'd first arrived. Something inside me loosened incrementally.

He set the mug down on the corner of the breakfast bar, a silent invitation. I accepted it wordlessly, slinking in and taking a stool. The mug was warm against my palms as I wrapped my hands around it.

"Unfortunately, the options are the same," Zalen said. "Hire a rent-a-pack, negotiate an informal arrangement with alphas you know— and by that, I mean *us*—or lock yourself in a room with a strong door and tough it out. Are you leaning in a particular direction?"

Still so neutral. Perversely, I almost wished he would do something impulsive, just so I wouldn't feel like the only one going crazy.

I fiddled with the handle of the coffee mug, breaking eye contact. "I don't feel like it's fair of me to ask you and Byron. Not with my heat coming right on the heels of Luca's."

There was a beat of silence.

"Mia, look at me."

It wasn't remotely a bark… almost the opposite, actually. Yet my eyes jerked up immediately.

Zalen gave a slow nod. "Listen. Your heat is not an *inconvenience*. Or, well, I suppose it is, to you. But it isn't to me. Not yours, not Luca's, not any omega's. Heat can be one of the most beautiful things in the world. Even when it's not an ideal situation, it's every alpha's responsibility to make sure that an omega in heat has everything they need — no exceptions."

My breath caught fast.

I would not cry.

I would not cry, damn it.

A pathetic whimper tore free of my throat before I could stamp on it.

"Oh, Mia." Zalen sounded unutterably sad. "I haven't done a very good job with any of this, have I. Is it all right if I hold you for a minute?"

I gave a tight nod, not daring to speak for fear of what other sounds might come out of my mouth. Zalen rose and came around to my side of the breakfast bar. A moment later, I was enveloped in strong arms and the scent of the tropics after a rainfall. Helplessly, I scrunched my eyes shut and buried my face in Zalen's shoulder. He said nothing, but a low purr vibrated beneath my cheek.

"Erm…" said a voice from the hallway.

I barely resisted the startled urge to shove myself free, as though I'd been caught doing something scandalous in a Regency romance novel. Instead, I pulled back more slowly, Zalen's arms immediately loosening as I put space between us.

My cheeks were burning as I turned to face Byron's raised eyebrow. The other alpha stood with his arms crossed, leaning a shoulder casually against the kitchen entryway. Unlike Zalen, he was dressed for the office, the picture of professionalism except for his loose tie and the undone top button beneath it.

"Something going on here I should know about?" he asked, the layer of dry humor in the words almost covering the tension beneath.

"Mia's heat is due to start not long after Luca's ends," Zalen said, unperturbed.

"I don't think anyone in the house is unaware of *that*," Byron shot back. "And that includes the cat."

I threw him a dirty look. It slid right off, like oil on Teflon.

"And I believe she was about to ask if we'd help her out in the event that her emergency blocker pill ends up being a dud," Zalen continued, as though he hadn't spoken. "Is that right, Mia? I don't want to put words in your mouth."

I swallowed hard. "Um, yes, that's right. I mean, if it's not too much trouble."

Byron's raised eyebrow twitched. "Another three to five days of nonstop sex? Oh, please, no… anything but that."

"He means yes," Zalen translated. "Byron, we may have to trade off that week. Alternating days."

Byron pushed off the wall and waved that away dismissively. "Emiel can handle things at the project. And Luca will probably be back to work by then. You know what he's like."

Zalen caught my eye and murmured, "Bad at being taken care of," by way of explanation. In a more normal tone, he added, "You'll have to forgive us for talking logistics. That part's nothing you need to worry about."

He thought I was going to be offended by the realities of having to be away from their jobs unexpectedly for almost two weeks? *Seriously*?

"Believe me, I get it," I said. "Things at the restaurant are going to be a nightmare if this pill doesn't work. Which reminds me, Nat needs to know what's going on, in case that happens. Is that going to be a problem?"

"Of course not," Zalen said.

At the same time, Byron snorted derisively. "As long as you're not planning on slinking back to him for your heat, tell him anything you want. Hell, give him a blow-by-blow account."

Gah. I did *not* need or appreciate the inappropriate burst of heat that came in the wake of that suggestion. *Fucking hormones.*

I cleared my throat. "Okay, good. I'll, um, give you his cell number, Zalen... so you'll have it in case anything comes up."

"Oh, I imagine several things will be coming up nicely," Byron said.

Zalen gave him a flat stare. "Or else your pill will be exactly what you expect it to be, Mia, and all of this will be moot. Either way, we'll make sure everything works out smoothly."

I nodded, daring to hope it would be true.

"Oh," I said. "There's one more thing, actually. This is a bit awkward, but... Luca asked if I'd be there with him for his heat. And I can't just bail out on work—not when I might have to miss next week, too—but I thought, maybe I could come by when I'm off? Like, in the mornings before I have to get ready? Just to, y'know, lend moral support."

"Of course you can," Zalen said. "Who's allowed in the heat nest and who isn't is Luca's call, not ours. Just knock first and let us know it's you, please. Even on dampeners, things can get a little intense."

"That's one word," Byron said.

"Okay, thanks," I said, even though the echo of that unsettled, panicky feeling from last night had returned. "Guess I should leave you to it and try to get another couple hours of sleep. Someone's staying here for Luca today, right? You know, in case—"

"I'm on heat watch today, yes," Zalen said. "So, I'll be around if you need anything. Get me that phone number whenever you have a minute."

I forced a smile and promised I would, draining my coffee cup before realizing that would probably sabotage my plans for a pre-work nap. Now, I just had to psych myself up to ask Luca if he'd be okay with me popping in and out of his heat nest around my work schedule. Followed by informing Nat of what I was mentally calling the Contingency Plan.

This day was going to be a real barrel of laughs, I could tell already.

FIFTY

Mia

"YOU COULD COME home." Nat's knuckles were white as he clutched the pen he'd been holding when I'd walked into his office at the restaurant. "We could close the place for a few days. And… it wouldn't have to mean anything more than that. Not if you don't want it to."

It sounded like the final words had been torn from him.

"No thanks," I told him. "I'm good. The others have already agreed to help, on the off chance that my replacement blocker pill is a dud. I just wanted to tell you so you'd know I might be AWOL if it doesn't work."

Silence fell for a moment.

"That's what the package was last week? Your blocker?" he asked, his tone cautious.

"Yeah," I told him. "It was. Is whoever destroyed it still going after our mail? Did you get anything else useful off the security camera?"

"I don't know if they're still going after the mail or not," Nat said. "Nothing has been delivered to the house since your package came."

I shook my head in frustration and started pacing, not that there was a lot of space to do so in the cramped, messy office. "There are too many weird things happening in our orbit. Something else is going on."

Nat loosened his death grip on the pen enough to tap it rapidly back and forth on the desk. "Maybe. I'm trying not to see a bunch of connections that aren't really there."

I'd always hated it when people spouted outlandish sounding conspiracy theories, so it wasn't like I could really argue the point.

'But, officer! There was a grease spill at a restaurant, and then a heavy rack fell off its hooks, and someone is stealing our mail, and the rival restaurant down the street is run by a gang!'

Yeah, I imagined the authorities would be *super* interested in that crazy-sounding story.

"I get it," I said. "I just wish there was some way to root out the cause so we can deal with it at the source."

"Well, for whatever it's worth—I have security cameras set up here at the restaurant, as well as the one at the house." Nat stopped tapping the pen and deliberately put it down. "And there haven't been any more incidents here, at least."

I fetched up against a set of wire storage shelves holding banker's boxes full of old records. "Thank goodness for small mercies." With a sigh, I scrubbed hard at my face. "I feel awful about maybe having to close things down for a few days."

"Meanwhile, I'm not happy about the idea of a bunch of alphas you barely know pawing all over you." As soon as they were out, Nat looked like he desperately wanted to pull the words back.

But I could be the bigger person here.

"Then it's just as well it's my decision and not yours," I said lightly. "Anyway, Zalen has your cell number. He'll keep you informed if anything comes up, and if I can't tell you myself for whatever reason."

I was pretty sure Nat was going to need reconstructive tongue surgery, given how hard he appeared to be biting it—but to his credit, he managed not to say anything else on the subject. Instead, he redirected the conversation to work stuff, as we discussed the last week's welcome increase in sales volume and nightly covers.

After close, I went home, where I discovered that Luca's heat hadn't started yet. He was miserable—twitchy and feverish—but I managed to get some crackers and broth into him.

"Do you want me to stay with you tonight?" I asked, still not entirely sure where the two of us stood after the past several days of mishaps and misunderstandings.

He shook his head, not meeting my eyes. "No. Better not. I'll just be tossing and turning all night. I'll keep you up."

I chewed my lip. "Have you thought about what I said this morning? About me sort of being in and out during your heat?"

It sounded wishy-washy to my own ears. Doubly so, since even the underlying concept of me popping in and out of Luca's nest at my own convenience was wishy-washy.

Luca hesitated. "I mean… you've got other things to worry about besides attending someone's free multi-day porn show as moral support. Honestly, the closer this gets, the less enthusiastic I am about people I care about seeing me like that."

My heart twisted in my chest, and not just because I'd be *all about* the free porn show if Luca didn't sound like he was being marched to the gallows. But I'd already made Luca's heat too much about me, and not nearly enough about him.

"It's whatever you want, Luca," I told him earnestly. "Whatever will make you most comfortable. Is it all right if I hug you now?"

The desire for physical contact during the run-up to heat was a bit of a mixed bag, but Luca only nodded tiredly and leaned into me. He was clammy and shaky and listless, but it was still a huge relief to wrap my arms around him and squeeze.

We would be all right, I told myself firmly. We'd just gotten sucked into a difficult situation, further complicated by the volume of hormones flying around — that was all. My pill would arrive in the mail on Friday, and it would work fine. Luca would get through his heat, and by this time next week, everything would be back to normal. We could pick up whatever pieces still needed picking up, and then we could all move on with our lives.

Wednesday came and went; Luca's heat still didn't start.

"Stress," Zalen said. "If it's bad enough, it can throw off the timing by a couple of days. Byron got some Gatorade into him earlier."

He and Byron were switching off, one of them going to the Hope Project as they normally would, while the other stayed home in case Luca needed them. I wondered, with a little pang, how many times they'd done this before. Luca skipped heats as often as he could. But unlike me, he listened to his doctor and had a natural heat once a year or so to reduce the likelihood of getting cancer of the reproductive tract at a young age.

In the past twenty-four hours, I'd convinced myself that Luca's change of heart about having me in the heat nest was a good thing. If the Mexican pill showed up on time and worked as advertised—which it *would*, damn it—then I'd only be torturing myself by playing at being part of a caring pack.

Better to keep things as they were, as much as possible. I was a guest here. It was a temporary situation while I figured out what the hell I was going to do about my marriage situation. I'd made a really good omega friend, whether or not that friendship came with sexual benefits attached. I'd played around with Byron, because Byron didn't do serious relationships. He was safe.

At some point in the near future, I would move on in my life and do... something else. I had no idea what '*something else*' would end up looking like, but that was just how life worked.

I'd figure it out when the time was right. In the meantime, I just had to make it through until Friday when my pill would arrive.

Luca was still stuck in his miserable pre-heat when I left for work on Thursday morning. Lunch service was slow. When the mid-afternoon lull hit, I went outside for a five-minute break, in hopes that some fresh air would calm my nerves.

Shaniqua looked up as I approached, smiling in greeting. There were no cigarettes in sight this time, the slow, easy day giving her no cause to break into her emergency stash.

"Hey, boss," she greeted. "You needed a bit of fresh air, too, I'm guessing?"

"Great minds think alike," I agreed. "How are you doing? All good?"

"Can't complain," she said, eyes crinkling at the corners before she sobered. "I'd been wanting to ask you, though—and do feel free to tell me this is none of my business. But the blocker shortage is all over the news these days."

"And my being in pre-heat isn't exactly subtle to anyone who isn't a beta," I finished, resigned. "Don't worry, I've got a pill arriving Friday. And if the worst happens, I promise everyone will still be paid."

Shani's dark eyes held mine. "That's not really why I asked, boss—though I'm sure the staff appreciates it. I asked because I need to make sure you're set up with something safe, just in case. Are you?"

I started to answer, and humiliatingly, had to pause when my throat closed up. I coughed and tried again, viscerally aware of the odd power dynamics at play in this conversation. I was Shani's boss. Shani was an experienced, middle-aged pack mother who'd shepherded her offspring through first heats and into adulthood. She couldn't have failed to notice the rift in my beta marriage to Nat, and she was worried enough for me that she was skirting the edges of our professional relationship to check on me.

My own mother—a loving beta—had done her very best for me while having no clue what it meant to come of age as an omega. For a horrible instant, my body tried to sway forward as though it wanted to collapse into Shani's arms and cling.

I took a deep breath, and then another. "Yes, I have a contingency plan in place," I said, in the most formal tone I could manage.

"Okay, good. That's good," Shani said. "As long as you're safe, then everything else will work itself out."

"I'm safe," I said. That much, at least, I was sure of. "And, Shani? Thank you for caring enough to ask."

Shani smiled. "Hey, now. We tough-as-nails omegas have to stick together, you know."

"That we do," I agreed, still a bit choked up.

The dinner crowd made up for the slow lunch service. The Elderflower Inn was hopping—every table occupied and a line of diners waiting. The kitchen was in fine form, sending the food out fast and delicious to hungry patrons.

Nights like this, I could begin to remember what had drawn me to this career in the first place. Not awards and star ratings, but the satisfaction of running a talented and dedicated crew of professionals, providing memorable meals to appreciative diners.

"How long on those potatoes?" I called, sliding a perfectly cooked pair of lamb medallions onto a sparkling plate decorated with an artful smear of gastrique.

Toby's reply was drowned out by a scream from the dining area. A second scream followed, and the entire line froze as complete chaos erupted from the front of house.

A jolt of adrenaline hit me so hard that I swayed.

No, no… oh, god, what now?

"Burners off!" I yelled over the noise. "Make everything safe, then get outside! Use the back door—don't worry about the food!"

I turned off my grill with shaking hands, feeling like I was about to pass out. Shani was pulling Toby away from the pass-through, where he'd apparently been trying to get a glimpse of whatever was going on up front. She pushed him bodily toward the back, where the others were already hurrying for the exit.

She gave me a questioning look.

"You too," I told her. "I'll find out what's happening and let everyone know if it's safe to come back in."

She gave a reluctant nod, worry shining from her eyes.

Straightening my spine, I pushed open the door to the dining area. I was prepared for anything from a patron having a heart attack to a fire. What I found was a virtual stampede of diners heading for the exits, with Nat and a gaggle of near-hysterical serving staff doing their best to make it as orderly as possible.

Very slowly, I turned to look in the direction everyone was running away from. The south wall and floor of the dining room was... *moving*.

Scuttling.

As I stared in abject horror, my brain reorganized the image into thousands of scurrying cockroaches, spreading across the room as they frantically tried to escape the light. I stood frozen in place, shuddering violently, my mind flatly refusing to take in the implications of what I was seeing.

It felt as though I was floating slightly above my own body as I turned on my heel and walked toward the employee entrance in the back. I didn't feel the heavy steel door as I pushed it open. Behind the restaurant, my kitchen staff stood in a tight huddle, their voices an undifferentiated buzz in my ears.

"Go home, everyone," I said blankly. "The restaurant is closed."

The buzz rose in a cacophony of questions I couldn't hear. A hand gripped my bicep. I shook it off and kept walking. I didn't remember getting to my car. I didn't remember unlocking it or starting the engine. I didn't remember the drive to Ladue, or letting myself into the house.

When I came back to awareness, I was standing in front of Luca's closed door. My face was a mass of tears and snot; my breath coming in choking, cut-off sobs. I raised my shaking hand and knocked weakly on the doorframe.

The door opened barely a second later. Zalen stood in the entrance, disheveled and bare to the waist. His eyes went wide.

"Mia?" An instant later, I was in his arms — not sure if I'd moved, or he had. "Mia, are you hurt? What's happened, what's wrong?"

I couldn't form words, so I only shook my head, pressing my face against tawny skin and weeping as though I would die.

FIFTY-ONE

THE OVERWHELMING WALL of spice, and summertime, and tropical drinks coming from inside Luca's nest hit me like Emiel punching out an opponent in the fighting cage, and I started crying even harder.

Everything was falling apart… everything was going to complete shit, and it felt like I didn't have the smallest bit of control over *any* of it. I just wanted someone to walk in and say, *hey, it's going to be all right; sit back and let me take care of this for you.*

Zalen's arms were strong and secure around my body.

"Mia," he said. "I don't know what's happened, but we're going to make it right, okay? But first, I need you to nod yes or no. Are you physically injured?"

It was so close to what I'd just been thinking that my heart skipped and kicked hard in reaction. Squeezing my eyes closed, I shook my head no with more intention this time. Zalen relaxed minutely against me.

"Good. That's good." He took a deep breath, his broad chest expanding beneath my wet cheek. "Can you tell me what's wrong?"

I shuddered hard in his embrace, trying to map out the right words to explain before I said them. But I couldn't. It was too big. Too absurd.

"*Everything*," I sobbed.

A whimper of distress penetrated my veil of misery, emerging from the depths of the nest. Luca's summertime scent had turned sour and curdled, while the sharpness of concern threaded through the alphas' musky pheromones.

"Mia?" Luca's voice was thin and scared. "*Mia!*"

That was enough to jolt me partway out of my self-absorbed fugue. Luca was mired in his heat after days of miserable waiting—trapped in the helpless state he hated so much. And I'd shown up at his door in hysterics, frightening the hell out of him at a time when he was operating on pure instinct.

An answering whine of distress escaped my throat. I pushed at Zalen's chest. He released me immediately, moving his big hands to my shoulders to steady me instead.

"Can you come in and show him you're not hurt?" he asked quietly, scanning my face with his earthy brown gaze.

I nodded, feeling tears drip from my cheeks at the movement. I swiped at them, smearing them across my skin even as more squeezed from the corners of my eyes. The cushions lining the nest were in total disarray, as though Luca had been obsessively moving them around in the run-up to his heat. Trying not to stumble over the uneven piles, I picked my way toward the source of Luca's voice.

My throat closed up as I knelt beside him in the low light. He was naked, curled on his side in the fetal position, the smell of sex hanging around him like a cloud. Byron was seated, nearby but not touching, on a low couch that normally sat against the far wall of the room. He, too, was naked—his tattoos half-seen shadows in the nest's dimness.

"Why aren't you holding him?" I demanded, my voice wavering. It sounded petulant even to my own ears, but weren't heat partners supposed to hold you and comfort you between peaks? Surely it couldn't be right to leave Luca curled miserably on the floor by himself!

Byron's face closed off as though it had been carved from marble.

"Because he refused," Zalen said gently. "He doesn't want that from us. Maybe he will from you, though."

My tears had stopped, but at that, they immediately started again. Why did everything have to be like this? Why couldn't the people I cared about be happy? Why couldn't I?

"Luca," I croaked. "I'm here, I'm okay. I'm so sorry, I didn't mean to scare you. Can I hold you?"

Please, please, let me hold you.

Luca made a choked noise and reached for me; his movements uncoordinated. I let him pull me down and wriggled close until we were tangled together in a messy clinch. He smelled like sweat and spunk and desperate neediness, his heat-soaked mown grass and honeysuckle perfume settling heavily across my over-stretched senses.

He sobbed once, and I swallowed against an answering sob. Maybe I could just… *not think about things for a while*. If Luca needed me, was there anything to stop me simply staying here and focusing on him? For tonight, at least.

The restaurant was closed. Hiring exterminators and dealing with the health department bureaucrats was in Nat's job description, not mine. I cooked the food, and that wasn't going to be happening again for the foreseeable future after word of the latest nightmare got out on social media and the news.

Before my brain could conjure up images of what the lurid headlines might look like, I distracted myself by tucking Luca's face against the crook of my neck. He nuzzled into me with a small noise of distress, but then his lips closed over my mating gland like a baby suckling at the breast to comfort itself.

The jolt that echoed along my nervous system from scalp to toenails was enough to drive away all other thoughts. I made an answering noise, but it definitely wasn't one of distress. The sourness faded from my scent, and a moment later, it faded from Luca's as well. His tense, trembling muscles loosened until it felt like he was melting in my arms.

Within moments, he was a warm and pliant weight pressed against me, our arms and legs entwined until I couldn't tell where he ended, and I began. I closed my eyes, my own tension easing as exhaustion rushed in to take its place. My nerves thrummed pleasantly beneath his lips, still pressed to the juncture of my neck and shoulder.

A faint rustle of movement sounded from nearby. "I need a minute," Byron said in a tight tone. His fennel-and-aniseed scent wafted past us, rife with a complicated knot of lust and emotional strain that I couldn't unpick.

"I'll guard the nest," Zalen said, solid and unflappable as ever. "Don't be long, Byron."

Tangy lime and coconut replaced the sharpness of spice, as Zalen settled in the place Byron had abandoned. Watching over Luca, but not touching him.

"He's between peaks right now," he said softly. "He needs to rest, and I think you probably do, too. Whatever happened outside tonight, none of it will reach us in here. You're both safe, Mia. I'll make sure of it."

The violence of my emotional reaction to his words took me by surprise. How long had I been waiting to hear something like them? I had to swallow hard, several times.

"Thank you," I rasped, when I could speak.

He shook his head. "You don't need to thank me. It's what I'm here for. Anything you need. Both of you. Now, get some sleep if you can. I'm watching over things, and Byron will be back soon."

Luca shifted against me, somehow managing to press another few square inches of our bodies together. Out of nowhere, I wished that I wasn't still in the clothes that I'd been wearing when I walked out of the restaurant. No way was I letting go of Luca long enough to wriggle out of them, though—especially with Zalen sitting right there watching me.

Before long, tiredness banished the minor irritation of cloth rubbing against my skin, and sleep overtook me.

⸻◆⸻

When I woke up, it was because Luca was rutting his erection into the crease of my hip, smearing precome against the black cotton-spandex blend. Sharp teeth nipped at the tendon running up the side of my neck, startling a gasp from me.

The air that rushed into my lungs still smelled like sex and summertime, but the minor annoyance of my clothing against my skin had roared into an untuned symphony of jangling nerves while I slept. I moaned, aware of the sweat prickling across my entire body. My womb felt heavy and bloated, aching with cramps.

"S-something's wrong!" I choked out, suddenly panicky.

"Mia?" That was Zalen's voice, but it sounded like it was reaching me through a tunnel.

"Oh." Byron's voice, this time. "Oh, *shit.*"

Then Luca moved, canting his hips so that his bare cock dragged directly over my clit through my work pants and underwear. Fireworks exploded behind my eyes, everything inside me igniting like a lightning strike catching a dry forest afire.

Without any further thought, I was pulling and tearing at my clothing, desperate to get the stale grill smoke and deep fryer smell as far away from my body as possible. Luca seemed to be thoroughly on board with this plan, tugging clumsily at buttons and pulling on pantlegs until I was completely exposed.

I was still half-smothered in my T-shirt, my bra hanging unhooked from my shoulders, when a hot mouth landed between my legs. Luca dove in as though my pussy had just gained its own Michelin star rating, devouring the slick that pulsed from my passage like a starving man.

Other hands helped disentangle me from the rest of my clothing, and I found myself blinking owlishly up at Zalen. His broad palm cupped my cheek as I panted, Luca's tongue curling inside me to chase the source of my honey.

"Mia," he said, slowly and clearly. "Being in Luca's nest triggered your heat early. We'll take care of you, but I need to get your birth control shot and give it to you. Do you understand?"

I licked my lips, arching when Luca's tongue rasped over a particularly sensitive spot, and tried to replay the words in my head. It wasn't time for my heat yet, was it? But the alpha was right. This felt like heat.

I nodded hesitantly.

"Good," Zalen said. "And you still want to be here? You want Byron and me to help you through it?"

This time, I nodded so fast I probably looked like a bobblehead doll—and it was only partly because Luca had fastened his lips around my clit and was sucking on it like a butterscotch candy. Zalen's hand moved to smooth my hair back from my face.

"Then we'll do that," he said. "Don't worry, everything's going to be taken care of. You and Luca can play with each other all you want while I get that shot for you, all right? He can't get you pregnant."

Luca gave a little growl against my folds and surged up the length of my body, wriggling his hips between my spread legs and thrusting his omega cock into me as though he'd taken Zalen's words as a personal challenge. I wailed as he slid home—an out of control, animalistic noise—locking my ankles around the small of his back as he pumped into me wildly.

"Yeah, so, you might want to hurry with that, Z," Byron said from somewhere behind Luca.

"Um… yes." Zalen sounded mildly taken aback. "I'll just be a minute."

FIFTY-TWO

Mia

THERE WERE THINGS I was supposed to be thinking about. Important things. The kind of things that it would be unforgivable to ignore.

I couldn't remember what they were. I kept getting as far as *'oh, god, the restaurant,'* and then Luca would snarl and snap his hips, making everything go hot and fuzzy again.

Even now, I could tell his almost violent rutting wasn't going to be enough for me. It felt good—no, it felt *amazing*—but my body craved more. So did his. The noises he was making sounded aggressive, but I could hear the desperation behind the growls. I could smell it in his scent, and in my own.

The door to the nest opened, and a jolt of alarm made my muscles twitch. But Luca didn't react, and I recognized Zalen's sharp, fruity pheromones an instant later. The door closed again, and a quiet presence crouched next to me among the cushions and blankets.

Luca made a warning noise and snapped his teeth at Zalen's approach, sending a strange surge of combined lust and protectiveness skittering down my spine. The alpha didn't back off, nor did he bark.

"No one's taking her away from you, Luca," he said, in a perfectly normal tone. "I'm giving her a shot, that's all."

"Insert joke about it 'just being a tiny prick' here," Byron muttered.

The words flew right over my head, but the reminder of Byron's presence drew a needy whine from my throat. Why wasn't he down here with us? This would all be even better if he was. I craned around Luca's shoulder far enough to see him, still seated on the couch with his cock standing at attention.

My passage clenched at the sight, and Luca gasped. A broad hand steadied my left shoulder, the skin-to-skin contact searing me like a brand. I moaned as something cool and astringent swabbed a circle high on my arm, barely registering the small, pinching pain that followed.

"There. All set for birth control," Zalen murmured, pressing a bandage over the tiny hurt.

The distraction brought me back to my body enough to notice my growing sexual frustration. I wanted to come. I *needed* to come, and I couldn't. I rolled my hips, meeting Luca's thrusts with equal fervor, wishing I could somehow roll over onto my hands and knees without stopping what we were doing.

Luca must've been feeling that same frustration. His growling grew broken, his breathing ragged and edging toward sobs.

"P-please," he moaned, as though the word had been wrenched from him. "I... I need..."

"Damn right you do," Byron rumbled. His lean, tattooed body loomed over me behind Luca's.

A heartbeat later, Luca's hips stilled, his omega cock twitching wildly inside of me. He made a strange, choked noise—not quite a protest, but not quite acceptance. I realized, with a fresh surge of lust, that Byron had entered Luca from behind and was fucking him while he fucked me.

The cadence of Luca's thrusts changed, and I knew he was no longer the one in control. Byron pressed Luca's hips into me—slow and deep, with none of the frantic edge from before. Alpha pheromones surrounded me in a cloud as Zalen slid a thigh under my head, supporting me half in his lap. My eyes glazed over as his fingers combed through my sweaty, tangled hair, rubbing patterns over my scalp.

"Let's give them a minute, okay?" he said. "You'll get what you need, Mia, don't worry. Think how good it'll be after waiting for it just a little longer."

I *was* thinking about it, that was for sure. I couldn't focus on much of anything else right now. Especially when Zalen's fingers trailed down to brush my lips. He didn't have to press between them. I was already surging up, dragging those fingers into my mouth to suck and nip.

That was better... 'filled at both ends' was always preferable to 'filled at one end.' I'd decided that not so long ago in Byron's room, with his big cock sliding in and out of my pussy while his hand held my head down, choking me on Luca's smaller dick until all three of us came in a rush.

The memory was almost enough to push me over the edge. I hovered there, not quite able to make the leap, my teeth digging into the meat of Zalen's fingers too hard to be anything other than a full-on bite.

He groaned. "God almighty, you two should come with a warning label. Not long now, Mia."

In the cradle of my thighs, Luca was coming undone. His muscles trembled. His head was thrown back, raven-dark flyaway hair flopping over one olive green eye. Behind him, Byron's expression was almost frightening in its intensity. Gone was the easygoing playboy, replaced by an alpha who looked like he could devour omegas for breakfast, lunch, and dinner.

His hand closed over Luca's mating gland, and Luca *screamed*, his entire body jerking into climax. I wanted to follow him more than I'd ever wanted anything in my life, even as his shudders dissolved into sobs.

Byron's eyes closed as he came silently, his teeth clenching in a grimace. I lay panting beneath them, Zalen's musk wreathing my head and his fingers still in my mouth. Byron somehow managed to manhandle Luca away from me and onto his lap, Luca's legs straddling his as he leaned back against the edge of the couch.

One inked arm secured Luca's torso, his back pressed to Byron's chest as they both breathed unevenly, knotted and flushed with exertion. Luca's eyes were tightly closed, and his dick was still hard, coated and shiny with my fluids.

Mindlessly, I pushed away from Zalen, scrambled onto my hands and knees, and made a beeline for it. Luca gasped and made a noise like he was dying as I swallowed him down, tasting myself on his oversensitive skin. His cock twitched weakly at the back of my throat, a little pulse of salty-bitter fluid dribbling from the tip.

"Christ," Zalen muttered.

I vaguely heard the sound of a plastic packet crinkling. In what felt like no time at all, hands grasped my hips and a hard, thick length pressed against my opening. Zalen pushed inside, and I cried out around Luca as a giant alpha cock nearly split me in two.

Dear god... Zalen was hung like a fucking *horse*.

My brain shorted out, my surroundings dissolving into tingling white noise. There was nothing except the scent of summer fields in my nose and the heat of a massive dick sliding in and out of my pussy.

I wanted someone to shove me down on Luca's cock like Byron had done before, but Zalen was probably too nice for that. Blindly, I rooted around for Byron's free hand—the one that wasn't holding Luca. When I found it, I tugged it clumsily toward the back of my head, groaning in relief when Byron took the hint.

After the barest hesitation, he fisted my hair and started controlling my movements, fucking my face up and down on Luca's unflagging erection. Luca writhed and keened, trapped between my mouth and the knot in his passage.

Zalen let out a sharp breath and fucked into me, deep and unforgiving, every stroke dragging that huge dick over the sensitive spot on my front wall. I was unraveling… my body spinning off in a thousand different directions. I wanted to burrow into the beating heart of this moment and live here forever, caught on the cusp of the biggest orgasm of my life.

When Luca's slender, shaking fingers joined Byron's on the back of my head, forcing me down until my nose was buried in his soft, crinkly pubic hair and holding me there, the moment finally broke. A massive wave of sensation crashed over me, swirling together with the feeling of Luca spilling down my throat as he climaxed a second time, still knotted with Byron.

Behind me, Zalen let out a surprisingly feral snarl and came hard inside me, his giant horse-dick swelling impossibly further. My body knew what was coming, the muscles of my passage clamping and stretching to catch and hold Zalen's expanding knot.

My heart pounded against my ribs in a frantic rhythm—*thudthudthudthudthud*. The hands tangled in my hair eased their grips. I backed off of Luca's cock—softening a bit now, but still half hard—not because I wanted to, but only because I needed to breathe.

"*More,*" I rasped, not sure how my body could possibly have the capacity for 'more,' but needing it anyway.

Luca whimpered something that sounded like agreement.

"You've been on blockers too long," Zalen muttered. "You both have."

But he carefully arranged me to lie on my side where I would have a view of Luca and Byron, his big body spooning me from behind. He threw my top leg over his, splaying me open and giving himself access to play with my clit, even as his knot shifted inside me with a slow, rolling rhythm.

I sighed in utter bliss as knowing fingers dragged circles around the tender nub, spreading my slickness and teasing me toward another lazy peak. I watched with swimming vision as Byron carefully worked Luca's half-hard cock back to fullness, pushing him toward another release as well.

Luca's head fell back to rest on the crook of Byron's shoulder as the alpha pleasured him, his green eyes staring wide and unseeing at the ceiling. Pants and cries filled the room, time passing in a slow current defined by the rise and fall of our pleasure.

Luca broke first, his body going limp and pliant under Byron's touch. His eyes slipped closed, his breathing sliding into the regular cadence of sleep. I watched him for a long time, taking in the blank smoothness of his face… the absence of worry lines around his eyes and mouth. He looked younger; somehow more vulnerable, but also at peace in a way I'd never seen him before.

That must be nice, I thought wistfully. Then Zalen's fingers plucked at my oversensitive clit, playing it like a delicate instrument and sending me into another gentle, rolling orgasm. This time, when I came down, everything inside my mind went quiet and shadowed, my awareness of the outside world slipping peacefully away.

FIFTY-THREE

Emiel

THIS WAS HELL. If it wouldn't have meant leaving Princess alone in the house with everyone else busy in Luca's heat nest, I'd've thrown a toothbrush and some clothes in a bag and headed for the nearest motel... or maybe crashed in the break room at the Hope Project for a few days.

I'd even got as far as checking for pet-friendly hotels on my phone before stopping myself. Princess was still way too skittish for that, and if I tried to take her to the Hope Project, I was afraid she'd slip out to her old haunting grounds, where that asshole a couple of blocks over was probably still trapping strays.

At the moment, I was huddling in a corner down in the basement after a sleepless night, while Princess rubbed against my shins, making concerned-sounding mewing noises. The scent of not one, but two omegas in heat was a bit fainter down here than it was up in my room. I was dreading going up for a shower before work.

I was dreading work, *period.*

It wasn't like we didn't have other people working and volunteering there. But me, Zalen, and Byron were the core crew when it came to day-to-day, hands-on stuff with the kids—and the other two weren't gonna be doing shit when it came to work for the next several days.

The world might not end if I called in sick or whatever. But it wasn't like I wanted to be *here*, either.

It was hard to think straight. I wanted to blame my problems on the pheromone dampeners I was taking, because they didn't seem to be working for shit. Not since Mia had come stumbling into the house last night and promptly gone into heat. It wasn't the dampeners' fault, though. They were from the same batch as the ones Zalen and Byron had taken, and I'd have been able to smell it if either of them had lost control and gone into rut.

Out of nowhere, the image of alphas in rut savaging Mia and Luca slammed into my head like a freight train. Naked bodies writhing, teeth flashing, bloody bite marks on tender mating glands.

"*Stop*," I gritted out, my jaw aching from clenching it so hard.

Princess made another worried noise and wriggled onto my lap, shoving her forehead against my chin and rubbing. I didn't understand why she wasn't afraid of me right now. She should've been afraid. Alphas weren't safe to be around when we got like this. I knew that better than most people.

I closed my eyes and tried to focus on the soft slide of fur against skin, the clean smell of a cat, rather than the summertime-in-heaven pheromones permeating the house. It helped, a bit.

A knock came from the door at the top of the basement stairs, nearly jolting me out of my skin. I'd locked it behind me when I came down, not even thinking about it as I did it. One more layer of protection between me and the two omegas I had no business getting anyplace near.

"*Emiel?*" The muffled voice was Zalen's. Good... I didn't think I could've handled Byron's punchable smirk and sex-tousled hair right now.

"What?" I called back, hearing the surliness in my tone.

A slight pause.

"*I need to talk to you for a minute. It's about —*"

"I know what it's about," I grumbled. It was about Mia's heat. What else could it be?

But Zalen was the head alpha of our group. He owned the fuckin' house. I got up and trudged up the stairs, unlocking the door and opening it. Princess trotted nimbly up behind me, darting out into the main part of the house. Guess even she'd had enough of babysitting me.

"What?" I asked again—still confrontational. I hated that. But the heat scent was already rolling into my sanctuary, stronger than ever. Clinging to Zalen's skin, to his hair, to the T-shirt and track pants he'd thrown on. The pants did nothing to cover the hard bulge of his dick.

"Sorry to intrude," he said. "I had to text Mia's husband and let him know what's going on. Otherwise, he'd be expecting her at work today, and she asked me to keep him informed if she couldn't for some reason."

"And?" I asked, not sure what any of this had to do with me.

"And he didn't take it well," Zalen said, with that same infuriating calm that surrounded him like an aura ninety-nine-point-nine-nine percent of the time. "If he shows up at our front door while the rest of us are busy, you're going to be the one stuck dealing with him."

I scowled. "What… you think he's gonna call the police on us or something if we just don't answer the door?"

"I wouldn't completely rule out the possibility," Zalen said.

My scowl deepened. "Am I your bouncer now or somethin'?"

Zalen's expression turned careful. "I'm hoping you're the housemate who can answer the door, tell the angry husband that Mia is here by choice and that she's safe, and then close the door again." Deep set eyes that saw too much fastened on my face. "Look… I know that Luca's heats are hard on you, even if I don't know why that is. Are you doing all right?"

"Yeah," I told him. "Peachy. Have I got time for a shower before this asshole shows up?"

"I assume so," Zalen said. "I just got his text rant about two minutes ago."

"Great," I said, and brushed past him, heading upstairs to my room.

<hr>

Even though it was more than the recommended dosage frequency, I took another dampener shot out of the medicine cabinet and injected it. At least when my face was under the shower spray, I couldn't smell what was going on downstairs on the second floor.

My hand ached to close around my cock, but that was a terrible idea. For one thing, I'd be stuck squeezing my knot for half an hour afterward, since popping a knot with nothing to hold it was a goddamned miserable experience. And for another, I didn't need even *that* much of a taste of what I was missing.

Plus, of course, Mia's ball and chain would probably show up soon.

Yeah... I could hardly fuckin' wait.

The universe did at least throw me a scrap. The extra dampener shot was kicking in, and when I got out of the shower, I didn't feel quite as much like I was about to go insane. I could still smell Mia and Luca, but enough of the receptors in my nose had been blocked now that I no longer had to fight the urge to scratch all the skin off my arms.

I got dressed for work and gave Princess a treat from the stash in my nightstand when she hopped up on my bed and meowed at me.

Right on cue, the front doorbell rang.

"We coulda been holed up at a posh, pet-friendly hotel somewhere, you know," I told my cat, who made a trilling noise of agreement.

I trudged down the stairs, holding my breath as I passed the second-floor landing, just in case. The doorbell sounded more insistently.

Maybe this guy would try to force his way in, and I'd have an excuse to punch him in the stomach. That actually sounded kind of appealing, now that I thought about it. I jerked the front door open, letting my bulk fill the doorway.

"Yeah?" I asked, making no attempt to rein in my belligerence.

I recognized the guy on the doorstep from the time Zalen and I had taken clients to Mia's restaurant, before we'd *known* it was Mia's restaurant. Gym bro, about five-foot-eleven, Asian or maybe mixed race. An accountant with weight-machine muscles, who'd probably never been in a real fight in his life.

"I'm Mia's husband," he said, and there was the faintest hint of a tremor beneath the words. "She wasn't due to go into heat yet. I need to know that she's safe, and that she's here of her own free will."

I glared down at him. "Ain't nothin' gonna harm a single hair on the head of any omega in this house while we're here," I told him. "And of course she's here because she wants to be. She's the one who told Zalen to keep you in the loop. It's not like he *had* to text your ass this morning."

The soon-to-be-ex-husband squared his shoulders. What the hell was his name again? Nate, or Nat, or something?

"I need confirmation of that. Not just your word. I need to see her for myself."

In a strange way, I kind of had to hand it to the guy. I'd figured this whole thing was some kind of a pissing match, like he thought the others were poaching on his territory even though Mia had already left him. But he was genuinely frightened, and I was pretty sure, based on his muddled beta scent, that it wasn't for his own safety when confronted with a surly alpha twice his size.

The idea that he'd drive out here and confront an entire pack of alphas, just to make sure someone he cared about was safe and not being taken advantage of, stabbed a needle someplace deep inside me. It was a place that I didn't dare look at too closely.

Still, that didn't change the reality of the situation.

"You tromp up to that heat nest uninvited, and you'll get your head ripped off your pretty shoulders whether the others are on dampeners or not," I told him. "You run that nice restaurant with Mia, don't you? So, I know you're not *actually* stupid."

"They're on dampeners?" he asked.

"Of course they're on dampeners. We're *all* on fuckin' dampeners."

A faint hint of relief loosened his shoulders. "And… you're not part of it?" he asked.

I stared at him. Maybe he really *was* that stupid.

"Do I *look* like I just walked out of a heat nest?" I gestured at my casual suit and button-down shirt.

"Right. No," he said, still on the back foot. "I guess not. But they'd let *you* in, wouldn't they? You live here. You could bring her down, just long enough for me to check that she's okay." His spine was ramrod straight. "I won't leave until I have it directly from her that she wants to be here. And if you try to throw me out, I *will* call the police for a wellness check."

The needle pierced deeper, digging into a well of old pain that had scarred over even as it festered.

Silence stretched for several long moments, as I tried not to think about the sensation of something inside me squeezing and malforming, threatening to erupt.

"Let me go see if she's lucid right now," I said eventually, and shut the door in his face.

He'd come here alone, ready to do battle and send in the police if he didn't get the reassurance he wanted that Mia was safe. Him, a beta whose marriage was already on the trash heap, and he still cared enough to come check on her.

Even after Mia had rejected him, he cared enough to do the one thing that no one in my early life had ever cared enough to do for me.

FIFTY-FOUR

Emiel

I COULD DO THIS. The second dampener shot was working okay. *Ish.* That idea lasted until I started down the hallway to Luca's nest. And… yeah. Maybe not. The scent of the heat nest hung in the air like fog.

That was all right, though. I'd tell Zalen, and he could throw on some respectable clothes and carry Mia downstairs so Nate or Nat or whatever could see she was safe. Zalen wouldn't rip the guy's lungs out. He never got upset about anything. Or, I mean, he *did* get upset by things. But he never showed it.

Based on the sounds and smells that I hadn't totally been able to avoid inside the house, I was pretty sure Mia was several hours into the recovery from her first peak, but not quite ready for the second. She was more likely to be lucid now than she would be later.

Okay. I could knock on the door, back up a few steps into the hallway so I wouldn't trigger their territoriality too bad, and tell Zalen what was happening. Then I could get back to the basement and pull myself together for a few minutes before I needed to leave for the Hope Project.

Easy.

I took a shallow breath of pheromone-laden air and knocked on the door. A low growl came from inside, followed by a rhythmic series of high-pitched cries. I froze in place.

The door opened, revealing Byron. His body filled the doorway in a way it had no business doing for an alpha as skinny as he was. His teeth were bared in warning. He looked feral. He looked like he'd swelled up to half again his normal size… like he was looming over me.

He looked like my ste—

I cut off that thought with extreme prejudice, even as fight or flight instinct flooded my muscles and nerves. My hands itched to clench into fists.

"What the fuck do you want, Emiel?" Byron snapped. Just like that, the illusion was broken, and he was my bitchy roommate again. "We're a bit busy in here."

Behind him, Luca let out a wail that sounded like he was dying. Completely against my will, my attention focused beyond Byron, to where Luca was writhing and panting on Zalen's dick.

I took two hasty steps back, even though moving felt like pulling three-inch nails out of my flesh.

"*Emiel.*" Byron's voice was a snarl. "What. The *fuck.* Do you *want.*"

My heart felt like it was pounding too hard for me to get words out. I tried anyway.

"Mia's husband is here. He's worried for her. Wants to see she's okay or he says he'll call the cops."

Byron stared at me. "Jesus Christ. Are you kidding me?"

"I thought maybe Zalen could…" I trailed off. Zalen was balls-deep in Luca, and probably knotting him by now. He wasn't going anywhere. "Or *you* could… take her downstairs. If… if she's lucid, I mean. And if she wants to see him."

Byron was looking at me like I needed a straitjacket. He wasn't far wrong.

"I can't do it. I'd punch him in the face," he said. "Or maybe throw her down on the floor and knot her right in front of him, to show him how it's supposed to be done. You can get back down there and tell him to go fuck himself, as far as I'm concerned."

"And if he calls the cops on us?" I asked, trying to keep my shit together. Luca was moaning and sobbing pathetically now, like someone exhausted beyond endurance from the throes of ecstasy. My dick throbbed, so urgent it was painful.

"Whass wrong?" Mia's voice slurred from within the nest. "Why is Emiel upset?"

At that point, my heart decided to get in on the action, stuttering and thumping. *She knew I was here. She was worried about me.*

Byron turned. "Your piece-of-crap husband is here checking up on you, rom-com girl. It's okay, though. You don't need to see him."

"Nat's here?" The words held a hopeful tone. "He came?"

"Yeah," I said gruffly. "He was worried."

"Like I said, you don't need to see him," Byron repeated, with a glare at me for good measure.

"I *want* to see him!" She sounded younger. Innocent. All her barriers stripped away.

Zalen's voice was a soothing rumble from deeper in the room. "Byron. She's not a prisoner in the nest. She can see anyone she chooses. Emiel. Can you take her down?"

Luca made a discontented noise, and Zalen shushed him tenderly. My throat ached.

"Yeah," I rasped, because that was the fastest option for me to get away from this room.

Byron stood poised, looking like he still wanted to forbid it. But he wasn't in charge here, and we both knew it.

"I'll get her one of my shirts to wear," he said eventually, and stalked back into the nest.

A few moments later, he reappeared with Mia cradled in his arms. She was covered to mid-thigh with a silk button-down the color of cranberries that smelled like fennel and anise. I cautiously came closer, aware of what a stupid, *stupid* idea this had turned out to be. She reached out toward me with a loopy smile, and the constriction around my heart squeezed tighter.

"Emiel," she said happily.

It felt like Byron had to force himself to hand her over to me. And I couldn't blame him. I wouldn't hand her over to me, either.

"Hi, Mia," I managed, as rich perfume like the flowers that used to grow behind our apartment building surrounded me.

"Hi," she said, snuggling into my arms and rubbing her cheek against my chest like a cat. "Why won't you come in the nest with us?"

"I don't do that," I told her, past the white noise buzzing inside my head.

She made another unhappy noise, and her slender arms wrapped around my neck.

"Emiel." Zalen was still speaking in that soothing tone designed to keep Luca calm. "Are you going to be okay with this?"

"Yeah," I said. "We'll just be a minute."

Mia hummed sleepily as I turned and headed back down the stairs, aware of Byron's rumble of displeasure behind us. Her perfume and her solid weight in my arms were all I could focus on.

"I wish you'd come in the nest," she said plaintively, pressing the words against the collar of my shirt.

I was going to have to change clothes after this to get rid of her scent. Probably shower again, too, before I'd be able to string two thoughts together. The cotton of my briefs dragged against my aching cock with every step.

The distance to the front door felt like it stretched on and on until it covered miles. When we finally got there, I made sure Mia was covered by Byron's shirt as much as she could be.

"Your husband's outside," I said. "That's where he's gonna stay, and we'll stay inside. Okay?"

She made an ambiguous mewling noise and rubbed against me again, her hair brushing the skin of my throat and sending sparks along my nerves.

I gritted my teeth and opened the door.

Whassisname was kicking his heels on the porch, looking like he was about ten seconds from crawling out of his own skin. I could relate.

He whirled on us. "*Mia*?"

"Nat!" she said happily, reaching for him.

His hand lifted to meet her, but he caught himself and jerked it back down to his side before I could even growl. It clenched into a loose fist, squeezing and releasing nervously.

"Mia, I had to check on you when that alpha texted to tell me you'd gone into heat early," he said. "Are you okay?"

I felt her nod against my chest.

"Nat, I'm *so good*," she said, earnest and unguarded. "It's *so good here*. I wish you could be here, too…"

I sent Nat a flat stare to reinforce just how much that would *not* be happening. I guess I didn't need to bother, though, because Nat already looked like he'd been kicked in the chest.

"Okay," he said. "Okay, Mia. I just had to make sure you really wanted to be here, and that they're treating you right."

Mia shifted in my arms, rubbing more of her body against me. My dick swelled, trapped painfully in the confines of my clothing.

"Of course I want to be here," she said dreamily, nuzzling at me. "This is my pack. You should have a pack, too, Nat."

I suddenly couldn't get enough oxygen.

"You need to leave now," I told the devastated beta standing on our porch. My voice was a hoarse rasp.

There was a heavy pause.

"Yeah," Nat whispered. "Okay. I'm leaving. Thank you for—" His voice cracked. "Thank you for taking care of her."

He might as well have been speaking Swahili, but I nodded like an automaton and turned, shoving the door closed with my foot and resettling Mia in my grip so I could engage the lock and deadbolt.

Mia purred, her body shifting and sliding against me with more focused intent. Her scent, already overwhelming, sharpened even further. I headed into the house, knowing in some distant part of my brain that I needed to get her back to the nest *right the fuck now*.

That didn't explain why every step felt like it was taking me closer to the gallows.

"God, Emiel," Mia moaned. "N-need you to touch me. Please, Emiel... I'm so horny. It aches so bad."

The staticky white noise in my brain rose higher, blotting out my thoughts. Elderflower and sumac were everywhere... in my nose, on my tongue, coating the back of my throat. The entrance to the TV room loomed on my left. There was a sofa inside. I had to put Mia down. Go tell one of the others to fetch her before—

A playful omega puppy growl was all the warning I got before sharp teeth closed on the tendon running along the side of my neck and bit down. *Hard.*

The world whited out.

FIFTY-FIVE

Emiel

SOMEHOW, I'D MADE it to the battered sofa with its piles of soft cushions. Mia was beneath me, moaning and wriggling. Cranberry silk gaped open, missing several buttons and torn below the collar on one side.

Had I done that? Had she?

It must've been me. She was pawing at my shirt and the fly of my trousers, but her movements were clumsy and uncoordinated. I needed our skin touching. I needed to wallow in that sweet elder-sumac perfume. I needed to bathe in it until anyone within a two-mile radius would know that this omega had wanted me, had claimed me with her scent.

I growled in frustration as the layers of clothing separating us confounded me. It was intolerable that I had to sit up and take my hands off her so I could tear everything off. Part of me wanted to lift her upper body so I could drag the remains of the shirt that smelled like another alpha off her. But I knew that scent, and as much as it made me want to howl with frustration, I knew she'd chosen that alpha, too.

But that other alpha wasn't here right now.

She was mine. All mine.

"*Emiel*..." she groaned. "God... touch me... I *need* you..."

She needed touch. I needed taste. I growled, untangling the last bits of clothing from my body and throwing them aside violently. Then my mouth was on her, repaying that sneaky bite that I could still feel throbbing on the side of my neck.

Her golden skin was unmarked, because apparently the other alphas in this house were stupid. I would fix that. I'd fix it right the fuck now.

She cried out as I started biting my way down her body, beginning with the hinge of her delicate jaw and trailing downward from there. Her mating gland smelled delicious. I paused, nosing against it, making her shudder.

Sharp fingernails dug into my shoulders, every little pinprick of pain skittering along the length of my spine, burning with icy heat. Her breasts were so *soft*. I was obsessed with the way the tender flesh gave way beneath my mouth… the way the hard peaks pebbled when I sucked on them, blood rising to the surface.

Mia sobbed with need and bucked her hips up, trying to rub her soaked folds against whatever part of me she could reach. I slid down the couch, abandoning those tempting tits in favor of the banquet waiting below. Her body was like a wellspring, gushing forth a never-ending feast of the finest manna.

No matter how much of it I licked up, there was more. I gave in to instinct, rubbing my face through the slick mess, reveling in the way it coated my cheeks and chin.

In what felt like no time at all, she arched beneath me, choking as a noise too big to escape caught in her throat. Her pussy clenched and twitched, the muscles of her passage fluttering around my tongue as I tried to lick deeper.

The choking noise became keening—a low, desperate sound that went on and on, worming its way straight to my painfully hard dick. Mia wriggled and shoved, and for a terrible moment, I thought she was trying to get away from me.

A black hole opened up in my chest at the very thought…but before it could swallow me whole, she slithered down to kneel on the floor, her pussy practically in my face.

"Please, please, please," she begged weakly, lowering her upper body until her ass was in the air. "Please… I can't… I need…"

I didn't actually remember ramming my throbbing dick inside her. I didn't remember lining myself up, or grabbing her hips hard enough to bruise, or making the decision to shove it inside her.

But somehow, between one moment and the next, we were joined together. Hot, silky muscle rippled around my cock, as though Mia's body would try to keep me from ever, *ever* leaving. I didn't want to leave… but I *did* want to recreate that first indescribable moment, again and again for the rest of forever.

I pulled back, and she groaned, bereft, then whimpered when I thrust back in, snapping my hips. How could anything feel this good?

"More," Mia demanded. "Need it so bad..."

I gave her more. I gave her *everything*, reveling in the little birdlike cries she made, the pitch rising with each thrust until she was singing for me, sweeter than the wildest songbird.

The scent of fennel and aniseed wafted into the room, sharp with surprise and something darker. I tensed, growling.

"Oh, fuck, you have *got* to be kidding me," said a familiar and unwelcome voice. "*Seriously,* Mr. 'I Don't Do That'?"

The instinct to keep thrusting into Mia's welcoming warmth warred with the instinct to pull out so I could lunge across the room and scare this rival male away from the omega beneath me. My growl deepened in warning.

But at the sound of the second voice, Mia's entire body went rigid, her muscles trembling and twitching. She let out a strangled, high-pitched cry, her passage clamping around my dick like a hot vise. I howled, taken by surprise, my release spurting out of me in rhythmic jets so intense that my vision tunneled in. When it cleared, my knot was already swelling, tying us together.

A moment of panic gripped me at the idea that we were vulnerable, but fennel-and-aniseed only grunted in disgust. "Unbelievable. Emiel, I swear to god that if you scare her at all, I'll hold you down while Zalen rips you a new asshole. I'll send him in here as soon as Luca unknots him and you can explain this to him, because frankly I don't even want to know."

I recognized the shape of the words, but he might as well have been speaking Swahili for all the sense they made. I rumbled another warning and hid as much of Mia's body from view with my own as I could manage. The other alpha muttered something else unintelligible and left, his scent fading slowly after him.

My shoulders unknotted, all my attention returning to the omega beneath me. She was making small, happy noises, still wriggling on my oversensitive dick. I wanted us to be in a den—someplace enclosed and secret. There was a blanket folded over the arm of the couch. I stretched out and grabbed it, throwing it over our bodies and the seat of the couch like a makeshift tent.

Mia sighed in utter contentment, going boneless. I eased us onto our sides and wrapped my body around hers as she continued to fuck herself on my knot with tiny, shallow movements. After a few minutes of this, a purr vibrated free of my chest. I couldn't help it. Mia shivered all over, her passage rippling again with a second, gentler climax.

As she hummed in contentment and went boneless in my arms, my purr grew louder. Had I ever made that noise before? I didn't think so. It just seemed like the only possible response to the feelings flooding through me. That, and…

Her mating gland was inches away from my lips. The dark and quiet space beneath the blanket-tent was thick with her pheromones, combined with a hint of the scent that I hid from the world—cinnamon and sour orange peel. The combination smelled like heaven. I wanted to tie those two scents together for the rest of our lives.

I licked at the little gland on her right shoulder. It was red and swollen, but she hummed contentedly at the contact and rolled her head to the side to give me easier access. My teeth grazed the skin and she shivered, but her breathing was already deepening into sleep.

I was salivating. It would be so easy. It would be so right. This was meant to be, wasn't it? She would want this as much as I did. She would *want* me to…

I froze.

She was asleep. She couldn't want anything right now, because she wasn't aware of what was happening. The faintest glimmer of wider awareness peeked through the haze of lust and instinct that had descended on me like a storm cloud. I was balls-deep in my roommate Mia, who'd helped me rescue Princess, and taken me out to lunch, and never, ever acted like she was afraid of me.

Mia, who hadn't agreed to having me drag her away from Luca's nest and stick my dick in her. Not until she was already heat-drunk.

Don't try to pretend, boy. I can tell you want it.

The phantom voice whispered in my ear, deep and dark and amused. Panic fluttered in my stomach, spreading outward in cold waves.

My hands began to tremble, clammy sweat breaking out on my skin as the sick, nauseating wrongness of what had just happened spread through me like burrowing worms.

I was trapped… she was trapped. We both were, until her muscles unclamped from my knot. Mia made a small noise of discontent in my arms, and it pierced through me like a prison-house shiv.

Oh, my god.
What had I just done?

500

FIFTY-SIX

Zalen

FEW THINGS LEFT me feeling as torn as Luca's heats. I hated the way his loss of control tortured him, both before and after the fact. *Hated* it. But when biology held its sway and finally brought down his barriers, it was the only glimpse I ever got of Luca as he might have been, if not for the cruelty of fate—and the gang that had hurt him.

Every time we did this, Luca began his heat by refusing any comfort once his body released our knots. After his passage unclamped, he would lie curled in a miserable fetal position among the cushions and blankets, flinching away from any attempt to hold him. Every single time, it broke my heart to see it.

But as the days wore on and his awareness of what was happening faded, he uncoiled by increments, until finally, during his last couple of peaks, he would accept our touch while he rested after knotting. It was a heady feeling—this fey, wild creature finally submitting to our care.

And I knew *exactly* why it unearthed those feelings within me. After losing Julie so unexpectedly... after feeling our mating bond snap in an instant while I was away on a business trip, leaving only a torn and bloody stump behind, I didn't think I would ever have it in me to sign up for that kind of heartbreak again. But, here and now, there was an omega who needed me. *Two* omegas, at least for this brief interlude of a few short days.

It was enough. It had to be.

I knew it was harder for Byron. He had his own set of issues. They were different from mine. Different from Luca's. Different from Emiel's—not that Emiel had opened up to any of us about whatever it was that had driven him to the Hope Project… or to the cage fights.

Byron sometimes looked like a knife was twisting in his heart when Luca relaxed into his care. I'd never been able to tell if it was a good kind of pain or a bad kind of pain. And, interestingly enough, that tortured expression had been completely absent from his features as he'd held Mia earlier.

I wasn't sure what that meant, or if it meant anything at all.

In my arms, Luca's scent shifted. If I hadn't been on dampeners, that shift would've signaled my alpha hindbrain to emerge from the rutting haze so I could care for my omega between peaks. As it was, it signaled Luca's silky-hot passage releasing its death grip on my knot, which immediately started to subside as the pressure went away.

Normally, Luca wouldn't have accepted my continued touch this early in his heat. But Mia's presence had changed the dynamic somehow. I'd felt the shift, watching them cling to each other when Mia had first arrived in the nest. And now, rather than squirming away from me, Luca cautiously settled into my embrace as I eased us down to lie on our sides.

Equally cautious, I let a low purr vibrate up from my chest. Luca went rigid for a moment, but then his breath sighed out, taking all his tension with it.

The moment I closed my eyes in relief, the doorknob turned. Dampeners or no, instinct flared at the sudden intrusion to the nest. A ridiculous response on my part—it was only Byron, back from checking on Mia and Emiel after they'd been gone longer than I was comfortable with.

But Byron wasn't carrying Mia back to the nest with him. He was alone, his scent bristling with something sharp that I couldn't quite identify. My purr cut off abruptly.

Byron drew breath in a way that said whatever words were coming next would be angry ones—but his gray eyes snapped to the dozing omega in my arms, and he caught himself at the last moment.

When he did speak, the words were a low monotone. Not emotionless—because his emotions still came through loud and clear—but controlled, at least.

"You need to go sort out Emiel downstairs. He's knot-deep in Mia, and I don't trust him not to flip his shit and scare her before she releases him."

Adrenaline shot through my veins.

"You're sure?" I asked tightly, as if that wasn't the single stupidest question on the planet. Of *course* he was sure.

Luca made an unhappy noise in my arms, wriggling restlessly. Byron raised a pointed eyebrow that clearly conveyed his disdain for the question. I took two slow, deep breaths, modulating my scent before Luca really started to get upset.

"Right. Okay. Can you get your reactions under control well enough to take my place with Luca?" I asked, keeping my voice low and calm.

"Probably," Byron replied through gritted teeth.

"*Probably* isn't good enough." I wanted to bark the words, but I didn't.

Byron hesitated. His bare, tattooed chest rose and fell on a breath. "Yes."

I stroked a hand through Luca's sweaty hair, soothing him while Byron stripped off the track pants he'd been wearing and crouched down next to us.

"Hey, Luca," I told him. "Byron's subbing in for a bit. He'll watch over you."

Luca made a little distracted humming noise and burrowed deeper into the pillows. Taking that as assent, I swapped places with the other alpha, keeping a hand on Luca to steady him until Byron was settled behind him.

"Did Mia seem upset at all?" I asked, keeping my voice low enough that it hopefully wouldn't penetrate Luca's post-knotting haze.

"Well, she was climaxing like a freight train at the time, so I'm going with 'no,'" Byron snarked. "I'm more worried about what'll happen when Mr. Knot-for-Brains realizes what he just did. He's on dampeners, but he sure as hell wasn't acting like he was on dampeners."

I nodded, not bothering with a reply before grabbing the joggers Byron had discarded and pulling them on. I closed the door of the nest carefully behind me and took the stairs two at a time, sending a prayer to the universe that whatever I was about to walk in on wouldn't be too bad.

It wasn't hard to follow the scent to the scene of the proverbial crime.

"Emiel?" I called as I approached the TV room. There was no reply, but I could hear ragged breathing coming from within. "Emiel. Mia. I'm coming in. Everything's fine, I'm just checking on you."

My reassuring speech was met with a low snarl as I passed through the open doorway. Mia's nervous whimper followed.

Okay, then.

"Everything's fine," I repeated, since that had worked *so well* the first time.

I took in the makeshift blanket-fort Emiel had tried to construct as a den. I kept speaking as I approached the opening where it draped from the couch seat to the floor.

"Hey, Emiel—you with me at all? I'm guessing this was a bit unexpected. Sorry, I shouldn't have asked you to bring her down here on your own. No harm done, though... heats can get crazy. Can you talk to me, please?"

I settled cross-legged a few feet from the opening, trying to make visual sense of the shadows huddled within. The silence stretched for too long.

"*No*," Emiel rasped, barely audible.

"Okay," I said, putting everything I had into projecting calm control of the situation. *What a joke.* "How about I just sit here with you both for a bit. We'll let Mia enjoy her knot."

More silence, broken only by that terrible, ragged breathing. It dragged on even longer this time.

"I shouldn't've."

And, oh crap. I'd never heard Emiel's voice shake before.

"I think your dampeners failed," I said, not sure what approach might make the situation better rather than worse. "And I'm guessing she initiated, to put it mildly. Again, I'm sorry, Emiel. But I promise this is going to be all right, yeah?"

Another long pause, and when Emiel finally spoke this time, he sounded like he was choking on something.

"I nearly... her mating gland..."

I went very still, because idiot that I was, that hadn't even occurred to me. But 'nearly' wasn't a bite. Nothing irrevocable had happened.

"But you didn't," I said. "And you *wouldn't*, because I know you, Emiel. So, you're both okay. She had a birth control shot, and the only repercussion is that she's likely to feel really bad about blowing past your boundaries. And that's assuming she even remembers this happened."

"*I raped her, Zalen.*" It came out as a whisper, thick with intensity.

It was all I could do not to recoil from the self-hatred beneath that shaky tone. I hated the couple of seconds it took me to center myself and choose what I hoped were the right words.

"*Emiel.* I have a feeling Mia's going to disagree strongly with that interpretation, once she's in a position to address it. But until then, you being upset is upsetting her." I saw the shadows inside the makeshift den flinch. "Right now, she needs you to be calm. We're going to do that box-breathing exercise we teach the kids. With me — in, two, three, four… hold, two, three, four… out, two, three, four… hold, two, three, four."

I repeated the sequence, feeling like a bit of an idiot at first, but fresh out of other ideas. Eventually, the ragged breathing from inside the tent evened out, falling into the right rhythm. I kept it up, the minutes sliding past until Mia's pheromones shifted.

"She's going to release you now," I said, striving to maintain that same calm. "I'll take her back to the nest with the others, but then if you want to talk —"

The blanket heaved and fell away. Emiel was on his feet in an instant; out the door in the next. I sighed, letting him go in favor of tending to Mia, who was whining low in the back of her throat.

"Hey, sweetheart," I said, gathering her in my arms. "You're okay. I've got you."

"*Emiel*," she whimpered. No fear or pain marred her sweet summer scent. Only sadness and confusion.

"He's okay, too." The lie left a bitter taste as it slipped past my lips, but the truth was that none of us could help Emiel until Emiel let himself be helped. I still had no idea what old injury lay beneath his behavior, and without knowing more, I was stuck. "He has to go to work now, so let me carry you back up to the nest in a few minutes, all right? Luca and Byron are waiting for us."

She burrowed into me unhappily, but she didn't protest. I kept her warm body bundled close to mine for a bit longer, making sure that she wasn't showing any signs of physical discomfort. When her breathing evened out into sleep with no indication of any problems, I sighed in relief and hauled her up in a bridal carry.

The stairs leading to the second floor reminded me how tired I'd been for the past few months. When the omegas were out of heat and recovered enough to look after themselves, my post-heat crash was going to be an ugly one this time around.

For now, though, biology meant that sleep wasn't in the cards.

I gave a couple of light knocks on the door of the nest with my bare heel and called, "It's just us, Byron. We're coming in."

Luca was out like a snuffed candle, with Byron still spooning him from behind.

The alpha raised his head as we entered.

"She doing all right?" he asked.

"Seems to be, yeah," I said.

"*He* doing all right?" Byron's tone was grudging.

"No fucking clue, but signs point to *no*." I carried Mia over and settled her in front of Luca, who immediately shuffled forward in his sleep and plastered himself against her.

I was just about to lower myself down next to her when the distinctive rumble of an eight-cylinder Detroit engine reached me from outside, followed by a squeal of tires. I hurried to the room's single window and tweaked the heavy blackout curtains a couple of inches to the side—just in time to see a familiar gray classic Bronco peel out of the driveway and slew down the quiet residential road.

"Well, *shit*," I cursed, watching it go helplessly.

FIFTY-SEVEN

Nat

"YOU NEED TO leave now." The alpha's tone was low and rough. His broad shoulders blocked the doorway. Tree trunk arms cradled the woman who'd once loved me with the same care one might hold a precious and irreplaceable work of art, for all that he claimed not to be involved with her heat.

There was a heavy pause, during which my mind helpfully supplied an annotated list of every terrible decision I'd made in the last six months. It was… an uncomfortably *long* list.

There was no place for me here, standing outside this expensive mansion in Ladue, where my wife had fled after I'd made our home too painful for her to bear living in.

My fault.

My choices.

My punishment, staring me in the face.

"Yeah," I whispered. "Okay. I'm leaving. Thank you for—" My voice cracked. "Thank you for taking care of her."

I forced out the final words, trying not to stare at Mia's blissful expression as she rubbed her cheek against the chest of this giant, aggressive looking man with the shaved head and the nice suit.

The scent of elderflowers surrounded me like a cloud, mixed with some kind of spicy cologne that smelled vaguely familiar. It was all I could do not to take a step back… or worse, a step *forward*—despite the sense that doing so might be the last mistake I ever made.

The alpha's expression was absolutely blank. *Disconcertingly* so. His head bobbed up and down once—a single nod of acknowledgement that he'd heard me agreeing to leave, even though I got the sense he'd already dismissed me from his awareness as though I'd never even been here. He took a step back, hooking the front door with one foot.

It swung shut, closing solidly in my face.

I stood there staring at it like some kind of a creeper for far too long after the lock clicked. Inside, the alpha would be carrying Mia back to a bedroom somewhere in the house, where other alphas would be waiting to have sex with her.

My hands began to tremble in earnest.

Ain't nothin' gonna harm a single hair on the head of any omega in this house while we're here, the man holding her had said, as though it was an unbreakable maxim. *And of course she's here because she wants to be.*

Of course she was.

She'd fled a home filled with constant arguing and long-buried resentment bubbling to the service, leaving it behind in favor of a pack of protective alphas who treated her like a queen. What omega wouldn't?

My breath had grown rapid and shaky. The houses in this neighborhood were set back from the road, surrounded by old growth trees for privacy—but I could still picture what I would look like to any nosy neighbor peering out the window through a set of binoculars.

Sad little cuck, staring at a locked door with his wife on the other side.

I could practically hear the words in my father's voice. And the rest—

A real man would have dragged her out of there by the hair...

Only a faggot would stand around while other men fucked his wife...

You might as well have bent over and begged them to take it up the ass...

I turned abruptly and nearly stumbled down the steps to the front walkway, my feet on a half-second lag from my brain. The door of the Jeep slammed behind me as I sat in the driver's seat and shook, my body hunched over the steering wheel like an old man's.

I'd been battered by these sharp moments of clarity nearly nonstop since receiving the text from that Zalen guy. *'Mia's heat came early. She's all right, but she'll be unavailable for the next few days.'* Until that message, I'd been working on the assumption that her blocker pill would arrive, and she would take it—just like she'd been doing every three months for longer than I cared to think about.

Since that message, I'd been clobbered over the head by a merciless series of painful truth-by-fours. First, *your pain and insecurity drove her away;* followed closely by *you don't know for certain that she's safe there while she's in heat.*

But the one on the alphas' porch had been the most brutal. *You've lost her for good. Mia is gone; she's not coming back to you.*

And now, the realization that my adoptive father's voice had wormed its way inside my psyche and set up shop there for thirty-one years without me ever noticing.

Mia had tried to make me see it over the course of our marriage, and I hadn't understood. I knew the man was rough around the edges. I knew he held opinions on some subjects that other people found crude and offensive. Frankly, he was an asshole. But that was *him.* I'd grown up and moved out. I was my own man now, and I had been for thirteen years and counting. His backward beliefs didn't affect *me.*

Except, of course, that they did. I just hadn't seen it before.

I straightened in the bucket seat, my joints creaking in protest. I had no business being here at this house, now that I knew Mia was safe. The Jeep's engine rumbled to life when I turned the key.

As I put the vehicle in gear and pulled forward around the circle drive, I couldn't help a final glance back at the house. The closed front door flanked by fancy carriage lights mocked me.

A toxic stew of negative thoughts churned inside my brain as I drove home, the trip happening on autopilot once I got back to the main highway.

I'd been twenty-five, and Mia had just turned twenty-two, when we originally met. She was fresh out of culinary school; I'd just sold my first business for a quarter-million dollars and was convinced I was hot shit. I'd known a few omegas over the years — most people did — but none had been like Mia.

She had no time for alphas who wanted her to be their little stay-at-home baby machine. We'd dated casually at first, but before long, we were deep in plans to open a restaurant together. We got married as much to become business partners as because we were lovers — but the sex had been okay at first. Sometimes, it had been positively spectacular.

I had a high sex drive, and she didn't, because omegas either needed to be in heat or use alpha pheromones to get horny. And back when Mia voluntarily had natural heats a couple of times a year, those interludes had been *explosive*. It was honestly the only time in my life when I'd been able to have as much sex as I wanted, and even then, we'd needed to keep a knotting dildo on standby in case my stamina gave out.

The periods in between were a bit rougher — she'd buy alpha pheromones a couple of times a month so we could have sex, whereas I'd have been happier doing it once a day.

But we muddled along for a few years, and things were okay... until the restaurant's success exploded, and suddenly both of us were completely consumed by the Elderflower Inn.

Mia stopped having natural heats, even though she knew perfectly well that using blockers for extended periods was a fast track to cancer. I started to resent the fact that I was married to someone who didn't care if we never had sex again... and to top it all off, needed sex aids in the form of another person's pheromones to even get wet for me.

It might've been stupid. Okay, it *was* stupid.

But it stuck a knife right into the hidden part of me that wondered if I really might be the *little pansy pussy* my father had always accused me of being as a boy. Could Mia somehow tell that I wasn't man enough for her? If I'd been more dominant, more masculine, more like an *alpha*, would our sex life have fallen apart just as our business life was shooting toward the stratosphere?

Did the fact that I sometimes found myself checking out other men mean that I'd been lying to myself—to *her*—the whole time, and she'd somehow subconsciously figured it out?

I'd pushed away those intrusive thoughts by turning my fear and resentment outward. I was just another frustrated husband whose wife withheld sex for whatever impenetrable female reason. It happened all the time. It didn't mean there was anything wrong with me.

This was the twenty-first century. I didn't have to stand for that shit for years on end. Divorce wasn't an option—I still loved Mia. We were partners. Business partners. Life partners. But there were other options.

If she didn't want sex, then fine. She could have the parts of the marriage that were important to her, and I could get the relief I needed elsewhere. God help me, when I was considering the plan, I managed to talk myself into believing that she'd be relieved at the prospect. No more getting pestered for sex. No more irritable, sexually frustrated husband.

Then 'plans' became 'action,' and everything fell apart.

Not only was Mia not relieved... she was devastated. Before I knew it, she was hanging out with a pack of alphas, proving in no uncertain terms that the voice in my head—the one that sounded like my adopted father—had been right all along.

It was me. I wasn't man enough to hold an omega's interest.

The bitter irony was that I hadn't even managed to sleep with a woman before my smoking hot, hyper-competent and hyper-talented wife had bagged multiple men. Instead, I'd done something much worse.

I'd gone out to bars and clubs, stayed out late—sometimes all night long—and ended up batting zero with the opposite sex. No one seemed right. If a woman flirted back, I immediately started comparing her to Mia.

And then, one night, I found myself staring at a hot guy for far too long, wondering if I wanted him or just wanted to *be* him. He was effortlessly magnetic; women and men orbited around him like moons.

It was fucking ridiculous. If I was gay, I'd *know*, wouldn't I? If I was actually the queer little loser my father had accused me of being, I wouldn't be attracted to Mia, right?

Suddenly, the uncertainty felt unbearable. I walked up to the guy at the bar and offered to buy him a drink. His sharp gray eyes raked me up and down before he shrugged agreement. Half an hour later, I was following his car to a nearby hotel, figuring that I'd either be repulsed by the whole thing once it started, or I wouldn't be, and I would at least have an answer about my own sexuality.

Two hours later, I lay on a too-soft, queen-sized mattress, sweaty and spent, without a single circling thought anywhere in my head. When the guy got up to leave, I asked for his phone number before my shattered brain caught up with my lips. He gave the same neutral shrug of agreement he'd given me when I offered him a drink, and then he jotted his number down on a hotel notepad.

Afterward, he walked out of the room, closing the door behind him.

I hooked up with him twice more that week at the same motel. Each time, I didn't find myself thinking, '*Oh, look, this is what I've been missing for the last two decades.*' It wasn't a life-altering experience at all. But for an hour or two, my brain completely shut itself off in a way it never did, otherwise. All the fucked-up stress in my life — so much of it self-inflicted — grew distant and unimportant. And afterward, the guy left without a word or a backward glance.

With the restaurant's reputation in tatters, our finances deep in the red, and my wife currently getting fucked by rich alphas in a West End mansion, right now my mind felt like an overheating engine on the verge of tearing itself apart.

I pulled into my driveway in Jennings, went inside the house, and collapsed on the sofa with a terrible, tight feeling banded around my ribcage. My hand shook as I pulled out my phone, desperate for an escape.

I brought up my contact list and opened a text window.

Hey, I typed. *It's been a while. I really need a hookup tonight. You free? Super 7 on Broadway, like before?*

I hesitated for long moments before hitting send. The phone made its little 'notification sent' noise, and I set it down beside me before letting my head fall back to stare blankly at the ceiling.

Minutes passed. An hour. Then two.

There was no reply.

End of Book One

Mia's story will conclude in *Knot Playing Fair: Book Two.*